More praise for Sue Henry's

DEATH TAKES PASSAGE

"Good stuff."
Library Journal

"Fun to read . . . Henry is adept at weaving a good plot with enough complexity to keep her readers guessing about 'whodunit' right up to the very end . . . Smart, strong, brave, vulnerable, thoughtful, and tender, State Trooper Alex Jensen becomes more appealing with every book."
Alaska Magazine

"Henry offers an opportunity for armchair tourists to travel the ordinarily peaceful Inside Passage . . . The scenery is marvelous."
Arizona Daily Star

"Hooray for Henry . . . [A] classic 'good read' . . . A believable plot, steady pacing, and characters that are comfortable and realistic."
Mystery News

"Alaska's spectacular scenery, intriguing history, and a well-engineered showdown should please fans of this series."
Publishers Weekly

"Fast-paced and extremely interesting . . . No one does Alaska (historical and present) better than Sue Henry does . . . Readers will want to book a ticket on the cruise ship *Death Takes Passage*."
Bookpage.com

Books by Sue Henry

SUE HENRY

DEATH TAKES PASSAGE

An Alaska Mystery

AVON BOOKS
An Imprint of HarperCollinsPublishers

This is a work of fiction. Though based on an actual event, in a real setting, with several very real people included as characters (with their gracious permission), it is an imaginary tale—never happened, or will happen, as written. Artistic license has been taken by the author in some details regarding locations and some law enforcement activities to allow the story to proceed smoothly, but every attempt has been made to make the rest as accurate as possible.

AVON BOOKS
An Imprint of HarperCollins*Publishers*
10 East 53rd Street
New York, New York 10022-5299

Copyright © 1997 by Sue Henry
Excerpt from *Deadfall* copyright © 1998 by Sue Henry
Inside cover author photo by Greg Martin 1996
Inside Passage map by Vanessa Summers
Library of Congress Catalog Card Number: 97-4002
ISBN: 0-380-78863-2
www.avonmystery.com

First Avon Books paperback printing: August 1998
First Avon Books hardcover printing: August 1997

Avon Trademark Reg. U.S. Pat. Off. and in Other Countries, Marca Registrada, Hecho en U.S.A.
HarperCollins® is a trademark of HarperCollins Publishers Inc.

Printed in the U.S.A.

10 9 8

M/V SPIRIT OF '98

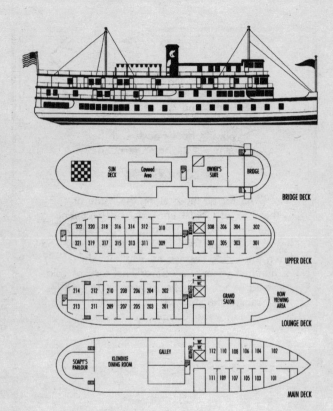

BRIDGE DECK

SUN DECK | Covered Area | OWNER'S SUITE | BRIDGE

UPPER DECK

322 320 318 316 314 312 310 308 306 304 302
321 319 317 315 313 311 309 307 305 303 301

LOUNGE DECK

214 212 210 208 206 204 202
213 211 209 207 205 203 201
GRAND SALON | BOW VIEWING AREA
WC WC

MAIN DECK

SOAPY'S PARLOUR | KLONDIKE DINING ROOM | GALLEY
112 110 108 106 104 102
111 109 107 105 103 101
WC WC

SPECIFICATIONS			
Maximum Capacity:	99 Passengers	Beam:	40 feet
Registry:	United States	Tonnage:	96
Length:	192 feet	Cruising Speed:	13 knots

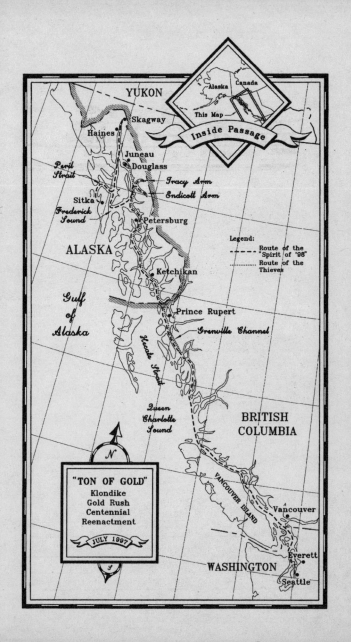

1

THE MOON WAS ALMOST FULL, BUT CLOTS OF CLOUDS SCUD-
ding darkly overhead persistently obscured it,
allowing only infrequent and mottled patches of pale
light to relieve the blackness of the waters of Gastineau Channel. It had risen just after midnight, from
behind the tall, sharp peaks that rose on the eastern
side of that slim arm of the sea like a wall. It would
soon disappear, along with the few stars that slipped
in and out of view.

The late breeze had quickened into a wind, which
sighed through the evergreens on a small hill that
stood between the Douglas Island boat harbor and
the channel. The hill sheltered the small marina from
the winter gales that frequently whipped the confined seas of the channel to an icy froth, driving inju-
dicious vessels desperately toward any possible
berth. This July wind, however, would more gently
blow itself out under the curtains of rain promised
by the threatening clouds. It was not unusual
weather for the Southeast Alaskan Panhandle—lush,
green, and intensely alive, home to rain and fog.

Within the harbor, no one noticed when one ketch

began to slowly, silently swing away from the dock. It gradually came about and headed toward the channel like a dark ghost, or the shadow of a huge waterbird.

The soft splash of a mishandled oar and a muffled curse revealed a man in an inflatable dinghy, rowing ahead at the end of a towline. As this smaller boat—conveniently borrowed from another vessel—gradually cleared the harbor, its oarsman became a brief silhouette against the navigation light that marked the harbor's entrance. His outline showed shoulders too broad to be hidden by the bulk of a dark slicker and a baseball cap with a brim that dipped and rose as he leaned to pull strongly against the weight of the water. He cast a glance over one shoulder to be certain that his line of exit from the marina was as direct and efficient as possible.

A second darkly clad man stood at the wheel in the stern of the ketch. A wiry knot of muscle, he was spare of flesh and small of frame, and the wind tugged contemptuously at the straggle of beard that thinly disguised a weak chin. Shifting his weight nervously from foot to foot, he turned once to assure himself of the continuing emptiness of the dock that fell slowly astern.

As the dinghy moved into the channel, the wind hit with enough force to make it slip southward, but the rower put more of his back and strong arms into the endeavor and managed to maintain a route that was mostly crosswise to the southerly flow of wind and tide. Ever so slowly, he pulled the boat away from the shore into open water, until the stern was completely clear. Then, with rapid and less cautious strokes of the oars, he rowed quickly back to the ketch, swung himself aboard, and left the purloined dinghy to drift away. Riding empty, high, and light, it quickly became a toy for the wind to toss, disappearing instantly into the dark.

The engine came abruptly to life, as the first man

encouraged the heavy boat away from the shore and swung it to starboard, into the deep waters of the channel. Within ten minutes the two men had managed to raise a single sail. They killed the engine and were gathering silent speed, still without lights, driven south before the wind toward the confluence of Gastineau Channel, Taku Inlet, and Stephens Passage. Beyond this, if all went as planned, it would be easy to lose themselves in the giant maze of the straits, sounds, bays, arms, harbors, and inlets of the Inside Passage, making pursuit an impracticality, except, perhaps, by air.

They fully expected it would be a long time before anyone learned there was any pursuit to be mounted. The boat they had commandeered was not local. Its home port, painted on the stern below its name, was Nanaimo, British Columbia, though, with traditional courtesy, the *Hazlit's Gull* flew a small United States flag on its stern. It had been chosen from among the many boats that occupied the southernmost marina in the area, more than two miles from the tall bridge that connected Douglas Island with Juneau to the east, across the channel.

The two men had masqueraded as acquaintances in search of the *Gull's* passengers, and they had gleaned, from the harbormaster's registry, the intended length of its stay—two weeks. Several days of careful but seemingly casual observation of the boat had told them that a young married couple owned and sailed the ketch, and that one of them—a factor in making it their vessel of choice—was no longer on board.

Clued by a duffel set onto the dock and a scene of affectionate leave-taking, one of the men had followed the young man to the Juneau airport and watched him catch a plane. From a casual question to the gossipy owner of a nearby boat, its watchers knew it would be several days to a week before the husband would return. By the time he reported his boat—and wife—missing, both would probably be as abandoned as the stolen and discarded dinghy.

Though making good time, the *Gull* rolled and pitched rhythmically in the rough waters of the channel. The heftier of the two men controlled it with an expertise that revealed prior experience. The older man joined his friend in the cockpit. Lowering himself into a seat, he turned to watch the lights of Juneau and its island neighbor, Douglas—a soft reflection of light to the west—fade in the distance.

"Can't understand why anyone would want to live in a place you can't get out of except by boat or plane," he said, cupping his hands against the wind to light a cigarette. "How long till daylight?"

"Oh, we got three . . . four hours yet. With this wind, we could be clear the other side of Taku and into the lower part of Stephens Passage by then."

"It's gonna rain." He looked up to assess the clouds that had now vanquished any sign of the moon.

"Yeah, looks like it, but it won't slow us down much. Besides, we could go half this fast and still have lots of time. We got a long way to go. We'll sail as long as we can, till it gets light, then put up somewhere till tomorrow night. But if this weather keeps up we could go longer. Won't too many people be out in it. Makes good cover."

As he spoke, the first few heavy drops spattered around them.

"Better go down and see if you can find some rain gear, Nelson. You'll get soaked without it. Should be a locker somewhere at the bottom of the ladder," he said. "And while you're down there, take a look at her. Make sure she hasn't worked her way loose somehow or got the blindfold off."

"Can I turn on a light now?"

"Yeah, should be all right. But turn it off when you come back up."

Tossing his cigarette overboard, Nelson moved forward and disappeared through the companionway. In only a minute or two he came scrambling back up, holding a pair of waterproof pants and wearing both a slicker and a frown of concern.

"She don't seem to be breathing, Rod."

"What?"

"I said, she ain't breathing. Still tied up good, and gagged with that duct tape, but I . . . ah . . . can't see that she's breathing. I . . . ah . . . I think she might be . . . you know . . . ah . . . dead?"

"Goddamn it!" the other exploded. "Get your skinny ass back here, Nelson, and take this damn wheel."

"Aw . . . you know I can't do that."

"Idiot. You can Goddamn well hold it like it is. I'll just be a minute. She's probably passed out. You just didn't check her right. How could she be dead?"

He vanished into the interior of the boat, leaving his partner fearfully clutching at the wheel as if it might suddenly come alive under his hands and send them crashing onto some hidden rock.

2

"IT MUST HAVE LOOKED A LOT LIKE THIS A HUNDRED YEARS ago," Jessie Arnold said to Alex Jensen, as they paused in front of the Red Onion Saloon to look up Broadway, Skagway's main street.

It was just after dark on a clear evening, and there were few modern streetlights in the historic gold rush town. Most of the warm glow between blue shadows came from the doors and windows of the small shops and boutiques lining the street. Several of these had false fronts, and a couple—including the famous Golden North Hotel, where Jessie and Alex had registered—sported round tower rooms on one corner, but most were boxy, single-story frame structures intended to look as if they had weathered a century, as many of them actually had. Most of the businesses that occupied them had already closed for the day, and the rest would soon follow suit.

A few tourists were still wandering the boardwalks, heading slowly back toward their giant tour ships at the town docks, or looking for some appealing place to have a late dinner. Silhouetted against the lights, they could have been gold rush stampeders from the late nineteenth century.

A pair of women laden with bulky plastic bags walked past, discussing their purchases with enthusiasm. Alex thoughtfully watched them head west toward the harbor, his mind still drifting back to the old Skagway, jumping-off point for the Klondike.

Someone whistled. A laugh rang out from down the street. The muffled ragtime rhythm of a piano drifted from the saloon, growing abruptly louder as someone flung open the door, releasing the sounds of conversation and the music.

"It's like stepping back in time," Alex agreed.

Jessie looked up and down the street again. "If you add a few more people, some horses and muddy streets, this would seem pretty much like 1897."

"Like it?"

"Even more than I expected. It makes me feel connected. Just imagine coming all the way from Seattle, or Portland, or San Francisco, ready to start for the Klondike, dreaming of excitement and fortunes in gold. It's no wonder they called it gold *fever*."

Alex agreed. "It was contagious all right. But they hadn't a clue how hard it would be to make it to Dawson, only to find out all the claims had been staked for over a year. A lot of them turned right around and went home."

"Well, I wouldn't have quit and neither would you. I still think it would have been great."

"Yeah, but *you*—who think nothing of thousand-mile sled dog races—would have fit right in. I'd probably have been at the top of the pass, freezing my tail, and helping the Mounties make sure everyone who went into Canada had enough equipment and supplies for a year."

Jessie laughed and turned toward the Red Onion. "Well, speaking of supplies . . . come on, trooper. Let's get something to eat before we die of starvation."

Closely followed by Jensen, she moved through the door into the immediate contrast of a large and well-lit room, full of cheerful sounds and the mouthwatering aroma of hot pizza. Aside from its thoroughly modern crowd of local and visiting customers, not to mention its twentieth-century cuisine, the Onion would have been right at home in the gold rush. In fact, it had been built in 1898 and was later moved to its current location. In the process, the movers had somehow turned it around, so that the back of the structure now faced the main street.

A long antique bar, backed with large mirrors and carved with scrolls of fancy woodwork, extended along well over half of one side of the long room, accommodating twenty-some people on tall stools. Another thirty or forty souls were seated on a collection of mismatched chairs at square tables only a little larger than checkerboards. The walls—except for the large windows facing the street—were decorated with an interesting assortment of artifacts from the 1890s.

"During the gold rush the second floor of this place was a bordello," Alex informed Jessie, as they quickly claimed the only empty table in sight. "It's supposedly haunted by Delilah, one of the former working girls."

"You're joking, right?"

"Nope. She has a reputation for not liking men— scares them if they try to go upstairs. I guess she sticks around to take care of the place."

A piano player in a collarless shirt, gartered into puffs at the elbows, teased an infectious honky-tonk from the yellowed ivory keys of an old upright piano, keeping patrons' toes tapping on the scuffed wood floor as they sang along with his old-time tunes. Jessie and Alex did some toe-tapping of their own, but there was little singing as they hungrily worked their way through a combination pizza and drafts of pale Alaskan ale in thick glass mugs.

When nothing remained but crumbs, they moved to tall stools at the bar, where they had a better view of the piano player, who paused now and then to add humorous comments to his music. Contented, they sat, enjoying the entertainment and sipping the last of their ale.

Alex drained his mug, lit his pipe, and looked questioningly at Jessie in response to the bartender's suggestion of another brew. She nodded. Then her attention was caught by a woman claiming the empty stool next to hers. Jessie smiled at the woman, who responded with only the slightest of nods and a twitch of her lips, and turned quickly away to lay a ten dollar bill on the bar.

The newcomer was short and had dark eyes and dark hair combed tightly into a knot at the back of her head. Small unruly curls of it escaped and stood out vigorously in a not unbecoming frame for her oval face. She was delicately built, and her expression was not particularly welcoming. Her thin lips were set narrowly together and she looked tired or worried—it was difficult to tell which.

Before Jessie had time to ponder the all but nonexistent acknowledgment she had received, the bartender set two ales before them with a flourish.

"Hey," he demanded with a self-satisfied grin, "Jessie Arnold—the Iditarod—right?"

"Right." Jessie reached to accept the hand he extended to her across the ancient, scarred surface of the bar, skillfully avoiding a collision with the full frosty mug he had just set down.

"Welcome to Skagway. We all cheered you into Nome a couple of years ago in the *gutsiest-ever* finish, and another in the top ten last year. Congratulations."

"Thanks," she smiled, pleased with his enthusiasm and the recognition of her effort.

"You going along on this big centennial boat run to Seattle?"

"Yeah," she confirmed, turning to introduce Alex. "This is Alex Jensen. He's the formal representative for the Alaska State Troopers on the trip."

"Don Sawyer," he offered, as the two men shook hands. "I'll be going along, too, as a bartender. So stop by Soapy's Parlour on the dining room level and say hello."

"We'll do that. It's really a vacation, since I'm just along to show off the uniform in the ceremonial parts, and not assigned to chase bad guys this trip." He laid a bill down to pay for their drinks.

"Naw." Sawyer shook his head. "These are on the house. Nice to have you both in town. Running this year, Jessie?"

"Planning to."

"Good luck then."

As he moved away to mix a drink for the woman sitting next to Jessie, Alex couldn't resist a comment.

"Glad we aren't supposed to be undercover. Why didn't I make you wear that fake mustache? Is there anybody in this state who doesn't know you?"

She grinned. "It's kind of nice that a few Alaskans know who I am—sort of a reward for all the work that goes into running the race. Besides, a fake mustache would make me look like a trooper. Right?"

Alex's reddish blond handlebar mustache was one of his few vanities. It was wide, with a half-curl at each end and he had worn it for so long he couldn't imagine what his face would look like without it. Periodically, Jessie waved a pair of scissors and offered to cut off half, so he could compare and see if he liked himself better without it. Pressed, however, she cheerfully admitted that she liked it and would prefer that he keep it.

They made an attractive couple. He was tall and slim, with the beginnings of smile lines around his mouth and eyes. She was a bit shorter, tan and fit from days spent running dog teams through the Alaskan wilderness, her hair a short honey-colored tumble of waves and curls, her eyes a calm gray.

The piano player stopped for a break, to the vocal disappointment of the impromptu and semi-harmonious chorus surrounding him. Eventually a quieter hum of cheerful conversation filled the room. The chess players didn't even glance up.

Don returned with a drink for the dark-haired woman and was reaching to pick up her money when a new voice interrupted him.

"I'll take care of that."

Jessie turned her head to see a stranger swing himself onto the stool beyond the other woman.

"Hi," he said. "I'm Bill Prentice. Don't want to sound like I'm just hitting on you, but I know you from somewhere."

The approach did seem sincere, but it was hard to tell. He paused, smiling quizzically, and waited for her response.

Plainly startled, she frowned slightly and gave him an uneasy glance before turning her eyes back to Don.

The bartender waited, still holding her money, giving her a very straight and level look, communicating silently that if she wanted this person gone, he would see to it. She raised her eyebrows, soliciting his opinion. Was he personally acquainted? He pursed his lips slightly, cocked his head, and, with a barely perceptible movement, shrugged his shoulders. It was up to her, he didn't know the guy.

Giving her uninvited companion one more contemplative look, with a tiny half-nod and answering shrug she allowed Sawyer to set up the drink. Without accepting payment, he returned to the tap to draw a beer for the newcomer.

Good man, thought Jessie, who had closely followed both the spoken and silent exchange. She was beginning to like this Sawyer person. A quick look at Jensen's amused twist of lips told her that he, too, had observed the byplay to their right.

"Thanks," she heard the woman say, "but I don't think you know me. I'm not from around here. Judy Raymond."

"Oh, neither am I," he answered. "Nice to meet you, Judy. Where're you from then?"

The bartender set up the beer and smiled. "These are on me," he told her.

Another bit of good, subtle work. Without being conspicuous, he had succeeded in giving the guy notice that anything out of line would not be tolerated, and he had explicitly canceled any obligation she might feel by making the beer on the house. As the couple resumed their tentative conversation, Sawyer met Jessie's watchful eyes, and she smiled appreciatively at him; another small conspiracy of silent communication. He grinned and went on down the bar in response to a customer waving an empty mug.

Jessie turned back to Alex, who was watching the piano player wend his way through the maze of tables back to his instrument.

"You about ready to go?" he asked. "I've had enough of the noise."

"Sure." She pushed back the last of her ale and slid off the stool to stand beside him. "The boat will be in by eight tomorrow morning and I'd like to see if we can get our stuff on board early. Then we can enjoy the day before we have to dress up."

"Great." Jensen laid a generous tip on the bar for Sawyer, who raised a hand in a brief farewell wave. "I'm tired. Too much bouncing around in the air between here and Juneau."

"Were you airsick? We weren't airborne very long and you fly in small planes all the time with Caswell."

"No, I just don't like it rough, and it's always rough over the Lynn Canal."

Jessie yawned as they stepped out the door. Alex took her hand, tucking it snugly under his arm.

The street was empty. They did not notice a figure that exited the Onion a few seconds behind them and slipped immediately into the dark shadow of a doorway to watch them stroll in step along the boardwalk toward the hotel.

3

10:15 P.M.
Sunday, July 13, 1997
Spirit of '98
Lynn Canal, Alaska

JENSEN LEANED ON THE STARBOARD RAIL OF THE *SPIRIT OF*
'98 and watched the black waters of the Lynn Canal
stream past the moving ship. Out of uniform, comfortable in jeans and a sweater with deck shoes on
his feet, he was enjoying the relaxation of a last pipe
before going in to bed. The fragrant smoke was
whipped away by the wind, disappearing almost instantly into the darkness. Jessie was already cozily
ensconced on one of the beds inside the cabin, reading a book on the gold rush.

The deck was quiet, and Alex could hear the rush
of water and see a bit of the white roil of the wake
as the ship ran south and west on the second leg of
the overnight trip to Sitka. Beneath these noises, the
throb of powerful engines was as much a sensation
as a sound, a deep rumble from somewhere
underfoot.

Not a single light was visible on the distant shore
of this particular stretch of immense and uninhabi-
table wilderness, but far across the wide waters of
the channel he could see the tiny lights of another

vessel moving, maybe a fishing boat headed for Juneau, or a sailboat unable to reach safe harbor before sundown. It looked incredibly small and lonely to Alex, giving him the same poignant, solitary feeling that he always had on hearing the haunting whistle of a train going anywhere at night. As he watched, the lights moved slowly away and were swallowed by the dark around some point of land.

The *Spirit* had sailed from Haines promptly at nine-thirty. Now, as it grew late, most of the passengers, pleasantly tired from the bon voyage celebrations aboard and ashore, had already yawned their way to their cabins. A few tipsy diehards, still too excited to consider an end to the festivities, had gone to the main lounge on the deck below for a nightcap, perhaps the last of the afternoon's champagne, but any sound of their small, continuing revelry was masked by that of the ship and the breeze its motion created.

A couple, senior citizens still in party dress, came up the companionway and passed behind Jensen, heading aft.

"Good night," he called after them, and the gray-haired man raised a hand in response, without looking back.

Turning his attention again to the dark beyond the rail, Jensen contemplated the barely discernible silhouette of the mountains that lined the shore of the channel, a solid barrier to the south. Behind them, glaciers filled the high basin of the St. Elias Range for hundreds of miles with a deep, interconnecting ice field, above which rose only the tallest peaks and ridges. Between each mountain, hanging glaciers spilled centuries-old fingers of ice over the edge of each lofty valley. In the sunshine, their broken edges reflected blue, so compressed by the annual weight of blanket after blanket of snow they absorbed all other colors of the spectrum. Though originally composed of airy snowflakes, all were now incredibly dense. The few massive rivers of ice that found their way down to the sea were so heavily compacted that, if they ever receded, the land they covered would rebound and rise inches in the absence of their mighty weight. Now, in the dark, these ice floes were as invisible as the peaks they divided, each with an unseen stream of ice-melt falling hundreds of feet to dilute the ocean's salt with freshwater.

It had been a long day, and Jensen was glad to catch a breath from his official duty of representing the Alaska State Troopers, though he was pleased to be a part of this unusual trip. The duty was also unusual for him; he was used to the continuing effort of solving homicides in South Central Alaska. For this trip he would be required only to dress in his best uniform and appear at all the official and cere-monial events, representing the state's law enforce-ment agencies.

He and Jessie had boarded the *Spirit* in Skagway early that afternoon, changed into appropriate period clothing in their cabin, and stood at the rail, watching other passengers come aboard, while he wondered exactly what he had volunteered for. Wearing his Alaska State Troopers dress uniform—medium blue tunic and darker blue trousers with a gold stripe that ran down the outside of each leg with a smaller red stripe in the center, blue Stetson hat, banded with gold braid and decorated with two small gold acorns—made it impossible to relax, always encour-aging him to stiffen his spine and draw back his shoulders.

Running a finger under his tight collar, he straight-ened his tie and sighed, longing for his well-broken-in jeans and soft cotton shirt.

"You look very handsome," Jessie told him with a glint of humor in her eyes.

He *did* look especially tall and official. The uniform was thoroughly modern, yet somehow it did not

seem out of place on the *Spirit*, a boat designed on
the lines of coastal steamers of the previous century.

"From the neck up," Jessie told him, with a glance
at his handlebar mustache, "you could have walked
right out of one of those old photos."

She was dressed in a costume she had made herself: crisp white blouse with leg-of-mutton sleeves
and a long, navy blue, gored skirt, pleated full in
the back. The lacy flounce of a white petticoat was
occasionally visible, swinging under the skirt as she
moved. A similar sea-foam of white lace cascaded
from a cameo brooch at her throat, and a small, flat,
straw hat, decorated with a pink rose, and carefully
pinned to her curls, completed the outfit.

"You need some of those high-button shoes,"
Alex suggested.

"Not a chance. Getting around the boat in this skirt
is challenge enough. I'm happy with these, thanks."
She raised the skirt and petticoat to reveal her everyday shoes, with a very low heel.

The day was sparkling, clear and warm. The snow
on the distant peaks across the Lynn Canal gleamed
pure white in the sunshine. Miles away, the glacier
faces exhibited a few faint suggestions of blue.
Spruce so dark they were almost black thickly covered the lower slopes; the millions of trees contrasted
sharply with the mountains that never lost their frozen cover.

The small town of Skagway was nestled in a narrow valley between the long arm of ocean and its
own surrounding promontories, little more than a
mile long and the width of four city blocks. A few
homes climbed the northern slopes, where a road
looped around eight miles of ridge that separated
Skagway from the starting point for the Chilkoot
Trail. Skagway was alive with the hundreds of tourists brought by the huge tour ships that docked at
the wharf. Its streets were festooned with banners,
flags, and decorations, which contributed to the rev-

elry of its seven hundred and fifty inhabitants, most of whom were on the street or dock.

"All this enthusiasm is catching," Jessie said.

The whole idea of the centennial reenactment pleased them both with its appropriateness. It seemed exceptionally well planned and orchestrated.

They couldn't have had a better place for watching the events preceding the sailing than the highest bridge deck of the *Spirit*, with its antique, coastal steamer appearance. From this position, they had a view of everything that was happening on the dock below and back as far as the main street, where they could see activity in front of the Old White Pass and Yukon Railroad Depot, currently a National Park Service Visitor Center. In a still impregnable hundred-year-old safe, the ton of gold designated for the trip had been secured the night before. A group of men were bringing it out now in wooden boxes, loading it onto a solid old baggage wagon for the short journey to the dock.

"Look."

A sharp, piercing cry drew her attention, and Jessie pointed out a bald eagle, drawing circles in the air high overhead, gliding like a hang glider on invisible thermals. Like everyone else, it seemed to be observing the dockside activity.

"Curiosity, do you think?" she asked Alex, watching it float.

"Probably looking for dinner." He pointed to a miniature poodle on a leash held by a woman on the dock. "One swoop and that pooch would be history, if there weren't so many people around."

Shouts of laughter turned their attention back to the crowd milling about on the dock and coming, single file, up the gangway. Jessie, an amateur photographer, had brought along her 35mm Minolta and a variety of lenses. Now she busied herself taking pictures of the activity below and those who were coming aboard.

It was a festive group, many in costumes of the late 1800s, representing the diversity of those who had come north during the gold rush a century before. Among them was a gang dressed as scruffy miners, one with a pickax over his shoulder. He waved at the crowd of Skagway residents assembled on the dock.

A married couple came up the ramp, he in miner's garb, she in the long skirt of the period. Between them they carried a blanket rolled around what was supposedly their wealth of gold. Feigning extreme difficulty in supporting its weight, they staggered laboriously and dramatically aboard, playing to their audience.

A bookish-looking man in gold-rimmed glasses seemed in studied contrast to the furs he wore and, from mukluks to hooded parka, appeared overheated and distinctly uncomfortable in the July temperature that hovered in the mid-eighties.

"Ho for the Klondike," someone shouted, and a cheer rippled through the crowd, followed by applause for a woman who swept onto the ship in a striking costume of deep red velvet. One by one, the passengers came up the gangway, excited to be embarking on the reenactment of a historic journey.

Boarding with the costumed passengers were some who had chosen to retain their modern mode of dress.

"Probably hated Halloween as kids," Alex speculated.

One of these, Jessie noticed, was the woman from the bar stool next to her in the Red Onion the night before. Dressed casually in beige slacks and a knit top, carrying a light blue windbreaker, Judy Raymond's dark hair was covered by a hat the color of her jacket, with a brim that shaded her eyes over a pair of dark sunglasses. She greeted the ship's captain with a conservative half smile, hurriedly escaped up the gangway, and immediately disappeared, as if she wished to separate herself from the celebration.

Alex and Jessie stared after her, curiosity aroused at the odd behavior. Why would anyone go on such a trip and not want to take an active part in it?

The captain, first mate, and several Centennial Committee members were at the bottom of the gangway, welcoming passengers. Among them were dignitaries coming aboard only for the first leg of the journey and planning to leave when they reached Haines, an hour and a half later, after a reception to mark the beginning of the cruise. For the most part, these—the mayors of Haines and Juneau, legislators, other officials and their wives—did not wear costumes but arrived in their everyday professional attire. The governor and his wife, however, had outdone themselves in dressing to suit the occasion as had the mayor of Skagway and his spouse.

As Alex watched the mayors glad-hand each other and everyone else within reach, Jessie used a zoom lens to capture the look of their authentic gold rush outfits. She was not alone in her photography, for half those in attendance, residents and tourists alike, were clicking shutters and using up film at a rate that would have pleased Kodak.

A bright yellow, old-fashioned vehicle, not quite recognizable as either a van or a bus, pulled up near the gangway, and its passengers began to clamber out through multiple doors along each side. The logo on the front door announced it as part of The Skagway Street Car Company. The driver, in black period suit with a gold watch chain across his vest, stepped out, still telling tales of Skagway history, and circled the vehicle to make sure all the doors were closed.

"Hey, Steve," someone shouted from the crowd. "You going on the cruise?"

He waved and smiled but only shook his head in answer, still engaged in the business of caring for his streetcar and passengers.

"What the heck is that taxi . . . bus . . . thing,"
Alex wondered aloud. You have any idea?"

"Yes!" Jessie crowed, "I do!" glad for once to be
able to tell him something he didn't already know.
"Ever see pictures of Yellowstone in the early days?
They used to have those in the lower-forty-eight state
parks to ferry tourists around." She explained that a
small fleet of the unusual vehicles had been pur-
chased and brought north when their usefulness became outdated in the parks. Reconditioned and well
maintained, they now fit right into the gold rush appearance of Skagway.

"Hey." Jensen pointed toward a man who had
exited the streetcar and was approaching the *Spirit*'s
gangway. "Someone's playing Soapy Smith. What a
great costume. He even looks like the old photographs. Get a picture of him, will you, Jess?"

Dressed in a broad-brimmed hat and dark suit,
with a vest buttoned high over a cravat, the man
wore a neatly trimmed beard and carried what
looked like a briefcase. From somewhere in the
crowd of observers came a hiss of disapproval, followed by laughter for this notorious Skagway con
man, now a century dead. The man with the case
turned, swept off his hat in an exaggerated bow to
the onlookers, grinned, and proceeded to shake
hands with the members of the welcoming
committee.

In less than an hour the *Spirit* would sail, but a
ton of gold had to be loaded first. This voyage would
commemorate the first gold—over two tons—that
had been brought almost exactly a hundred years
earlier on the SS *Portland*, from the rich Klondike
claims to Seattle. For this centennial trip, an actual
ton of gold had been amassed by miners still working in the Dawson City area; it was now being
brought down to Skagway for transport to Seattle.
Watching the passengers, Jessie and Alex had forgotten its approach. Now, in fifteen wooden boxes

stacked on the antique baggage cart and pulled by a
modern cargo tractor, it was eased slowly and carefully down the long vehicle ramp and onto the dock.
Clearly, no one wanted to risk having somewhere
between thirteen and fourteen million dollars in gold
plunge over the side of the concrete dock into the
frigid waters below.

Even in the wooden boxes that had more than dou-
bled its size, it didn't seem possible that it could
weigh over two thousand pounds.

"Is that all?" Jessie asked. "Looks awfully small."

"Gold's heavy," Alex told her. "A ton in one con-
tainer would be about the size of a footlocker, or
three five-gallon cans, maybe. Of course you couldn't
lift either one . . . but . . ."

Laboriously, with hand trucks, each hundred-and-
fifty-pound box of gold was carried aboard, disappearing onto the *Spirit* through a door that opened
onto the Main Deck, making it unnecessary to move
it up the gangway.

Throughout the morning, one of the boxes had
been open for display in the visitors center, under
the watchful eyes of a pair of guards who had accompanied it down from Lake Bennett on the narrow
gauge railway. Alex and Jessie had gone to take a
look, and they'd been rewarded with a view of the
assorted kinds of gold that made up the ton: dust
and nuggets in canvas bags, opened for the curious,
and bars or ingots, both professionally made and
smelted into rough shapes by the miners themselves.

"Where are they keeping it for the trip?" Jessie
asked.

Jensen was carefully watching the progress of each
box onto the ship, a slight frown of concentration on
his face. For a moment or two he made no response
to her question, then he turned with a distracted expression. "What?"

She grinned at his distraction and asked again,
"Where is it being kept on the boat?"

"Ship," he corrected, absently. "I don't know. Must be somewhere on that lowest deck."

"Hey, Jensen," someone yelled from below.

Alex looked, grinned, and waved a hello.

Moving close to the rail, Jessie saw a pleasant-looking man in dark glasses, who had been helping load the ton of gold.

"Have a great trip," he called.

"You bet," Alex answered. "Thanks again for the tour."

"Who was that?" she asked as the man walked away behind the baggage cart that was now being pulled up the vehicle ramp.

"John Mielke, chief mechanical officer for the narrow gauge. Took me on a tour of the railroad maintenance shops this morning, while you were exploring the hotel."

"I thought you were gone a long time."

"Well, don't often get invited to ride in the cab of a steam engine."

"You got to ride Number 73? I'm green with envy."

Alex waved as Mielke saluted from the top of the ramp and climbed onto the back of the tractor, hitching a ride back to the station.

It was almost three-thirty. Below them, the last box was carried on board, the last of the passengers had boarded, and the crew was in the process of stowing the gangway. In a very short time they cast off the lines, and, amid cheers and shouts from the crowd on both sides of the widening separation of water, the ship glided away from the dock into Lynn Canal. Almost everyone on the vessel lined the rail to watch as they left with waves and shouts of *bon voyage*, tossing colorful paper streamers. The *Spirit of '98* was on its way.

Alex looked down at Jessie, not surprised to see a satisfied expression on her face, and he found it matched his own. It promised to be a remarkable week.

"Can I get out of this monkey suit now?" he asked.

"Well . . ."

Over their heads the ship's public address system crackled to life.

"Ladies and gentlemen. We will arrive in Haines at five o'clock, where you are encouraged to leave the ship for a celebration given by the Haines Visitors Bureau at the Halsingland Hotel. Please be back aboard no later than nine-fifteen, as we will depart promptly at nine-thirty, on our way to Sitka. For the next hour and a half, the Spirit of '98 *invites you to join our captain and special guests in the Grand Salon on the lounge deck for a champagne celebration of this Gold Rush Centennial Reenactment Cruise."*

"That's it—special guests, the governor and all," Jessie smiled. "Command performance. You'll have to wear the uniform till the ship leaves Haines, I think, Alex."

4

11:00 P.M.
Sunday, July 13, 1997
Spirit of '98
Lynn Canal, Alaska

THE HAINES RECEPTION HAD BEEN AN ENTHUSIASTIC SEND-
off party. From the Port Chilkoot dock, passengers
from the *Spirit* had had only a short walk up the hill
to historic Fort William H. Seward, where a generous
and varied buffet supper had been laid out. Half the
population of Haines had waited to greet them at the
Halsingland Hotel, at one time quarters for officers
of the fort.

The governor of Alaska and his wife, along with
the mayors of Skagway and Haines and their
spouses, had greeted guests in a receiving line at the
door of the hotel. The place, mazelike, with smallish
rooms on various levels, had filled quickly, celebra-
tors soon overflowing onto the porch and grounds.
The noise level had quickly increased, punctuated
with whoops of laughter and boisterous voices.

As Alex and Jessie had moved slowly toward the
buffet table, he'd noticed one heavy, florid-faced man
attempting to sing what must have been the only
Alaskan song he knew—or, rather, didn't know, for
he'd tunelessly intoned over and over, "Squaws

24

along the Yukon are good enough for me." Each repetition had been echoed by the exasperated voice of
his female companion, "Shut up, George. Just *shut
up.*"

Plates in hand, Alex and Jessie had hurriedly escaped outdoors to find a quieter and cooler place.
They'd joined a friendly mixture of Haines residents
and passengers from the ship on the grass of the
parade ground. Many had changed from their costumes to more casual clothes, but several had still
looked as if they had stepped from the previous century. After this party, the costumes would be put
away until they reached Seattle, where they would
add, once more, to the festive gold rush flavor of
the celebration.

Jessie had insisted it wouldn't be fair to change
hers while Alex was still expected to wear his dress
uniform. He'd thought she looked especially attractive, with her long skirt spread on the grass and the
pink rose on her hat matching the color in her cheeks,
and he'd told her so. She'd looked up from under
the brim and smiled.

"Thanks, but don't get the idea I'm going to adopt
this rig when we get home. It's hot. I don't know
how they did it."

The sun *had* been bright and warm all day, unim-
peded by clouds, and, even as it had settled toward
what would prove to be a spectacular sunset, the
temperature had remained warmer than usual for
Southeast Alaska. The ice tea they'd drunk with their
meal had been welcome.

"Would it be all right . . . I mean . . . could I . . .
join you?" a hesitant female voice had asked. Looking up, Jessie had found a round-faced woman of
perhaps sixty looking down at her. She was round
all over, fifty-extra-pounds-plump, and pale enough
that her makeup had vaguely suggested a painted
doll. Still in costume, a dress of period design, made
of cotton fabric with small blue forget-me-nots scat-

tered across a peach background, she'd stood waiting, clearly uncertain of her welcome.

"Sure," Jessie had invited with a smile. "Pull up a section of grass and make yourself at home."

"Oh, thank-you. I really do appreciate it. I'm Edith . . . Edith Johnson. Are you from the boat, too?"

Jessie and Alex nodded and introduced themselves.

"O-o-h," she'd breathed, her eyes widening. "I know who you are."

Alex had suppressed a smile, thinking, as usual, that she had recognized Jessie, but he'd been surprised to learn that he had been the object of her identification.

"You're that policeman from Alaska that rescued that poor man on the Top of the World Highway last fall. I'm from Dawson City. It was all in the newspaper."

She had been referring to a case Jensen had shared with an RCMP inspector, involving a suspect who had tried to escape, wearing unsuitable clothing, over a high mountain pass. The resultant frostbite had been a horrible punishment, far worse than the law would ever have demanded.

Edith had begun to recount the whole story to a couple sitting next to them. Unseen by Jensen's obvious fan club of one, Jessie had winked at him.

"Gotcha," she'd commented, mouthing the word.

"Are you on this trip by yourself?" Alex had asked Edith, when she'd finished her story—and flattery.

"No. Wayne, my husband's, with me . . . though he didn't really want to come on this trip. Doesn't like boats."

"Where is he?"

"Ah . . . he didn't get off. He's . . . ah . . . not feeling well."

"Oh. I'm sorry," Jessie had told her. "Can we take

him something to eat? He'll be hungry. They're not serving dinner on the ship tonight."

"Oh, no . . . no. No . . . really. That's not necessary . . . shouldn't disturb him. He'll be fine in the morning. Really."

The almost panicked response from Edith had startled them both enough to drop the subject. She'd seemed frightened, embarrassed, and almost in tears.

Jessie had exchanged a look with Alex that Edith, suddenly focused on pushing food around on her plate, did not see. Let's talk about this later, it had meant, and he'd nodded.

Trying to think of something to say that would defuse the sudden tension, Jensen had called their attention to a crowd gathered on the porch of the Halsingland. Over the heads of the group, he'd caught a glimpse of a broad-brimmed hat he'd recognized as belonging to the man who had earlier boarded the ship dressed as Soapy Smith.

"Hey, let's go see what's going on," he'd suggested, standing and reaching to help Jessie up.

Assisted to her feet, she'd brushed crumbs and bits of grass from her long skirt before turning to Edith, but the older woman had stayed where she was, with her plate on her lap.

"You go ahead," she'd told them, waving her fork. "I think I'll finish this."

Alex had taken Jessie's hand, and they'd moved across to the hotel steps, tossing their paper plates and cups into a convenient trash can on the way. From the back of the crowd they could see little, but it had soon thinned, allowing them to move closer.

The briefcase the Soapy Smith imitator carried had revealed itself as a small folding table that opened up and was supported by a metal rod with a triangular base, much like a music stand. He had been entertaining the people around him with the well-known find-the-pea shell game, rapidly switching the positions of the cups and challenging a man who had laid a dollar on the edge of the table to select the cup under which the pea was hidden. Faster and faster his hands had flown, the three cups a confusing blur that had stopped suddenly, inviting speculation. When the victim's guess had been wrong, the observers had laughed, and the dollar had vanished into a pocket of the con man's vest.

"Try your luck," he'd enticed the others. "Just three little cups. Watch the pea carefully. Your eye must be faster than my hand. Who's next? It's really very simple. Double your money with one guess. Try your luck. Who's next, folks?"

One of the costumed passengers from the boat had stepped forward and laid down another dollar. The pea had been placed under one of the cups, and the game had begun again.

"He's really good," a familiar voice had commented from behind Alex and Jessie. They'd turned to find Don Sawyer peering over their shoulders to watch the shill.

"Hi," Jensen had greeted him. "Who is he? He looks pretty authentic."

"Oh, Jeff's all right. He's Soapy Smith's real great-grandson, Jefferson Randolph Smith IV. Lives in California and inherited all Soapy's games through his father and grandfather. That folding stand thing he's using? Same one Soapy used himself in Skagway during the gold rush. Jeff's brought his ancestor's three-card monte game, too. Neat, huh?"

Alex had agreed, and Sawyer had continued.

"He's scheduled to give a talk about Soapy Smith and a demonstration of the games for the passengers on the ship. Should be interesting, since he doesn't believe Soapy deserves his infamous reputation."

The game had continued behind them as the three had strolled off across the parade ground.

"Here comes someone I want you to meet," Don had said, waving a hand at an approaching couple.

The woman, as tall as the man with whom she

walked, had been easily identifiable, in her striking velvet costume and feathered hat, as the one Alex and Jessie had watched boarding the *Spirit* earlier in the afternoon. The deep burgundy red color of her dress, Jessie had noticed, complemented her dark complexion and hair.

"Alex Jensen and Jessie Arnold, meet Jim Beal and Laurie Trevino, two of our actors for the Thursday night mystery."

Beal, a slender six feet, had been wearing the thin mustache of a riverboat gambler, and the costume as well. His string tie had been fastened with what appeared to be a large gold nugget, though it had been a little exaggerated to be real. It had matched several smaller ones that had hung from a watch chain across the front of his green brocade vest. His black coat had been stylishly cut for the 1890s, and the outfit had been completed with a top hat and brass-headed cane meant, obviously, for show, not support, for it had been as slim as the rapier blade Jensen suspected it concealed, having once seen a similar device in a museum.

Beal had grinned as his awareness followed the trooper's inspection of his walking stick.

"Familiar with these?" he had asked, offering it for Jensen's inspection.

As Alex had flicked a small switch on the handle, the cane had slid easily apart into two pieces, one of them the foil he had expected. Upon closer examination, Jensen had realized it was a stage prop, collapsible, with no sharp edges.

"Clever," Jensen had grinned, handing it back to the actor.

"You might also be interested in this," Laurie Trevino had smiled, opening the drawstring bag she carried and handing him a very small lady's pistol.

Again, it had been a fake weapon, but one that would shoot caps to provide the report required in stagecraft.

"Are we going to see the *Shooting of Dan McGrew?*" Jensen had joked, handing the gun to Jessie, who had hefted its slight weight in the palm of her hand before giving it back to Laurie.

"Well, something similar," the actress had confirmed. "Starting tomorrow, we'll do three short scenes—one each day—leading up to a big finale scene at the Mystery Evening on Thursday. All the passengers may then submit their solutions to the whodunit."

"Are there other actors in this play?"

"Oh, sure," she'd answered, "and some of the Centennial Committee members—and Jeff Smith—are going to help out."

"Smith, I would imagine, will be playing his great-grandfather?" Alex asked.

"Right. He's pretty good. You see him do his shell game?"

"Yeah. Amusing."

"We could still add a character or two. With that mustache you'd be perfect for Arizona Charlie Meadows. Interested?"

"No thanks," Alex had told her. "I'd be better as part of the scenery. Not dramatically inclined, I'm afraid."

"Oh, Alex, you'd be great," Jessie had encouraged. "Why not give it a try?"

"It's really just a suggested script, with a certain latitude for ad-libbing," Laurie had told him. "Just having fun for an audience."

"Maybe for you," he'd grinned, shaking his head. "I'd probably freeze solid with stage fright."

"We could write your part out for you. It's an introduction for my part, really nothing more. Would you do it? It would add a lot."

"Well . . ."

"Oh good. Your part won't be till the second scene, on Tuesday. That means you can watch on Monday and get the idea. We'll get together and go through it. Thanks so much. Now, we've got to go. Nice to meet you both."

As the pair of thespians had walked away across the grass toward the hotel, Jessie and Sawyer had grinned, and Alex had wondered exactly what he had agreed to do.

Celebrations over, the *Spirit* was now quiet, with no one on deck. It was time for bed. Carefully knocking the dottle from his pipe into his hand, Jensen cast the dead residue of ash and its crumbs of singed tobacco into the wind, away from the ship. He put the pipe into his pocket, took a last look at the stars brightening overhead, and opened the door to the cabin. Jessie looked up from her book and smiled.

"Hey, trooper. Did you know that when the *Portland* docked in Seattle and started the gold rush, the mayor of Seattle was in San Francisco at a meeting, and didn't even bother to go home? He just wired his resignation and took off for the Klondike. Can you imagine?"

As he drifted toward sleep, vaguely aware of Jessie's soft breathing from her bed across the narrow stateroom, Jensen continued to recall the day's activities and the fascinating assortment of passengers he found himself with for this week-long trip down the Inside Passage to Seattle. Drowsily he recalled Laurie's enthusiasm about the play. Could he really be an actor?

Maybe I shouldn't have agreed to it. He turned over and yawned. *Well, what the heck?*

He drifted off to sleep, imagining himself as Arizona Charlie Meadows, striding across a stage in a fringed leather shirt and large, white Stetson, with a pair of pearl-handled six-shooters—famous western scout and sharpshooter for the Buffalo Bill Wild West show. *Shoot the spots off a playing card from thirty feet,* he mumbled and began to snore.

5

6:00 A.M.
Friday, July 11, 1997
Hazlit's Gull
Tracy Arm, Holkham Bay, Alaska

"DAMN IT. WHAT THE HELL ARE WE GONNA DO NOW?
She's sure as hell dead."

Once again the older man swore, as he had continued to do for the last four hours, with the same result—silence or accusation from his partner. This time it was the latter.

"Oh, *will* you shut the fuck up, Nelson? I *know* she's dead. Wouldn't be if you hadn't screwed it up. She must have thrown up and, with that tape over her mouth, choked. I think she had the flu or something. There's that medicine next to the bed. Just shut your trap. I'm thinking."

"But how was I supposed to know she was sick? I had to keep her quiet or she would've woke somebody up when we left. What're we gonna do? Nobody's gonna care if we *meant* to kill her or not. They'll just say . . ."

The younger man gave him such a menacing glare that he broke off what he was saying and looked down at the deck. Fumbling in his slicker pocket, he retrieved a crumpled package of cigarettes and lit one. It leaked a tiny ribbon of smoke from an infinitesimal tear in the paper, so he concentrated on carefully pinching the rip between finger and thumb and avoided looking at Rod while he smoked. "Damn it, anyway."

The rain had stopped, but clouds still hung low, obscuring some of the tallest peaks, and thin wisps of fog had begun to develop here and there over the channel as the wind slowly died to nothing. Rod had started the engine and they were again on their way, more slowly than they had been under sail, with the strength of the storm behind them, but still moving steadily to the south.

Ten minutes later Rod finally spoke.

"Look. We've got to get rid of her somewhere nobody will find her—somewhere really deep. So here's what we'll do. You go down and wrap her up in the sheet, or something, before she stiffens up too much . . ."

"Aw, *Rod* . . ."

"Don't start, Nelson. You want to run the boat? No? Well, then, just do it. Find some line and tie her up in a real good package. Then get that extra anchor that's in the sail locker in the bow and bring it up here."

"You gonna dump her overboard?"

"Yeah, but not here. With that anchor, she'll sink like a stone, probably would anyway, but I want her to stay sunk in deep water. We're almost to where Tracy Arm takes off out of Holkham Bay. There's a couple small coves back in there where we can tie up for a while and sleep till tonight. But, best of all, it goes straight down, practically to China. We'll dump her and that'll be that. Nobody'd ever find her, even if they knew where to look. Which they won't."

Not pleased with his assignment, Nelson reluctantly went down to follow his instructions, since the idea of running the boat appealed to him even less. In the forward sail locker he found the anchor, a large Danforth, which he lugged back to the cockpit and left on the deck, along with a coil of line. He then disappeared below decks, where he remained for the better part of half an hour before reappearing, face wet with sweat, an open bottle of whisky in one hand.

"Goddamn, I hate stiffs. Gives me the willies to touch 'em." He shuddered and tipped the bottle to take a long pull.

Rod had run the boat into Holkham Bay and was now heading up Tracy Arm, a confined passage that was walled on both sides by high cliffs, scraped and scored by the glaciers that had formed it long before. If the steepness of what could be seen above the water was any indication, the bottom must be hundreds of feet down, Nelson thought, with an uneasy feeling.

"There's gonna be no place to put down an anchor to lay up here," he said to Rod.

"Don't intend to. The only anchor I care to see slide over the side is the one that goes down with her. I'll tie us off between a couple of rocks. Don't panic. Haul her up here and get that anchor tied on."

"Hey. I can't carry *that* by myself. She looked little, but she's a dead weight now. You gotta help."

"Drag her, damn it. I'll help lift her up the steps. Hurry up before we get too close and I have to mind the boat."

The woman's body, bound with its anchor, made a remarkably small splash as it fell from the stern of the *Gull*. Both men watched it vanish into the depths of Tracy Arm until a wisp of fog crept around the boat, obscuring the surface of the water.

"Gone," said Rod, turning to recheck the lines he had used to secure the sailboat between a large boulder and a stunted scrub of a tree on shore. Moving to the boat's inflatable dinghy, upside-down on the cabin roof, he began to untie it. "Get me those two

cans of paint out of the galley. Before we sleep I got to change the name on this thing."

In a short time and with a little less than professional effort, he had cleverly transformed the *Hazlit's Gull* into *Harry's Doll*. Climbing back aboard, he left the dinghy floating from the stern of the larger boat.

His partner sat morosely smoking, the level of the whisky in the bottle fallen to three-quarters.

"Jesus, Nelson. Why did I bring you? You're drunk, you S.O.B. Go get some sleep. It's over—she's gone forever. Nothing to worry about. Nothing to prove she was ever here."

The old man staggered to his feet and tossed his cigarette toward the side, where it fell short, hung up against a cleat, and smoldered until Rod snatched it up and tossed it overboard. Without looking back, Nelson shuffled to the companionway and down into the cabin, toward the head and a bunk, in that order.

Rod stared after him, shaking his head in disgust, then reached for the bottle and took a deep swallow of his own. Carefully checking the boat to be sure all was secure, he soon followed his own advice and went below.

But forever is a long time, and far beneath their somnolent oblivion, the hasty knots Nelson had inexpertly tied began to loosen as they were dragged against the steep rock that angled into the depths. The body tumbled through the water, scraping stones in slow motion until the line caught on a sharp protrusion, giving the anchor just enough slack to slip free and continue the long, silent fall on its own.

For a time the body remained where it had paused, swaying gently. Then the determined current of the incoming tide twisted it with curious fingers, the line holding it pulled free, allowing it to drift languidly away into the frigid waters of Tracy Arm, rising a little nearer the surface, toward a fate neither of the sleeping men could have imagined in their worst nightmares.

6

7:45 A.M.
Monday, July 14, 1997
Spirit of '98
Peril Strait, Inside Passage, Alaska

MOST OF THE TIME HE SPENT PILOTING HIS SHIP THROUGH
the deep icy waters of the Inside Passage, Captain
Dave Kay's face was more inclined to smile than to
frown. Close observation disclosed a glint of farsight-
edness in his eyes, the result of guiding the *Spirit of
'98* through roughly a thousand miles of uncertain
waters on an almost weekly basis during the tourist
season. He was, quietly and competently, totally
aware of whatever was happening around him at any
given moment. At this particular moment on Monday morning, however, he was quite uncharacteristi-
cally frowning.

Jensen was not anticipating a frown when he was
ushered into the captain's office just behind the
bridge, though the frown faded as Captain Kay rose,
offered his hand, and indicated a chair. Alex lowered
his tall frame into it. Having enjoyed a hearty breakfast, he and Jessie had been leaving the dining room
on the lower deck when the first mate appeared to
relay the official request for his presence.

"Thanks for coming up, Sergeant. Glad to have
you aboard."

"Thank you. It's a fine ship."

The captain glanced down at a sheet of paper in front of him on the desk and was silent for a minute before he gave Jensen a serious, thoughtful look. "Do you consider yourself on or off duty, Sergeant?"

Jensen qualified his answer, hoping to ascertain the purpose behind the query. "On . . . a special kind of duty, I guess, sir," he equivocated. "I was instructed that I should be present, in uniform, for all official functions on the trip, but otherwise to enjoy the cruise. But, in a way, I'm always on duty. All troopers are." Then, anticipating, "Why? You have a problem?"

Kay hesitated a moment and pursed his lips slightly before answering. "Ah . . . well . . . unfortunately, it would seem so."

Weight on his elbows, the captain leaned forward on the desk with an air of restrained frustration.

"In the last few hours three passengers have come to me with reports of pilfering in their cabins last night. All of them claim that while they were ashore in Haines for the reception, possessions they left aboard were disturbed. The cabins weren't vandalized or trashed. Carefully, skillfully searched and several items are apparently missing: a gold nugget chain necklace of some kind, cash and a silver money clip, and an antique pocket watch of sentimental and historic value. Two of them didn't even notice the thefts until this morning—one came to me last night, here on the bridge, after everyone had already gone to bed."

As Kay spoke, Jensen straightened in his chair and gave the captain his complete attention, his law enforcement awareness taking over. His air of respectful deference vanished, the "sir" in his vocabulary forgotten. They were suddenly two equal individuals with a shared predicament.

"Who came last night?"

"Judy Raymond, from 305. The necklace was hers."

"One might indicate a simple misplacement or loss, but three is too many to be anything *but* theft. Is there any way they could be related?"

"Yes. The three cabins involved are next to each other on the forward starboard side of the Upper Deck—301, 303, and 305."

"Just forward and on the opposite side from ours, 314. Isn't there another one in that group, and who are the passengers in those cabins?"

"Yes, but 307 wasn't touched. Occupied by a Mr. Stanley and his daughter." The frown returned to the captain's face as he glanced unhappily at the paper between his elbows. "Who those passengers are compounds the problem. All those cabins are occupied by the descendants of Klondike miners, three of whom—including Stanley—had relatives on the *Portland* in 1897 and are all honored guests for this centennial thing. The others are Bill and Nella Berry, Charles . . . Chuck . . . Lovegren and his wife Carol, and Judy Raymond. The worst part of this is that the necklace and the watch were family heirlooms, handed down from the gold rush. As you can imagine, they're not too happy about it."

"What about the clip? Not an heirloom?"

"No, thank God. It was on the money that was stolen."

Stolen. The word lay between them like a most unpleasant tangible thing, and the captain's frown emphasized his reluctance to define the problem so explicitly.

"Look, I'd really appreciate your help on this," he told Jensen. "You're better trained and equipped to deal with it than I am. Critical incident training is one thing—identifying potential situations before they happen. I've had to take care of an alcoholic passenger or two, a crewman with a warrant for a hit-and-run in Seattle . . . once somebody took home a life ring . . . we never did find out who, or how they got it off the ship. But never serious theft. The cabins are open, no locked doors, but everybody has always respected that. Never a problem. We suggest that any real valuables go in the hotel manager's safe."

"Anyone *could* just walk into any cabin at any time?"

They could, but don't. It's an honor system, company policy . . . establishes a certain friendly, trusting atmosphere that we encourage. Passengers don't have to carry keys, misplace them, forget and take them home accidentally. It also makes it much easier for the crew to get in for cleaning. It isn't that large a ship, room for just under a hundred passengers and a crew of twenty-five. There's almost always someone on deck. You'd have to be just about invisible . . ."

"Unless everyone is ashore . . . at a reception, say? Maybe not too smart security-wise. How about lunch and dinner? Everyone's served at once, aren't they? All in the dining room at the same time?"

"Well, yes . . . but late morning and during lunch the cabins are being cleaned . . . faster when they're empty and unlocked . . . and at dinnertime there are crew members turning down beds, going in and out of all the cabins. There's no time it would be easy."

"How about someone who is neither a passenger nor a crew member? An outsider? Someone who could slip aboard and off again without being seen."

"Not possible. When we're in any port, we keep someone posted at the dockside end of the gangway to watch for just that sort of thing. Only passengers are allowed on board. Anyone else must be identified, have special permission, and be accompanied by someone from the ship."

"So . . . it probably isn't an outsider."

"I don't think so. But now, realistically, without other options, you're about to come to a conclusion that really bothers me—whoever did this is either one of the passengers . . . or one of my crew. And I don't like either one."

There was silence for a moment or two, while the two men looked at each other with concern. Jensen could sense a slight shift to port. The faint scream of a gull drifted in from somewhere outside.

"Obviously, the passengers, including those who were robbed, were off the ship in Haines."

"Yes."

"Did any passengers stay on board?"

"Only three, as near as I can figure. A Mrs. Blake, in 302, which backs up to the Berrys in 301—elderly woman who uses a wheelchair most of the time. Her niece, Rozetta Moisan, did get off for a quick walk on the dock, but she got right back on and was never out of sight of the crew member, at the gangway. The other was a retired man, Wayne Johnson, in 308—drank too much between Skagway and Haines, went to bed. His wife went to the party without him."

The penny dropped for Alex concerning Edith Johnson's discomfort over her husband's *illness.*

"Oh, yeah. We met her. Heavyset woman in a pink-and-blue dress."

"Who was the crew member at the gangway?"

"My first mate. Totally trustworthy woman . . . no question."

There was a long moment of hesitation, during which Captain Kay took a deep breath, let it out, got to his feet, and walked over to look out a starboard window.

"Who was responsible for turning down the beds in those cabins?" Jensen asked. "That was done while we were at the reception. We'd better start there."

Kay turned to face him, misgiving unmistakably etched on his face, though he nodded agreement. "I've already sent for her," he said, stepping to open the connecting door to the bridge. "Julie, would you come in, please?"

A young woman in her mid-twenties came into the room. Perhaps five feet two, she had shoulder-length brown hair tied back with a blue ribbon, and intelligent eyes the color of coffee. She wore tan slacks and a white cotton shirt under a navy blue anorak with the same tan lining its collar. *Alaska Sightseeing/Cruise West* was machine-embroidered on her top left jacket pocket, a name tag with *Julie* and the company logo—a polar bear in profile within a bright blue circle—pinned to the pocket on the right.

"Jensen, this is Julie Morrison, one of our CSRs. Ah . . . that's Customer Service Representative. Julie, Sergeant Alex Jensen, Alaska State Troopers."

Alex noted with a glance that Kay was also carefully watching the woman's reaction to the introduction of his official position. Her response *was* interesting. For a bare fraction of a second she was still, and something very like apprehension seemed to move in her eyes; nothing overtly identifiable, more an impression than anything conclusive. Then, so quickly and smoothly that it left Jensen wondering if he had imagined her initial stillness, with a nod to the captain, she stepped forward and held out a hand. "Nice to meet you, sir." Her smile transformed her face with a cheerful openness—a completely likable, innocent person.

They shook hands, and, still smiling, she stepped back and turned her attention to Captain Kay.

"Julie," he began, waving her to a chair and sitting down behind his desk, "you didn't leave the ship last night in Haines?"

"No, sir. There really wasn't time. The crew waited to eat dinner until the passengers had gone ashore, so we were a little later than usual. Then we had the party cleanup in the lounge, cabin check and bed turndowns to do, plus some extra printed information that the centennial committee asked to have distributed along with the usual pins and welcoming information we put in the cabins. It was after eight when we finished. Didn't seem worth while to get off. I went to the lounge."

"Anyone help you turn down the beds?"

"No, sir. I did the Upper Deck alone."

"Anyone else around on that deck?"

"No, sir, not outside. Mr. Johnson was in 308. He was asleep and didn't answer, so I thought the cabin was empty and went in. I left their things on the other bed. Mrs. Blake and her niece were awake in 302. Everyone else was gone. It was pretty quiet."

"No one else at all?"

"No, sir. Not that I saw."

Kay looked at Jensen, who had remained silent. The captain nodded an invitation to the trooper to question Morrison.

The woman also turned to look at him, and, once again, uneasiness flickered in her eyes, though her expression of pleasant helpfulness did not change. It altered the tentative approach Jensen had been about to take with his questions, motivating him toward a more aggressive interrogation.

"Three cabins were burglarized last night, Ms. Morrison. All three on the Upper Deck—your deck. Were you aware of this?"

The congenial expression left her face along with its color. For several seconds, mouth open, she simply stared at him without answering, recognition of their suspicion abruptly dawning.

"Well?"

"*No*, sir. I wasn't," she at last responded, shaking her head.

"It seems you may have been the last, perhaps the only, person to enter and leave those particular cabins before their occupants returned. Can you explain that, in light of the thefts?"

Apprehension was now clearly apparent in more than her eyes. It tightened the line of her lips and drew vertical marks between her brows as anger began to mix with it. She glared at him defensively, started to speak, cleared her throat, and finally all but spit the words out.

"*No,* I can't explain that. But I didn't take *anything* from anyone's cabin." Her voice rose in indignation, real or feigned. "I don't take things that don't belong to me. *Ever.*"

Jensen let the tension stretch itself out for a few moments as he looked at Julie Morrison without speaking. For perhaps thirty seconds, she held his gaze, then looked down at the hands rigidly gripping each other in her lap, fingers tensely interlocked.

"You should be aware that we will need to search your cabin, Ms. Morrison," he told her in a more conversational tone.

Her attention returned abruptly to his face, and, though it seemed impossible, she appeared to turn even more pale.

"I don't think you can do that without my permission. Not without a warrant."

"Julie," Captain Kay broke in, "if you didn't have anything to do with this, then let Sergeant Jensen do his search and prove it."

She bit her lip and shook her head.

"I can get a warrant in Sitka, if you force me to do it," Jensen told her. "Why not just get it over with now?"

"No," she all but whispered. "I can't."

"Why?" the captain asked.

Her only answer was to shake her head, refusing to look at him.

"Julie . . ."

"No. *No.* I didn't do it. There's nothing there."

"Then let us look."

"No."

She remained adamant, and they had little choice but to let her leave. She went out through the bridge, white-faced, arms folded defensively in front of her, and she disappeared toward the work she was assigned in the dining room."

"What do you think?" Captain Kay asked as the door shut behind her.

"Pretty upset. She's hiding something," Jensen answered. "Just didn't quite seem the reaction I would have expected if she's guilty. Why wouldn't she just deny it? What was all that refusal of a cabin search? She's right about the warrant, but . . ." He grinned suddenly. "Not much to do, after all, you don't have a brig, do you?"

Captain Kay shook his head and couldn't prevent the ghost of a smile.

"If she *took* those things, she *could* get rid of them before we get to Sitka. Lot of ocean out there."

"Risk we'll have to take. She been aboard long?"

"New this season. Replaced a veteran crew member who left to get married."

"Where'd she work before?"

"One of the big cruise ships . . . Princess, I think. Came with a good recommendation."

"I'd better take a look at it and check with Seattle for any wants or warrants. Of course it doesn't have to be her at all. There are plenty of other passengers in cabins on other decks, with their own crew members to take care of them, and other crew members as well. She just seems suspicious. May be some completely different reason for not wanting her quarters searched."

"That's true, all right."

"With your approval, I'd like to get an officer with a fingerprint kit to come aboard in Sitka, to take prints in the cabins where the thefts occurred. He probably won't find much, considering how many people are in and out, but who knows? It's worth a try. I'll go talk to the folks in those three cabins. I'm sure they can't tell me much more, but it will give me a more complete picture, and let them know we're onto it," Jensen suggested. With Kay's agreement, he headed for the door.

Just short of it, he turned back. "I'd like a list of everyone who was on board during the reception," he said. "Crew, passengers, everyone—even for part of the time. Crew members should list the time they went ashore and came back, if they did. Okay? Later, I'd like to have a look at the security for that gold we've got on board?"

"Sure. I'll get the list for you. You really don't need to worry about the gold. We had it checked by the trooper in Skagway after it was loaded, and the security company that provided the guards is bonded and gave us a record of their work."

"Still . . . when we have time, okay?"

At a nod from Kay he went out onto the bridge. The first mate gave him a smile as he passed through the quiet room, where the dials, wheels, and technology it took to sail a ship this size worked constantly. Who first, he wondered, and where would he find the passengers he needed to see?

This, he suddenly realized, was not turning out to be the relaxing cruise he had anticipated.

7

9:00 A.M.
Monday, July 14, 1997
Spirit of '98
Peril Strait, Inside Passage, Alaska

COMING DOWN AN OUTSIDE STAIRWAY, JENSEN WALKED
along the rail, past the owner's suite, which lay just
behind the bridge and captain's office. Together these
three adjoining facilities filled the forward half of the
Bridge Deck. The rear half of this deck was not en-
closed, though it was partially covered with a blue
canvas awning protecting a dozen or so weatherproof
tables and chairs. Aft of the awning, open to the sky,
a shuffleboard and giant checkerboard had been
painted onto the sundeck. A small skiff with an outboard engine was secured next to the port rail and a
paint locker was farther to the rear.

At the corner of the owner's suite, he turned right
to a stairway and went down it to the next—Upper—
deck. There, with elbows on the rail, he found Jessie,
with her camera, viewing the northern shore of Baranof Island as it passed by at surprisingly close range.
During breakfast, through the picture windows of the
dining room, they had seen the mile wide lower
reaches of Peril Strait, into which they were headed.
Now, the strait had narrowed by half, making it plain

why larger ships dared not venture into this slim passage. The smaller *Spirit* could easily and safely glide through the waters of the strait, a shortcut that reduced the required travel time by almost half a day, and allowed its passengers a closer look at the flora and fauna of the region.

Small islands littered the shoreline, heavily forested like the mainland. Yesterday's sunshine had disappeared behind a low layer of clouds that threatened rain before nightfall, something for which this part of the state was famous. A pair of eagles—silent predators—drew lazy circles against the pearly gray of the overcast, searching with keen eyes for any fish unfortunate enough to swim near the surface of the strait. A salmon, too large to interest them, leapt from the steel gray water midway between the ship and the shore, attracting Jensen's attention, though the sound of its splash was covered by the deep rumble of the *Spirit*'s engines.

"Like to get a hook in that one."

"Hi." Jessie smiled up at him as he leaned on the rail beside her. "Did you know that Disney's Scrooge McDuck supposedly made his fortune in the Klondike during the gold rush?"

"Nope. Didn't know that. Where'd you collect that bit of trivia?"

"Don Sawyer. Ran into him in the lounge a while ago. I told him about the mayor of Seattle, and he told me about McDuck."

"Are there a lot of people in the lounge?"

"Yeah. You want to go . . ."

The public address system interrupted, coming to life over their heads:

"Consider the bow of the boat as twelve o'clock and you will see several sea otters at ten o'clock on the port side of the ship, about a hundred yards out. Though the adults weigh sixty to seventy pounds, these are the smallest of all marine mammals and have the densest fur, which was why they were hunted almost to extinction until they be-

*came a protected species in 1911. There are now approxi-
mately a hundred and fifty thousand of them in the waters
of Alaska. They are extremely social animals, sometimes
floating together in rafts of several hundred. Usually they
swim on their backs, but they will quickly dive underwater
if startled. Look carefully. This time of year there should
be some with babies that are often fed as the mothers drift
in the water. Sea otters eat lots of clams, mussels, urchins,
and crabs, which they break open by pounding them on
rocks that they balance on their stomachs as they float."*

By the time the disembodied voice had completed
its recital of information, the ship had slowed until
it was barely moving through the channel, giving the
passengers, who had flocked to that side of the ship,
a better look at the otters. With her most powerful
zoom lens, Jessie focused in on a few of the closest
animals. Some disappeared, as predicted, at the
ship's approach, but the rest remained, rocking comfortably on the surface of the water, lifting their
heads, curious, to observe their observers.

"Look at them watching us," Jessie laughed.
"Aren't they great?"

"Always bigger than I expect," Alex remarked.
"Photographs make them seem the size of teddy
bears, and about as cuddly, if a little damp."

"What did the captain want?" Jessie asked.

"Nothing good. Come inside and I'll tell you,
while I find my notebook."

Their stateroom, though not large, was comfortably
arranged with two single beds, a small desk and
chair, and a compact bathroom with a shower. No
space was wasted. Even the suitcases fit neatly under
the beds, after Jessie and Alex had unpacked into
two generous drawers at the foot of each. Green glass
shaded reading lamps over each bed added a touch
of the antique. Once inside, he told her why the captain had invited him to the bridge.

Jessie deposited her camera bag on her bed and

sat down beside it. Alex found a notebook and pen in his gym bag and looked at her.

"Were you aware that these cabin doors are never locked?" he asked.

"Yes. Weren't you? They mentioned it at breakfast, when the cruise coordinator told us the specifics of the stop in Sitka. She went over the things we needed to know about the ship and scheduling, things we didn't hear last night because the reception in Haines took the place of dinner on board."

"Well, I must have been talking to someone and missed it. I'm not completely comfortable with what the captain calls *company policy*, for obvious reasons. But, also, I can't leave this here, unsecured." He took a holstered Colt .45, the semiautomatic side arm he had carried as squad leader of a Marine airborne team years earlier, from the gym bag. He had learned to prefer it over the .357 Magnum that was usually part of his uniform.

"You can't carry it around all the time. Isn't there a safe in the hotel manager's office for passenger use?"

"Think I'll ask the captain if he has one on the bridge. There's always someone up there. It'd be more secure and easier to get at if I need it." He slid it into the pocket of his jacket, where it lay, a heavily obvious lump.

"What are you going to do about the thefts?" Jessie asked. "Can I help? I'd like to see you in action for a change, instead of hearing everything secondhand."

He thought about this. In a community of just over a hundred people, in this small, confined area, it would be difficult to investigate with any anonymity. Jessie's natural curiosity could be a big help.

"Why not?" he agreed. "But you have to understand I'm the officer in charge. Let me ask the questions. Okay?"

"Yes, sir . . . *sir*." She saluted, with a grin. "And what are my orders now, sir?"

"Here." He tossed her the notebook and pen. "We

find and talk to Judy Raymond, the Berrys, and the
Lovegrens, who lost items from their staterooms.
Then Stanley and his daughter, who are in the last
stateroom of that group of four. I also want to meet
Mrs. Blake and her niece, and Mr. Johnson, all of
whom skipped the reception, for whatever reason,
and stayed on board. I'll do the interviews, and you
can take notes for me, please."

"Okay. I can do that, but I don't take shorthand,
you know."

"That's okay. Just get the particulars accurately—
times, locations, item descriptions—important stuff.
Use your own judgment. If I want anything specific,
I'll look over at you, or nod."

With that, they were off to the lounge to see who
they could locate, with a side trip to the bridge,
where Jensen left his .45 in the safe the captain did
indeed have in his office. While they were there, Jensen made two phone calls. He was then ready to
begin his investigative interviews.

On the deck below their stateroom, the Grand
Salon, or main lounge, *was* comfortably filled when
Arnold and Jensen entered. There was an attractive,
dark wood bar to the left of the door, and tables
in a variety of sizes were informally arranged and
surrounded with matching chairs. A few sofas and
armchairs completed the furniture. Old-fashioned
lighting fixtures and a player piano added to the
turn-of-the-century atmosphere. A display case in
one corner offered blue-and-white *Spirit of '98* mugs,
T-shirts, sweatshirts, and other souvenirs.

Though most of the passengers were watching the
scenery glide by through wide windows on three
sides, a few seemed oblivious to what was going by
outside. Two couples were playing bridge at a
smaller table near the center of the room, the player
with the dummy hand refilling empty coffee cups
and juice glasses. Two women, at a table near the

perpetual coffee urn, were working on stitchery pieces, their bright-colored yarns spread out in a rainbow on the tabletop. Another, at the same table, was knitting what looked like a fuzzy orange sweater.

On a sofa on the port-side of the lounge, Jessie noticed Judy Raymond talking to Bill Prentice, the man who had offered to pay for her drink in Skagway. Intent on their conversation, she did not appear to notice that Alex and Jessie had come in. Jessie pointed her out to Alex.

"I'll talk to her later. Right now I want to start with the Berrys and the Lovegrens. We met them at the Haines reception, remember? See any of them?"

"Yes, both. Over there, in front, by the windows."

A low cabinet served as a divider about three-quarters of the way forward from the doors of the salon. Beyond it were a collection of armchairs, from which the passengers had a good forward view of whatever they were passing. In four of these, the couples they sought were talking together.

"Shared history, I'll bet," Jensen commented, as he started across the room toward them. "Ancestors in the gold rush."

"You're not going to talk to them here?"

"No. In their cabins. I want to see the crime scenes."

8

10:00 A.M.
Monday, July 14, 1997
Spirit of '98
Peril Strait, Inside Passage, Alaska

BILL AND NELLA BERRY, COOPERATIVE AND FRIENDLY, WILL-
ingly accompanied Jensen and Arnold to cabin 301.

"Captain Kay said you would want to speak to
us," Bill Berry told Alex. "Whatever we can do to
help, just ask. I'm very concerned about getting that
watch back. My grandfather carried it to the Klondike during the rush. It means a lot to me."

"He one of the Bonanza and Eldorado Berry brothers?" Jensen couldn't resist asking.

"Yes," the other man said, nodding, "Fred, the
youngest. Frank was the oldest, and Clarence and
Henry were the other two, all a part of Klondike
history because they struck it rich on both Bonanza
and Eldorado Creeks. Clarence and his wife Ethel D.
were on the *Portland* when it reached Seattle, with a
hundred and thirty thousand in gold. You must be
interested in gold rush history, Sergeant."

"It's a thousand great stories. I've done a lot of
reading. Clarence was one of the only successful
stampeders to put his money to work and build it
into a family fortune, along with his brothers,
wasn't he?"

"That's right. The companies he started are still in the family."

"I'd like to compare notes sometime, if you don't mind, but we should get back to the watch. Is there any way to identify it, sir?" Jensen asked, as they entered the cabin.

"I never turn down an opportunity to talk gold rush, but only if you'll call me Bill."

"Alex, then," Jensen agreed. "I think this situation is casual enough to dispense with the formalities."

Jessie was looking around with interest. The cabin was larger than the one in which she and Alex were staying. Most forward of eleven along this side of the ship, its outer, windowed wall was curved to follow the shape of the hull. The door opened to the outside, as did all but a few on the lowest deck. It held a queen-sized bed, though the rest of the furnishings were similar to those in all the cabins. As Bill waved them to chairs, she took one farthest from the door and made herself ready to take notes.

The Berrys were an attractive couple in their forties, with a hint of smile lines in the right places. Honey blond hair curled softly around her face, while his hair was darker and had receded to expand his forehead. Small courtesies between them—a touch of hands, a quick glance of communication—spoke of respect and affection that repetition had worn smooth and rich into a gratifying marriage. Tucked into the frame of a mirror above a built-in vanity was the picture of a pleasant-looking young man in his twenties, evidently their son, and another of a young woman, a daughter. That these should be a part of their trip was another clue to family solidarity.

"Yes," Berry said, answering Jensen's question about the watch. "An inscription inside the cover, 'Love, Mother to Fred.' My great-grandmother gave it to him the year before the rush. You might be surprised that it still runs."

Jessie noted the inscription and the working order of the timepiece, as Berry pulled open one of the built-in drawers under the bed to show Jensen where the watch had been placed before it was stolen. The black, hinged, velvet-covered box that had held it remained in the drawer. He opened it to show the impression of a pocket watch on the velvet lining.

"It was a good watch for its day—steel, no precious metal or jewels. The brothers were doing a lot of prospecting, and she must have known he needed one he could depend on, that wouldn't be easily damaged. There wasn't anything to make it different from a hundred others, but the inscription will identify it."

Next to the velvet box lay a soft-sided roll of chamois leather, a travel case for jewelry.

"Was this in the drawer when the watch was taken?"

"Yes. Funny *it* wasn't touched."

"May I?"

"Certainly."

Alex picked it up and turned to Nella Berry.

"This must be yours."

"Yes, it is."

He laid it on the bed beside her, untied and unrolled it. In its divided compartments were several pairs of earrings, a silver and turquoise necklace, a gold bracelet.

"Nothing missing?"

"Not a thing, and these ruby earrings weren't in the case. They were over there on the vanity, in plain sight."

Alex retied and replaced the case, with a thoughtful glance at Jessie, who was busily taking notes.

"You might want to put this in the ship's safe, Mrs. Berry. At least until we solve this."

"You don't think whoever it was will come back?"

"No, not really. Word will have filtered out by now, making the thief cautious. Is there anyone on board, besides yourselves, who knew the watch was here?"

They both shook their heads. "We've just met the Lovegrens, and the watch hasn't been mentioned," Bill offered. "Anyone could have seen it when I came aboard in my costume, or at the reception in the lounge, I guess, but it's not worth much, really . . . except to me. If it were gold . . ."

Jensen hesitated, then asked, "Have you met the CSR, the crew member who takes care of your cabin?"

"Julie? Yes. She introduced herself yesterday, not long after we came aboard. Nice girl."

"Anything out of the ordinary about her behavior?"

Nella Berry frowned slightly, following the direction of his questions. "No. Do you really think . . ."

"Probably not, but I'd appreciate your not mentioning that possibility to anyone else. I'm just dotting the i's and crossing the t's. Don't worry about it. We'll keep you posted."

As there was little more to ask or see, Jensen excused himself and Jessie, and they went next door to the Lovegrens' stateroom, which was smaller than the Berrys' and was arranged as a twin. Their interview was similar, but, while the theft of his money had obviously raised Chuck Lovegren's temper, he was also sheepishly embarrassed.

"My fault. Shouldn't have left over four hundred dollars lying around. Wouldn't do it in a hotel room. Why should I do it here? Felt like no one could get at you on the water. Dumb. Real dumb. Still, it really burns me. You got any ideas yet?"

"Was it . . . lying around?"

"Well, not really. In one of my jacket pockets." He pointed to a maroon waterproof jacket hanging over the back of one of the chairs. "That's just like I left it last night when we went ashore. I hope you catch the bastard, *and* get him what he deserves."

Jensen assured them that he would let them know if the money clip and cash turned up, though Jessie noticed that, to her relief, he did not mention Julie Morrison. Lovegren, short and generally round, with hair tending to wisps of graying-brown, and a florid complexion that practically announced a struggle with blood pressure, seemed just the type to confront the CSR directly. His wife, Carol, was friendly and quiet. She had nothing new to offer, nodding agreement with her husband's statements. When Alex closed the door on their stateroom, he found himself wondering which one of the two, Charles or Carol, was somehow related to a gold rush stampeder.

Neither Judy Raymond nor John Stanley and his daughter were in their cabins.

Not knowing what the Stanleys looked like, Alex and Jessie headed down to the next deck, hoping to find someone who did. Judy Raymond, Jessie remembered, had been in the lounge, reading. As they reached the foot of the stairs and were about to enter the lounge, the door to the elevator opened, and an elderly woman in a wheelchair was pushed out into the corridor by a younger woman wearing slacks and a blue *Spirit of '98* sweatshirt.

A pompadour of pure white hair, pulled into a knot on top of her head, was the first and most noticeable thing about the older woman. After that came the piercing, unfaded blue of a pair of remarkably confident, intelligent eyes. Though she was thin, in her prime she had apparently been tall, for despite her fragile appearance she was not at all childlike in the chair. Her shoulders and neck were hunched slightly forward in the suggestion of a dowager's hump, reminding Jessie of a great blue heron she had once seen near an island while sea-kayaking. Dignity and watchfulness were words she could easily attribute to both.

"Please," the older woman called out in a strong, low tone. "Wait. I want to speak with you, Sergeant."

Seemingly dissatisfied with the speed at which her niece was moving her, she waved both hands in the air to indicate her impatience, then demanded a halt just short of the toes of Alex's deck shoes.

"Thank you, Rozie, love," she said. "You go ahead, now. I'll be along in a minute. Pour me a coffee, please, dear, if it's not weak as dishwater. None of that whitener stuff, either. If there's no cream I'll drink it black."

Her niece, a tall, dark-haired woman in her mid-thirties, with a build similar to that of her aunt, nodded, smiled vaguely at Alex and Jessie, and disappeared into the lounge.

"There," the aunt remarked with the air of having disposed of a minor problem. "Now." She waved toward the door leading to the outer deck. "We could, I think, talk there." Without waiting to see if they followed, or asking for assistance, she wheeled herself across, locked the wheels of the chair, rose to her feet, and pushed open the door. "Coming?"

At the astonished looks on their faces, she threw back her head in a bray of gratified laughter. "One of life's small pleasures—surprising people," she said, as they came through to join her by the rail, the door closing behind them. "I confess I use that one on a fairly regular basis. People do tend to make such quick assumptions don't they? I'm not quite a cripple—just becoming more of one by the day. Rheumatoid arthritis." With more impatience than self-pity, she exhibited hands that displayed some of the characteristic deformation of the disease. "It's in my hips and legs, too. By the time I'm seventy-five—in two years—my doctor thinks I'll be confined to the damn chair. It'll make traveling more difficult, so I'm doing a lot of it now, with Rozetta's help. Why not? My husband left me well taken care of. I have more damned money than any of those Klondikers—

all Texas *black* gold. What'll I spend it on later, or ever, for that matter? You'll pardon my not shaking hands, Sergeant.''

Alex had to grin in spite of himself. He had already warmed to this feisty woman, with her practical, positive outlook and sense of knowing exactly what she wanted and how to get it. He noticed that she retained enough vanity to still wear two rings of unmistakable value on those somewhat twisted fingers: a significant diamond next to her wedding band, and a large natural blue sapphire.

"You *do* say what you think, don't you, Mrs. Blake?"

"*Exactly*, Sergeant. One of the only benefits of getting old is the right to be eccentric as hell. What can they do—take away my birthday? And it's Dallas—for the place I was born—not Mrs. Blake. That was my mother-in-law, who's been dead a long time, thank God. Just Dallas, please."

"Just Dallas, then. I'm Alex . . . Jensen, and this is Jessie Arnold, my . . . ah . . . assistant."

"If you say so." Dallas's expression was amused. "Nice to meet you, Jessie. I've heard the Iditarod mentioned in the same breath with your name, have I not?"

The concentrated wattage of her smile elicited answering grins from both Jessie and Alex, pleased with her delight in recognizing Jessie's achievement in the famous sled dog race.

Alex broke the spell. "The captain says you didn't leave the ship last night in Haines. Is that right?"

"Yes, it is. I'd had enough champagne and excitement for an old broad," she answered. "Got as comfortable as possible in my bed and read a good book between catnaps for a couple of hours. I tried to send Rozetta, but she wouldn't go. She went for a few minutes' walk, but came right back.

"Now . . . from what I understand, there was some

kind of a robbery in a couple of cabins while everyone was gone, and you're looking into it, right?"

"That's right," he told her. "Why? Did you notice something?"

"No, but while my niece was gone I heard someone walk quietly past my cabin."

"What time was that?"

"Must have been about seven, maybe a little later.
I thought it was Rozetta coming back, but whoever
it was went on by. I didn't see, of course. Could have
been anyone. There was something familiar about the
sound of the steps, but they were gone before I could
figure out what. Then Rozie came back and a few
minutes later the girl came to turn down the beds.
Might have been her, I suppose, but she seems to
have a specific order to her work. This other one was
going the wrong direction and didn't sound the
same."

"Anything unusual about CSR Julie's behavior?"

Dallas gave him a sharp look. "Makes sense she'd
be the initial suspect, but no, nothing out of the ordinary. She came in politely, did her job, and left. She's
got a problem, though."

"Problem? What do you mean?"

"Personal kind. She reminds me of someone I used
to know. When I asked her if she'd ever lived in
Phoenix—that's where I moved after Calvin died
twelve years ago—she said no, but stiffened up some.
Got to watch people. They'll tell you more by the
way they move than by what they say. She brings to
mind a bird I had once that never lost an opportunity
to get out of its cage. She knows what the inside of
a cage feels like, that one. She watches everything."

It was an interesting and insightful observation,
and Alex, remembering the earlier flash of apprehension in Julie Morrison's brown eyes, didn't doubt her.
He wondered briefly what Dallas Blake's intuition
had told her about him. She'd already figured out
his relationship. He glanced to where Jessie was lean-

ing on the rail, following the conversation with interest. They were a little alike—this up-front Texas
lady—and she was a *lady*—and Jess, in the genuine-
ness of their approach to life, though Jessie's style
was gentler, less obvious. Still, if she was going to
be anything like Dallas at seventy-three, he thought
he'd like to stick around to see it.

"Tell me a little about your niece, Rozetta . . . Moisan, is it?"

"Yes . . . well . . . to be honest, Rozie's a bit fragile
at the moment, Alex. Had a bad patch the last two
years. Lost a baby she wanted desperately. Then they
found a lump, and the pig of a surgeon had got
permission from her husband to do whatever was
necessary while she was still under. What he thought
necessary was a radical mastectomy. Her husband—
a Houston development shark—couldn't handle it.
Refused to touch her, treated her like she was contagious, or something. Sued the doctor and everybody
else involved, and, when he lost, divorced her—
though he was in the process of doing that anyway.
Left her with nothing but a house she couldn't pay
the mortgage on.

"I found her hiding in her bedroom closet. She'd
lost thirty pounds, looked and acted like a concentration camp victim. So, now we're helping each other.
She's better—beginning to see she's better off—but
it's going to be a while yet."

Alex and Jessie were silent for a long minute,
contemplating the injustice Dallas had just described.

"You've got a lot on your plate, Dallas," Alex
said finally.

"Well, life's like that sometimes. Nobody promised
tea and crumpets, did they now? What can I do to
help?"

Jensen's laugh was full throated and admiring.
"You've already helped, more than you know. Just
keep your eyes and ears open, okay?"

"And my mouth shut?"

"Would I ask a creek to stop flowing? I think you're as well acquainted with discretion as I am. Let's go get that coffee you mentioned."

"We'd probably better consider lunch instead," Jessie observed. "It's eleven, and they're serving early so we can finish before we get to Sitka."

"Good idea. Let me get back in that damned chair, find Rozetta, and we'll make it a party of four."

"I'll get her." Jessie headed for the lounge.

This time, Alex held the door for Dallas.

9

Afternoon
Monday, July 14, 1997
Spirit of '98
Sitka, Alaska

NORTHERNMOST OF THE LARGE ISLANDS OF THE INSIDE PAS-
sage, Chicagof and Baranof form a long triangle like
the blade of a knife just south of Glacier Bay, wider
at the northern end and horizontally divided by Peril
Strait. This slender channel separates the islands as
if the knife had been fractured two-thirds of the distance from the southern tip.

Sitka, on the west side of Baranof Island, faces
open ocean and Mount Edgecumbe, the perfectly
symmetrical cone of an extinct volcano that rises over
three thousand feet on Kruzof Island fifteen miles
west across Sitka Sound—one of the most spectacular
settings in Southeastern Alaska. Known as the Paris
of the Pacific when San Francisco was still only a
ragged frontier town, Sitka was originally called New
Archangel by the Russians, who first sailed into its
waters in 1799, and established a center for fur trade
that brought opulence to this new capital of territo-
rial Alaska. In 1867, having dangerously diminished
the fur-bearing sea otters, the Russians sold the territory to the United States for 7.2 million dollars,

though their influence still hauntingly lingers in Sitka.

The *Spirit of '98* reached Sitka as Dallas, Rozetta, Alex, and Jessie were finishing dessert and coffee in the dining room. Through the picture windows, as the ship docked, they watched a dozen bald eagles flying touch-and-go's from a rock in the harbor, scooping up small fish from the waters of the incoming tide and returning to the rock while another eagle took a turn.

"Formation flying," Alex commented. "They've sure got that down pat."

Dallas chuckled. "I can't believe how many eagles I've seen on this trip. Our *noble* national bird? Scavengers, from what I've seen. Unless they're fishing, they seem to haunt garbage dumps. If the founding fathers had paid attention . . ."

"We could have had the wild turkey instead," Jensen grinned. "Somehow I don't see that as an improvement. At least the eagles are magnificent-*looking* birds of prey."

The loudspeaker woke suddenly to life:

"The Spirit *will be in Sitka from now until six-thirty. Anyone who is going ashore should be back aboard ship no later than six o'clock. Buses are waiting in the parking lot to transport you to the downtown Visitors Center, and will be there to bring you back. Please don't forget to turn over your cabin number on the going-ashore board as you leave the ship and when you come back. Dinner will be served at seven. Have a great time in Sitka."*

"Let's get our jackets and take a look," Jessie suggested, eagerly, getting up from the table. "I've never been here, and it's supposed to be an interesting little town. Can you take the bus, Dallas?"

"Could do," the older woman said. "But, with this chair, it's easier in a taxi. They said they'd call one for me. Why don't you two share a ride with us?"

"That sounds good," Alex agreed, "but I have

some business to attend to first. Won't take more than a few minutes. I'll meet you at the taxi, okay?"

Through the window, he had noticed a uniformed trooper standing by his car in the parking lot, waiting for the ship to tie up so he could come aboard. This, he knew, would be the officer with the fingerprint kit he had requested. The man would not need Jensen present to do his job, but he wanted to fill him in on the details of the thefts. The prints would be forwarded to the Anchorage crime lab to be put through the system. All the occupants had agreed to the captain's request for the procedure and were going ashore, leaving their staterooms empty.

Half an hour later, Dallas had made it carefully to the dock, up a ramp to the parking lot, and was waiting with the two younger women when Jensen came up the ramp at a trot, carrying her collapsed wheelchair. He deposited it in the trunk of the waiting taxi, and in ten minutes they were on the sidewalk of downtown Sitka.

The town was full of tourists, from the *Spirit* and at least two huge cruise ships. Shops along the main street were doing a profitable business in trinkets and souvenirs. Restaurants and coffee shops were crowded, though the hour for lunch was past. Jensen had been to Sitka before—the police academy, where troopers were trained, was located here—but his visits had all been during the winter months, when visitors were few and tour boats nonexistent, a time of cold, gray, rainy weather. Now the streets were full of bright banners, signboards, and flowers cascading from attractive planters. Visitors in colorful clothing roamed the streets, appreciating ground that was not in motion, spending their time and money on items of local and historical interest. The flavor of Sitka's Russian origins was evident in the displays of store windows, along with the complex patterns of Haida and Tlingit native arts and crafts.

Jessie immediately made use of the camera she had

slung around her neck to take a few shots of the vivid, picturesque surroundings. She then turned her lens on her three companions. "Cheese?" she suggested, and they amenably obliged.

"Now," Dallas said to Jensen, "you and Jessie run along and don't wait around for us. You want to see as much as you can. Thanks for the help."

Alex, however, had another idea.

"I've been here before. Jessie hasn't. Why don't you and Rozie go exploring and shopping, Jess? I'll spend some leisurely time with Dallas. Okay with you?" he asked Mrs. Blake, with a tilt of his head toward her niece—who had drifted to a shop window, where she was examining a display of silver Haida bracelets—silently suggesting that she might enjoy some time on her own. "Can you put up with me?"

With quick comprehension, Dallas colluded in urging the two younger women to go off on their own.

"I want to see the onion-dome cathedral," she informed them. "I'm sure Alex can help me get up the stairs in front, chair and all, if necessary. You two run along and see what you can find that appeals to you. Rozie, dear, you could do me a favor, while you're at it. Pick up some Jack Daniel's and spring water. There are times I'd rather have my toddy in the stateroom than that crowded lounge, and tonight is going to be one of them. Get yourself whatever you like. Maybe Alex and Jessie would join us for a predinner drink, yes?"

They agreed to meet in two hours for coffee at a cafe near the cathedral, and, when they had gone, she turned to Jensen with a conspiratorial smile.

"Thanks, Alex. That was a great idea. Rozetta uses me as an excuse, sticks like glue, so she won't have to socialize. Your Jessie will be just the thing for her."

"You're welcome, and I agree with all but the last. Jessie belongs to no one but herself. Can't say I'd like it different, though. We do pretty well at keeping a balance."

"Smart. You'll both be better for it."

With that, she gestured to the east, and he wheeled her off toward St. Michael's Cathedral, which lifted its copper onion-shaped dome, turquoise with patina, from the very center of town, where it divided the street so that traffic split into one-way single lanes on either side of it. Painted a neat gray with white trim, the small, gracefully shaped building gave no hint of the riches they discovered within.

"Incredible. Absolutely lovely," Dallas said, softly, gazing at an outstanding display of glittering Russian Orthodox icons. The luster of silver gilt *riza* overlaying and protecting the religious oil paintings on canvas was astonishing and unexpected in the small, quiet cathedral.

As they went out, Jensen noticed that, at the counter where postcards and booklets were sold, Dallas unobtrusively slipped a bill of large denomination into the hand of the priest, avoiding the obvious donation bowl.

Out on the street again, he mentioned a half-forgotten detail the act had pulled from his memory.

"You know, Dallas, in Southeast Asia they refer to quiet good deeds as *putting gold leaf on the back of the Buddha*."

Looking up at him over her shoulder, she smiled, but shook her head. "That was not a *good deed*, Alex," she told him. "There are just things, as you go along in life, that need doing."

He nodded. "Like Rozetta, you mean."

"Yes. Like that, too."

Dallas had only one additional request, a return to the shop where Rozetta had admired the silver Haida bracelets. There she inspected several and settled on one that featured stylized eagles on its graceful crescent—one she said she hoped would remind Rozie of the eagles they had noticed in the harbor and a pleasant trip. Alex couldn't resist a pair of silver ear-

rings for Jessie, and they left, gratified with their purchases and the anticipation of gift giving.

At the other end of the street, Jessie and Rozetta
were admiring prints by Alaskan artists, as they
drifted through a small art gallery.

"Oh, I love that one," Rozie pointed to the sketch
of a sea otter on its back in the water, a clam in its
paws. "How much is it?" she asked the clerk.

Jessie turned toward the door, catching a glimpse
of a person she had noticed twice before in the last
half hour: a man in a short dark blue jacket with an
elasticized waist, tan pants, dark glasses, and a cap
with a bill that hid most of his face. From across the
narrow street, he seemed to be staring into the shop,
straight at her. When she stopped moving, trying to
get a good look at him, he froze, then swung away,
and hurried off up the street.

Instantly, without a word to Rozie, Jess darted for
the door, stepped out, and, raising her camera, fired
off a quick shot in his direction. But he was already
turning a corner, and she knew she had missed him.
Who the hell was he? Why was he following them?
She was now almost sure it was not coincidence that
she had seen him for the third time, but it didn't
make sense. Who would want to know where they
were and what they were doing?

Opening the gallery door, she called to Rozetta.
"Rozie, I'll be right back. Wait for me."

"Okay, I'm buying this print. It'll be a few
minutes."

Jessie took off in the direction the man had disappeared. Nearing the corner, she walked close to the
buildings, then quickly stepped around into the small
side street. Nothing moved but a dog, trotting away
from her, tail swinging from side to side. She waited,
but no one appeared.

Damn. Who, and where, was he?

She went back to the gallery, watching for him
every step of the way, but he had vanished. She said

nothing to Rozetta, seeing no reason to upset the younger woman, who already had problems of her own. Pleased with her purchase, Rozie chattered away as they walked back toward the place they had agreed to have lunch, never noticing the thoroughness with which her companion was assessing other people on the street.

Almost there, Jessie once more caught a glimpse of a blue jacket at the edge of her peripheral vision to the left, across the street. This time she went on answering Rozie, pretending not to have noticed him. Then, between one step and the next, she abruptly stopped, swung up the camera, and took another picture.

He was quick. Before Rozie could turn to see what Jess was recording on film, he had ducked into a doorway and was gone again. But, this time, she thought she might have caught him in profile, if not better.

A minute later, he was back. Grabbing at Rozie's arm, Jess steered her into a needlework shop they were passing and, just as they were going in the door, tried for another picture. He was ready again and stepped behind a passerby.

When Alex and Dallas reached the cafe, the younger women were already waiting, arms full of the shopping they had done, including Dallas's bourbon. At the door, Jessie let Rozetta enter first with her aunt's chair, took Jensen's arm, and held him for a moment outside. He looked at her, puzzled, as she glanced up and down the street, frowning.

"Someone's been following us, Alex," she told him. "I don't like it."

"Who?"

"I'm not sure. He didn't get close enough to identify—if I could identify him. He's got a dark blue jacket, tan pants, and a baseball cap that sort of hides his face, wears dark glasses. He's been there, off and on, for at least an hour, and I don't know how long before. Everywhere we went, he went too, but never came close. I tried to get a picture, but he was too quick for me. May have caught him once, though."

"Do you see him now?"

"No. But he was there not ten minutes ago—up there by that T-shirt shop."

"Rozie see him too?"

"I didn't mention it. Seemed better to leave her out of it."

"Good thinking. Are you sure it's a man?"

"Yes . . . well, I guess it could be a woman. Hard to tell. Moves like a man. I tried to fake him out, turned Rozie around to go into a needlework shop once, and ran after him out of an art gallery, but he disappeared."

"Needlework? You going domestic on me?"

She grinned. "I haven't done any in a long time, but there was a great needlepoint kit of a killer whale that caught my eye. Thought I might get it started between here and Seattle."

Serious again, Alex thought for a minute. "Let's go in and sit by the window. You watch, and, if you see this guy again, point him out to me. Okay? He may feel safe enough to come closer with us inside."

He put an arm around her shoulders to give her a half-hug along with his smile. It was good to have her along, within reach, and be able to give her the reassurance of touch.

They went in to find Dallas and Rozetta conveniently seated at a window table.

Though both Jessie and Alex cast suspicious glances at the street outside as they drank their coffee, there was no sign of the man she had described.

"Maybe I was just imagining it," she told him in a low voice, as they left the cafe. "There's a lot of people on the street, in a relatively small area. It could have been coincidence."

Nevertheless, the incident made Jensen uneasy, his thoughts turning to the large amount of gold in the lower section of the *Spirit of '98.* It was time to take a look at just how it was situated and guarded. Foremost in his mind, however, was a concern for Jessie's safety. Why would someone follow her . . . or Rozie?

For the next hour, they watched the New Archangel Dancers, an all-woman troop, entertain a large audience with authentic Russian folk dances; whirling, stamping, leaping about on the stage of Centennial Hall. Their last stop was Jessie's suggestion, a rehabilitation center for raptors, where volunteers treated injured bald eagles, rehabilitating them for release back to the wild, if possible. Those birds that were unable to survive freedom would have homes found for them in zoos. The group of four moved quietly between large cages, enjoying the chance to take a close look at the birds they had previously seen only from a distance.

"They seem much larger up close, don't they?" Rozie said. "Aren't they beautiful? Look how that one watches us, but never ruffles a feather."

The bird she referred to clung with razor talons to the broken limb of a dead tree trunk close to their side of its cage. It stared at them with attentive yellow eyes, the only thing about it that moved. Never for an instant did its concentration break.

Disdain, Alex thought, staring back. It watches as if we were insignificant, but possibly threatening, creatures. Maybe we are. There can't be much to kill eagles besides man.

"Well," Dallas said, when they were on their way back to the ship in another taxi, "they may be scavengers, but seeing the one that woman had perched on her heavy leather glove was certainly impressive. Fiercesome critters, aren't they—all sharp talons and scimitar beaks?"

Jensen noticed that Jessie was still closely examining people as they drove past, searching the crowd of shoppers for her mysterious stalker. She seemed glad to reach what was becoming the familiar home-away-from-home of the *Spirit*, though he was less certain of its security. Jessie and Rozetta went on ahead in the crowd of returning passengers, carrying everyone's packages to their staterooms. He was considering his next step in the investigation of the thefts when Dallas spoke from her wheelchair, which he was guiding down the ramp.

"Jessie's worried about something, Alex. I'm no idiot. Something happened this afternoon, while she and Rozie were gone, didn't it? What?"

She stood up to step carefully across the gangway onto the ship, as he followed with the chair. Once on board, she turned to face him, waiting for an answer.

"Not much gets by you, does it, Dallas?"

"Well, I do more watching than participating these days. What is it?"

"Probably nothing, but I tend to trust Jessie's instincts. She says someone followed them, but not close enough to identify. Could have been a coincidence. Lots of people around."

"But you don't think so." She sat down in the chair.

"I don't know. So I tend to err on the side of caution."

"Connected to the robbery?"

Jensen shrugged. "Who knows? Could have been someone who recognized Jessie from a picture of the Iditarod."

The elevator opened, he wheeled Dallas in, and they rode up the two decks in thoughtful silence. At the door to her stateroom Alex left her. "See you at dinner?"

"Drink before?"

"I think we'll pass tonight, thanks. I've got a couple of things to do."

"Rain check," she smiled, and he went off to find Jessie, with the pair of silver earrings in mind and pocket, already envisioning them against the gold of her hair.

10

6:30 P.M.
Monday, July 14, 1997
Spirit of '98
Leaving Sitka, Inside Passage, Alaska

THE FORWARD LOUNGE, BEFORE DINNER, WAS CROWDED
with people hungry after their afternoon of dis-
covering Sitka and anxious to make their way to the
dining room for a relaxed evening meal. Slipping in
among them, Alex and Jessie stopped for a minute
to say hello to Bill and Nella Berry, who insisted on
buying them a drink. The enticing aroma of hot hors
d'oeuvres floated through the air, drawing Jensen in
that direction, as Bill went to the bar for their gin
and tonics.

When the men returned, bearing refreshment, Jessie and Nella were comparing notes on their Sitka
visit.

"What a great location," Bill enthused. "I don't
think I ever saw such a spectacular setting for a city.
Be a great place for a summer home, don't you
think?"

"Did you get those earrings this afternoon?" Nella
asked Jessie. "They're wonderful."

Pleased at the compliment, Jessie admitted they
were indeed from Sitka. "Alex found them for me.
He says they're a July fourteenth present."

"Is that an anniversary of some kind?"

"No," Jensen answered, with a grin. "Just July fourteenth, and the day of the eagles."

Raising a hand to touch the ornate, stylized silver birds that gleamed on her ears, Jessie smiled at Alex.

"That," commented Bill, "is a trick we should fire you for, Jensen. I have enough trouble remembering real anniversaries, right, Nella? Jensen will ruin our absentminded male reputation."

"Would you recognize John Stanley?" Alex asked, changing the subject. "I need to talk to him about the thefts last night."

"Sure. He's right over there." Berry pointed across the room.

"Maybe he'll know something that will lead you to get my watch back!"

Stanley, who was quietly watching the evening colors on the waters of the strait, turned out to be the bookish, gold-spectacled man they had seen boarding the *Spirit* in Skagway. Relieved of his bulky prospector's clothing, his frame was smaller than anticipated. Jensen, long interested in the physical elements that sometimes seemed to shape a person's character and psychology, wondered if Stanley's myopia might not have been diagnosed late in his childhood, for, from behind the thick, concave lenses of his glasses, Stanley exhibited a vague, soft-spoken, patient attitude that could easily have been the result of a long period of perceiving the distance as a blur. He greeted them politely, completely willing to answer questions.

The day before, their attention had been so focused on Stanley's outfit of fur parka and mukluks that they had all but overlooked his daughter, Louise, who had preferred jeans and a sweatshirt to a costume. Lou was an enigma of sorts, a tiny, sylphlike girl with enormous green eyes and carrot red hair permed to an electric halo that floated around her head in a dense cloud of crinkles. Following her father's lead, she said a quiet, courteous hello, but instead of sitting down she meandered off across the lounge.

Later, with more attention, she would strike Jessie as intentionally ambiguous, appearing and disappearing—seemingly out of nowhere—at odd times and places, drifting about the ship, usually in motion. Looking younger than her fifteen years, she listened constantly to music through the headphones of her CD player, apparently ignoring nearly every adult, including her father.

A conviction grew with Jessie that Lou saw and heard much more than she revealed. Jessie suspected that, as the teen wandered from one end of the ship to the other, she might actually be aware of more of what went on than anyone else aboard, though she might not realize its significance. Passing Lou on one deck or another, it was at times possible to catch a faint rhythmic thread of music, just enough to make one wonder if it was real or imagined. Regardless, Jess began to wonder whether Lou's music was as uninterrupted as it appeared, or if she sometimes wore the headphones to surreptitiously listen to the conversations of other people.

"My great-grandfather, William Stanley, brought what, at that time, was a fortune out of the Klondike on the *Portland*: a hundred and twelve thousand dollars," John told them.

Her jeans and fuchsia sweatshirt a couple of sizes too large, Lou Stanley was wandering around the room, a Coke in her hand, looking out the windows. Jessie noticed, however, that Lou never moved completely out of earshot.

"I'm proud to represent him for this reenactment," Stanley went on. "He sold books in Seattle and wasn't making enough to support his wife and seven children, so he took his son, Samuel, and went north. They were practically destitute, and the trip north to search for gold was a last resort. He had a gimp leg, but he made it down the Yukon and was there, close enough to stake a claim when the Bonanza strike was made." He'd started his small, unsuccessful business with money from a gold strike in the Rocky Mountains, but lost it during the depression of the mid-1890s.

Jensen had listened with honest interest, but now, with only ten minutes left before dinner, he changed the subject.

"Last night," he said, "you went to the party in Haines—both of you?"

"Yes, sure. Wouldn't miss any part of this once-in-a-lifetime celebration."

"And when you came back you didn't notice anything unusual, or that your stateroom had been disturbed?"

"No. Not a thing."

"You knew that three other staterooms next to you had been robbed?"

"Oh, yes. Everybody knows that. There aren't that many people on this boat—less than a hundred, not counting the crew. Information spreads fast."

Lou made one of her nomadic, seemingly unintentional trips past where they sat, and Jensen reached out a hand to stop her roaming.

"Did you notice anything at all last night, Miss Stanley?"

She pulled the headphones off.

"Nope. I went to bed early, after I watched the ship leave the dock."

"So you were on deck for a while before you went to your cabin?"

"Yes."

"Did you stay on your deck? On the side nearest the dock?"

She frowned. "Not all the time. I walked around some—went up to the top deck, where the chairs and tables are."

"Talk to anyone?"

"No." She fidgeted, resistance to his queries plainly growing.

"See anyone suspicious?"

"No."

Jensen ran out of questions and nodded to the girl that she could go. "Thanks, Ms. Stanley."

A sudden, brilliant, and beautiful smile spread over her face, transforming her looks completely, allowing the others a glimpse of the lovely woman she was about to become. Then she giggled. *"Ms. Stanley?"*

Alex grinned back at her, surprised, but pleased.

Passengers around them were leaving the lounge for the dining room one deck below. Alex and Jessie rose to join the exodus, but the Stanleys were swept ahead in the hungry throng.

"Nobody knows anything," Jensen said under his breath to Jessie, as they went down the stairs and paused in a narrow hallway leading to the dining room. "That search warrant for Morrison's cabin will be faxed in this evening, when the judge flies back in from Juneau. The magistrate's gone to Hawaii on vacation. Maybe there'll be something there. What'd you think of Lou Stanley?"

"Interesting. Smart. She might be more open with another woman."

The line started to move as Alex thought about that for a minute.

"You could be right," he agreed. "Take a shot, if you get a chance."

"He get to Ketchikan?"

"No message from Walt on the machine."

"Damn it."

"Yeah. If they don't get going soon, they won't make it on time."

"Another day's cutting it pretty close."

"Right. But we'll have to wait till tomorrow, after five. I'll try again later, but can't go up there too often. Some-

one will wonder why I'm making so many calls. You keep your act together. Don't forget what's at stake here. I didn't take you on to have you blow it."

"How the hell would I do that?"

"Just don't. That business last night was real stupid."

"Wasn't my fault. That cop go to the office in Sitka?"

"No. We watched them both play tourist all afternoon with that Blake woman in the chair. His girlfriend had a camera, though, and somehow knew we were there. Tried to take a picture and we had to move fast. It's okay. Now, get out of here."

The Klondike miner was ragged and unkempt, a full, bushy beard covering the lower half of his face, a fur hat on his head. His coat, homemade out of a gray wool blanket, overlapped in front and was secured around his waist with a piece of rope. Boots, stained and stiff from supposed encounters with the waters of Bonanza Creek, appeared lacking in comfort. He stomped between the tables of the *Spirit*'s dining room—a grubby contrast to the sparkling clean white of their tablecloths and napkins, waving a piece of firewood, threateningly, in one hand.

"You slippery sidewinder. You jumped my Eldorado claim. Yer a cheat and a damned snake. I'll not let you get the better of me yet. I'll set the constable on you. We was partners! You miserable . . ."

"So you say," a second, similarly dressed man replied. *"I don't recall any agreement to partnerin'."*

Heads raised, dessert forks and coffee cups suspended in air, passengers craned their necks to see what was going on in the center of the dining room to justify the loud, angry voices that had interrupted the leisurely completion of an excellent meal.

As the first furious miner stepped forward to take a swing at the other with the firewood, a third voice halted the action.

"Hey, you two knuckleheads. That will do, unless you'd

*like to spend a week cutting wood for the Northwest
Mounted. What's going on here?"*

Jensen, sitting with Jessie at a table for eight that
included Dallas and Rozetta, the Berrys, and the
Lovegrens, recognized the tall, red-coated policeman
moving into the room as Jim Beal, the riverboat gambler from the parade grounds in Haines, now playing
another role. This was evidently the beginning of the
drama they had been promised.

"He stole my claim," the first miner shouted.

"I never."

"You lousy skunk."

"Enough," the red-coat demanded. *"We'll get Ogil-
vie up here to survey and verify your claims, both of you."*

A fourth voice, this time a woman's, added itself
to the discussion.

*"He's right. Johnson is a claim-jumper and a thief as
well. My gold nugget necklace disappeared yesterday, and
he's the only one who could have taken it. I want it back,
you hear?"*

Laurie Trevino, transformed into a gaudy dance-
hall girl, advanced into the room from Soapy's Parlour, the bar in the stern of the ship. Once again she
was clad, appropriately, in red, this time a shade
closer to that of a fire engine. The dress was an adap-
tation of 1890s risqué: bodice held up by tiny shoulder straps, allowing a daring display of décolletage;
a full, flounced skirt swinging provocatively over
frothy, lace-trimmed petticoats; old-fashioned black
boots laced halfway up her calves; a headband supporting a fluffy ostrich plume, red to match the dress.

Swinging a beaded purse by its strings, she sa-
shayed closer to the center of the room and paused,
hip-shot, swaying slightly, as if to music only she
could hear.

Jessie grinned to herself, reminded of Lou Stanley,
but what caught Jensen's attention was the mention
of a gold nugget necklace. Quite a coincidence. Could
this somehow be related? Could the thief have been

one of the players? The immediate mental image was that of Jim Beal and his riverboat gambler costume. Well . . . he returned his attention to what was going on between the players.

"Think you can call me a thief?" the miner yelled at Laurie. *"There's a dozen other men could have stolen your baubles, Alice, you tramp."*

"Hey," Alex whispered to Jessie, in sudden recognition. "That's Jeff Brady, Skagway chairman of the Reenactment Committee."

The rest of the diners, now realizing that a drama, not an actual altercation, was taking place, had settled back to enjoy it. A few hisses at the supposed villain signaled their growing involvement.

"I'm no tramp, you weasel. I work hard singing and dancing at the Palace for every ounce of dust I get. That chain of nuggets and charms was a birthday present from several good friends of mine. Search him, please, constable." Alice from the Palace turned indignantly to the red-coated policeman. *"I'm sure you'll find my property."*

"Search him. Search him," called someone from the back of the audience, followed by laughter and applause from the rest.

The miner-suspect snatched the piece of firewood from the first prospector and waved it threateningly toward the constable, who had unexpectedly drawn a handgun and was closing in, along with the other miner, who had also pulled a firearm from somewhere inside the blanket coat.

Lifting her skirt, Alice retrieved, from a fancy, beribboned garter, the miniature pistol she had shown Alex and Jessie in Haines. Stepping toward the other three, she took careful aim.

Abruptly, and without warning, all the lights in the room went off, and the sound of a shot rang out in the gloom. A scramble . . . a shout . . . the crash of a chair falling over . . . running feet.

Then, as suddenly as they had gone off, the lights

were on again. All four players in the scene had vanished, leaving only the up-ended chair in the center of the room to show they had been there. A rush of excited conversation and laughter filled the room. Several diners stood up to look, but resumed their seats as the cruise coordinator plugged in her microphone and stepped forward.

"Please, ladies and gentlemen. May I have your attention, please."

The passengers settled back to listen.

"As you have probably guessed, this has been the first of several scenes from an ongoing mystery, which will reach its conclusion on Thursday night in the upper lounge. Pay close attention, as you will be invited to submit your solutions to the puzzle, in writing, at the end of the drama.

"Here are the rules. You must decide whodunit, a motive, and how the crime was accomplished. You may ask questions of any of the cast members if you find them in costume, but please refrain from asking if they are not in costume. They need a little time off once in a while. Be aware that all of the characters must answer your questions truthfully, except for the villain, who may lie at any time. Prizes will be presented when judging of your solutions is completed on Thursday night. Good luck."

Enthusiastic conversation resumed as soon as the announcements were finished. Who was shot? Who shot whom? What would come next? And when?

Alex chuckled. "Wish I had this much assistance in some of my cases."

"Well . . . who do you think fired the shot?" Jessie asked. "Got any early leads?"

"You shouldn't ask me," he grinned. "Remember what you always tell me, when I . . ."

"Yeah . . . I know. Do it—whatever *it* is—yourself. Guess it has to backfire on me sometimes, huh? Okay."

"One hint. Were you so engrossed in the action

that you missed that shadowy figure with the shot-gun in the door to the galley?''

"Really?''

"Yup. It's not actually fair for me to work on this. I'm trained to see the whole scene, not just the pieces.''

"Was it a man or woman?''

Jensen grinned as answer.

"Rats! Well . . . I'll look more carefully at the next scene. Shall we go to the lounge?''

"You go ahead. I need to see the captain . . . and find Judy Raymond. She's never in her cabin—I've tried three times already, and she disappears when-ever I get her in sight outside of it.''

"Okay. I'll catch up with Dallas and Rozie. If you're sure you don't need me to take notes.''

"I can handle it for once. I'll join you in not too long, or see you in the cabin.''

He was thoughtful; the necklace mentioned in the play reminded him of his responsibility to find out who had made free with the staterooms and stolen the items belonging to the occupants. He suddenly found the whole thing an imposition. The trip was supposed to be an official appearance for the troop-ers, himself the representative, not a case to be solved. He frowned in irritation, then sighed. After all, it was his job, though at times he wished it would stop long enough to draw breath. He had imagined this cruise as a breathing space. The problem, how-ever, seemed so petty, small-time theft, really . . . only the value of the necklace and the cash made it more important.

The dining room was almost empty, as people moved slowly in the direction of the hallway and stairs, still conjecturing about the mystery. The wait-staff members of the crew were working steadily at clearing the tables.

"Great meal," Alex told one of them, a tall, red-haired young woman near the door, as they went past her on the way out.

"Thanks. That's Eric, our new chef—the company lured him away from a classy Seattle restaurant. Our cooks are always good, but he's the best, with Carla, the assistant's, help. Even the crew's meals are super."

"Give him my congratulations, but if this kind of food continues, I'm going to need some serious exercise soon."

She laughed as they exited the room, but Jensen had no idea how little effort he would need to expend on an exercise program in the next few days.

11

11:00 P.M.
Monday, July 14, 1997
Spirit of '98
Return through Peril Strait
Inside Passage, Alaska

AT ELEVEN O'CLOCK THE *SPIRIT OF '98* WAS ONCE AGAIN
cruising smoothly, returning through the dark eastern waters of Peril Strait, heading for Stephens Passage and, across it, a side trip next morning up Tracy
Arm with its two huge glaciers. The decks, lounges—
even the bridge—were quiet and peaceful. Captain
Kay was on duty and the first mate was catching a few
hours' sleep before she was to take over the watch.

A few of the staterooms showed soft light around
the edges of their window curtains, passengers still
awake, but not for long. Sunday's send-off celebrations and today's outing in Sitka had been tiring for
most. Adding to that time spent outside on the decks
of the *Spirit*—more fresh air than many people were
used to—meant everyone had eaten better and was
sleeping earlier and sounder than usual.

The air was not only fresh; it was so clear and
clean that, short of rain or fog, the incredible scenery
of the northern Inside Passage could be seen for
miles in layer after layer of mountains that grew blue

with distance, wide expanses of salt water altering their color with every shift in the weather. Rich with spruce and hemlock forests on the lower slopes, the peaks were laced with ice that had shrunk over the centuries from covering, to flowing between, the ridges in wide rivers that recorded their powerful passage in deeply scored walls of stone. The constantly changing panorama was captivating to out-of-state people who had seldom seen such relatively young, rugged mountains still in the slow process of rising.

Plates of the earth's crust are most dense under the oceans. Where these collide with less dense plates of continents, the land plates are shoved upward, growing mountains and additional land mass. Twelve million years ago, in southeast Alaska, one result of the collision of the Pacific Plate, which moves north, and the North American Plate, which moves south, was the long uplift of the St. Elias mountains, including Mt. Logan, tallest peak in Canada and second tallest in North America. Terranes carried by the Pacific Plate have been, and are still in the process of being, added to the land mass. Part of what is now Southeast Alaska was once within fifteen degrees of the equator and was added to the continent as another result of the ongoing collision of plates. Between and through terranes, among the islands of the Alaskan Inside Passage, run numerous underwater faults, one of which formed Peril Strait, through which the *Spirit of '98* was now returning, on its way back to the sheltering Inside Passage.

It had been late, almost ten, when the necessary warrant had arrived by fax from Sitka. Jensen and the captain had come to the reluctant decision that it would be more sensible to wait for morning to search Julie Morrison's cabin. To disturb her two cabin mates, one of whom was the hardworking assistant chef who had to rise early to prepare breakfast, seemed like punishing the innocent. Besides, there were no stops, no way for Julie to leave the ship. If she had rid herself of evidence, it would undoubtedly have been done before now, anyway. Alex still did not think her a likely thief. She was hiding something, but what? Perhaps it was not associated with the thefts at all.

In transit between the captain's quarters and his own, Alex paused outside Judy Raymond's dark cabin and knew his talk with her would also have to wait for morning, though he wondered if she was avoiding him. Letting it go, tired as the rest, he returned to his stateroom to find a light burning and Jesse asleep on his bed, curled up with her head at its foot. Still in the clothes she had worn to dinner, gray slacks and a green sweater, shoes on the floor beside the bed, she slept on her side, both hands under a pillow like a child. As he stood looking down at her, she stirred, turned over, and looked up at him, drowsily.

"Hi," she said, yawned, and sat up. "Get your warrant?"

"Yes, but we decided to wait till morning to serve it."

He sat down beside her, pulled off his jacket, and, without untying them, pushed off his deck shoes with his toes. As he moved, something crackled under him, and he pulled out a sheet of paper with printing on it.

"Oh, I meant to show that to you. Every night they leave one of these when they turn down the beds. It's a newsletter that tells us what to expect the next day. Good idea, huh?"

Jensen took a look at the single-page sheet of information. Called "Adventure Update," it gave the schedule for the next day and some information about what they would be able to see.

ADVENTURE UPDATE

Itinerary:

6:00 am	*Continental Breakfast available in the lounge.*
7:00 am	*Breakfast is served.*
9:00 am	*Sail into Tracy Arm.*
12:00 noon	*Lunch is served.*
1:00 pm	*Sail into Endicott Arm.*
6:00 pm	*Cocktail hour in the lounge.*
7:00 pm	*Dinner is served.*
8:30 pm	*Entertainment in the lounge.*

Stephens Passage:
Before we reach Tracy Arm this morning we will be traveling through Stephens Passage. Be on the lookout for humpback whales feeding in these plankton-rich waters. If you would like to be awakened if we spot whales, be sure to sign up on the wake sheet in the lounge. (Wake up calls may start at first light, 5:30 a.m.) If we don't see whales here, you can be sure we will when we reach Frederick Sound late today. Sometimes they move between these two areas, following the food supply.

Tracy Arm:
You will see harbor seals near the glacier in Tracy Arm. There is a page of information on these seals in the lounge. We will also tell you about them over the PA system when we arrive at the Sawyer Glacier.

Tonight's Entertainment:
Jefferson Randolph "Jeff" Smith IV, Soapy Smith's great-grandson, will give his version of his famous relative's history from research he has done for a book, The True Story of Jefferson Randolph Smith. *He will also entertain with demonstrations of sleight of hand, shell and card games, using the*

*original equipment Soapy used in Skagway during
the gold rush, and which he has inherited through
his father, Soapy's grandson, Jefferson Randolph
Smith III.*

*"It's not so much the destination as the voyage itself
that matters."*

When he had finished reading the newsletter, he
agreed with her that it was a good idea, but that if
anyone woke *him* to look at whales at five-thirty the
next morning, they would be in for real trouble. Jensen
lay back on the bed with a weary sigh.

"I was really hoping for a vacation on this trip,
not an investigation."

She smiled sympathetically. "Maybe you'll solve
this one in a hurry. At least we're getting to know
some of the people on the ship."

"I can think of more pleasant ways to get
acquainted."

"Anything new?"

"No. We don't know much more than we did this
morning. It's really hard to know where to start on
this one."

"You don't think Julie Morrison is responsible?"

"I don't know. She may be, but so far we have no
proof of anything. It just doesn't fit somehow."

Yawning, Jessie got up and went to retrieve the over-size
T-shirt and crew socks in which she slept. Sitting
on her own bed, she pulled the green sweater over her
head, asking another question in the process.

"You have . . . ugh . . . anyone else in mind at all?"

Alex smiled as her light hair flew away from its
usual neatness and fluffed out around her head. He
never tired of looking at her.

"That's part of the problem. There doesn't seem to
be anyone else. Or it could be anyone, except for the
fact that they were all ashore. I suppose any crew
member who was on the ship at the time could have

done it. We'll have to start with Morrison's cabin first thing tomorrow, and go from there."

In the extra-large T-shirt and socks, Jessie stepped into the bathroom and began to brush her teeth. But, as soon as she had toothpaste on the brush and the brush in her mouth, she came out again.

"A-ow bow mis-r-r ons-on?"

"Right." Alex dropped his shirt on a chair and turned to attempt a long-suffering look that he quickly lost to a grin. "And I understood every word of *that?*"

"Sorry. I said, *'How about Mr. Johnson?'* "

"Supposedly, he was alcoholically out for the count, but we'll check it again."

She returned to the bathroom sink to spit out the mouthful of frothy paste.

One of the things Alex liked most about Jessie was a decided lack of physical self-consciousness. At ease in her own body, strong and supple from practicing an active sport, she moved in whatever manner was most comfortable or efficient, seldom aware of her appearance. It lent her a certain grace that was appealing and direct. He paused, one leg still in his jeans, to admire the curve of her back and hips as she bent over the small, stainless steel sink, rinsing her mouth.

She turned and smiled at him, suddenly mindful of his appreciation.

He smiled back and returned to the task of getting ready for the night. "Let's go to bed. I'm tired. You?"

"Yeah, me, too." But, sitting down on his bed again, she looked up at him with a grin. "Just how tired are you, trooper?"

"Not *that* tired."

Half an hour later, they were both asleep, though Jessie had complained it wasn't fair that they had both warmed his bed, while she had to warm hers alone.

*   *   *

Sometime in the middle of the dark, Alex slowly became aware of a soft but insistent knocking on the stateroom door, and the deep voice of the captain quietly calling his name.

"Jensen? Wake up, Jensen?"

"What? Okay. I'm awake."

Switching on a light, he glanced at his watch. Four-forty. He padded barefoot to the door in his underwear, opened it, and stuck his head around to find Kay and a woman crew member standing outside.

Something was wrong.

"What?"

"Sorry to have to wake you, but . . . look, can we come in? I don't like to talk from out here."

"Sure." He reached for his jeans and pulled them on, as they entered and closed the door.

Half-awake and confused, Jessie sat up in her bed.

"Sergeant Jensen, this is Carla Hodges, our assistant chef, and one of Julie Morrison's bunkmates. She got up half an hour ago and discovered that Morrison's not in her bed and it hasn't been slept in."

"Anywhere else she might have spent the night?"

"Not unless she spent it sitting up somewhere on deck, and I made a quick tour as we came here. Carla's been up since four. She looked everywhere she could think of—heads, galley, decks, lounge—before coming to me."

Jensen frowned, trying to think, then looked to Carla. "Hate to ask, but you would probably know this better than Captain Kay. Is there someone she might have spent the night with? Any suggestion of a relationship?"

The assistant chef shook her head. "No. No one. There isn't room on this ship for that sort of thing. Anyway, there's always three or four crew in each cabin. Not much privacy, except . . ." She glanced at the captain, hesitantly. "There *is* the engineer's cabin, sir."

"Not the engineer's. Ray's awake, down below—

some kind of problem with a valve—and the new guy's asleep . . . alone. I took a look." He turned to Jensen to explain. "The engineers have their own separate sleeping space a deck above, but right across from the door to the engine room. They work seven to five, but are on-call twenty-four hours a day, for obvious reasons. A crew member on night duty, checking for fire, leaks, that kind of thing, woke Ray over an hour ago. There's one other, the hotel manager's cabin. We'll check, but it doesn't make sense. Our current manager's . . . well . . ." He paused, diplomatically, but unsuccessfully, searching for a word. "He's sort of . . . singular. Doesn't spend much time with the other crew members."

Morrison's roommate spoke up to clarify. "He's a bit older and just doesn't get along well with most of us. He keeps to himself, kind of antisocial, has a pregnant wife at home that he phones at every port. Julie wouldn't be there, but I just can't imagine where she'd go." Her brows tightened in a worried look. "There's no place to just disappear."

"No place at all?"

"Not that I can think of. To disappear, she'd have to . . ."

"No," Captain Kay abruptly stopped her. "We haven't exhausted all the odd nooks and crannies yet. There's still a few of them, actually. Did you look in the linen storage rooms, for instance?"

"What would she be doing . . . ? Well, no, sir. I didn't."

"There's food storage rooms, freezers, the anchor chain locker, laundry, the fan room, the steerage compartment. Still lots of small maintenance spaces."

As Alex reached for the rest of his clothes, Jessie threw back her own covers and got up to dress herself as well.

"A passenger's stateroom?" he asked, putting on his jacket.

"They're all occupied this trip, and fraternizing with passengers is against policy."

"Well," Jensen said, considering this. When had *against policy* ever stopped a determined romance? Fear of being fired could explain Morrison's flash of apprehension in the captain's office. "I guess we'd better start with those odd places. Have you got some flashlights, Captain? Who, besides yourself, has the best knowledge of the whole ship?"

"Ray McKimmey, the engineer."

They had searched every corner of the ship they could think of when McKimmey, who had been called up from the engine room to help, found the first clue. Hanging around a bottom rail at the stern, outside Soapy's Parlour, the aft bar to the rear of the dining room, was the blue ribbon Morrison had been wearing in her hair the day before. There was no mistaking it. Why it hadn't blown or fallen off into the waters of Peril Strait was a minor miracle, since it just hung there, with the ends fluttering gently. On one end was a small stain of reddish brown.

Further search in the same location turned up a small gold earring in the angle formed by the deck and the superstructure of the ship. In the deck lights, they could all see the uneasy frown on the face of the assistant chef, as she held it out in the palm of her hand.

"Yes, it's hers. One of a pair she wore all the time."

"And here," McKimmey said, pointing with his flashlight to the half-smoked butt of a cigarette lying in a protected pocket of the deck. "Is this her brand, Carla?"

"Yes. I think so."

"She smoked?" the captain asked. "This is a passenger area."

"Well, it's a rule that's bent a little, since *all* the deck space is passenger area. This was one of the few places smokers in the crew probably wouldn't meet passengers, especially late in the evening. She only smoked one or two a day. Liked to come out here just before going to bed. Said it gave her a chance to relax and be alone for a few minutes . . . see where she'd been."

Jensen got up from where he had been examining the deck nearest the rail with his light.

"There's a few scuff marks, but it's hard to tell if they're the result of a struggle."

McKimmey moved over to take a look. "These are dark," he commented analytically. "No one on the crew wears dark-soled shoes, because they do this."

He and Jensen looked at each other for a long minute, and, though McKimmey said nothing, Jensen identified angry comprehension and regret in his eyes.

"What time did Morrison come out here last night?" Jensen asked Carla.

"I think it was a little after ten-thirty when she came back to her bunk for her cigarettes. On our last run she usually came out here sometime between ten-thirty and midnight, for maybe half an hour."

In sudden silence, Alex stared out at the churning white wake the *Spirit* left behind. What he *didn't* say was now clearly understood by everyone who followed the direction of his gaze and thoughts.

Straight from the ice and snow of a hundred glaciers, the waters through which they were passing were so cold that anyone falling into them unprotected could survive for only a few minutes before surrendering to hypothermia. In the dark . . . in the cold . . . suffering from shock . . . a thin scream, drowned by the rumble of the engines . . . perhaps a weak cry from the water that no one would hear . . . swept away, tumbled under the roiling wake in an instant. At least it would be quick.

He turned back as Captain Kay spoke hesitantly. "She was . . . pretty upset this morning, but I don't think she would have done . . . something like this . . . herself."

"I doubt it. All the facts point to enough resistant force to pull off an earring and the ribbon. I'll have to have it tested, but I know that this blotch on the ribbon is blood."

McKimmey agreed. "It looks like someone caught her off guard. She didn't finish her cigarette and wouldn't have left it to go out on the deck."

"Shouldn't we go back?" Carla asked, suddenly. "Shouldn't we try to find her?"

They stared at her, caught up in sharing her feelings and the futility of them.

Alex spoke gently. "Where?" he asked. "How?" He glanced at his watch. Five-thirty. "It's been about six hours, at a guess. Time enough for the tide to move a body a long way from where it went into the water, but nowhere close to where we are now. We don't even know exactly where it happened. We'll have to leave it to the coast guard. All the passenger staterooms still have to be searched, just because they *are* possibilities we haven't covered, but . . ."

But, he was thinking, it was also possible that whoever had committed the stateroom thefts had had something to do with this disappearance. The very fact that the two incidents had happened so close to each other in time created a conditional and suspicious link between them. Was Morrison, or someone else, responsible for the thefts? Could someone have overpowered her, hit her, and taken her, unconscious, to a stateroom, rather than shove her overboard? Very unlikely, yes, but motive might provide the answer. Why would anyone want to kill her in the first place? Had she seen something, heard something? Was she involved in something incriminating? What had the flash of fear in her eyes meant in the captain's office yesterday?

"Damn it." Carla turned away, distressed, reached

out to Jessie, found the other woman's hands, and clung, shaking her head.

Jensen watched her with sympathy. He was proud of Jessie, as the two moved away a little, exchanging a word or two, but mainly holding to each other.

McKimmey walked a space apart along the side of the vessel and stood staring out across the rail into the dark. Confronting this kind of thing wasn't easy.

Alex glanced after him and found himself identifying with the younger man's response. Ray McKimmey had intelligently and capably handled himself throughout the search and its regrettable result. Tall and slender, a quiet sort of man in his thirties, he seemed thoughtful, speaking when he had something specific to say. He appealed to Jensen's concept of merit. There was something solid about him that inspired confidence and reliance. He could be helpful, Alex thought, should there be a need to include an ally in the investigation into which he had been drawn.

Carefully, he collected the three pieces of evidence and put them in plastic bags from galley storage. They would go into Captain Kay's safe for the time being.

As they walked back through the dining room to the elevator, leaving McKimmey to his thoughts and Jessie to accompany the assistant chef to the galley for a cup of tea and sympathy, Dave Kay shook his head, looking older and tired.

"Pardon the expression, but I can't fathom this. It scares the hell out of me. Theft is one thing, murder—and you think it *was* murder, don't you?—quite another. What are we going to do now, Jensen? Got any ideas?"

Alex thought of the response that a friend and fellow trooper would give in this situation.

"Let me knock it around for a little, Captain. There's something we're missing here. This doesn't quite make sense. Pretty extreme reaction to something, by someone. Let's go make the calls, take care of business, then we'll talk some more."

It angered and discouraged him to admit, even to himself, that he *had* no specific idea as to motive or perpetrator; only a few people on board raised questions in his mind, but no suspicions could be directly linked to either of these crimes. None. *Not enough information,* he thought. *I need more time and information.*

On the stern of the ship with only a few fragments of evidence, he had felt the world shift in a strange understanding, almost as if Morrison had tried to communicate. He remembered her pale face in the captain's office. *"No. No,"* she had said, refusing a search of her possessions. What had she been hiding? It was time to find out. Time to get a grasp on what had happened—what was still happening. *Right now,* he thought, *I have only one finger touching this and I need to grab hold of it.* It was time to know what the now-useless warrant would have told them.

As they stepped out of the elevator on the Bridge Deck, he suddenly stopped and turned to Captain Kay.

"What time does Sawyer close Soapy's Parlour?"

"It varies," Kay said slowly. "Depends on when the passengers leave, but usually not later than eleven—possibly midnight, if there's a reason. The Parlour isn't even busy enough to be open about half the time. This trip, though, I think it will be, most of the time." He paused, thinking hard. "I suppose the timing might mean that Sawyer saw something, Morrison and someone else—maybe—or. . . . You think he might have something to do with it? He's an extra bartender for this particular run. We haven't had him on board before but he was recommended by the committee and has excellent references from Skagway. I've watched him work, and he's very good with people."

Alex nodded. "I noticed that at the Red Onion the

night before we left. I liked him, but I'm just trying to cover all the angles. Where does he sleep?"

They walked on toward the bridge as the captain answered. "Well, since he was hired as extra, there wasn't a space in the crew quarters. We have just enough for the number of regular crew. The Centennial Committee has three staterooms assigned to them. From what I understand, he's sleeping on a cot in one of those occupied by a committee member and one of the actors. I'll have to look at the list to see which one."

Jensen followed Kay through the bridge, where the first mate was now on duty, to the office. *What next?* he wondered, as he sat down to call the coast guard. How were the thefts and the disappearance of Julie Morrison related—or were they? Intuition and the proximity of their timing made him suspect that they were, but his facts were still insufficient, and what had to be done now would easily fill most of the morning. At least they would not stop again until Ketchikan on Wednesday—tomorrow—twenty-four hours. How much could he uncover in that much time? And would it be enough?

12

Morning
Tuesday, July 15, 1997
Hazlit's Gull
Clarence Strait, Inside Passage, Alaska

AS THE *SPIRIT OF '98* TRAVELED EAST ACROSS STEPHENS Passage, close to two hundred nautical miles away, the rechristened *Harry's Doll* sailed smoothly through the waters of Clarence Strait on a freshening morning breeze, headed for Ketchikan, southernmost city of the Alaskan Inside Passage.

Rod and Nelson had fled toward this location for three successive nights following their nefarious pause in Tracy Arm, sailing through the dark in an attempt to pass unnoticed, anchoring or tying up to sleep during the daylight hours in small coves and inlets where they could, hopefully, remain undetected by boats in the main channels. So far they had been successful, the only other vessels they sighted too far away to be a threat.

For most of Monday night it had rained, but an improvement in the weather had come with a rising wind. They now clipped along at a steady speed, sails, deck, and gear drying in the morning sun. So close to Ketchikan, Rod had elected to continue the journey during daylight hours. Nelson was uneasy with this decision, and ill-tempered, for he had not been drunk or hung-over since Saturday night, as Rod had successfully hidden the whisky bottle.

"What if they're looking for us?" he called up from the galley. "What if they found her? We're right out here in the open, where they can see us easy."

"*Will* you cut it out? They couldn't have found her. You know where she is. You helped put her there, watched her go down, and that's where she's going to stay. By the time the body's ripe enough to float, the fish and crabs and stuff will have left nothing *to* show up on the surface. Bones don't float, Nelson. Think about it."

"Yeah, you're right. I know you're right, but, even so, he's not gonna be happy," the older man said, appearing at the top of the companionway with a plate of scrambled eggs, bacon, and toast.

"Oh, stuff it, Nelson. I'm fed up with hearing it. We both *know* he's not going to be happy, whoever *he* is, so keep it to yourself." He reached for the plate. "Goddamn it. You burned the bacon *again*. How do you *do* that?"

"That propane thing cooks stuff too fast. I turn around to get the eggs ready, and it's already fried the stuff. I like electric better."

"Well, try cracking the eggs into a bowl *first*, then you wouldn't have to turn around. Watch the damned bacon. Flip it over a time or two. I hate it burned."

"I use a bowl, I'd have to wash it," Nelson whined. "*You* cook, if you don't like it."

"And leave you to run the boat, I suppose? At least burned bacon won't put us on the rocks somewhere." Rod crumbled the offendingly charred bacon with his fingers and mixed it into the eggs before shoveling a forkful into his mouth.

Nelson disappeared into the galley again, exhibiting an unspoken delusion of safety that he only felt when out of sight below decks. The warmth and sunshine of the day was inconsequential to him. He wished it were midnight.

Rod, on the other hand, was pleased to be traveling in the daylight for a change, and to have reached this lower part of the Alaska Panhandle, where the country temporarily spread out into a gentler, more open landscape. Having crossed through Stephens Passage and the waters of Frederick Sound, slipped past Petersburg at midnight, and threaded the twenty-four-mile constriction of the Wrangell Narrows into Sumner, then Stikine Straits, it gave him confidence to finally sail down the middle of this wide arm of ocean, a mile on either side between boat and shore. Being able to see the shape of what he was passing didn't hurt his feelings or frighten him.

He loved to sail, and the boat he had stolen was a pleasure to handle, sleek and quick to respond to an experienced hand on the tiller. His enjoyment was mitigated slightly by the knowledge that a sailboat had not been ordered and was probably not well suited for whatever specific task it had been liberated for, that choosing it was his own indulgence and would not be appreciated by the person to whom he was responsible. Still, it was such a fine boat, a fine day, that recriminations could wait till later. So they really *should* have been in Ketchikan yesterday. What could one more day matter? As usual, little given to anticipation, Rod was living pretty much for the moment, taking care of whatever business was at hand and letting the rest be someone else's worry.

By midafternoon the two were proceeding down Tongass Narrows with the Ketchikan airport in sight across the channel from Alaska's fifth largest community. As they drew nearer, a small ferry could be seen, regularly transporting airline passengers back and forth between Gravina and Revillagigedo Islands, where Ketchikan was located on one of the largest of the many pieces of water-surrounded land in Southeastern Alaska that almost fit together like bits of a scattered jigsaw puzzle between the mainland and the Pacific Ocean.

Rather than dock at any of the city marinas, where they would be observable even in the mix of local and transient boats, Rod swung west, around the far side of small Pennock Island, half a mile across the water from downtown Ketchikan. As the city disappeared behind the island, he lowered the sails, started the engine, and motored slowly along the shore, looking for a quiet place to anchor. Halfway along the island, in a tiny space more depression than cove, he slid in close and anchored just deep enough to keep from going aground should the wind shift to blow from the west at low tide. Leaving the *Doll* to swing on its Danforth tether, he untied the inflated Zodiak dinghy from the cabin roof and slid it into the water. Tying it to the stern, he attached a small outboard motor, then turned to Nelson, who was watching from the cockpit.

"Where're we goin'?" he asked, with a frown.

"Not *we*," Rod told him. "*Me*. I'm going into town. We need some supplies, more eggs, for one thing, and if there were such a thing as unburnable bacon, I'd get that, too. It's time for me to make a phone call."

"What about me?"

"You stay here and keep an eye on the boat. That's what about you."

"But . . ."

"No buts. One of us in town is enough. I want to find out if this boat's been reported stolen yet, and check with our contact."

"Who *is* he?"

"No idea, but he's obviously got something pretty solid going on, if he's willing to pay good money just to get us down here."

"What do I do if somebody shows up—police— somebody—you know?"

"Aw-w, they won't. Don't know we're here, and

aren't looking for us. Bet on it. But just play dumb. You won't see anyone."

He stepped from the stern of the *Doll* into the Zodiak, started the motor, and was off, leaving Nelson to watch the small inflatable grow smaller in the distance. The older man did not stay on deck for long, however, but once again vanished below in response to his personal paranoia.

Rod left the dinghy tied up next to a launch that ferried passengers back and forth from cruise ships forced to anchor out when the dock was filled to capacity, though most of the huge floating hotels that visited Ketchikan moored at the long central dock, towering over the majority of its buildings, and allowing passengers to walk directly into the oldest part of the city. The streets were lined with a variety of stores designed to attract a tourist's attention and interest—art galleries, T-shirt shops, restaurants, bars, bookstores, bakeries, and more.

In a specified phone booth on the dock, Rod dialed a memorized long-distance number and waited while it rang several times, after which a recorded message spoke in a strange, distorted voice:

"At five o'clock go into the Sourdough Bar next to this phone booth. On the farthest stool from the door a man in a blue shirt will be sitting with a newspaper on the seat next to him. Ask him if it is today's paper. If he says it is, picks it up, and lays it on the bar, sit down on the stool and order a bourbon and water, which he will pay for. He will then give you the information you need to proceed. Don't screw this up, Rod, or you'll be sorry, and you won't get paid."

He hung up with a frown on his face, crumpled the paper list of numbers, and stuffed it into his pants pocket. "If I choose to accept this assignment," he muttered to himself, "the Goddamned message will probably self-destruct in five seconds. Right!"

Stepping away from the telephone, he stood staring at the door to the Sourdough Bar. What had he gotten himself into? It had all sounded so simple on the telephone in Juneau. Steal a boat, take it to Ketchikan by Monday, make the phone call, and collect his money—or so he had anticipated. *"Information you need to proceed."* What the hell did that mean? *Proceed?* He had proceeded as far as he intended to— right here to the dock to find out where to deliver the boat. Now what did this unknown guy want? This didn't sound like it had anything to do with drugs, which he had half-suspected. Serves me right for taking a job when I don't know who I'm working for and don't get the money up front, he thought unhappily. Well, I'll just have to make it clear that enough's *enough.*

He glanced at his watch—ten after five—and headed for the door to the bar.

It was darker inside, with no windows but one beside the door, and he blinked for a minute as his vision adjusted. It was a small place, a couple of minuscule tables with a couple of chairs each, and the bar itself was against the west wall. The walls were covered with pictures of shipwrecks, unlucky vessels that had sunk in the Inside Passage, probably since the beginning of time.

The bartender looked up and nodded. Rod nodded back, then looked past him and a couple of fishermen in working clothes and rubber boots, who perched on stools halfway down the bar. In the seat farthest from the door, as the message had indicated, a man was sitting, watching him. He wore a blue shirt.

As he passed behind the fishermen, Rod could see a folded newspaper on the stool next to the man in the last seat. All right, he'd play along—for now.

"That today's paper?"

The stranger nodded and, as expected, took it off the stool, allowing Rod to sit down. Then he laid the paper beside him on the bar.

He was big. Because he was sitting down, Rod

couldn't tell if he was tall, but under the denim of the shirt his upper body was solidly muscled in a way that did not indicate a man who lifted weights to satisfy his vanity—fishing nets or the local lumber mill was more likely. He said nothing, but assessed Rod from under wiry gray brows, with eyes so dark it was impossible to distinguish iris from pupil. His hair was mostly gray, though he did not look much over forty.

"What'll you have?" The bartender waited, a towel in one hand.

"Bourbon and water." Rod tossed the words at him out of the corner of his mouth, still staring at the stranger. "Now. What the hell . . ."

"Wait," the man interrupted.

When the drink was set up and the barkeep gone, he turned, abruptly accusing. "You're late."

"Only a few minutes," Rod shrugged. "Who're you?"

"No, damn it, I mean you were *supposed* to be here yesterday. Where the hell have you been?"

"It took a little longer than I thought. So—we're here today instead. What's the big deal? Was that you on the phone, making weird with the voice?"

"We've got a schedule to keep. That's the big deal. And what do you mean *we*? You were supposed to come alone."

"I didn't get it that way. I brought a boat and some company—an old partner. You won't have to pay him, I'll split my money. *Listen!* What the fuck is your problem? Who's running this show?" Rod almost yelled.

The bartender and both fishermen turned to stare.

"Shut up. Keep your voice down, stupid. Let's get out of here." Blue shirt threw some money on the bar and walked out, newspaper in hand. Rod, caught off guard, half-ran along behind.

As they cleared the door onto the dock and were beyond the window, the stranger turned, grabbed

Rod by the collar, and slammed him backward into the wall next to the phone booth.

"You listen to me, you worthless turd. You're a day late, with someone else along. What else have you screwed up on your own? I'm Walt—just Walt—and I'm *not* the voice on the phone. Don't know who it is any more than you do, but I've worked for him and his boss before, and he's treated me right when I follow his instructions. Okay? I don't want this deal blown. It's the biggest one yet. He said you were okay. I don't know who the fuck you are, or anything about you, except you were damned well supposed to have a powerboat down here from Juneau yesterday. Whatever he has in mind, he obviously wants it spread out from here to Canada, because from here he said for us to go on down to Prince Rupert on the boat you've brought. You *have* brought a boat, right?"

"Right," Rod agreed between gasps, as his collar was released, allowing him to breathe—and speak. He considered, with dread, what this guy's reaction would be to the stolen sailboat—not, by any stretch of the imagination, a powerboat. It was obviously imperative that this . . . Walt . . . must never find out about the woman they had sunk in the depths of Tracy Arm. He'd have to warn Nelson to keep his damned mouth shut—if that was at all possible.

"All right. Now, we start for Prince Rupert as soon as possible. Should have left this morning. You go over there while I make a phone call. And don't you fuckin' dare disappear on me either."

Rod shuddered, and wondered if there was any way he could abandon the *Doll* and steal another boat from somewhere in Ketchikan. This was not turning out the way he liked. Prince Rupert was Canada, for God sakes, too far from home, and not where *he* had any desire to go. But, if he wanted to be paid, it looked like they were headed south, and Walt intended to stick like glue until they got there. Goddamnit!

13

7:30 A.M.
Tuesday, July 15, 1997
Spirit of '98
Stephens Passage, Inside Passage, Alaska

"THE PARLOUR WAS FAIRLY BUSY LAST NIGHT," DON SAW-
yer told Jensen and Captain Kay. "Those who didn't
want to join the sing-along in the upper lounge came
down for a quieter drink or two after dinner. I had
fifteen or twenty people wander in and out between
eight and eleven, when the last couple left and I shut
down. Why? What's wrong? There wasn't any trouble. Everyone was pretty low-key."

Summoned from the cabin he was sharing—when
Jensen and Captain Kay had completed the officially
required notifications of Morrison's disappearance,
along with their conclusions regarding its time and
location, and initiated a discreet stateroom search—
Sawyer had appeared in Kay's office wearing jeans
and a *Red Onion* sweatshirt, flip-flops on his feet. His
hair was wet from a shower, and he had either been
shaving when called, or he had shaved in a hurry,
for Jensen noticed a small uneven triangle of whisk-
ers that Sawyer had missed on the jawline below his
ear. He came in, took a chair, and gratefully accepted
a cup from the pot of coffee Kay had requested earlier from the galley.

Alex politely glanced at the captain for permission and, at Kay's nod, responded to Sawyer's question.

"Before I answer that, let me ask you a couple of things, Don. This was the first night that Soapy's Parlour was open, right?"

"Right. We didn't open Sunday because there was already so much other celebrating."

"You know any of the *Spirit*'s crew before you came on for this trip?"

"Sure. Probably a dozen of them to speak to and three or four pretty well. They come into the Red Onion when they're in Skagway. We're closest to the dock and have good pizza."

"Who?"

"Who do I know, or who comes in?"

"Who do you know?"

"Well, Brad Francis, Gordy Hanners, Ellie Davidon, Jo Anne . . . ah . . . Don't remember her last name. Steve Broughton—he's not on this run—and Ray McKimmey come in pretty regular. There's a couple more I don't know names for . . . and what's her name, starts with an H, the one who does the talking on the loudspeaker."

"Any of them in Soapy's last night?"

"Ray, for a couple of minutes, when I couldn't get the cooler latch to work. I went to the engine room, and he came up to fix it."

"What time was that?"

"Oh, I don't know, nine-thirty, ten?"

"What was McKimmey doing in the engine room at that hour?"

"Working on something on the engine. Have no idea what, really. I'm not much on mechanics."

"Anyone else?"

"Ah . . . no. All passengers in the Parlour last night."

Jensen noticed the slight hesitation. So did Kay, and he leaned forward, ready to ask a question that Alex forestalled with a lifted hand. Rather than ask one of his own, however, he simply stared at Sawyer . . . waiting to see what response silence would produce.

Sawyer stared back, blinking rapidly, changing the direction of his gaze to the floor after a few seconds.

"No one?" Jensen challenged.

Sawyer shook his head. It was obvious from a slight uncontrollable flush that spread over his face that he was uncomfortable. He looked tired, discouraged, and somehow resigned.

Again, Jensen waited.

Again, nothing from Sawyer.

"Julie Morrison?" Jensen asked softly.

Sawyer's attention whipped back to the trooper as swiftly as the color left his face. "What? What about her?"

"You might as well tell us what you know about Morrison, Don, how you know her, and how well. Did you see her last night, for instance?"

The bartender took a deep breath, then slowly nodded. "Yeah, I saw her, but not in Soapy's. On the deck outside. Why?"

"Did you talk to her?"

"Yes, for a few minutes after I closed up."

"What about?"

"Ask her. It's her business. It's not my practice to break a confidence."

Jensen turned his head to look at the captain again. Kay shrugged his shoulders. "You'd better tell him, I guess."

"What? Tell me what? Is she okay? Is Julie in some kind of trouble?" Anxiety rose as the look on Jensen's face told him something was wrong.

"Some reason you think she might be?"

Sawyer said nothing, waiting in rigid attention for Jensen to answer his questions.

Alex sighed and began.

"Morrison's missing. Since sometime last night. We found her hair ribbon and an earring on the deck outside the Parlour almost two hours ago now. We've searched the ship thoroughly, and she's not on it. Her roommate saw her just after ten-thirty, when she came back for her cigarettes, headed for the stern. Her bed wasn't slept in. You may have been the last to see her."

Sawyer's reaction was, for a moment, shocked silence, then swift and unexpectedly virulent anger. "That fucking bastard! Goddamn him. He said he'd kill her. *Damn* him. Damn him. How could he know where she was? How did he find her? Who did he hire?"

His fury astonished both the other men, as did the accusatory nature of his words. For a moment after Sawyer stopped speaking the only sound in the room was that of his rough breathing. Almost hyperventilating, he covered his face with his hands and groaned.

Jensen waited for him to regain control, and, at last, he dropped his hands and looked up, his face wet with tears.

"Don," Alex asked gently, "what is Julie Morrison to you?"

"My cousin," he answered tonelessly. "My aunt—my mother's sister—her girl. We grew up together when my mother died, and I went to live with her family when I was six. She was two years older. She took care of me. I thought I could take care of her."

"Who do you mean *he*? Who said he would kill her? Who was looking for her?" Jensen peppered him with questions.

"Her husband—ex-husband—Gary. Gary Holden, the bastard."

"Why?"

"She left him. He made her life a misery—beat her, intimidated and embarrassed her, threatened her. Said he'd kill her if she left—kill her—and Josh, if she took him. Oh, shit—Josh! I've got to call and see about Josh, warn Marie." He leaped to his feet and stopped. "But I'll have to tell her about Julie. God, how can I do that on the phone?"

"Marie?"

"Julie's mother. She's in Vancouver. She has him there. He's only four. Julie sees . . . them . . ." He stumbled over the words. ". . . *saw* . . . them when she could. When she had days off, she'd take the train from Seattle, with care to make sure she wasn't followed—that Gary, or someone he sent, hadn't found her."

He sat down again and the rest of the story came pouring out.

"Julie's real name is Donna Lyons Holden—she was never able to get a divorce. My real last name's Carpenter. Marie's husband died ten years ago of a heart attack, so she didn't have trouble disappearing with us. She took her grandmother's maiden name, Roberts, and we left Josh his own first name and gave him hers as a last name, too, so it was easier for her to take care of him when we weren't around—if anybody asked questions.

"Julie came to me for help, when she knew she had to get away. We all left Arizona together, spent a month traveling around, afraid Holden would track us. We didn't tell *anyone* where we were, or where we were going. Bought, sold, and rented several different cars, took three different airplanes, finally split up and went into Canada three different ways. By then we all had fake IDs and had spent just about every dime. We hooked up in Vancouver, found a place for Marie and Josh, Julie went back to Seattle and found work on one of the Princess boats, and I came up to Skagway on the ferry. I was going on up to Anchorage, but they hired me at the Onion, so I stayed. That way I could see her every so often, when the boat came in. Then, she got the job on this boat that came in every two weeks, and when there was this chance to be on the same trip, I jumped at it."

He looked down at his hands and slowly made them into fists.

"But Gary must have found out somehow where Julie—Donna—was. Someone on this boat pushed her overboard. She didn't fall, didn't jump. She had Josh. Somebody here did this, and he has to be behind it. I'll find out who it is if it's the last thing I do." Sawyer—Alex found he couldn't see him as Carpenter—jumped to his feet.

"Whoa," Jensen cautioned. "Let's get our ducks in a row here, before we make mistakes that could cost us exactly what we need most. We need to figure out just how all this fits together. There are still some pretty awkward pieces to this puzzle, some we want to know and some that you haven't considered, Don, because you don't know about them. There's more to it."

"What?"

"Well, for one thing—not that I don't believe you, but—I've got to find out just where Gary Holden, Julie's ex-husband, is, though he's still her husband, from what you've said, which could complicate things."

"He's not on the ship or I'd have seen him . . . recognized him. So, whoever he sent has to be someone we don't know. You'll need to dig out just who it is."

"You can't know that for sure. There are other possibilities. It could be coincidence, you know. We had thefts in three staterooms night before last. What if the reason she was killed was related to them?"

"How could it be? Julie's no thief."

"She was responsible for those staterooms," Captain Kay told him, from where he sat behind his desk. "She might have seen something as she turned down the beds that caused this whole thing. It seems to get more complicated all the time."

"Sit down, Don," Jensen told him. "Let's talk this thing through. I hate to say this, but we might as well get it out of the way, so we can go from there. I like you, and I'm inclined to believe you, but the way to do this is to make absolutely sure of every fact. We can't know for sure that what you've told us is true unless we verify it. Have you any way of proving you are who you say you are—or were? Can you prove who Julie Morrison—Donna Holden—is, or was?"

Anger once again altered the color of Sawyer's face. "Who the hell else could I be?" he asked, resentfully, and learned immediately that Jensen could play hardball if pressed.

"Well," the tall, rugged trooper told him, in a voice startling in the quietness of its intensity, "for all I know you could be Holden, having disposed of Sawyer *and* Morrison, telling me you are Sawyer in order to avoid exposure. That do?"

Though the scenario he sketched didn't quite fit the situation, it was enough to stop Sawyer. Wide-eyed, he nodded, hostility vanishing. "There's a secret pocket in Julie's suitcase for our real ID. It's down in her cabin, under her bunk. You'll find Josh's birth certificate there, too. Marie has a copy of everything in Vancouver, too, just in case anything went wrong and she needed it."

"You have anyone outside the family who will vouch for you?"

"There's a lawyer in Phoenix who knows all about it, but it's confidential. He won't tell anybody anything without a phone call, or a letter, from me or Julie."

"Okay. Give me the name. You'll have to call him, so it can go on record." Jensen thought about that for a minute, before turning to Kay. "You satisfied with that, Captain?"

"Yes, I think so. It would be a good idea to bring Morrison's personal things up here anyway, don't you think? I'd better call a crew meeting as soon as breakfast is over. They'll have to know something. Any suggestions?"

"Since we don't know who's responsible for this, it'd probably be better to say she's missing and presumed overboard during the night. I've got a hunch it would be smarter not to let the perpetrator know

we suspect foul play just yet. Let them think they
got away with it for as long as possible. Maybe
they'll make a slip as we proceed with an
investigation."

"How about the passengers? They'll have to know
why we've been searching staterooms."

"Right. Same thing, I think. Tell them it's part of
routine procedure—company policy—in such circumstances."

"I'll talk to them at breakfast. You want to be
there?"

"You can handle it. I've got a bunch of other things
to do." Jensen turned to Sawyer, who had more or
less tuned out the conversation and was sitting in
the chair, staring at his hands again.

"Don? I'm really sorry about your cousin, but you
could really be a help, if you would. Probably
wouldn't hurt you to have something to do anyway.
Will you?"

"Yes, I guess. If I could help do something to
catch . . . whoever . . . you know . . . I'd feel better
about it. What do you want me to do?"

"Right now, I want to find Jessie. I need her help
too. She's been with Carla, the assistant chef who
found Julie missing, and may have something new.
We'll have to caution Carla to keep what she knows
to herself. I'd like you to find Judy Raymond and
ask her to meet me in her cabin."

"Oh, yeah. I remember her from the Onion—when
you guys were there. She was in the Parlour last
night, too. Early, for one beer. With that guy she met
at the Onion."

"She's the only one of those who were robbed that
I haven't been able to talk to yet, and I want to tie
that up." Without turning, Jensen spoke to the captain. "I don't think I really need to interview Wayne
Johnson. Three people have said he was too drunk
to walk and watched him get that way. After Raymond we'll get Morrison's personal effects. Okay?"

"Sure." Sawyer got up from the chair, but he hesitated as Jensen now turned to face the captain.

"Is that all right with you?"

Kay nodded. "Don't worry so much about asking me about everything. Just keep me informed, and I'll back you up. You have my authorization, if anyone asks."

"Thanks. I might need it. One other thing. I need someone on the ship to answer questions. You seem to have a pretty good opinion of McKimmey, that engineer of yours. I was impressed with his good sense. And, because he already knows about some of this, he might also be some help. You've had him on board quite a while, seems to know everybody, and you trust him, right?"

"Yes, he's been aboard as long as I have. He's solid and smart. But you have to remember I have a ship to run here. Ray McKimmey is as important to that engine room as anyone on the bridge. Maybe more."

"Does he have to be there all the time? Isn't there an assistant that you spoke of?"

"Yes, but he's new this run. The usual assistant was in a car accident just before sailing, and he replaced him at the last minute. Doesn't know the ship like McKimmey. He'd be okay for short periods of time, but I couldn't rely on him for more than that. Besides, Ray wouldn't hear of it. That engine room is his baby, and he wouldn't have it any other way. Knows every nut and bolt, piston and pump in it. Can tell just from the sound exactly what's going on. He talks back to it."

"Okay, so, with your permission, we'll work around that. Don, let's go find Jessie and McKimmey, and see if we can start to figure this out before anything else happens."

14

9:15 *A.M.*
Tuesday, July 15, 1997
Spirit of '98
Tracy Arm, Inside Passage, Alaska

JULIE MORRISON'S PERSONAL POSSESSIONS HAD BEEN
brought to the captain's cabin, where the papers in
the secret pocket of her suitcase verified Don Sawyer's account of their identity and that of her son,
Josh. By the time it was done, and Sawyer and Jensen
had made calls to the attorney in Arizona—who
agreed to check out the situation with Gary Holden
through the Phoenix police and get back to them—
and Julie Morrison's mother, Marie, in Vancouver,
they were both wrung out. Sawyer's grief had partially settled into an intense, cold desire to find whoever had killed his cousin.

Alex had a private conversation with Ray McKimmey, asking for his assistance with both the situation
and keeping an eye on Sawyer, who was deeply
angry, but was probably not an impetuous hothead.
Even outraged, his usual instinct and method of han-
dling problems was one of even-tempered reason,
not violence. Should he be faced with whoever
caused Julie's probable death, however, Jensen suspected that Don might be inclined to abandon his

customary moderation in favor of physical retribution; for that he could not honestly be blamed. If it had been Jessie in Julie's place, Jensen was sure his own spirit of reprisal would put him on automatic pilot, and he would, if possible, and without a second thought, beat the bastard responsible to a bloody pulp. The idea shook him a little.

When they were finally alone in their stateroom—where he had meant to fill her in on everything that had transpired in the time since they separated on the lower deck—Jensen found that he wanted more than anything just to stand, holding her close, feeling a huge and somewhat guilt-ridden gratitude that it had been somebody else's loss and not his own. In fact, for the rest of the trip, he would find himself seeking reassurance, reaching out to touch her, appreciating the familiar look and warmth of her presence in a way that reminded him of the early days of their relationship, when every encounter was somehow new and amazingly physical. Now it was precious and seemed fragile, a valuable thing that could, in an instant—as suddenly as Morrison had vanished—be gone. He was, he realized, overcompensating, aware of the transience and frightening mortality of the woman he loved and valued, for whom there were no guarantees or perfect protections. There were, he was learning, again, incredible, unexpected prices to be paid for caring, and a sense of awesome helplessness was one of them.

When he knocked, Judy Raymond opened the door and allowed Alex and Jessie into her stateroom with nothing more than a half-nod of her head. Immediately, she crossed the room to take the only chair, effectively leaving them to stand by the door, rudely discouraging any further intrusion.

Jessie gave Alex a look that spoke volumes in its blankness, braced herself against the wall, and took out her notebook.

Alex was less inclined to passively accept Raymond's behavior.

"Ms. Raymond, is there some reason you would rather not talk to me? I was under the impression you were interested in getting back what was stolen from this cabin.

Judy Raymond didn't move from where she had leaned back in the chair. She slightly lifted her chin and didn't answer for a second or two, as she stared at him haughtily.

"And *I* was under the impression that *you* were supposed to be interested in getting it back *for* me," she said finally. "It has been *two* nights, and you're just now finding the time to look me up? Except for that fingerprint person in Sitka, nothing's been done."

"I have looked for you several times, Ms. Raymond, between other duties and interviews. You weren't the only person I had to talk to, and you have been *very* difficult to find."

"Interesting. It must be a *much* larger boat than I realized. I've seen *you* a number of times." She turned her head just enough to glance at Jessie. "And this is your girlfriend, right? Is she a usual and necessary part of your work, officer? I find that decidedly unprofessional."

Jessie straightened and took one step away from the wall, feeling her face flame in resentment, but she bit back a retort and left the response to Jensen, who didn't let it pass.

"Whether Ms. Arnold is, or is not, a personal friend has no bearing here. She is assisting me, on a completely *professional* basis, in an investigation requested by the captain of this ship and with his full approval.

"Now . . . may we get down to business, or should I inform Captain Kay that you refused to help us out?"

They glared at each other, then Raymond, elaborately, shrugged and moved one hand in a dramatic, dismissive gesture.

"Whatever. Like, what is it that you want to know?"

"May we sit down, please?"

Another shrug.

He deliberately half-sat, half-leaned against the vanity, nodding Jessie to a seat on the bed.

"Will you describe the gold nugget necklace you found missing from this cabin when you returned from the reception in Haines on Sunday night?"

"Well, to begin with, it isn't a necklace."

"A chain, then, I think you told the captain."

"Yes . . . no. It's a belt."

"A gold nugget *belt?*"

Raymond looked at him as if he were an idiot, a condescending half-smile, lacking humor, on her lips. "You don't know much about the gold rush, do you, officer?"

"Sergeant," Alex said, in a softer than normal voice. "*Sergeant* Jensen, Alaska State Troopers, ma'am."

She said nothing, sitting very still, watching him.

"I do know a fair amount about the gold rush. It's a hobby of mine. Would you mind telling me how your gold nugget *belt* fits in?"

"It's a gold rush artifact," she said. "Any number of the dance-hall girls had them as gifts from the miners. My grandmother was Violet Raymond Stander, the Queen of Burlesque in the Klondike in 1897, first in Juneau, then in Dawson City. It was mine when she died."

"I didn't know Violet and Antone Stander had any children," Jensen commented.

"They didn't. That's why my name's Raymond. She gave her own to my mother, adopted her after they split up and he died."

"Describe this *artifact*, please."

"It's like a chain, or rope—real solid gold, thirty-four inches long and about half the diameter of a pencil, with large—half to three-quarters of an inch—gold nuggets attached along it—nine of them. It has a gold brooch clasp two inches wide with smaller chains hanging from it with gold charms on each: a gold pan with a pick and shovel, a little gold pencil in a gold case, a perfume bottle with a top that unscrews, a windlass with a handle that turns, a lady's watch with *Violet* engraved on it, a miniature riverboat, a gold champagne bottle.''

"Cad Wilson had something similar, if I remember right,'' Jensen said, glancing at Jessie to be sure she had all this recorded. She nodded.

"Yes, she did . . . lot of them did. Cad's was the biggest, most spectacular, the one you read about. This is about two-thirds as big. It weighs almost 17 ounces.''

"My God. What is it worth?''

"Artistically . . . historically, I have no idea, really. By the weight of the gold alone, last time I checked—a year ago—around six thousand five hundred dollars. But, as a unique piece of jewelry with historical value, it's insured for fifty thousand.''

He stared at her and whistled. "Your insurance company is *not* going to be pleased that it's gone missing from an unloc . . .''

Judy straightened in her chair and frowned. "I beg your pardon, *officer*. It hasn't 'gone missing'—like I lost it or something. It was stolen . . . remember?''

"And you brought it along on a cruise where the doors are never locked, and left it in your stateroom?'' Jensen shook his head. "I'd have to call that irresponsible. There's a safe for passengers' valuables, you know?''

"Well—'' she almost spit at him, defensively. "I only took it out to wear to the party in Haines, but forgot to put it on at the last minute. I was late and in a hurry.'' Once again the dramatic gesture with the hand. "I want you to get it back. It was my *grand-*

mother's. It has sentimental value to me that far outweighs the monetary considerations. What are you *doing* about it?"

"Everything I can, Ms. Raymond, considering that I also have a crew member missing at the moment. We're working on it."

Raymond did not respond to his comment about the missing crew member, and she cast a disdainful glance in Jessie's direction. "Yes. "I'm *sure* you are, *Sergeant.*"

This time Jensen chose to ignore her, not rising to the bait. "You were at the reception in Haines until what time, Ms. Raymond?"

"About eight-thirty. I walked back with a friend."

"Who? Please."

"Prentice. Bill Prentice."

"And when did you find the belt was gone?"

"I stopped in the lounge for maybe half an hour, came up here, took a shower, and got ready for bed. I read for almost an hour after we left Haines. As I was about to turn off the light, I noticed that I hadn't put my earrings back in my jewelry case. Then I remembered that I hadn't worn the belt. It was supposed to be in my suitcase under the bed. I found the case for the belt open and empty."

"What did you do?"

"I got dressed again and went up to tell the captain."

"Was anything else disturbed or missing?"

"No. Nothing."

As Alex and Jessie left Raymond's stateroom and stepped out on deck, the public address system crackled to life.

"Ladies and gentlemen, we have now entered Holkham Bay, named by Captain George Vancouver in 1794. It has two branches, Tracy Arm to the north, and Endicott Arm to the south.

"We are heading first into Tracy Arm, which was named by Lieutenant Commander Mansfield of the U.S.

*Navy, for Benjamin Franklin Tracy, Secretary of the Navy
from 1889 to 1893. Mansfield, commander of the survey
vessel, Patterson, in Alaska from 1889 to 1913, also
named Sawyer Glacier, which you will see at the head of
this arm, and which calves the hundreds of icebergs you
will see floating in the waters of the arm. This passage
was carved centuries ago during an ice age by a massive
glacier which completely filled the channel. You can see
the signs of its passing in the scoring of the bare rock
walls. Avalanche chutes further scar the walls each spring
and, as you can already see ahead of us, these are occupied
by spectacular waterfalls. We will shortly stop near one
of these so you can view it close up and feel how cold the
water is coming directly off an unseen glacier at the top.*

*"After visiting Sawyer Glacier, we will go back and
turn up Endicott Arm, named for William Endicott, a
member of the Massachusetts legislature and the U.S. Sen-
ate, to see Dawes Glacier. He was secretary of war from
1885 to 1891. Part way up Endicott Arm we will come
to Ford's Terror, a branch of Endicott Arm which has very
strong tidal currents."*

Jessie had been looking forward to this particular
part of the trip as she had never been to the foot of
a glacier that calved directly into the sea.

"Oh look, Alex," she caught his arm and tugged
him to the rail.

He laid an arm around her shoulders.

Three icebergs floated past the ship a few yards
away. One of them was as large as a small house,
and all were delicately shaded in the azure blue of
massively compressed, centuries-old ice.

"How long till we get to the glaciers?"

"Oh, a while yet. We're only four or five miles in.
We'll turn east soon." High cliffs of stone walled
each side of the arm of water, scarred by the force
of the long-gone ice.

"Feel the wind. It's already colder, coming off the
ice. Come on, let's go get jackets and find a place
to watch."

Back in the stateroom Alex quickly reviewed the notes Jessie had taken.

"Good job, lady. What're you doing messing around with dogs when you could be a secretary?"

"Hey! Careful. I'll quit, and you'll have to be your own stenographer."

"The notes would be unreadable."

She laughed. "That's true. You're making a cryptographer out of me with those notes you leave on the refrigerator at home. You should have been a doctor. All prescriptions are supposed to look like that, aren't they?"

When the jab did not bring a light, humorous response, she gave him an inquiring look. "What?"

He was still reading the notes, one finger tracing slowly down the page.

" 'Remember the eyes.' You've underlined it as a comment. What did you mean?"

"Oh, yeah." She dropped onto her bed and sat there thinking for a minute, her lips pursed, a slight frown lowering her brows.

As he waited, Alex felt, rather than heard, the *Spirit*'s engines lose power, and the ship began to slow a little.

"It was kind of a feeling," Jessie said, at last. "Hard to explain exactly. Let me just talk around it for a while, okay?

"She was such a bitch, but it was like she was trying to be one, sort of. Then, when you got into the description of the belt—chain—thing, it was like she forgot and only remembered later, just before we left, to get back into her role-playing.

"The thing about the eyes was that every time you weren't looking directly at her, she was watching you very carefully. Like she wanted to see how you were taking it—to see if you were buying what she was selling. You know? Does that make sense?"

"You mean the bitch bit was just an act? Covering something? I know that all of it except the description bothered me. But I hadn't evaluated it because she pissed me off so much with her patronizing attitude."

Jessie nodded and, standing up, began to walk around the small space, as if being in motion helped her to think. Once again the ship's engine changed the frequency of its vibrations, half-attracting Alex's attention. Before he realized it, however, Jessie had answered his question.

"Yes, exactly. But was she trying to make you—us—angry for some reason, the most likely being, of course, to hide something else?"

"What?"

"I've no idea. There was something else that made me feel uneasy, like she was playing a part. All those big words and la-di-dah pseudo-sophistication. Underneath it she seemed to be something else. There were a few times her vocabulary seemed to slip into words that wouldn't cost a dollar and a half—more like a quarter."

"Interesting. You're right. That part about, *like she lost it or something?*"

"Yeah. Little things, hard to put your finger on."

"Hm-m . . ." Jensen paused, concentrating. "I wonder if . . . that belt she described might not have been stolen at all? That's a lot of insurance money. Wouldn't be the first time someone wanted to have something and the money for it, too. Right?"

Jessie held up a finger to stop him. "Go you one better. Did anyone see that seventeen ounces of gold belt—*fifty thousand dollars'* worth of gold belt? You have only her word it was stolen—that it ever existed. Lifting the Berrys' watch and the Lovegrens' cash and money clip would make a great cover for something of her own's supposedly disappearing, wouldn't it? Maybe she never brought it in the first place. She certainly wouldn't have worried about leaving something on the ship unguarded that wasn't really there, would she? That seemed a really strange and careless attitude to me when she shrugged it off and didn't answer you about it."

Alex was now on his feet. "Jessie, you could have something. I don't see how she could have done it and still have been at the party in Haines, but . . . it's not impossible. More difficult things have been pulled off with a little maneuvering. What if . . ."

A pounding on the door interrupted what he had been about to say.

Don Sawyer stood outside, a stricken expression on his face.

"You'd better come, Jensen," he said in a strained, flat-sounding voice. "One of the passengers just spotted a . . . a . . ."

"What, Don? What?"

" . . . b-body."

"What?"

". . . a bo . . ." he couldn't say it again.

"A body? Where?"

"In the . . . water." He was practically hyperventilating.

Jessie grabbed his arm and pulled and shoved him to a seat on Alex's bed. "Put your head between your knees," she told him over her shoulder, heading to the bathroom for a glass of water.

Alex suddenly realized that as they talked the *Spirit* had come to a complete stop. He grabbed his jacket and promptly left Jessie to take care of Sawyer.

The ship had turned a dogleg into the passage and was now headed east. Looking down from the rail of the Upper Deck, Jensen could see that there was a human form in the turbulent currents beneath a waterfall that tumbled hundreds of feet down the side of the southern cliff. It was floating low, with shoulders and back barely showing above the surface, dark hair swirling like strands of weed around the head that bobbed gently in the agitation. Dark shirt, or jacket, possibly blue, with a hint of something red where the collar would be, hardly visible.

On the lower level, one of the deck crew had opened the outer door, caught one of the arms with a boat hook, and stood, holding on, keeping it from slipping away, his pale face betraying his aversion to this responsibility. Ray McKimmey struggled beside him to get a rope around the clearly female form, before it was pulled loose from the hook by the rolling pressure of the churning water that had drawn it in close on the surface and still tugged at it.

Jensen swallowed hard and ran down the stairs to the lower deck. A floater. He hated floaters—bodies of people that had been in the water for some period of time after they'd died. Some were worse than others, but all were water soaked and swollen. He would almost rather be faced, as he often had been, with blood—shootings, knifings, violence that many law enforcement personnel considered the worst. Bodies taken from the water were too revoltingly clean.

As he reached the bottom level, he wondered how long this one had been moved to and fro on this arm of the ocean's all but frozen tides, and he hoped it had not been long. It could not be Julie Morrison; the currents could not possibly have moved her body so far. Who, then, could it be? And what a wretched coincidence.

15

10:30 A.M.
Tuesday, July 15, 1997
Spirit of '98
Tracy Arm, Inside Passage, Alaska

JENSEN REACHED THE LOWER DECK IN TIME TO ASSIST McKimmey in lifting the body up and through the door that opened amidships a few feet above the surface of the water. The crewman who had laid the boat hook aside held tightly to a line they had secured under the arms and around the upper torso of the corpse, so that it would not fall back into the sea.

Together they strained at the weight, which was exaggerated by the water-soaked clothing and hair. Both men were panting with exertion by the time the woman's body lay on its side on the deck, water draining in pools around it.

The dark hair had lost the floating appearance given it by the support of the water and clung suddenly to the head, hiding the upper part of the face. The mouth was covered with a strip of duct tape. The same material tightly bound knees and ankles, and the wrists were taped together behind the woman's back. A length of line, with a few inexpertly tied knots, trailed in several loose loops around her. Luckily it had caught on her arms, but Jensen could

see that just a little longer in the turbulent water
would probably have pulled it loose. It was an interesting combination of colors, blue and pink, he
thought, remembering white or yellow on the boats
he had seen before. Perhaps she had fallen or been
put into the water not from a boat but from the land
somewhere. It was something to have the lab check.

"Get a mop," McKimmey told the deck hand, "and
a blanket, or something to cover her." He looked up
at Jensen. "God, what the hell is going on here?
Who's this? It's not Julie Morrison, though Sawyer
went off to get you in panic and confusion—afraid
that it was."

"Yeah, I know. He's in the cabin with Jessie for
the moment. It obviously can't be Morrison. We're
too far from where she could have gone in. Let's take
a look."

He stepped forward and knelt by the body, carefully lifting away the hair that obscured the face.
Eyes open, staring, this woman was a complete
stranger to him, blue eyes, medium brown hair, dark-
ened with water, and young, perhaps twenty-five, he
thought. He glanced up at McKimmey questioningly.

"I don't know her." The engineer shook his head
and turned away to find Captain Kay coming down
the stairs. Above and behind him, a couple of passengers peered curiously down.

"Who is it?" he asked. "Not Morrison."

"It's not," Jensen agreed. "We have no idea. You
recognize her?"

Kay leaned over to look. "No idea. There've been
no reports of anyone missing. How can we possibly
have just lost one woman and found another? Got
any ideas, Jensen?"

"No, sir, I haven't. She didn't come from this ship,
that's clear. You'd better get out another coast guard
communication, though they're going to think something's really strange about all this. There's more
happening on and around this vessel than I can even

begin to understand. I guess, right now, we'd better deal with the problems at hand and worry about the rest later. For instance, where can we put this body until we can get it to the authorities? We can't leave it here."

The captain frowned, thinking hard. "No, we certainly can't, but the whole ship is packed. We have no empty staterooms and, although it should probably be kept cool—right?—I can't put a dead body in with the food in the only cooler, or freezer, we have."

McKimmey had a suggestion. "We're right next to the engineer's cabin, sir. We could wrap her in sheets to absorb the water, and plastic to keep a bunk dry, and put her there. We'd only have to move her a few feet, and we could stay on this deck."

Jensen nodded. "That's a good idea, but where would you guys sleep, Ray?"

"Actually, we wouldn't need to put it on a bunk," the captain considered. "We can put it in there, but on the floor. It won't be that long, because we can make an unscheduled stop in Petersburg tonight and turn the body over to the authorities. They can take turns borrowing the extra bunk in the hotel manager's cabin in the meantime. It has the same arrangement as theirs—a bunk and a Pullman that's almost never used."

"Okay. I want to examine the body to see if I can figure out what killed her, but then I think that's the best course of action, if it's all right with you, Ray."

Captain Kay went back up to the bridge to make the necessary notifications. In less than half an hour, Jensen had completed his examination, and they had placed the woman's body, successfully contained in plastic and several sheets, on the floor of the engineer's cabin. He had found nothing to confirm violence in his scrutiny of the body, which was limited; he had hesitated, then decided not to remove the tape to make a thorough inspection. It was obvious she had not applied the tape to her own face and extremities then jumped overboard from whatever boat she had come from, and it was fairly certain, in this area, far from any town or community, that she must have come from one. Someone had meant her to die. A postmortem examination would reveal more about her death, and he determined to leave her as she was, to give the pathologist a better chance at any evidence. For now, he elected to leave what he could do nothing about and focus on the other problems on board the *Spirit*.

Before Jensen went back up to his cabin, he asked Ray McKimmey to show him the stateroom where the gold was being kept, with two guards, who even slept with it at night, in shifts, so one was always awake.

In the forward section of the same lower deck, the stateroom dedicated to the treasure was located along the only interior corridor on the ship that had staterooms opening into it. The rest, on the top three decks, all opened outward. Six staterooms lined either side of this corridor, and the rest of this deck was occupied by the galley, dining room, and Soapy's Parlour. Three of the staterooms held two single beds, two held double beds, and the last, forwardmost of the six, surprising large, held not only a queen-sized bed but also a sleeper sofa, so it could be used for triple occupancy.

The gold, in its fifteen wooden boxes, was in the first twin-bed stateroom on the port side of the long hallway. This door, when Alex tried it, was locked. He knocked. Someone from inside called out, "Who is it?"

"Sergeant Jensen, Alaska State Troopers, and Ray McKimmey, ship's engineer," he answered, and the door opened a few inches.

"Trooper, you say?"

Holding out his wallet with identification and badge, Alex waited till the guard was satisfied he was who he said he was, and opened the door a little wider. McKimmey stood behind Alex in the corridor.

The guard wore sweats and was in his stocking feet. Jensen didn't blame him. A week confined to the inside of a stateroom, no matter how comfortable, with all your meals delivered from the galley, and little chance to relieve the boredom, would assuredly not call for a uniform. He grinned.

"Taken to playing poker for the cargo yet?" he asked.

The door opened completely, and the guard smiled, yawned, and scratched his head. "No, but that's not a bad idea. No matter who won, the pot would stay where it is."

"How's it going for you guys? Everything okay? Any disturbances or problems?"

"Naw. Nothing but peace and quiet, damn the luck. The dancing girls haven't shown up yet."

Beyond the guard, Jensen could now see the boxes of gold stacked up along one wall, three high. They took up a fair-sized section of the smallish stateroom, leaving the beds for relaxing and a narrow strip of the floor in which to move around. A window showed the scenery they were passing.

"You alone? I thought there were two of you."

"There are, but we take turns going up for short breaks, just to get a little exercise and fresh air, periodically. Jim's gone for a smoke. Should be back any minute. As long as we're underway it's unlikely anyone would have a try at the gold. Where would they go with it? Besides, who could carry it away without help?"

It made sense, and they couldn't be expected to stay cooped up completely. A little fresh air would keep both of them more alert.

"Well," Jensen told him, "if you need anything . . . help, someone to relieve you once in a while, or whatever . . . let me know. Okay?"

"Sure. Nice of you to offer."

The door closed, and Jensen turned with McKimmey back toward the entrance to the corridor. As they reached it, a man who was unmistakably the second guard, in a similar pair of sweats, came toward them from the direction of the dining room. As he came closer, the condition of his face stopped Jensen in concern.

"What the hell happened to you?"

An angry, recent bruise reddened one of the man's cheekbones. His eye was swelled half-closed and looked as if it had every promise of soon turning black. His lower lip was split and also swollen. All in all, he was not an attractive picture.

"What business is it of yours?" he growled.

"Hey. Every business. I'm a State . . ."

"Yeah, I know. You're that trooper aboard to be gorgeous for the muckity-mucks. So what?"

"So it might be a good idea to get rid of the attitude and tell me what happened. Unless you'd like me to see about having you replaced."

"Oh, shit. I fell on the stairs. Okay?"

Jensen looked dubiously at this statement. "Which stairs?"

"Those." He pointed to the ones leading to the next level up. "Slipped about halfway down 'em last night."

"Do you need medical attention?"

"No. Hell, no. Just leave me alone." He turned away and headed down the hall they had just left. They watched him knock on the door to stateroom 112. As the door opened, he cast a resentful glance in their direction before disappearing within.

"Real sweetheart," McKimmey commented.

"A honey," Alex agreed, frowning toward the stateroom into which he had vanished. He hesitated, then turned to the engineer. "There's no way that damage was done in a fall. I know the result of a beating when I see one. Somebody competently worked that guy over, and I'd like to know who. I know you've got things to do, but I'm going to look up the captain. I want to know who he is and see if I can find out who pounded him."

"Any word?"

"No. Stay away from me. I'll let you know when I hear."

"Goddamnit. It's too long. They're gonna screw it up."

"Don't get your tail in a twist. There's time. Go. When I hear, I'll leave a note, yes or no, in your stateroom."

"Okay."

"Now listen, you imbecile, stay clear. If anyone sees us together . . . I don't intend to have you wreck this. I'll . . ."

"Don't threaten me."

"Hey. Who's in charge here? And who's in the most trouble now? Just shut up and go."

"I'm gone."

Jensen took the elevator to the Bridge Deck, favoring speed over exercise, and he was startled, when the door opened, to find a large number of passengers collected along the rails, where they could get a good view of the glacier they were approaching. Working to examine and secure the body of the woman they had found, he had completely dismissed the fact that the *Spirit* had continued its trip to the upper end of Tracy Arm. Now he wondered if Jessie was still in their stateroom with Sawyer, or if she was somewhere on deck where she could see the wall of ice that rose over a hundred feet out of the water. It was hard to believe that something so large and solid could be a river in motion, but numerous icebergs, of various sizes, bore witness to the fact that they had been forced by its massive weight and flow to calve off into the sea.

Dozens of seals, many with pups close to them, lay on the pieces of floating ice, their dark spotted coats distinctly visible in contrast to its light color.

"*Ladies and gentlemen. The seals you see on the ice-*

bergs are harbor seals. They can be identified by their spotted appearance, though they may vary from dark to nearly white. They haul out here on the ice in groups of a few to several hundred, to birth their single pups where they are safe from predators, particularly orcas—killer whales. The pups are a silvery color, but still blotched, and they darken as they mature.

"Adult harbor seals average six feet in length, weigh as much as two hundred and fifty pounds, and may live to be thirty years old. They can dive to depths of up to six hundred feet and stay underwater as long as eight minutes before they must surface to breathe. They eat a wide variety of fish, squid, and crustaceans. They do not migrate, but may follow the movement of their prey. They can be seen anywhere from California to the Bering Sea."

Jensen found Captain Kay on the bridge.

"Message from Sitka," the captain said. "Reported that there were only the anticipated prints—passenger occupants and crew members—no one unexpected, even around the items that were stolen."

Turning away from the instrument panel, he picked up a fax message which he held out to Jensen. "The coast guard found Morrison's body," he told him. "In Peril Strait. I won't bother explaining the technical information on the location, that doesn't matter anyway, since it was about where you would expect. What matters is that they say she wasn't just thrown overboard. Report says she was dead before she went into the water. There was a penetrating fracture of her skull. She was hit with something heavy and sharp. Their preliminary guess is an ax."

Jensen looked up sharply from the fax. "An *ax*?"

"Yes."

"There wasn't any blood on the deck."

"There wouldn't be much, but . . ."

"There was one small blot on the ribbon we found."

"From the angle of the wound, they think she was leaning on or over the rail."

"Where the hell would anyone get an ax? The tool locker? The engine room? Wait . . . there was a fire ax on the wall of the deck where we found her hair ribbon. No. That deck had the windows to Soapy's, so it had to be the one above it."

"No, two above," Kay told him. "The Upper Deck, one down from the checker board."

"Right. Bright red. Clamped to the wall. Let's go get it. If it's still there."

"Make you a bet it's not. Probably thrown in after her. You go. I can't leave the bridge right now. If, by some incredible luck, you find it, bring it back up here and we'll make sure it gets locked up till we get to Petersburg."

Jensen was already halfway out the door.

Almost sprinting around the owner's stateroom, Jensen collided with Jessie coming up the amidships stairway.

"Whoa," she cautioned, throwing out a hand to clutch at the rail. "Where're you going so fast?"

"I'll show you. Come on."

Unbelievably, the ax *was* there, tucked securely into the clamp that held it to the wall under the stair. It was bright red, with *Spirit of '98* in black block letters on the long handle, the sharp edge of the heavy blade resting in a protective metal sleeve also fastened to the wall, a typical fire ax, with a spike on the head opposite the blade.

Amazed, Jensen simply stared at it.

"What is it, Alex?" Jessie asked, as they stood in front of it, backs to the wide wake that churned white foam out behind the ship. "What's going on?"

Still looking at the ax, he told her in short, terse sentences how Julie Morrison had died.

"My God, Alex," she said, when he finished. "I hope she didn't see it coming. This isn't going to go over well with Don Sawyer."

"She couldn't have. The blow came from behind, above and a little to the right, which indicates a right-

handed person, taller than she was. She was leaning
on the rail. It was probably the ax that pulled off her
hair ribbon as she fell overboard and left that single
patch of blood. It also means that someone knew she
was there. Whoever it was planned it, took this off
the wall two decks up and was waiting for her, or
crept down the stairs behind her after Sawyer left.
Any sound would have been covered completely by
the rush of the water.

"Afterward, they wiped this and put it back, thinking, maybe, that its absence might be noticed before
hers—by a crew member doing a security check.
They check the fire equipment—part of the routine."

Carefully, using a handkerchief from his pocket so
as not to leave his own fingerprints, Jensen lifted the
ax from its clamp and metal sleeve. Carrying it
nearer the rail, where there was better light, he exam-
ined it closely. There was no evidence on the sharp
blade that it had been used for the purpose he suspected—it had been wiped clean—but between the
head and the handle it was very slightly discolored,
a brownish tinge, hard to see against the red paint.
One short strand of hair was caught there, too.

"The lab will have to test it, but I think there's
enough there for type and DNA," he told Jessie.
"There may be fingerprints on the handle, though it
looks like it has been wiped down—the blade, for
sure."

Nevertheless, he knew it *was* the weapon that had
caused the death of Julie Morrison. *Why* and *who*, he
had no idea.

Together, they took the ax back around to the elevator, rather than up the stairs, to avoid taking it
through the crowd of passengers on the Bridge Deck
above them. There was no need to upset them—yet.

16

12:30 P.M.
Tuesday, July 15, 1997
Spirit of '98
Tracy Arm, Inside Passage, Alaska

WAS SERVED AS THE *SPIRIT* RETURNED DOWN TRACY ARM
and into Endicott Arm, headed to the second glacier.
Don Sawyer had refused to come to the dining room,
saying he wasn't hungry. Jensen could understand
why, considering the events of the morning and the
loss of Julie Morrison. It was all the man could do
to keep on track with everything that was happening.
Alex and Jessie ate with the Berrys, the Hemlins, a
couple they had not met before, Laurie Trevino, and
Jeff Brady, the committee member from Skagway,
who had been one of the miners in the mystery play
the previous night.

Everyone at the table asked questions about the
body of the woman retrieved from the waters of
Tracy Arm, but they changed the subject when Alex
explained to them that no one knew who she was,
what had caused her death, or how she had come to
be there. "I think Captain Kay will make an announcement about it in a little while," he told them.
"We'll be making an unplanned stop in Petersburg
later this evening to turn the body over to the
authorities."

Jessie helped steer the conversation away from the corpse by turning to Trevino. "You all did a wonderful job in the play last night, Laurie."

"Thanks. It's a lot of fun for us, too."

"Was that a real Canadian mounted policeman?" Nella Berry asked.

"We're not supposed to ask Laurie questions, are we? She's not in costume." Jessie smiled. "Not even hints, Laurie?"

"Don't worry. There'll be another scene at dinner tonight that'll give you a couple more clues, and we'll be in the lounge for questions later."

The actress turned to Jensen. "Are you ready to play Arizona Charlie Meadows, Alex? It's just a few lines that you could read if you needed to. It's an introduction for my part, hardly anything else. You're so perfect for the part. It's going to be great."

Astonished and embarrassed, Alex remembered that he had promised to play Meadows. The thefts and murders had driven it completely from his mind, and now he was too busy trying to solve them. Recalling his half-asleep fantasy of Sunday night, he couldn't help smiling ruefully. *Be careful what you agree to, Jensen,* he thought.

"I just don't see how I can," he told her. "There's so much going on right now that I hadn't planned for."

"Oh, do it," Jessie urged. "It would only take a few minutes if you can read it and don't have to memorize lines. You'd be so perfect."

"You are," Brady seconded her enthusiasm. "I promise to make it easy for you, and we really need you. There's nothing to it."

Alex chuckled. "And just how much do they pay you to recruit inexperienced amateur actors?" he asked. "You don't know what you're asking—or what you're liable to get, but . . . okay. Just don't expect Shakespeare. And I'll take you at your word, to make it easy."

"Hey, no problem. Come to our cabin after lunch and I'll give you your lines and the costume. We eat early—five o'clock to five-thirty—with the crew, if you don't mind, and do a quick run-through just before dinner. And, best of all, we won't even have to glue on Charlie's famous signature mustache—yours would put his to shame anyway."

"Good for you," Jessie whispered to him, as the waitress set a bowl of mushroom soup, with an inviting aroma, before each of them. "Be good for you to do a little bit of something besides this investigation for a while."

He had to agree that a digression wouldn't hurt. With all that had happened, plus his lack of sleep the night before, he was beginning to feel a little overwhelmed. Things just didn't seem to stop happening long enough to think them over. The idea of eating with the crew was an unexpected bonus. Someone might have an idea about the thefts or murder that would be helpful. It couldn't hurt.

Resolutely, he tried to put the whole thing out of his mind. For a few minutes, he focused on a conversation between Bill Berry and Jeff Brady, about the work of the centennial committees in setting up the whole reenactment. But soon his thoughts had slipped back to the problems on which he was working, and he couldn't seem to help turning over in his mind all the disparate elements in the confusion of the last day and a half. Twice, he had to ask his lunch companions to repeat their questions.

Before lunch, he had spent the better part of an hour with Captain Kay, in his office, trying to make some sense of the events, and sending out communications to several agencies. He had spoken to the Scientific Detection Laboratory in Anchorage, which took care of crime analysis for the whole state of Alaska. Answers he needed from postmortem investigations on both dead women would not come quickly, nor would fingerprint information or test results. The ax with its tissue samples could not even leave the boat until they reached Petersburg later that evening.

He had called ahead to that community, to let them know what to expect in terms of the body retrieved from Tracy Arm, and to request that a fingerprint kit be put together to take with him on the ship.

"I want to dust that ax myself, before it leaves the ship. Takes too long for the prints to go back and forth. I want a set here in case we need it. I'll make photocopy enlargements of any I find and send the originals with the weapon. They can check them through AFIS."

The captain had raised a questioning eyebrow at the acronym.

"Automated Fingerprint Identification System. The lab has a whole roomful of computers that talk to— well, the national system.

"Who hired those guards?" Jensen had asked, switching gears to focus on his earlier encounter with the surly man in the lower corridor. "There's something about the one that claims he *fell* on the stairs. He's got a real attitude, and it seems odd to me that they would send someone like him on a job this important. Someone pounded him pretty good, from the condition of his face."

"They were hired by the centennial committee, but double-checked by the company."

"Do you have paperwork—contracts on them?"

"No, but I can get them faxed from Seattle. Important?"

"Maybe. Don't know. At this point everything's important—or not important. Until I know more I won't know what is and isn't. Go ahead and get them for me, will you?"

"Sure."

Jensen was yanked back into the present during dessert, a chocolate mousse with raspberry sauce, which he realized he had half-eaten without any idea of what he was putting in his mouth. As he stared at it, Kay rose to address the passengers, and he stood looking silently around the room for a moment. He was an imposing, noticeable man, every inch a captain in his white uniform. The room grew still. His deep voice easily reached everyone in the quiet room.

"I am sorry to have to speak to you concerning the unpleasant occurrence this morning. Some of you are already aware that we were obliged to retrieve the body of an unknown woman from the waters of Tracy Arm during the time we stopped at the waterfall. We have no idea who she was, or how her body came to be at that location. I assure you that this has nothing to do with the crew member who was reported missing from the ship early this morning. Julie Morrison's body has been found in Peril Strait, where we believe she fell from the vessel in a manner we have not yet discovered."

This, he and Jensen had agreed, was the best way of informing those aboard who had nothing to do with Morrison's disappearance, without alarming whoever was responsible.

"I want to reassure you that you needn't be concerned in either case, both of which have been tragic and the last kind of thing we would hope to have occur on this trip. Both incidents are being taken care of through the authorities, and we will be making an unscheduled docking in Petersburg later tonight. However, no one will leave the ship at this short stop. We will turn the unidentified body over to the police and continue on through the Wrangell Narrows toward Ketchikan, where we will arrive at approximately nine o'clock tomorrow morning, for a stopover of five hours.

"I have one request. If anyone knows anything at all about the disappearance of Julie Morrison, our crew member, we would appreciate your reporting it. Otherwise, please continue to enjoy your trip and the wonderful scenery that Alaska and the Inside Passage provide. If we can do anything to make your stay with us more pleasurable, please let us know. The bridge will be open for visitors this afternoon, if you would care to see how the *Spirit* operates. During the next hour or so, we will pause briefly at Dawes Glacier and return down Endicott Arm before turning south across Frederick Sound toward Petersburg. Be sure to keep an eye out for whales, as there are often dozens of them to be seen in the open waters of the sound."

As soon as Kay had finished his speech, passengers began to leave the dining room. Jessie stood up, declaring her intention to spend some time with her camera.

"I'd like to get some pictures of the seals, if there are any on the floating ice at the next glacier. You want to come?"

"No," Alex told her. "I'm going with Laurie, to get the costume for *whatever* I've committed myself to. I wish now I hadn't agreed, but how could I have known I wouldn't have the time? Then, I think I'll go hide out in the engine room. Ray offered to give me a tour, and I'd like to see the power that runs the ship. You're invited, if you want."

"Nope. I've ignored my camera long enough. There's a lot of good opportunities for shots out there."

They separated, Jensen going with Laurie to a cabin on the same deck as the dining room, along the corridor where the gold was secured. He tried on a fringed leather jacket very similar to the one he had imagined. "We must have seen the same picture in the gold rush books," he told her, as she handed him a broad-brimmed white western hat so big it rested on his ears.

"Oh dear. Well, you can stuff the inside band with some folded paper until it fits," she decided. "The jacket looks great, though, doesn't it? Have you got a pair of pants that will go with it? I wish we had some boots. Here's the six-shooter and gun belt." It was a huge pearl-handled gun, but not any more real than her small pistol. "Don't worry. It's for looks. You won't have to pretend to shoot anybody."

"Hey, with this, I might like to practice drawing and fancy twirling for the impression it would make."

"Good idea," Laurie laughed. "Do it while I sing and I'll use it, improvise. You're a born actor," she told him. "Already getting into character. Arizona was a real showman for Buffalo Bill's Wild West Show. Have I created a thespian that will give up law enforcement for a life in the theater?"

"I doubt it, but this could be fun," he grinned and tipped the hat, which, without padding, pressed his ears out like handles on a jug. "I do have a pair of western boots. No proper Idaho cowboy would travel without them."

"Oh, you're one of those! Great. Wear them."

Something occurred to Jensen, as he remembered the performance of the night before. "Listen, Laurie. Last night, in the play, you mentioned that it was a gold necklace that was supposedly stolen by one of the miners. Right?"

"Yeah. We're trying to put as much authentic gold rush material into this as we can. A lot of the dance hall girls had them. They could be worn as necklaces, or belts, and had . . ."

"A lot of charms and gold nuggets attached to them," he interrupted. "Do you actually have one that will be used later in the drama?"

"Is this a real Alaska State Trooper question?" she wanted to know. "It sounds as though it's something more than just wanting to know about the performance."

"Well, yes. Could I see it, please?"

"Sure. We made one up of an assortment of cos-

tume jewelry. Made nuggets like beads, out of that
bakeable clay, and painted them gold."

As she spoke, Laurie opened a case that Alex could
see contained an assortment of jewelry, stage
makeup, and other odds and ends necessary to her
acting job. Reaching into it, she pulled out a long
chain and held it out to him. "Here."

Without taking it, Jensen frowned, still staring into
her case.

"Is that other chain part of it?"

"What other chain?" She looked back, puzzled, at
the sight of another gold chain that had been under
the one she lifted out, and she reached to pick it up.

He caught her arm to stop her. "No. Don't touch
it."

From a handy box of Kleenex, he pulled one tissue
and carefully raised the second chain from the case.
It wasn't really similar to the first, clearly well
crafted, with a thinner chain, and hung with what
appeared to be real gold nuggets and charms: a tiny
gold pan with a pick and shovel, perfume bottle, a
windlass, a champagne bottle, and others. A gold pin
or brooch hung from one end, meant to fasten it together at whatever length the wearer desired, leaving
the rest to dangle. But it was a lady's watch that
caught his attention, and, when he turned it toward
the light from the window, he found that it had a
name engraved on it—*Violet*.

"Where the hell did that come from?" Laurie ex-
claimed in bewilderment.

Jensen looked at her in silence, waiting.

She shook her head. "Not mine. This is the only
one I've used—had. It was not there when I put this
one in. That thing is real, isn't it?"

As far as he could tell, she was honestly astonished
and telling the truth. However, he couldn't ignore
the fact that she was an actor, and a good one, from
all he had seen. The item of jewelry he held in his
hand was, obviously, the missing chain that had re-

portedly been stolen from Judy Raymond's stateroom two days before. How had it turned up here? Who could have known about the false one made of bits and pieces of costume jewelry, and then been smart enough to slip it into Laurie's case, where it would lie undisturbed until she needed the fake one for the play? Would she have pulled out the fake, if she had known the real one was right there, under it?

She now looked frightened, as comprehension dawned. "Is that one of the things that was stolen while we were in Haines? It couldn't have been me, Alex. I was off the ship for the whole party. Jim and I came back just before we sailed. We were some of the last people to get back on. I don't know where that thing came from, but I did *not* put it there."

He wondered where the watch and clip and its money were. Should he search this cabin? He looked back into the case, but neither of the other items was there. Glancing around the room, littered with personal clothing and professional costumes and props for both Trevino and Beal, he knew there were dozens of places the other items could be hidden—the pockets of the red mountie's coat hanging from the closet door, a suitcase under a bed, the mattress of the bed itself, beneath which any small item could be secreted. The list was endless. It would take time to search it properly, even with cause to do so.

He looked down at the chain he still held suspended. There was no chance of finding prints on it, and it was senseless to send it to the lab in Anchorage. It had no surface adequate to hold enough of a print to identify anyone.

Reluctantly, he gave up any idea of searching Trevino's room. Perhaps the clip and the watch would soon surface. Maybe the thief, wary of being caught, was trying to put the items where they would be found and throw suspicion on someone else, hopeful that the search would stop if the items were returned. Putting them back where they belonged seemed an

obvious choice. If it was possible they could be put
back in the staterooms from which they had been
stolen, a stakeout of some kind could be fruitful in
catching the pilferer. Not knowing the thief's identity, it was also the only place he *could* watch.

Wrapping the real gold chain in a scarf Laurie
loaned him, Jensen laid a hand on her shoulder.
"Don't be upset. It's pretty obvious that someone is
trying to get rid of this before they're caught with it.
It doesn't make much sense that you'd lead me right
to it. I think you'd have hidden it. I wonder why it
was left here."

"Maybe because I mentioned one last night in the
play." She smiled weakly and sank down on the bed
in relief, as he headed for the door. "Thanks, Alex.
See you here at four?"

She was probably right, he thought. He assured
her he would remember and picked up his costume
as he left, though he was more concerned with crime-
solving than the play.

On an off chance, he went up to have a look in
the staterooms of the Berrys and Lovegrens, but neither the watch nor the money clip had been found.
Both couples were interested and almost apologetic
that their possessions had not turned up, obviously
wishing he could find them and stop everyone's
worrying.

Four possibilities occurred to Jensen. The watch
and clip were long gone over the side of the ship
and would never be found or returned; they were
still in the possession of the thief and would remain
so; they would turn up later in the Lovegren and
Berry staterooms; or they might have been, or would
be, returned to someone else on the *Spirit*, like Laurie,
who either had not yet found them or who had no
idea where they came from, or what to do with them.
If the thief kept the two still missing items after returning the chain, it might be because they were
more anonymous, though without authenticity from

the Berry family the watch was just another old time-piece. The gold nugget chain was a one-of-a-kind item, and anyone who was offered the opportunity to buy it might question where it came from and how this person came to have possession of it. It was worth, according to Raymond, fifty thousand dollars—at least it was insured for that much.

The likelihood that an attempt might be made to return the watch and clip to their owners inclined Jensen toward setting some kind of watch on their stateroom, but how and who? Anyone watching the door from the narrow passageway outside it would immediately be seen by anyone attempting to enter. The watcher would have to be someone in motion, and someone who would not be considered and recognized by the thief as an observer. The other prospect was to put someone inside one or the other of the staterooms. In either case, the waiting could be long and unsuccessful. However, with the gold chain returned, waiting had a reasonable chance, but it would have to be done soon if it was to be done at all.

17

2:00 P.M.
Tuesday, July 15, 1997
Spirit of '98
Frederick Sound, Inside Passage, Alaska

JESSIE FIRST WENT TO THE BRIDGE DECK TO TAKE SOME pictures of Dallas and Rozetta against the scenery they were passing, and to wait till the ship drew closer to the glacier, which they could now see in the distance. Rozie had also brought her camera along— a neat little pocket variety with a zoom lens, which she said, with a laugh, was supposedly foolproof.

"I just can't get the hang of a camera like yours. Every time I want to change lenses I am convinced that I'm exposing all the film inside," she said. "I've also got a lot of pitch-black shots of the lens cap— when I wasn't losing it."

"You ought to take a class on the basics," Jessie encouraged. "That's what I did. It really isn't as hard as it looks."

"Did you get some pictures of the glacier this morning?"

"No, I missed most of it. We were pretty busy."

"Look," said Rozetta, turning. "There *are* more seals on the ice, Jessie. Aren't they something? If you can get some close-ups, would you send me one? I can't understand how they can tolerate lying on that ice, even the babies."

"The water is hardly any warmer than the ice, and they swim in that, too. They're well protected with fat and warm coats—more than they look."

Jessie went to the rail and began to snap photos of the harbor seals.

"Speaking of cold," Dallas volunteered. "I'm damn close to freezing. You two are moving. I'm just sitting here, so I'm going down where I can get some hot coffee and watch it all through those wonderful lounge windows."

"I'll come, too. There's hot chocolate." Rozetta moved to push her aunt's chair. "Jessie?"

"Not yet. I think I'll see how close we get. That glacier is pretty awesome."

The other two moved away toward the elevator, leaving her to watch the fantastic river of ice grow slowly larger as the *Spirit* moved tentatively between the icebergs the glacier had produced.

Photography was not the only attraction for Jessie, however. As Dallas moved, Jess had been able to see, for the first time, Lou Stanley, sitting with her back to where they had held their conversation. Slumped down in the deck chair, she was so tiny she had been almost invisible until Dallas wheeled away. Her headphones were, as usual, on her head, but, as she walked nearer the girl, Jessie noticed that none of the telltale whisper of sound spilled over to let her know that Lou's music was turned up to the volume relished by teenagers who didn't value their hearing.

"Lou," she asked, "would you stand by the rail and let me take a picture with the glacier behind you, so there's some perspective? Otherwise no one will know how big it really was."

The girl turned to look at her, then got up and came to stand leaning on the rail. "Sure. Why not?" She pulled off the headphones, releasing her thick, crinkled hair, which sprang up, an attractive, wind-blown frame around her face. "That's a cool camera."

"Do you like photography?" Jessie asked, as she focused in on her, also taking the measure of her cooperation.

"Don't know. I don't have a real camera—just a couple of those phony ones that you give back the whole thing and they develop the pictures. With one of them, though, you can take a really wide picture. Like you could get in the whole glacier and everything."

Jessie took the picture, then moved to take another, a close-up of Lou, having noticed how striking the contrast of her red hair was against the bluish white of the glacier ice. The girl did not smile, the ordinary "Say cheese" reaction being absent. But a pleasant glint of humor in her eyes and the slight tilt of her head revealed much more character than any wide smile could have.

"Would you like to see how this camera works?" Jessie asked, when she had finished for the moment.

Lou came to sit down and, after a little tutoring, was taking a picture of Jessie, as the woman guided her through the intricacies of 35mm camera settings. Lou was a quick study and seemed truly interested in what she was learning. When Lou had taken one or two more shots, Jessie showed her how to change lenses and was gratified at the girl's delight in looking through the different lenses.

"This is like the one I have that takes wide pictures," Lou enthused, peering through the viewfinder. "Except you can see a lot more with this. But I like the one that's like a telescope best. You can see the seals as if they were up close, then closer."

"The one you have now is called a wide-angle lens," Jessie told her. "The other one you already know is a zoom lens. And you're right, it lets you sort of sneak up on things that are a long ways away. There are stronger, bigger ones, but that one's my favorite. It goes from 35 to 70mm. That means like looking through an ordinary camera lens, then it makes things seem much closer. I have one more that goes from 70 to 200mm that I use once in a while, when I want to get in really close. Those two and the wide angle make it easier than carrying a whole bagful of lenses."

"Can I try the one that lets you get really close?"

"Sure. You can take some pictures of the seals for me with it."

They had just attached the long zoom lens, and Lou, with enthusiastic concentration, was focusing the camera back toward the glacier, when Jensen got off the elevator and crossed the deck to where they were standing. He was holding two paper cups full of coffee.

Jessie grinned and raised a finger to her lips to warn him to stillness.

"Hold it very still, Lou. Any movement of yours will spoil the picture. A long lens is very sensitive to movement. When you're ready, take a deep breath, then let it out. Just as you finish exhaling, take the picture."

Lou followed her advice. Still looking through the camera, she spoke excitedly. "Oh, Jessie. Come and see this baby with its momma. It's so cute . . . and with this lens it fills the whole picture."

Lowering the camera, she turned and was surprised to see Jensen standing with Jessie.

"Hi . . . ah . . . sir," she greeted him, obviously confused as to what to call him.

"It's just Alex, Lou. This is supposed to be a vacation. We'll save the sergeant stuff for some more formal occasion, okay?"

"Okay . . . Alex." She grinned.

"If I'd known you were here, too, I'd have brought you something to drink. Sorry."

"Oh, that's okay. I'm not thirsty. Can I take some more, Jessie?"

"Sure. There's about half a roll of film, maybe fifteen or sixteen frames left. You can take them if you want."

"Can I change the lens?"

"Yes. You know how. Just be careful that the one you put on is locked into place so it doesn't fall off. Check that before you use it and put the one you remove back in its case."

"I'll be very careful, thanks."

Alex and Jessie moved to a table, where they sat down to watch her and savor the warmth of the coffee on their hands, as well as mouths, as they drank it.

"Looks like you've made a friend," Alex observed, as Lou competently changed the lens on Jessie's camera and conscientiously put it away.

"She's really sharp and pretty easy to get to know."

"Listen," he told her, "you'll be glad to hear that Judy Raymond's gold chain turned up."

"Hey, that's great. Who took it?"

"I've no idea. And the Berrys' watch and Lovegrens' money clip are still outstanding."

He told her how and where the chain had been found and his suspicion that the others might be returned as well, possibly to the staterooms.

"Cash is impossible to identify, but that clip is one of a kind, as is the watch. Whoever has them will probably try to get rid of them. I'm surprised the chain wasn't tossed overboard. Whoever put it in Laurie's things risked being seen. Someone went in and out of her stateroom, sometime during lunch would be my guess. But it's perilously close to the dining room."

Concentrating on their conversation, neither Alex nor Jessie had noticed Lou as she approached the table, camera in hand.

"There was a man, dressed like a deckhand, only not, that started to go into the stateroom of that man who had his money stolen, while you were all having lunch," she said. "But someone came along and it looked like he changed his mind, because he went away fast."

Startled, they both stared at her.

"Good lord. You saw him, Lou?" Jensen asked her.

She nodded.

"What did he look like?"

"I don't know. It was too far away and I only saw him for a second, then he was walking away from me, see? Before he tried to go in, I mean. Then he went the other way, around the front of the ship and I couldn't see his face at all."

"Where were you, Lou? Why weren't you at lunch?" Jessie questioned.

"Well, I looked at the menu by the dining room and it said they were having Mexican food. I hate Mexican food . . . yuk . . . so I didn't go to lunch. I had some hot chocolate and cookies instead."

"And where were you when you saw this man? If you saw him, why didn't he see you?"

"Come and I'll show you." She handed the camera back to Jessie. "I only took six. Maybe I could take the rest later?"

"Sure you could."

Jessie put the camera back in the bag and went with Lou and Alex, as they headed for the nearest stairs. One level down, on the Upper Deck, the girl led them toward the stern on the starboard side of the *Spirit*.

"It was kind of cold," she said, as they walked back, "but kind of nice, too, because everyone else was in the dining room. There wasn't anyone going up and down the stairs, so I could sit on the bottom step and just watch the scenery go by."

She pointed to the stairs that came down on a diagonal from port to starboard of stern. Looking through the metal steps that were empty of risers, Jensen could see the clamp and sleeve that had held the red

fire ax in place. This part of the ship was consistently
and closely curved, and the rail that ran around outside the strip of deck followed the same line. The
stairs took up most of the space within that curve,
so that there was enough room for one person to
pass outside it easily, but not for two people to pass
each other, as there was elsewhere on the deck. Still,
from the bottom step, it would not be possible to
look down the corridor made by the deck as it
straightened to pass the length of the ship.

"Lou, you couldn't have seen anyone go into the
stateroom from here."

"I know. I didn't. Pretty soon I moved and got
more comfortable, with my back against the wall,
facing out. I sat there," she pointed again, farther to
the starboard this time, "and when I leaned a little I
could look around and down that way."

It was true. Jensen could see that she could have
done just that.

"Just as I looked around, he came out of that sort
of hall in the middle of the ship, by the elevator. He
looked this way for just a second, then went straight
to the stateroom door and had his hand on the door
handle. Just then a woman came up behind him,
walking toward the front of the ship, in the same
direction he had. He let go of the door handle and
moved away forward in a hurry, like he didn't want
her to see his face, like I told you."

"Will you sit down there again, for me, Lou?"
She did.

"Now lean around, like you did at lunchtime."
She leaned.

Jensen walked back up the deck till he was standing at the place where Lou said the man had looked
toward the stern. There he looked in that direction.
In a moment or two, he walked on to the Berrys'
stateroom and looked back again. Then he came back
down the deck and paused at a place between two
of the rear staterooms, where an interesting collection

of red pipes and fire equipment was attached to the wall. An alarm that would ring with a clapper inside was fastened next to a red pipe that ran from the deck they stood on almost to the overhead ceiling that was the Bridge Deck above. Midway down, the pipe branched. With a faucet handle to control water flow, it was connected to a fabric-covered firehose that folded in loops into a rack. Below the alarm was a break-the-glass-in-case-of-fire-type alarm box. Everything that had to do with fire was red, except the hose.

"You didn't duck back when he turned this way, did you, Lou?"

"No. It didn't seem important for him not to see me."

"You're wearing a red jacket. You must have been almost motionless. On this inner side of the walkway, sitting down close to the deck, you blended right in with the red of that fire equipment. He must not have noticed you at all."

"You said he was dressed like a deckhand—*only not*," Jessie said. "What did you mean by the 'only not' part, Lou? What made you think he wasn't a deckhand?"

"I didn't. I mean I thought he was, but it seemed kind of funny, his going in. They had already cleaned the staterooms and he wasn't carrying anything, like towels or stuff. You know. I just heard what you said about someone going into someone's stateroom during lunch, and I remembered. He was the only one who went in during lunch. Well, maybe not—I was sitting on the stairs part of the time—but he was the only one I saw.

"I don't remember why I thought he looked different from the others. There was something, I guess, but I don't remember. Sorry. Maybe I will. I'll think about it. Okay?"

Alex smiled at her. "Yes, it's more than okay, Lou.

You've been a big help. If you think of it, tell me or Jessie. Right?"

"Right. Bye." She sprang to her feet and waved as she walked off toward her own stateroom, two doors away from the Berrys', putting on her headphones as she went.

"I told you she was sharp," Jessie told Alex. "I like her . . . a lot."

"Yeah, me too. I just hope somehow we can catch this thief before he—she—gets rid of, or returns, that clip and the watch. We'll have nothing to rate a trial or conviction if we don't."

18

3:00 P.M.
Tuesday, July 15, 1997
Spirit of '98
Endicott Arm, Inside Passage, Alaska

"YOU KNOW, ALEX, I'VE BEEN THINKING."

Jensen lay on his bed in their stateroom, hands behind his head, long legs stretched out, relaxing for the moment and trying to make some sense out of the tangled web of the events of the last two days. He had decided that while passengers were circling the decks to walk off their lunch, watching the passing landscape as the *Spirit* left Endicott Arm on its way to Frederick Sound for a possible look at whales, no one would risk being seen entering the Berry or Lovegren stateroom: there was the chance that either couple might, at any moment, return for one reason or another, as most passengers went in and out of their rooms throughout the day. If the money clip was to be returned, it would more likely be during a time when the passengers were gathered for a meal, or later in the evening, when entertainment would draw them to the lounge. Any watching should be done then.

Jessie interrupted his thoughts.

"Are you just wool-gathering, or are you considering something specific?" he teased.

When she didn't respond in kind, with a tossed pillow or some other equally retaliatory action, but instead sat down on her bed, frowning thoughtfully, he concluded she was serious.

"Didn't Judy Raymond say that Violet Raymond Stander adopted her mother?" she asked.

"Yeah, she did," he answered slowly. "Why?"

"Well, that seems impossible to me. Isn't she too young to have had a mother adopted by someone who was in Dawson a hundred years ago during the gold rush? Jeff Smith is the *great-grandson* of Soapy Smith, not his grandson. Right? For the sake of discussion, let's say that Violet was maybe twenty in 1898. That means she would be forty in 1918. Somewhere between is when most women would most likely adopt a child. Even if she was in her forties when she adopted a child, it would make that child, Judy's mother, in her seventies now, if she had been a newborn or very small child at the time she was adopted. If Judy's mother, in turn, had a child at, say, thirty, in 1948, that child would be almost fifty now. If she had one at forty, in 1958, it would still be almost forty. Does she look almost forty or fifty to you?"

Alex sat up and stared at her, following her thought process.

"Damn. That one slipped right by me. Too many things happening at once. She's nowhere near either, of course. Thirty, at the most, but more like middle twenties. Maybe that's what she was trying to hide with her hostile attitude."

"Maybe. But what it really means is that she's a generation off in her estimate—it's out of whack."

"You're right. Well, she told me one lie, why wouldn't she tell another? Where *did* she get the gold chain? She presumably wasn't given it by her mother, who had it from Violet, was she? Stole it from someone? Who?"

"I'd really doubt it. But why would she lie? Seems

like it would have been easy to count on her fingers, though, I'll admit I had to sit down and think about it for a while. *Did* she steal it somewhere? Does it belong to someone else? Could she be playing some game? It could be any number of things."

Alex shook his head in bafflement. "She's using Raymond, which, I *think*, was Violet's maiden name before she married Antone Stander, one of the gold rush kings, who died broke after giving her all his money. This gets more complex by the hour. I'm beginning to lose track of all the details. Could you get that notebook?"

Jessie got up to retrieve it, along with a pen, from the dressing table.

"Let me go through everything I can think of, in the order it occurred. Maybe if I can see it all written down I can make some connections—some kind of sense out of it. I wish I had a blackboard. It's easier to get a big picture when you can see it all spread out, can erase and fill in when you need to. However . . .

"Okay, what all has happened? Write just the specific happenings, not speculations about them. Then we'll go back and go over them one by one. Help me out here, if you think of anything I've missed.

"First, during the party the watch, money clip, and gold chain were stolen from the Berrys, Lovegrens, and Judy Raymond, respectively. I met Julie Morrison in the captain's office and she refused to let us search her things. You and I talked with the Berrys and Lovegrens, but didn't find Raymond till later.

"Then we met Dallas and Rozie, and spent the afternoon with them in Sitka, where you saw someone following you. There was . . ."

The loudspeaker broke in, interrupting him:

"Ladies and gentlemen, there are three whales on the starboard side of the ship at approximately three on your imaginary clock."

Jessie dropped the notebook, stood up, and grabbed

her jacket and camera. "Oh, let's go see. These are the first ones they've spotted."

Passengers were crowding to the rails from everywhere on the ship.

"These are humpbacks, one of many varieties of whales that migrate north in the summer, though most stay farther from land. Humpbacks, northern right whales, and minke whales, all come in among the islands of the passage to feed. Orcas—killer whales—may also be seen, but they are not true whales, being in the same family as dolphins.

"Humpback whales are medium-sized, averaging forty-six to fifty feet and twenty-five to thirty-five tons in weight. The babies are sixteen feet long at birth and weigh only two tons. The adults are black, with some white on the throat, belly, flippers, and tail. Each whale is unique and can be identified by the difference in coloring and shape of its flukes.

"These whales usually stay together in groups up to a dozen, and are among the most active whales. You may see them breach—rising out of the water to fall back in—slap the water with their flukes, or spyhop—coming up to look around them with only the head showing. They can stay deep in the water for as long as twenty-eight minutes without coming up for air. In groups of two or three, they sometimes engage in a cooperative effort called bubble-net feeding. One takes a large breath of air at the surface, then dives under a school of herring. Rising in a spiral, while exhaling to release a circle of bubbles, it drives the herring, which are afraid to swim through the net of bubbles, to the surface, where another whale opens its mouth and eats the frantic ball of tiny fish.

"Humpbacks are still an endangered whale, with a worldwide estimate of perhaps ten thousand. They have been protected since 1966."

Jessie was busy with her camera, as the whales rose and sank in the ocean. Several times they breached, falling back to create an enormous splash as they hit the water. Coming slightly closer, one raised its head just enough to take a look at the ship, including the people lining the rails, with a huge eye.

"Wow," Alex said. "Wish they'd do that bubble-net thing. That's something I'd really like to see."

They watched until the whales fell behind the ship as it sped up to continue its trip south.

Back in the stateroom, Jessie picked up the note-book and settled herself on the bed, getting them back into the list by reading the last entry.

"We went into Sitka with Rozie and Dallas."

She stopped writing and looked up at him thoughtfully. "You know, I think I just might have got a picture of that guy who was following us, from a long ways away. It might be worthwhile to have that film developed when we get to Ketchikan tomorrow morning. There must be a place that develops in an hour. If there's anything at all in the pictures, we could have it enlarged. Maybe they have one of those machines that lets you do enlarging yourself."

"Good idea. Do you know which roll of film it is?"

"Yes. I mark them with tape and number them, so I know which one is which. That one was number four: Sitka."

"That's pretty organized."

"Well, I got tired of finding odd rolls of exposed film in the back of the suitcase, or in the bottom of my purse, and having no clue what they were."

"Well, get it out and we'll make sure to get that done."

"Okay. What next? We were talking about the af-ternoon in Sitka."

"Right. Next we interviewed John Stanley and Lou in the lounge."

"And saw the first part of the Mystery Play at dinner."

"How's that relate?"

"It doesn't, I guess. But a mystery is a mystery, so I threw it in."

Jensen grinned and went back to his mental list.

"Early Tuesday morning Morrison was missing and we searched until McKimmey found where she had gone over the stern outside Soapy's Parlour. Then we talked to Don Sawyer and found out who she really was. How's Don taking it all now, by the way?"

"Finding that other woman was a shock, but he seems to be getting it back together. He's pretty angry about it all. Still thinks her husband had something to do with her death. I think it helped when they found her body in Peril Strait. He hated the idea of her in the water somewhere." Jessie shuddered. "So did I."

"I'll talk with him again soon. Don could be right about that husband of hers. Even though the attorney says he's not our man, he could be wrong. I asked Commander Swift, in Anchorage, to see what he could find out about the guy—see if he's really been in Phoenix, or if he could have been elsewhere—or sent someone to do his dirty work. If anybody can check it out, Ivan can.

"Now . . . we interviewed Judy Raymond, finally, and she was hostile. We talked about the possibility of her attempting some kind of insurance fraud—stealing the other things as a cover-up. I'd like to know where she was when the chain and watch were returned, or at least found. All that you figured out about her age fits in here. Good going, by the way, Jess."

"She was in the dining room at lunch. I saw her with that Bill what's his name, the one from the Red Onion," she told him, with a smile for the compliment.

"Prentice. Bill Prentice. She seems to be spending a lot of time with him. Maybe I should see what I can find out about him, too.

"Then we found that woman's body in Tracy Arm and took it aboard. I checked on the guards for the gold, and the second one has been beat on by someone."

"We found the ax that was used on Julie Morrison," Jessie interjected.

"Right. That will go to the lab in Anchorage, along with the body we found. Two bodies—what a confusion.

"The gold chain reappeared and. . . . That's it, I think. Now, does any of it fit together? Come over here, so we can both look at your list."

Jessie was sitting against a pillow at the head of her bed, with her legs stretched out, at ease. She leaned back, sighed a comfortable-sounding sigh, and gave Alex an amused look, raising an eyebrow.

"Okay . . . okay. I get it," he replied. He stood up and crossed to join her, bringing his pillow along. "You don't take dictation, make coffee, or respond well to demands, right?"

"Right." She moved over to make room for him to sit next to her.

"Oh, I forgot, Lou told us about seeing the man going into the Berrys' stateroom."

Jessie added it to the list.

"Okay. Let's examine each item and the people who were involved, or affected by it.

"The watch, money clip, cash, and gold chain. Whoever stole them had to either be on the ship, or come back aboard during the party in Haines. Dallas and Rozetta stayed on board, as did Wayne Johnson, and all of them were on the deck the thefts were committed on. Makes sense, there are more cabins on this deck than the others. We also have all the crew members that were aboard.

"When Captain Kay asked for my help the next morning, I met Julie Morrison. She refused to let us search her things, but now we know that she was probably protecting her identity and Sawyer's, as well as the names and location of her mother and son. A letter from her mother was with the identification papers. It didn't have a return address, but, from what she wrote, it wouldn't have been too hard to figure out that they were in a large northern city on the West Coast."

"Then we met Dallas and Rozie," Jessie read from her list. "But they aren't part of this, are they?"

"No, but Rozie was with you when you noticed someone following, so I think it's sensible to put down everyone involved in any way, suspicious or not. I'm just trying to see if there are any connections between what's been happening."

"Okay, you're right, that's reasonable. We'll get the film developed and see if I got anything. Probably didn't, but you never know. It's worth a try."

"I'd sure like to know who was following you."

It may have been my imagination, you know. A coincidence."

"I doubt it. You're usually pretty aware of what's going on around you."

"Yeah, I don't think it was a coincidence either. I find myself looking at all the people on the ship to see if I recognize anyone."

"Keep looking, Jess. There've got to be a few you haven't seen, or at least focused on, yet.

"We talked to John Stanley and Lou in the lounge. Nothing helpful there. But Lou actually may have seen the thief outside the Lovegrens' stateroom. I wish she remembered what it was that made her think it wasn't a crew member."

"Maybe she will."

"Right. Just have to wait and see. I still want to have someone watch the Lovegrens' stateroom. It's the easiest, since it's closer to the rest of the ship. If Judy Raymond should turn out to have something to do with this, she's right next door, and it would be convenient to slip back into the Lovegrens'."

"I was wondering about that stakeout you're thinking about. You know Don Sawyer didn't come

to lunch . . . stayed in his stateroom. Isn't it possible
he won't want to come to dinner either?"

"Oh, I don't imagine . . ."

"You're missing the point, Alex. If he stayed in his
stateroom once, he *could* do it again. But this
time . . ."

". . . he could stay in the Lovegrens' stateroom,"
Jensen finished for her. "Good idea, Jess. Only one
problem. I haven't removed the Lovegrens or Berrys
from my list of suspects. We don't know that any of
them are cleared for sure."

"Oh, you don't really think one of them did this,
do you?"

"No. I know they were at the Haines party, because I saw them there. The first mate confirmed that
no one came back aboard during that time."

"Well, if you want to set up a watch, you've got
to trust somebody, and it might as well be the
Lovegrens."

"Intuition has been wrong before, Jess. But I think
you're right. Okay, let's see if they'll go along. We
could even arrange for dinner to be sent to Sawyer's
own room early, while passengers are still around,
drifting toward the dining room, so people see it arrive and think he's there."

"Yes. And just in case someone's keeping an eye
on the Lovegrens' stateroom to see when they're
gone, let's disguise him going in. Chuck Lovegren
wears a green jacket and a cap with a bill. They're
close to the same size. Let Don wear it going in with
Carol, and I'll bet they'd think it was Chuck."

"Good. But we've got to have Chuck come out so
the stateroom appears empty. If Chuck and Carol go
in and out several times, together and individually,
between now and dinner, Chuck could eventually
stay in. Who would be counting every entrance,
without seeming obvious? Carol can bring out the
jacket and cap folded inside a coat of her own, and
we can slip Don in wearing Chuck's clothes. Then

Chuck can put them back on, come out with her, and we're set."

"But what if somebody really does go in to return the money clip? Are we forgetting that this may be a killer we're dealing with?"

"No. I'll figure out a way to stay close enough to get there if there's any trouble."

"You're in the play tonight. Did you forget?"

"Oh, damn. Yes. What time is it? I told Laurie I'd be there at four. Why did I ever agree to do that thing?"

"Only three-thirty. Don't panic."

"I'll just have to cancel my part in the play."

"Alex! You can't now, it's too late for them to get anyone else."

"Well, you do it."

"How could I? Borrow your mustache?"

He had to laugh at the thought of Jessie trying to play Arizona Charlie Meadows in his mustache. "Guess not, huh? Okay, I'll do it. It won't take very long. It's just a few lines."

"Couldn't I stay in the Berrys' stateroom next door and watch?"

Jensen shook his head and stood thinking for a minute.

"No," he said. "I'm not putting you into this. If they go into one stateroom, they'll likely go into the other as well. Don's enough. But I've got a better idea. If you and Lou were at the stern, and she was sitting just where she was during lunch, she could look around and be hidden by the fire equipment, like she was before. She's such a tiny little thing."

"She's tough, I think. Fragile looking, but strong. You don't think they'd notice we weren't at dinner either."

"With a hundred people going to dinner, who'd know which ones to count? And who's to watch, if they're going back into those staterooms? No, I don't think so. Waiting and watching to make sure the Lovegrens' stateroom is empty makes more sense."

"You keep saying *they* and *they're*. Do you think there's more than one?"

"Now there's a thought. But, no, I didn't mean that, but I suppose it's possible. Usually this kind of petty theft is just one person, though."

"Well, I'll find Lou and ask if she'll help. What shall we do if someone does go in—if there's any kind of trouble?"

"Send Lou for me, on the double—the captain, if she can't find me, or I'm right in the middle of my thespian thing. But I doubt there'll be trouble, since whoever it is is more concerned with not being seen—caught—than anything else. Don't get in the way, or try to stop anyone, just identify them and get away from there. Up the stairs to the Bridge Deck would be fastest. No, down to the Lounge Deck, then to the dining room."

"Right. Darn it. I wanted to see you in the play."

Jensen stood up and began to pace around the cabin, his rising enthusiasm and energy making it impossible for him to sit still on the bed.

"Believe me, you won't miss much. I'm no Kevin Costner. Anyway, let's finish this list. I've got to get going in a minute, and so should you, to find Lou. I need to talk to Sawyer before I go for that run-through."

Jessie turned back to the notebook. "The mystery play at dinner had nothing, really, to do with anything else. Next they found Julie Morrison missing the next morning, and Ray found her hair ribbon—then the earrings and cigarette butt."

"Can't understand why someone would kill her unless it really is somehow connected to her ex-husband. It's a strong motive, but so is the Raymond insurance fraud idea. They may not be divorced, but to her he was clearly an ex, and it sounds like he was anything but happy about it. What other reason would anyone have for getting her out of the way? Could she have seen the thief and been able to identify that person? Seems a bit extreme to kill her for that—unless it's somehow connected to something else, and I can't see what. Have to wait till Ivan gets back to me on the husband.

"Judy Raymond is next, right?"

"Well, yes, except for interviewing Don. You truly don't think he had anything to do with this, do you?"

"No, I don't. He's too shocked—stupefied, actually. That's hard to counterfeit. The physical symptoms of shock don't show up the same if it's not real, and his did—in fact he threw up twice. Difficult to fake."

"Raymond."

"Lies—more than one, it seems. She's got something going on, but I cannot for the life of me see how it connects to the rest, can you?"

Jessie considered. "Not really. She and Bill . . . ah . . . Prentice? . . . keep hanging around together. Is he on the list?"

"No, but it won't hurt. Who else is not on the list that should be? Got any candidates?"

"Not at the moment. Oh, yes. The guard with the bruises."

"Okay. The woman's body in Tracy Arm doesn't connect at all. Complete coincidence. Has to be.

"The ax may give us something, but not until the lab is through with it. We're doing what we can with the reappearing gold chain, but it's no good for prints."

"Have you given the chain back to Raymond?"

"Not yet. Don't know why, except she was so conspicuously careless with it. I will, after dinner. She's not very nice."

"Nope. But I guess it's hers, isn't it?"

"We have no reason, so far, to say positively that she can't claim it. Well, so much for that. Didn't get far, did we?"

"We'll keep plugging. It's more Morrison's death than any theft, now, isn't it?"

"Yes. Homicide alerts all my law enforcement instincts. Still, somehow, I do think there's an association between it and the thefts. However, I'm doing it again—trying to solve it without enough information. You're right—keep plugging."

While they talked, he grabbed the fringed leather jacket, the western hat he had padded till it fit, his own boots, and the gun belt with its pearl-handled six-shooter.

"Got to get on my horse and ride, or I'll be late."

Jessie laughed. "You'll be great. I love the hat. You should have one of your own like it."

"I do. You just haven't seen it because I don't like to look like a drugstore cowboy in Alaska. It's at my folks' in Idaho. I wear it when I go to visit. You'll see it one of these days."

Jensen went out, then leaned back in the door. "See you after dinner. Don't take any chances."

She stood up from the bed and kissed him. "I won't. Promise. Break a leg, trooper. That's . . ."

"I know. I will. But it better not take too long. Bye."

He was gone, and Jessie collected herself before going to find Lou Stanley to see about getting some early dinner for the two of them and Don Sawyer.

19

9:00 A.M.
Wednesday, July 16, 1997
Stolen powerboat
Revillagigedo Channel, Inside Passage, Alaska

"*IDIOTS!* A GODDAMNED PAIR OF TOTAL FUCKIN' IDIOTS.
And I have to baby-sit you two assholes. Should
leave you to figure out what the fuck to do with your
idiot sailboat."

Walt steered a constant stream of scathing invec-
tive toward his unwelcome companions. Since he and
Rod had picked up groceries and beer, crossed the
channel from Ketchikan in the inflatable Zodiak,
rounded Pennock Island, and come close enough for
him to get a good look at the renamed *Hazlit's Gull*,
he had hardly stopped swearing.

Nelson vanished below, where he could pretend he
didn't exist. Rod maintained an apprehensive silence,
fearful that the larger man might take another swing
at him. It was the first thing Walt had done, as soon
as they were aboard the *Doll*, and Rod's ribs and
stomach still ached, but he ignored it. Calling attention to his discomfort was definitely not the wisest
thing to do at the moment.

"What the *hell* were you thinking?" Walt yelled
furiously at him. "You were told to snatch a *pow-*

erboat, not grab one from some rag-bagger. How the fuck do you think we can get to Prince Rupert on time in this thing?"

"Hey," Rod ventured. "It was the easiest one to get away with. I like sailboats."

"*So you like sailboats!* Big fuckin' deal. Where does that leave us? Now we've got to decide where and how to lift another damn boat—and that's going to put it too close to what we want to do, shit-for-brains—as well as take time we can't afford."

But they took the time, as soon as it was dark. Slipping back across in the Zodiak to one of the town's largest marinas, Walt casually searched the docks, looking for a suitable candidate, while Rod waited, holding the line to the inflatable in case they needed to get away in a hurry. Walt, however, was lucky. A large powerboat sat alone at the end of one of the outer docks. From its looks, it had been there for some time without use, for its decks needed cleaning, and the windows were dingy. He broke in, and, with a little rewiring, it started on the first try. It wasn't new, but inside it seemed well maintained, and the tanks were half full of gas.

"Good," said Walt. "We won't have to fill up here and risk being spotted, or someone recognizing this tub. I've got a stash of gas in cans that should take care of us for the time being. We'll drain what's left in that worthless piece of junk you brought and add to the store. Now, tie the dinghy to the stern and let's get the fuck out of here."

Nobody seemed to notice when they moved it away from the dock, Zodiak trailing behind on its tether.

Draining the gas tanks of the *Doll* into cans, transferring the food and other things they might need, and taking the Zodiak on board took another hour. Nelson sighed in disappointment when he saw Rod retrieve the whisky from under the navigation console, a space he hadn't searched, because he hadn't known it existed. The bottle vanished again into the other boat before he could see where Rod hid it this time.

When everything had been moved, before they left the sailboat anchored where it was, Walt took one of the full cans of gas and emptied it over the interior of the cabin, obviously intending to set it afire.

"Hey," Rod objected. "What the hell are you doing? Why burn it? We don't need to. We'll be long gone when they find it."

"Idiot. Ever consider the hundreds of fingerprints you've left on everything?" Walt asked, carefully balancing a saucer on the very edge of the table. "We don't want to leave them anything to identify us. This'll make sure they damn well don't."

He poured the saucer full of gas and carefully lit one of Nelson's cigarettes, which he set in the gas and held, lighted end up, pinched in a clothespin he'd found in the galley. "It'll burn down and, after a while, light the fumes or the gas it'll suck up through the filter, which'll set off the rest. Probably, before that, though, another boat'll go by, and the wake will rock it off the table and set it off. Works real good either way. But you're right, we'll be long gone."

Rod tried again to argue, hating the thought of such a great boat going up in smoke, but Walt threatened to hit him again and shoved him up the gangway onto the deck.

"Get in the other boat, and don't give me shit. It's your bacon I'm saving. Get out the back—I'm right behind you—and don't rock this thing when you do. I don't want that cigarette tipping over and the thing going up before we're gone. We gotta hurry and get going, thanks to you two boobies. We'll have to pour it on—barely make it—and if the weather turns bad . . . I gotta be there in time to meet . . . well, just get going."

He started the powerboat and, very slowly, pulled

away from the sailboat, being careful not to create a wake large enough to set it rocking. Keeping the speed low until they were far enough away for the waves they made not to reach the other boat, he then throttled up, making the powerboat fly down the channel.

They made one more stop, at a small rickety dock below a shack with brown paint peeling from its siding, and, with the assistance of an outside light, loaded a dozen more cans of gasoline, more food—more than necessary, it seemed to Rod—in ice chests and boxes, along with a case of whisky. Nelson's eyes lit up, and he stayed close to this, until Walt noticed and backhanded him away.

"Don't get any fuckin' ideas, old man. I catch you anywhere near those bottles, and, I swear, I'll toss you overboard, after I hammer your head knotty. Piss off."

The last thing loaded was a locked box, which Walt carried aboard himself, very carefully, and put under a bunk in the forward sleeping compartment. His scowl was warning enough to leave it alone. Even Nelson could tell it wasn't whisky and steered clear of it.

They were on their way again in maybe fifteen minutes, speeding down the channel until they reached the south end of Annette Island. There they had altered to a more easterly course, passing the end of Revillagigedo Island and its two inlets, George and Carroll, and, finally, Thorne Arm and the Behm Canal, in the dark. Only the faded brilliance of one of Southeast Alaska's most vivid sunsets allowed a glimpse of the dark, shadowlike fingers of the inlets, in contrast to its last glowing reflection on the water between them.

After that, they powered on throughout the night, Walt at the wheel. Rod offered to relieve him, but he was abruptly refused.

"Be just my damn luck you'd run us onto a rock

somewhere. I know these channels, been fishin' them all my life. You go down and get me something to eat—anything that's fast—I'm starving. Eggs, maybe. Yeah, bacon and eggs—some bread with lots of that jam. And don't fuckin' burn the bacon. If there's anything I hate . . ."

Rod didn't know whether to laugh or cry at this coincidence. Instead, he went below, where he found his buddy staring pitifully at the unopened whisky. Then he laughed.

"Sorry, Nelson. Some days you eat the bear, some days the bear . . . you know. You hungry? I'm cooking."

The older man nodded. "Yeah, I could do with a little somethin'." He helped Rod find the skillet and supplies to make a meal.

"You can stir some eggs while I get the bacon going. But I'll do the cooking. He hates it burned too."

"What's going on, Rod? You know where we going?"

"Nope. Just someplace near Prince Rupert. Might as well stay with it, ya know. Sounds like something we might make a buck or two off of."

"Well, I don't think I like it much. Didn't know we'd have to go somewhere besides Ketchikan. Don't like going into Canada."

"Might as well get used to it. That's where we're goin', from the looks of it. Ah, don't whine. It'll be okay. Just . . ."

"How long is it gonna take you two dummies?" Walt yelled from the cockpit. "Get it going and cut out the damn chatter."

They ate, and Nelson washed up. Then he and Rod slept, since Walt seemed to want no assistance. It would take hours of cruising down Revillagigedo Channel, past Misty Fjords National Monument—a natural wonder of narrow channels, like the fingers of a giant hand—before they reached the wide water that was open clear to the Pacific Ocean, where they would hope for calm weather. Rod was certain Nelson would be seasick in rough water, and he was not completely confident of his own ability to keep a settled stomach.

"Listen, Nelson," he told the older man. "If it gets rough and you get seasick, stay as far away from me as possible, okay? All I'd need is to watch you lose your biscuits and I'd do the same."

They slept till Walt slowed the boat and kicked them out to fill the gas tanks.

"We're in Canada," he told them. "Now we've committed a real felony, and, if they catch us, we're fuckin' done for. So don't forget, you're in it up to your eyeballs, just as much as me. Hell, more. You brought that beast all the way down from Juneau. You've stole *two* boats."

"Shit," said Nelson, blowing his nose on a grubby gray handkerchief he then stuffed back into a pants pocket. "I didn't even think of that. *Canada.* Goin' across the border makes it worse, don't it?"

Rod said nothing, not particularly concerned with that specific state of affairs. Angry that Walt had insisted on burning the sailboat, he wasn't about to challenge him about it now. There were, after all, other sailboats. He was relieved the other man knew nothing about the dead woman they had sunk in Tracy Arm. No one must ever know.

"Whatever happens," he warned Nelson, "you keep your mouth shut. You hear? Don't you dare tell *anybody*."

Nelson promised.

20

JESSIE AND LOU ATE DINNER IN JESSIE AND ALEX'S STATE-room, having carried it up themselves—plates wrapped in foil to keep the roast beef, baked potatoes, and vegetables hot—in a box that had once held paper for the captain's fax machine.

"I usually hate carrots," Lou commented, as she finished hers, "but these are okay."

They were good, julienned very thin, with sun-dried tomatoes and a hint of garlic that Jessie thought she might be able to duplicate. She agreed with Lou, however, that ordinary plain cooked carrots were not an item on her wish list.

"The food's been great, though. O-oh. Try this!"

A cream puff filled with Amaretto-flavored custard, topped by a drizzle of chocolate sauce, more than satisfactorily completed the meal.

They both ate every scrap, then sat waiting till the time came to assume their watch location. As they waited, Jessie explained to Lou how the different settings on her camera were adjusted for different kinds of light and depths of field.

174

"I wish someone would have told me all this before," Lou said. "I could have been taking pictures of my own. I'd like to have a camera like this of my own."

"Maybe you should ask your dad about it . . . a birthday, Christmas?"

"Oh, I'll think about it, but maybe I could earn some money and buy it myself. I don't think I want to bother him with it." She frowned, then confided in Jessie. "He's been worried about the bookstore. It's not doing very well right now, and he's afraid he'll have to sell it, I think. I don't like to ask him for stuff, and this would be expensive, wouldn't it?"

Jessie nodded, thoughtfully.

"I've had some part-time jobs, I'll work on it myself. And I think I'll see if there's a class, like you said. I'll never remember all this."

"Well, there are books that help, too." Jessie had to smile to herself at this confirmation of the girl's eavesdropping. She knew she had mentioned the class to Rozie, not Lou.

"Hey, Jessie. Why don't we put the smaller zoom lens on the camera and take it out to the back of the boat with us? Maybe we could get a picture of that guy I saw, I mean, if he comes back again."

Jessie considered. "I don't know. He might notice a camera."

"I don't think so. It isn't *that* big. I could look through the . . ."

"Viewfinder," Jessie prompted.

"Yeah, that. Anyway, I could get it all focused and ready before I look around the corner. If I hold really still, I don't think he would see. And he can't hear from there, because of the wind."

"Okay, if you want to try. He may not even show up, though, Lou. Don't get your hopes up too high."

"Oh, yeah. I won't. But, maybe he will."

The ruse of getting Don Sawyer into the Lovegrens' stateroom seemed to have worked well. He was there now . . . also waiting . . . its actual occupants gone to dinner.

It was almost time for Jessie and Lou to take their positions on the stern.

"Will you be warm enough?" she asked the girl. You can borrow one of these, if you want." She held out a plaid wool shirt belonging to Alex, similar to one she was putting on herself.

"No, I'll be . . ." Lou stopped, frowned, staring at the blue plaid shirt. Then her eyebrows raised in excitement. "That's *it*. That's what was *different* about him. He had on a plaid shirt and his jacket was open, so I could see it. The crew people don't wear plaid shirts, do they? Or caps like he had on, either." She turned to Jessie, her eyes shining with pleasure in her own remembering.

"No," Jess agreed. "I haven't seen one who does. I think you've got it right, Lou. So it probably wasn't a crew member. Good going. We'll tell Alex as soon as we see him."

"Got your note. They made it?"

"Yeah. They'll be there. Those idiots brought a sailboat from Douglas. Had to find another one."

"Shit. Who the hell have you got working for . . ."

"I've got you, too, stupid. And you already made a bigger mistake, killing that woman. Don't start. I've got to get back in there, before someone starts to wonder what's taking me so long."

"They'd never suspect you."

"Don't count on it. I'll talk to you later."

In the dining room, the rest of the passengers were having dessert and coffee, settling back for the second installment of the mystery play, and speculating wildly on the identity of the victim and killer.

The players, including Alex, were all in costume and ready to begin as soon as the waiters let them know they had finished serving.

Jensen was emotionally pulled in two directions, shuffling from one foot to the other. The place he felt he really should be was up two decks, waiting with Jessie and Lou to see if a thief showed up. But, before any of these incidents happened, he *had* promised to be in the play, and he would have felt just as bad skipping out on it. On top of all that he was convinced that *butterflies* was too gentle a term for the nervous condition of his stomach.

"It's okay, you know," Laurie told him. "All of us put up with nerves before a performance. You'll be fine once you get started. The run-through was great and you've got the script right in your hand, disguised as a playbill. If you forget, just read it. It will look as if you intended to."

Jensen took a deep breath and nodded, as the waiter stuck his head into the passage from the galley.

"They're ready and waiting for you," he said.

"Okay. Go ahead, Alex. When the coordinator is through making announcements, she'll hand you the microphone. Just remember, everyone in the room wants you to do well, they're on your side."

Gripping the playbill-script tightly, he walked down the narrow starboard passage and into the dining room, leather fringe swaying, hat pushed back at a cocky angle, holster lightly slapping his thigh with the weight of the impressive pistol. At the door he waited a minute as the coordinator finished her speech, inviting the diners to the evening's entertainment in the lounge, to hear tales of the infamous "Soapy" Smith.

She paused, and the man who had elicited hisses and boos on the dock in Skagway stood up and bowed to the diners. She went on:

"As you know, there are several other descendants of the stampeders who went to Dawson City in 1897 and '98. Tomorrow night some of them will talk about their ancestors and show some of the things brought home from the gold fields and passed down in their families.

"Now, let us take you back to the actual time of the great Klondike gold rush. I have the pleasure of introducing someone from Dawson City, who, in 1898, built the most famous of all its saloons and theaters, The Palace Grand. He is also renowned as a member of Buffalo Bill's Wild West Show, so watch out because he's a crack-shot with that pearl-handled pistol. Ladies and gentlemen, I introduce to you Arizona Charlie Meadows."

She handed him the microphone with a grin. "Great getup," she whispered, leaving him alone in front of what now seemed to be several thousand people. He cleared his throat and began his sideshow barker routine.

"Ladies and gentlemen. I, Arizona Charlie Meadows, owner of the Palace Grand Salo-on, proudly present—for your entertainment and satisfaction—a very special performer of ex-ceptional talent and breathtaking beauty."

As he warmed up, the butterflies disappeared, and his voice grew stronger.

"Dy-rect from the West Coast of our U-nited States . . ."

He was really into it now, throwing in a gesture or two with the playbill.

"It is my privilege and honor to bring you that well-known and loved songbird of the South, Miss . . . Alice . . . La . . . Belle."

With an exaggerated bow that practically brushed the floor with the huge western hat, he welcomed Laurie into the dining room, handing her the microphone as she passed.

She swept in with the air of an empress appearing before peasants, with her head held high, sporting one more extravagant costume. Silver fabric clung lovingly to her slim form, and fell in a straight line from her hips to the floor, ending in a flounce of white ostrich feathers. She carried a large, matching ostrich-feather fan and was an impressive sight, inspiring a round of applause from the *Spirit*'s delighted spectators.

Stepping back and replacing his hat, Alex stood proudly with self-satisfied approval.

"Thank you, Charlie, for that sweet introduction, darlin'."

Alice curtsied deeply to the audience and stepped forward.

"The song I am about to sing tonight is dedicated to my dear friend Jake, who was shot last night by some skunk of a sidewinding rat."

She spit out the insult, then paused to dramatically wipe a tear from her eye with an artfully poised finger.

"We can only hope that the Mounties are able to bring the perpetrator of this gruesome crime to swift and much deserved justice. I—we—will miss him terribly—just ter-ri-bly. So—for Jake, who used to call me his songbird."

From somewhere in the room—the result of a tape recorder hidden earlier behind a potted palm—came the sound of a rinky-dink piano, playing the intro-ductory bars. Clasping her hands together around the handle of the fan and clutching it to her breast in a gesture pantomiming heartfelt emotion, she began to warble.

"She's only a bird in a gilded cage . . ."

This musical antiquity solicited a murmur of recog-nition and laughter from the audience. A few people sang along softly.

"Haven't heard that one in years," Jensen heard one white-haired lady half-whisper to another.

". . . happy and free from care. She's not, though she seems to be . . ."

As "Alice" sang, Meadows drew his pistol and began quietly playing with it—twirling it, whipping it in and out of the holster. The spinning silver gun flashed in the dining room's overhead lights, and drew almost as much attention as the singer. The audience was forced to divide its concentration be-tween the two actors.

Shooting him a dirty look or two as she sang, Alice

from the Palace reached the end of her highly dramatic musical rendition.

". . . her beauty was sold for an old man's gold. She's a bird in a gilded cage."

Laurie gave it everything she had, imploring and beseeching her listeners to sympathize with the much maligned bird. Her performance brought wild applause from the passengers as well as cheers and whistles from the kitchen staff, who had all come out to watch.

"Encore! Encore!" came cries from all parts of the room. Alice bowed her bejeweled and sparkling thanks, wafted her feathered fan gracefully through the air, laid down the microphone, and turned to Arizona Charlie.

"You dog," she hissed. *"How dare you interrupt my song for Jake with your feeble attempt to show off your less than average control of that ostentatious pistol? Have you no respect? It might lead some to think you aren't sorry he is dead. Perhaps, even, that . . ."*

"Hey," Arizona Charlie started to object, but from the back of the room came a new voice, and one of the miners from the night before came up through the tables.

"Well, Alice. Some of us ain't so sorry he bought the farm. Whatever you say, he warn't such a choir boy—he was a louse. And I'm just glad to see shut of him."

"Me, too." The second miner followed the first one into the room. *"He cheated at cards."*

An argument ensued, filled with clues to the identity of the criminal who had shot Jake—in the back, it turned out. Two others entered and took part in the debate, including Jim Beal, in his red jacket as the Canadian mounted policeman. Threats were made, accusations hurled. Between them, the red-coat and Arizona Charlie finally brought the confrontation to a halt—one by promising to throw them all in the hoosegow if they didn't desist, the other by reminding them that this was, after all, a saloon, not a street corner on the boardwalk, and Alice wasn't getting paid for standing around, consorting with riffraff.

The audience took great delight in joining the fracas with hoots, hisses, and applause. When they heard there might be another song from Alice, the response was overwhelming. Alex, the red-coat, and the rest left the room, still growling at each other, leaving Laurie, who launched into another turn-of-the-century tune. She finished to another loud ovation and swept from the room, swishing her skirts, waving her fan, and promising to return again soon to the Palace stage.

She met the rest of the cast in the hallway, and they all headed for the lounge, where they would give the passengers a chance to ask questions.

"Alex, you were tremendous," Laurie told him. "Anytime you want to change professions, just let us know, okay."

He grinned at her. "I had a great time. Thanks for persuading me."

He slipped out and hurried up the stairs to the deck above the lounge, meeting the first of the diners, but waving off their questions with a laugh.

"I'm just a stand-in. The cast is in the lounge, to answer your questions."

He headed for his stateroom, changed back into his own clothes, then hurried to the stern.

There he found Jessie and Lou still in position, the girl leaning out, as she had demonstrated earlier, Jess on her knees behind her, out of sight from the long walkway along the side of the ship. Lou was very still with Jessie's camera held up to her eye, a zoom lens attached. Jess spoke in a sharp whisper.

"Alex, he's there. He just went in. He's been in there with Don for maybe a minute, couldn't be more."

21

"WHAT ARE YOU DOING?" JENSEN ASKED LOU. "HE might have been able to see that camera."

"I'm going to get a *picture* when he comes out," Lou whispered fiercely. "I'm all ready for him. I think I got one when he went in."

"Well," Jensen decided. "I'm not waiting. Anything could be happening in there. I'm going in." He stood up from where he had knelt down next to them and clapped a hand to his hip. "Oh, damn. My .45 is still in the captain's safe."

"What's that then?" Jessie asked, pointing.

In his swift stateroom change of clothes, he had neglected to take off the pearl-handled pistol he had worn as Meadows. It was in the holster he was still wearing. Familiar with wearing one gun or the other, he had simply ignored it.

"Well . . . it'll have to do. Whoever this guy is, he probably didn't see the play and won't know it's not real. I haven't got time to go after mine now."

"Lou, you stay here. Jessie, go see if you can find some help, Captain Kay, or Ray McKimmey, in a

182

hurry. This might take more than two of us. And ask the captain for my .45, please."

"Right," she said, and raced around the port side of the ship, heading for the bridge, where the captain could call down to the engine room for McKimmey.

Lou hadn't moved from her position with the camera, and no one had come out of the Lovegrens' stateroom. Jensen walked forward toward it, down the long deck walkway, Lou watching him grow smaller through the viewfinder of the camera.

The door was closed. He listened carefully outside it but heard nothing from inside. Crouching down, he cautiously turned the handle and pushed. Slowly, soundlessly, the door opened a crack. Through it, he could see Sawyer sitting on the bed, but Don did not notice the open door, his attention on someone Jensen couldn't see.

Jensen pushed it a little more and, this time, it initiated a sudden reaction. The door was snatched from his hand, and he found a man he didn't recognize staring down at him. Rising quickly to his feet, Jensen took a step backward to assess the situation from a less precarious position. He was immediately glad he had, for the man was holding a large hunting knife and looked eminently capable of using it.

He was, as Lou had described, wearing a crewman's jacket, zipped halfway up, slacks the color required by the company, and a cap with a bill that partially hid his eyes. He had a narrow chin and a thin mouth, but he was as heavy through the shoulders as a weight lifter. He had pulled the cap so far down that, until he slightly raised his head, Alex had trouble seeing what the upper half of his face looked like—ordinary, quite ordinary, except for a tiny tattoo next to the corner of his left eye. It was impossible to ascertain hair or eye color, but he appeared to weigh about a hundred and seventy pounds.

"Who the hell are you?" he snarled at Jensen. "Never mind. Get in here." He brought the long blade, wickedly sharp, forward threateningly, and assumed a stance that reminded Jensen of gang members used to street fighting—feet apart, weight centered over them, arms wide and forward, ready for instant motion. The knife was blade up, positioned for slashing, not stabbing. This was not a man who thought knives were kitchen utensils—had probably never chopped a vegetable in his life—and any meat he cut had likely been alive and kicking.

"I don't think so," Alex told him, drawing the pistol loaded with caps from its holster and trying to draw attention to his face, away from the fake firearm. "Now, we'll get along just fine, if you drop that right out here on the deck, please. I'm Sergeant Jensen, Alaska State Troopers, and you, whoever you are, are under arrest."

"You gotta be kidding, right?" the other questioned. "I'm supposed to believe that a trooper would just appear on this boat in the middle of . . . wherever the hell we are."

Who on the ship, at this point, could possibly not know there was a trooper aboard?

"No," Alex told him, "I'm not kidding. Nevermind how I got here, just put down the knife. I can reach farther with a bullet than you can with that blade, and I won't have to move at all." He hoped he sounded more confident than he felt. "Drop it."

The stranger considered his demand, then his eyes narrowed slightly and he blinked. With that, Jensen realized this was not going to go smoothly. The man was about to move, and dropping the knife was apparently not on his agenda. As he prepared himself, Alex caught a hint of movement behind the knifeholder. Then, before the man could take a chance that a state trooper wouldn't shoot him—or wouldn't shoot him anywhere extremely important—and before he could lunge and make a break for it, Sawyer simply reached around him, made a fist with one hand, and grabbed his own wrist in the other, effectively pinning the knife-wielder's elbows to his body.

Quickly, before the intruder could attempt to escape or stab at Don's arms, Alex stepped forward and brought the handle of the pistol down on his hand, numbing it, and causing him to drop the knife.

Running feet pounding the deck made Jensen glance quickly to his left, as the man began to twist and struggle in Sawyer's grip, but it was McKimmey who showed up at his shoulder.

"Jesus, Glen," he declared in a shocked and disbelieving voice. "What the hell are you doing?"

As the three of them worked to subdue their captive, Alex questioned Ray. "You know this man?"

"You bet. He's my . . . ugh, damn it . . . assistant engineer."

"The one who replaced . . . the guy who usually travels . . . with you?"

"Yeah. Hell . . . Glen . . . stop it. You can't get away. Steve Broughton's my usual man. He got banged up pretty good in a car wreck a couple of days before we left Seattle. Glen . . . ah, Carlson's a new guy, his first run, took over temporarily, just for this trip. What's going on?"

They sat Carlson down in the room's only chair, Sawyer standing behind him, hands on his shoulders in a clear warning that any attempt to leave it would be met with stiff resistance. Jensen used his handkerchief to pick up the knife that still lay on the floor, and met Captain Kay coming in. Directly behind him, Jessie and Lou appeared in the doorway. There was a sudden flash from the camera.

"Better take Lou back to her stateroom," Alex suggested to Jessie.

"Aw . . ." said Lou, clearly wanting to stay.

"Sorry, Lou. Official policy. I'll explain later, okay?"

"Yeah, I guess."

He had to smile at her disappointment, as Jessie

handed him his real gun and led Lou away. He closed the door. Though the girl had earned the right to know the outcome of their trap, he was sure her father would have other ideas.

Carlson stared in astonishment at the counterfeit pistol as Jensen put it back in its holster and casually trained the Colt .45 in his general direction.

Don Sawyer's eyes widened. "Is that what I think it is?" he asked, pointing at the holstered pistol.

Alex confessed. "Yeah. A gun is a gun, right? Acting isn't an art limited to a stage."

Ray grinned, but it was a little weak. "Remind me to check before I depend on *you* for protection."

Sawyer, however, had been incubating a deep and personal anger, and, before anyone could interfere, he grabbed Carlson by the shirt collar and shouted at him, "You son-of-a-bitch. You killed my cousin."

The assistant engineer held his tongue, but he might not have been able to speak even if he'd wanted to.

Jensen and Captain Kay moved together to separate the two.

"Don. *Don.* Stop it. We've got to talk to him in a legal and organized way. If he did it, you don't want him to have a reason to slide out of it, do you?"

Sawyer, his fury turned to frustration, shook his head and backed off, as advised.

Alex read Carlson his rights, including the part about not having to talk if he didn't wish to.

He obviously didn't. For, aside from a blink and half a nod, when asked if he understood his rights, they got nothing from him—they might as well have been in a different room.

"I think," Jensen told Captain Kay, "that we should take Mr. Carlson up to your office. The Lovegrens will be wanting their stateroom back."

He agreed.

"First, however, we need to search him. Did you

see the money clip, Don? Or can we just assume he came in to leave it or take something else?"

"I didn't see it."

Another struggle ensued, but against four other men Carlson had no chance. When Sawyer threatened to grab him again, he quickly gave up and let Jensen empty his pockets, one of which yielded up the silver money clip, empty of its cash, of course.

"So," Alex confronted him. "How and when did you pick this up, Mr. Carlson?"

There was no answer. Carlson sat stubbornly glowering at them all, refusing to speak. It seemed they were unlikely to get anything in terms of explanations or confessions from him.

Jessie and Lou went down to the lounge, where they found that Jeff Smith had already started the presentation about his famous great-grandfather, Jefferson Randolph "Soapy" Smith. Tiptoeing in quietly, they found a place to sit in the back of the room and wait for him to finish, before seeking out Lou's father.

One on either side of Rozie Moisan, they sat on the bench for the player piano, and Jessie was pleased to find Dallas, in her wheelchair, beside her. She reached out, laid a hand on the older woman's wrist, and they smiled at each other.

With a humorous lift of her eyebrows, Dallas silently inquired why they were late.

"Catching crooks," Jessie whispered in her ear, earning an *I'm-impressed* mime from Dallas, who then pointed at Lou with a questioning look.

Yes, Jessie nodded, *she helped, too.*

Lou caught the gist of the all but silent conversation and grinned around Rozie at Dallas, who mimed applause and a thumbs-up.

During this exchange, Jeff Smith had continued to tell stories about Soapy from the front of the lounge to a fascinated audience. Directing only half her attention his way, Jessie really wished they were somewhere else, where they could talk. She was too energized, after the exciting capture of Carlson, to want to sit still and listen to more gold rush history. Maybe I've been reading too much, she thought, consciously directing her concentration back to what was going on.

"Some of you," Jeff said, "saw my demonstration of my great-grandfather's shell games at the reception in Haines on Sunday night. For those that missed it, here it is again.

"This case, which appears pretty much like an ordinary briefcase, is actually a small, self-supporting stand. It opens up like this, to become . . ." He opened the fastener that held the case closed and began to unfold it, to show the crowd in the lounge exactly how clever this piece of hundred-year-old equipment really was, ". . . a table." The case opened suddenly, as Jessie and the rest watched, and something dropped to the floor from inside it. It hit with an audible thump that was heard by everyone in the room.

There was a sudden pause in his narrative, as the room filled with silence and the audience waited for him to go on. He did not, however, immediately continue, but stood, still holding the half-open case, staring down at the item that had fallen to the floor. In a second or two, he bent to pick it up and examine it.

Then Jessie could see what it was that had surprised and startled him into abandoning his presentation. A watch had fallen from the case. Its steel case showed in his fingers.

"Well," he said, curiously. "I wonder where this came from. It's not mine. Do any of you know who this belongs to?"

He held up the watch and looked out in appeal to the audience.

Many of them thought it was part of his act—strange, perhaps, but, maybe if they waited long enough it would become clear just where he was headed with the odd interruption in what he had been about to show them. Others weren't so sure, including Bill and Nella Berry, who were sitting half-way between Jessie and Jeff Smith. Bill Berry abruptly stood up and addressed Smith.

"I believe that's mine. Could I see it, please?"

Without a word, Smith handed the watch to someone in front, and it was then passed back from person to person until it reached Berry, who accepted it and opened the cover. He stood for a moment, reading the inscription inside the lid of the watch, then looked up at Smith, a puzzled expression on his face. In a carefully controlled voice, he said, "It is. It belonged to my grandfather, Fred Berry. He carried this to the Klondike with him. How did you happen to have it, Mr. Smith? It was stolen from my stateroom Sunday night, while my wife and I were attending the reception in Haines."

A murmur of astonishment swept through the crowd, as they realized what Berry was asking, or intimating.

"Not by me, it wasn't," Jeff Smith returned, in swift denial.

Jessie suddenly found herself on her feet, propelled there by a slight shove from Dallas, but only, she was sure, because all her body language had told the other woman that she wanted to get up anyway.

"Mr. Berry?" she said, in a low tone that carried straight to him, for he swung around to see who spoke.

"I think Sergeant Jensen is, perhaps, the person you want to speak to. Don't you?"

Many people in the crowd didn't hear exactly what she'd said, but it brought a startled expression of awareness to Berry, who had only been asking an honest question, in the sudden consternation of having his watch back in such odd circumstances. He realized that what he'd said had sounded like an accusation, and why Smith had taken offense at his words. He turned back.

"I'm sorry, Mr. Smith," he apologized. I didn't mean that the way it came out. I think you were as surprised as I was when this fell out of your case. We can talk about it later, if that's all right with you."

Smith nodded. "Sure." Then, ever the performer, he proceeded to finish setting up the table for his shell games and went ahead with his demonstration for the crowd.

Jessie sat down and sighed in relief, realizing she had been holding her breath.

"Thanks," she said to Dallas, who grinned.

"I could tell you just needed a little push," she said. "You were the one who could rightly keep those two from starting something neither of them really meant, or wanted to get into. You did well, Jess. Pulled their irons right out of the fire. The more I get to know you, the better I like you. You've pretty much got your act together, girl."

The unexpected endorsement and approval drew a flush to Jessie's face, coming so close behind an action that she now realized had filled her with fear, even as she went ahead, following her impulse.

"Thanks, Dallas. I like you, too, a lot."

With all her heart, Jessie hoped that the end of this cruise would not see Dallas Blake disappear from her life. She was determined to make sure it didn't happen.

The Berrys came to stand beside her, Bill with a word of gratitude.

"Jessie, you saved me a bad moment there, and I appreciate it. Thanks."

"Hey, it was just a thought that I acted on without consideration, really. We should let Alex know the watch is back, though."

"Where is he?"

"Oh." She leaned forward, inviting the rest to do likewise, so that what she told them would remain fairly confidential. "They caught someone trying to return Chuck Lovegren's money clip to his cabin, and they're questioning him right now, I think. I don't know much, actually. Lou and I just kept watch for a while."

She glanced at Lou, who once again offered a conspiratorial grin, pleased to be a part of something important.

"Good going, Lou," Nella congratulated her.

"Thanks. I got to go tell my dad, Jessie."

"Okay. You go," Jess laughed. "I'll come along in a minute or two."

She was gone in an instant.

"She's like a fairy child," Rozie observed. "What a beautiful girl."

"She's almost sixteen."

"Really? She's so tiny."

"You should be a teacher, Jess," Dallas spoke thoughtfully. "You're really good with young people."

Jessie smiled. "Lou is awfully easy to be good to," she said.

"Hey! Don' you tell me I can't have 'nother drink!"

The loud, angry, inebriated voice of a man at the bar brought all other conversations in the lounge to a halt. It was followed by an assertive hammering sound, and passengers turned to see what was going on.

"Wayne. Stop . . . honey." A woman's voice, hesitant and embarrassed.

An unfamiliar large man with a red face stood in what appeared to be a face-off with the easygoing bartender, each on his side of the bar, the complainer holding an empty glass. He pounded it on the surface of the bar and yelled again. What was left of the ice it had contained flew out and skittered along the smooth surface.

"Wayne. Come on now. Let's go . . ."

The two people next to him on bar stools moved

away from the couple, and, for the first time, Jessie recognized Edith Johnson, the woman at the Haines party in the forget-me-not dress. And this must be her husband—an alcoholic, from the look of it, and from what she remembered of their conversation on the grass of the parade ground.

"I don' *have* a problem," Johnson stated. "But you will, if you don' put some of that vodka there in here—an' a squirt of tonic. Who you think you-u-re? I'll come 'round and do it m-shelf, if I got to."

"Sir. Sir?" Totally ignored, the bartender tried to placate him. "I'll give you coffee."

"Coffee be damned, damn it! You gimme what I ast for. No right . . ."

With a last vicious pound, the glass shattered in his hand, fragments tinkling onto the top of the bar. Immediately, blood began to pour between his fingers.

"Oh, Wayne," Edith wailed. "Oh, help him somebody."

A tall, completely bald man with fuzzy, gray eyebrows, stepped out of the silently watching crowd and went to Johnson, who was now standing still, staring at his bleeding hand in amazed, drunken stupidity.

"I'm a doctor. Let's take a look at that."

Like a child, Wayne Johnson offered his injured hand, palm up, as he was told, frowning in consternation. "I didn' mean . . ."

"No. Of course you didn't. Let's go up to my stateroom. That's not as bad as it looks, I think. I can put a few stitches in it. It'll be all right."

He led Johnson toward the door, with a glance at the bartender and a motion for Mrs. Johnson to come along. The bartender raised a hand from toweling the glass and blood from the bar to give him a small salute of thanks, and turned back to the passengers who were left.

"Hey, it happens sometimes. It's over. Don't let it

spoil your evening. Can I give anyone a refill on the house? Why don't you start the player piano?"

The room relaxed, and conversation picked up again. Several people took advantage of the offer of a refill, and, soon enough, cheerful music was rolling out of the piano, its keys moving up and down on their own, as if they were being played by an invisible man.

"I love this kind of piano, don't you?" Rozie asked, and Dallas answered.

"Yes, but probably because it plays music I recognize from what my mother used to sing. Not your generation, dear."

Jessie excused herself and went across the room to speak to John Stanley, who, with Lou, was watching Jeff Smith's games with rapt attention. She grinned. At the rate Louise learned things that interested her, Stanley had better anticipate the emergence of a con-artist in his house in the near future.

22

10:15 P.M.
Tuesday, July 15, 1997
Spirit of '98
Petersburg, Inside Passage, Alaska

JESSIE TOLD ALEX ABOUT THE INCIDENT WITH WAYNE Johnson, later, when they were back in their stateroom.

"No wonder she was so adamant about not taking him food in Haines. Evidently he can get aggressive when he drinks, and he seems to drink a lot, most of the time. I wouldn't be surprised if she catches a lot of it. She was so anxious."

"Damn it," Alex growled, wearily. "I really *hate* that kind of drunk. I suppose I should have talked to him after the thefts—not that I think he'd have noticed anything. I've seen too much of that kind of behavior. He needs help."

"Well, he's probably asleep again now. That doctor took him to put some stitches in his hand, and they didn't come back to the lounge."

Alex filled her in about the unsatisfactory session with Carlson.

"So, that was it. The four of us finally stopped trying, and decided to lock him up till we reached Petersburg and turn him over to the authorities."

"What'd you do with him?"

"We handcuffed him to a heavy pipe in the engine room, where Ray can keep an eye on him, and maybe get something out of him. Wouldn't say a word, even to confirm his own identity. Nasty piece of work, I think. Wouldn't talk even when Judy Raymond showed up."

"She came up to the bridge?"

"Yes. Walked in with Prentice in tow, again, took a look at Carlson, and said, 'So this is the bastard who stole my gold chain,' and demanded to know who he was. He took a look at her and turned his face to the wall. He seemed almost afraid of her."

"Maybe he was."

"Doesn't make much sense."

"Does any of it?"

"Not really. I'm not getting any smarter, I guess." He knocked a fist on the dressing table, more in frustration than heat, and walked on.

"So, you don't really know if he was the thief or not."

Alex turned from pacing the stateroom to stare at her.

"I'm going on that assumption, since he had the clip in his pocket, and wouldn't deny it."

"Well . . ." she frowned, thoughtfully. "Maybe. Or there could be someone else involved, maybe Judy, and he's taking the blame—he could've been putting the clip back for her or somebody else."

He nodded, listening carefully.

"What makes you say that, Jess?"

"Nothing specific, really. Maybe that he was afraid of her. You'll find out something soon, when you see if he's got a record, right? But don't small-time, petty criminals usually try to talk their way out of this kind of stuff? Since you can't prove he stole it, wouldn't he at least say he found it somewhere and wanted to return it—didn't want to be accused of stealing it?"

Jensen thought about it. She was more quick than he was to examine the reasons *why* people reacted the way they often did. He had to agree.

"Yeah, they do. Many of them talk themselves right into a cell."

Having set him thinking in this direction, she left it and sat quietly on the bed, where she had been reading another of the books about the gold rush.

"How's Lou?" he asked her. "I hated to shut her out, she did a good job. I couldn't let her in and state categorically later that there was no reason for Carlson to clam up."

"I know. I told her something like that. She's fine. Got a real kick out of watching and having him show up so she could get her pictures."

"She actually *got* some?" He laughed and sat down on Jessie's bed, pulling one of his long legs up to wrap his arms around it. He prepared to listen.

Jessie looked at him for a moment before she spoke, thinking that his posture and eagerness revealed the boy still lurking in this tall, accomplished man she loved. She smiled.

"She sure did. Four, I think she said, including that last one of the four—no, five of you, staring out at us before you shut the door. A real photo-essay. She could hardly wait to tell her dad."

"Did he mind that we let her help?"

"Not after I explained that there really wasn't any danger. He seems pretty lenient with her. I was impressed.

"I mentioned how pretty I thought her hair was. He said last year it was shorter and dyed black, but as long as she's clean and reasonably neat, he lets her look the way she wants and choose her own clothes. Her mother died when she was just a baby and she's an only child, so they're close."

"Sounds perceptive and reasonable to me."

"Sort of like the way your parents raised you."

"Well, they weren't that liberal. Actually my mom

did most of the raising. My dad's pretty quiet and mostly went along with her. I grew up chasing cattle up and down hills and riding a school bus to town every day, but I had chores to do when I came home—milking cows, feeding calves, forking hay. Summers I worked with mom's brother, bachelor Uncle Ed, who ran the ranch and lived next door. My brother and I had pretty strict rules, but ranching keeps kids so busy they don't have much time to run wild."

"Your mom did a pretty good job, I'd say."

"Well, she's third-generation Scottish, with flaming hair and a temper to match. Real stereotype, but, fast as her temper flares, it dies. She's very warm and mothering, you'll see. She'll feed you to death if you don't watch out. I think my mother and yours would get along great. They'd live in the kitchen."

"Yeah, they would. But you stayed thin. I still don't see how her hair and temper missed you?"

"Well, you know my brother got it—the hair. I got the Danish half of the family, from my dad."

"And the mustache?" she teased. "He have one, too?"

"Naw. He just teaches his classes at the high school and lives in his book world most of the time. Been a teacher for almost thirty years."

"He always sounds sweet, but a little vague on the phone."

"That's him. But he's a pretty good teacher. His former students show up from time to time to see him."

Jessie thought for a minute. "I had rules—curfews and chores, too—but my dad always encouraged me to try whatever I was interested in. I've already told you I think that's what got me started sled dog racing. It never occurred to me that I couldn't, or that anyone would think I shouldn't, until I was already really involved in it. Then some of the men who race made me aware of the fact that they thought women didn't belong in the sport. Well . . . you know all about that. I told you during the Iditarod."

"That's right, you did. I hadn't thought about it. I've met your parents. One of these days you'll have to meet mine."

"Did they really only come once to Alaska?"

"Yeah, only once, right after I moved up here. Dad's school schedule gets in the way, and he doesn't like to travel much. We'll have to go to Idaho."

"Never been there."

Alex paused for a minute, thinking—back on the case, just wishing he could figure out what exactly *the case* was.

"Sure wish I knew how this Carlson guy fits in. He's giving us absolutely nothing to work with."

"And you're going to turn him over to someone in Petersburg?"

"Yes. I want him off this ship. We'll be there before too much longer, between midnight and one o'clock."

Jessie yawned, turned out her reading light, and put aside the book that had been resting upside down on her lap. "You going to stay up till we get there?"

"May nap a little, but I've got to be up for it. Interesting—we've got an engineer who won't talk at all, a guard that didn't tell the truth, Morrison, who refused a stateroom search, and Raymond, who lies—a lot of equivocation. It would be easier if, like the play, everyone had to tell the truth except the perpetrator. We also have a dead body, a live one, and an ax to put off the ship. The ship will move on as soon as they're put ashore, but getting them off won't solve anything. This gets more complicated all the time. There's something I'm just not seeing here. Probably several somethings. Whatever. I'm tired. Disappointing to go through Wrangell Narrows in the dark. I wanted to see it. You know, we'll have

to come back. Remember the sailboat that belongs to
that friend of Delafosse's? He mentioned it in Dawson? Maybe we could . . ."

"Is it really narrow?" Jessie muttered, drowsily.

"Yes, really narrow, but not rushing water—more
like a lazy river . . . smooth." Watching her eyes
close, he grinned. "But we'll throw out a rope and
you can water-ski behind the boat as we go
through."

"Sure. And you can ride a bicycle over the captain's bridge. I'm not asleep yet, trooper. No tricks,
cause I will be soon. Go read a book or something
and don't plague me." She yawned again, without
opening her eyes, and, shortly, as Jensen watched,
she began to snore softly.

Still smiling he moved to his own bed, lay down
with his clothes on, and did start to read. But, long
before the first mate knocked softly on the door to
let him know they were about to dock in Petersburg,
he was matching Jess snore for snore.

"He still okay?"

"Yeah. We got him loose, no trouble."

"They'll take the boat apart."

"Won't find him. It'll work."

"How the hell did they catch him?"

*"Because, you fuckup, your other guy couldn't keep his
hands off other people's property, and you compounded it
by sending Glen to put the stuff back. That's twice. Should
have tossed it."*

*"Had to do something to take the heat off. How're you
going to hide him?"*

"It's taken care of. Don't worry about it."

"He should get off."

"Not here. They'd catch him for sure."

"I don't like it."

*"Tough. I'll do whatever I have to to make this thing
work, and you'll just have to go along with it. Liking it
isn't a factor. We've got to pull this off."*

"I know why I'm in, but why do you need it so much?"

"Shut up. It's none of your business. I've got my reasons."

"What'll you do with him until . . ."

"Don't fret. It's all settled."

"Right."

"What I'm concerned with now is the pictures that trooper's girlfriend took in Sitka. If she did manage to get anything, it might be trouble—for him and me. Got to keep an eye on her and see if I can get the film . . . or the pictures, if she decides to get it developed in Ketchikan."

"Shit. Just what we need."

"I'll get them somehow."

The unscheduled stop in Petersburg was quiet, but it took longer than planned, and all that was removed from the *Spirit* to the dock was the ax and the body of the woman found in Tracy Arm. Glen Carlson, supposedly safely confined in the engine room, was nowhere to be found.

The handcuffs Jensen had used to secure him had also disappeared, but Ray McKimmey was very much in evidence—unconscious at the foot of the stairs that went down into the hold. Whatever had been used to hit him had disappeared with his attacker, but the assault was clearly intended to put him out of the way while Carlson was liberated from the pipe to which he had been shackled. A deep cut on McKimmey's chin said he had fallen at least partway down the stairs and was out cold when he hit the floor, where he lay, loose-limbed, on his face.

Jensen, intending to collect Carlson to turn over to Petersburg law enforcement, was shocked to see him there when he came through the door and started down the stairs to the hold. Ray started to revive as Alex reached him, and he had soon struggled to his knees, against the trooper's advice.

"Stay still, for God sake, Ray. You've been hit pretty hard, from the look of it."

"What happened?" he asked groggily, stubbornly insisting on gaining a sitting position, his back against the newel post of the stairway. He was very pale, and his chin continued to bleed through his short beard and down the front of his coveralls. He smeared at it, in a dazed fashion, with one hand. "I fell."

"That's pretty clear. You've got a bad lump on the back of your head . . ."

McKimmey reached up to find it and winced when he touched the sensitive spot.

". . . and that nasty cut on your chin."

Another wince.

"Who . . ." turning his head, carefully, ". . . where the hell is Glen?"

"Gone. Whoever hit you turned him loose. You don't remember anything?"

"Nope. Not even . . . coming down here. Just a . . . vague . . . feeling that . . . I fell."

The first mate, who had disappeared at the first sight of McKimmey, returned with a first aid kit, a towel, two bags of ice, and a man wearing sweats and carrying a medical bag. He introduced himself, while examining Ray's head, as Vern Repasky, and he fit Jessie's description of the tall, bald doctor with fuzzy, gray eyebrows, who had stepped out of the crowd in the lounge to help Wayne Johnson. "We need to get him upstairs to his bunk," he said, "but he's going to need X rays, I think."

Jensen agreed.

McKimmey did not.

"There's nobody to mind the store," he objected. "With Carlson gone, I'm it."

"Forget it," Alex told him. "First, before this ship goes anywhere, we get a doctor from Petersburg with an X-ray machine. If he says you're hurt too bad to stay aboard, you get off. If you're okay to travel, until tomorrow morning at the very least, all you're going to be doing is taking care of yourself."

"Isn't there someone else who can take care of the engine room?" Repasky asked.

"There isn't anyone. I'll rest down here."

"Nope. Sorry. What you've got isn't to be messed with," the doctor replied.

Alex also shook his head. "The engine room gets checked regularly by a crewman at night, while you sleep. They can check it now. If you stay aboard and there's any problem, I'll wake you up for it. Promise . . ."

"There's a valve that keeps sticking. Got to keep an eye on it."

"Where?"

McKimmey pointed.

"I see. Okay. I know a fair amount about engines and machinery. I was raised on a cattle ranch that grew its own hay, and we had a few of them, all right? I'm not your caliber, but I can pinch-hit . . . a valve's a valve. If it sticks and I can't keep it unglued, I *will* wake you—if you go on with us. Okay? Check it every half hour, between the crew checks."

McKimmey gave in. "But I'm not leaving the ship."

Between the doctor and Alex, he managed to get to his feet, up the stairs, and into his bunk, though his face was white and he was wet with sweat by the time they reached it. "Bastards," he breathed, gingerly holding a bag of ice, wrapped in a damp towel by the first mate, to the back of his head.

"You got that right," Alex agreed. "I'll be back, but I've got to see the captain and a cop waiting on the dock for Carlson, and find out about waking up another doctor. You're in good hands till we can find one." He smiled at Repasky and the first mate, who nodded.

They were carefully cleaning and dressing the wound on Ray's chin, when Jensen left the engineers' quarters and headed for the dock.

*   *   *

"Damn it!"

It was the first time Jensen had heard the captain come even close to swearing. With him it seemed overkill somehow.

"So, he's still somewhere on the *Spirit?*"

"Yes, somewhere, and we certainly don't want him to slip off without our knowing." He turned to the Petersburg policeman listening to the conversation. "We need a doctor with an X-ray machine. Got one? And we need a couple of men to stand guard on the dock, and one to put in a boat on the other side."

"Okay, I'll set it up and get the doctor."

"Great. I'll set a couple of watchers on deck for now."

The officer went off to use the radio in his patrol car, and Jensen sent two crew members up to find a good view of the opposite side of the ship to make sure Carlson didn't attempt to make a water escape.

"He may have already gone. It's been half an hour."

Jensen disagreed. "I don't think he'll try at all. This is a small town, on a wilderness island. In a couple of hours' time everyone in Petersburg would know there was a fugitive on the island and be out looking for him. These people are Scandinavian fishermen and their families. They're used to hard work and hard weather—tough guys, with a real sense of tradition and values. They'd get him. Where could he go? I doubt he's stupid enough to climb off. Think he'll wait for an easier answer—Ketchikan, probably. I'm just making sure. I want to leave him here, but on my terms, not his."

Captain Kay frowned, considering. "A search of the ship is going to take hours, Jensen. We've got to go on. This particular trip, more than any other all summer, is so important in terms of its timing that I don't see how we can stay here long enough to make a total search. Tomorrow's stop in Ketchikan is our last before Seattle. Passengers need time ashore before two whole days on board. Can't skip it. The only thing that will make me delay much longer is if these doctors say McKimmey is too badly hurt to continue and I *have* to wait for another engineer. Even then, I would expect the company to advise me to go on to Ketchikan, where we could pick one up tomorrow from a Seattle flight. We'd have him faster that way than waiting for him to get *here* by air."

As he spoke a police car showed up, and a short, graying man got out with a medical bag in one hand. Alex came close to laughter, the man so utterly fit the comic image of a doctor disturbed in the middle of the night. His hair, what there was of it—a fringe around the sides of his head—stood out in every direction. He was wearing running-shoes without socks, and a raincoat over a pair of striped pajamas. He had remembered his glasses, though, and his slightly sleepy smile.

"Hi. I'm the doc . . . Richards. They tell me I've got a patient who's been hit over the head with something hard?"

"Right." Alex smiled back. "The ship's engineer was assaulted about an hour ago by someone who wanted to free a prisoner we had arrested. He's on board in his bunk, with another doctor who's a passenger aboard, waiting for your opinion as to whether he needs a hospital or not. Don't let him push you around, he'll try. He doesn't want to leave his engine."

The doctor nodded. "I don't push easy, sir. I'm used to patching up commercial fishermen."

As a crewman led him aboard, the three men on the dock watched him go in silence.

"How bad is Ray?" the captain asked shortly.

"Touch and go. He got hit pretty hard."

"Well, if the doctor says he goes, that's the end of it. He's too good a man and engineer to risk."

Surprisingly, the doctors did not say he had to

remain in Petersburg. They insisted on a quick trip to Richards's office for the anticipated X rays, which McKimmey fought, afraid they were suckering him into a hospital. But Repasky and Richards brought him back, complete with a couple of professional bandages and the report that he was only slightly concussed, with no fractures or intercranial bleeding.

Repasky helped McKimmey back onto the ship, headed in the direction of his bunk, while Richards gave them the report.

"He'll have one hell of a headache for the next couple of days. I've given him something for that, and orders to get as much rest as possible. Threw a couple of stitches in his chin. Will that do?"

"You bet," the captain told him with a grin, as they shook hands. "Thanks, doc. We'll treat him right. We owe you for a midnight ship-call."

"Oh, your company'll get a bill. I've seen a couple of your crew in the past for small stuff, cuts and bruises, now and then. Don't worry."

He turned to Jensen. "Take care of that young man, Sergeant."

"Yes, sir."

Off he went, yawning, to the police car. He climbed in, and it drove away, taking him back to a bed now undoubtedly cold.

"Okay," Alex told Captain Kay. "Here's what we'll do, if it's all right with you. We'll borrow one of Petersburg's finest, here, to go with us as far as Ketchikan and fly back. I'm sure your front office will be willing enough to front him a plane ticket. He and I will each take a partner, senior crewmen, who know the ship well, and, while we do the Wrangell Narrows and get on down the road, we'll search from bridge to bilges until we find Carlson. Okay?"

Once again Kay smiled. "Better than okay. A good solution, if one of these cops will agree to the plan. I'll personally guarantee that plane ticket."

One of them did, and within half an hour the *Spirit*

was once again underway. Petersburg's streetlights winked out one by one as the ship made a slow turn to the south that hid them behind the edge of a hill. The ship entered the famous Wrangell Narrows's twenty-four miles, advancing slowly, but steadily, from one navigation marker to the next, all in the dark, to Alex's disappointment—though he would have seen little of it anyway, since he and officer Tim Torenson worked with two of the senior crewmen to cover every spot on the ship that might be even remotely large enough to hide Glen Carlson.

23

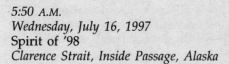

5:50 A.M.
Wednesday, July 16, 1997
Spirit of '98
Clarence Strait, Inside Passage, Alaska

FOR THE REST OF THE NIGHT, THE QUARTET SEARCHED THE
Spirit from top to bottom, but when the sky began
to pale with morning light, they were still empty-
handed. Carlson had vanished into the ship . . .
somewhere . . . and they had looked everywhere they
could think of. But Jensen was sure, doggedly and
unconditionally convinced, that Carlson had not left
the ship—that, somewhere, on board, he was lurking.

At five o'clock, starving and discouraged, they
paused for coffee and food. Alex was thankful to find
that Carla, the early-rising assistant chef, was already
in the galley. She insisted on cooking them the
works: eggs and bacon, hash browns, toast—though
Jensen assured her they could easily make do with
whatever was available, if they could have fresh
coffee.

From Carla's comments, word of Carlson's escape
had obviously already filtered out on the crew's
word-of-mouth information system.

"Nobody works well on cold food," she told them.
"I can't do much to help find this guy who killed Julie,

can I?" she pointed out, looking up and smiling a teasing, quizzical sort of smile. She continued, "But this is my territory, and you'll eat what I give you, right?"

Her expression hit him, somehow, as sort of a challenge, a whole different attitude than her frustration of the day before. Seeing that he had no choice, he grinned back at her with his thanks. "We don't really *know* that he's the one, you know."

"Who else? Got any more candidates? I think he robbed those staterooms and killed her because she saw him someplace and was afraid to tell because of her background. We all know about that now." She paused, then went on with a frown and an increase in intensity. "I'd like to get my hands on him."

"You liked her."

"Yeah," Carla replied, with a grimace of sympathy, "I did. She was one of the good ones. I feel bad for her little boy."

"Sawyer told you?"

"Yeah, I wanted to know, so I looked him up when I found out he knew her before. Was that okay?"

"Sure. How long have you been working on the *Spirit*, Carla?"

"Three years now. Why?"

"You're really familiar with the food stores, right?"

"Yes. It's all planned ahead for each trip. We have to be sure we have everything we need, even though we always repeat some of the menus from the last trip to use things up."

"If anything was missing, would you notice?"

"Probably. But there's extra of some things—staples, mainly."

"What do you do with leftover cooked food?"

"That depends on what it is. The crew eats a lot of it. Whenever possible, things like sauces or specialty dishes and desserts are frozen for later."

"Watch, will you? This guy, Carlson, can't exactly walk into the dining room, or sit down with the crew. And he's going to get hungry . . ."

"*Right!* Good idea. I'll tell the kitchen staff, and we'll keep close track of it. Now, the coffee's ready in the waiter's station in the dining room. Take that toast, go sit down, and let me scramble these eggs."

Gratefully, the weary searchers practically inhaled the food Carla soon set before them. After they had eaten, Alex sent the senior crewmen Captain Kay had assigned to him to get some sleep, and he and Torenson, the Petersburg officer, discussed the negative results of their night's work.

During the last hour of the hunt, Jensen had been thinking, in addition to climbing around in various sections of the hold, becoming more and more irritated with their singular lack of success. He was now ready to vent some frustration. Failure didn't ever sit well with him.

"There's no way this guy could have made his escape alone. Somebody got him out of those handcuffs, and it took a key. You can't use bolt cutters on the new ones like you could on the old kind. There wasn't time to do anything but unlock them. Somebody hit Ray, then got Carlson loose, and that somebody's making sure he isn't found. He had help, and still has, I think. Who? Why?"

The officer from Petersburg nodded slowly, holding his cup for Carla, who was providing refills from a second fresh pot of coffee. They had emptied the first so fast that she accused them of carrying canteens.

"I agree, but we haven't found him. Where the hell is he? Could he possibly have made it off the ship *somehow?*"

"I don't believe it. I know he's here someplace. *Know it!* We'll start with staterooms next, but I think it's a waste of time. We'll give it an hour or so before we start, and catch some sleep ourselves. I hate to bother the passengers again. Let them wake up and go to breakfast, so Captain Kay can make an announcement to keep them from getting too rattled about it. I really didn't think he'd try to hide in a stateroom—too much risk of an accidental outcry but we've looked everywhere else. At least he doesn't still have that knife."

"Unless whoever turned him loose gave him another one."

"Yes, damnit. That's possible. He knows how to use it, too."

They *had* looked everywhere they could think of, almost foot by foot—every stateroom, linen locker, generator room, on every deck—including crew quarters, and all their lockers. They took particular care in the engine room, with its huge, powerful engines, so noisy that they put on protective earmuffs before peering into, over, under, and around each and every corner and cranny. They searched it all, then went forward to the bow, where they did the same with the chain locker for the anchor. Even the bridge was thoroughly searched, and, through it all, no sign of Glen Carlson did they find.

Jensen decided they would next have to look at the passengers' staterooms. But a respite was definitely in order. He found an empty bed for Torenson in the crew quarters; when Jensen left him, Torenson was taking off his shoes, but leaving his firearm firmly buckled on as he lay down with a relieved sigh.

On his own way to snatch an hour's nap, Alex made another quick inspection of the engine valve—it had given no trouble during the night—then went back up the engine room stairs and stuck his head in to check on Ray McKimmey. He found him sitting up in his bunk, with a tray of breakfast on his knees, courtesy of Carla. From the color that had returned to his face and the hungry welcome he was giving his food, Alex could tell a little rest had done him a world of good.

"Feeling better?" he asked, going on into the engineer's quarters, which were narrow and included their own head with bath. They also had two bunks—one a Pullman that folded down from above.

"Yes, thanks." A forkful of eggs followed a large bite of jam-covered toast.

"How's your head?"

Ray reached up one hand to gently prod the bandage on the back of his skull.

"Not too bad, considering. The pills Doc Richards gave me helped, but spaced me out. I'll stick with aspirin for now, unless it gets really bad. Everything aches, of course. For some reason, I feel like I fell down a flight of stairs."

"No kidding. Chin?"

"Pills took care of that, too. Stitches pull a little. No big deal."

"You look like you'd been through a Golden Gloves exhibition, and you'll look worse before you look better. But, you'll be glad to hear that your valve behaved like a champ all night."

"Good. Maybe I finally managed to get it fixed yesterday."

Tired, Jensen slumped onto the single chair the room had to offer, and he leaned an elbow on a small dressing-table-chest-of-drawers piece of furniture across from McKimmey's bunk.

"Listen, Ray," he said. "We've gone over every foot of this ship, except for the staterooms—which we will do next—and there's no sign of Carlson. Got any ideas of a place we could possibly have missed? Some small corner, just large enough? You know the *Spirit* better than anyone aboard, even Captain Dave. I'm at my wit's end, and I really think he's still aboard somewhere."

"Why?"

"Why do I think so?"

"No, why would he still be on board? He *could* have gotten off in Petersburg as soon as we docked. Be a dope not to, given the chance. It's possible. Cold swim, but short and possible. Did you check the outer doors on this deck, the lowest one?"

"No, and at least one of them's been opened and shut since then, but I'll look."

The door was immediately outside the engineer's quarters, so Jensen was only gone a minute or two. When he came back, he was shaking his head. The door was closed tight, and it was impossible to tell anything from it, except that it would have been difficult to close from outside and away from a dock. An accomplice, however, could have taken care of that.

"I assumed he wouldn't want to strand himself in a place he knew he'd have trouble getting away from—where everybody would know he was there and be on the lookout for him."

"How would he know that?"

"Isn't the crew familiar with the stops you make, even the places you usually pass?"

"You're forgetting, he's not one of us. He's a replacement. Never made this run, as far as I know. Might not even realize it was an island."

He was right. Alex sat staring at him and inwardly cursing his own tired forgetfulness and stupidity.

"Dumb, dumb mistake," he said shortly.

"How could you know?"

"You mentioned it when we caught him, for one. And I seem to remember it being referred to once before by somebody."

"Oh . . . well, something in passing . . ."

"Confusion—none of this seems to fit together, but I don't believe in this much coincidence. There's got to be a link between some of the things that have been happening on and around this ship. I've never had a case where every piece is singular, isolated, making no picture at all—no edges to fit together."

"All the pieces for the thefts in the staterooms fit, now that you've caught Carlson, don't they? Well, sort of caught him . . . I mean we know who the thief is."

"Maybe. But there has to be more than one person involved, from the look of it. We were assuming Carlson was the thief and that he was trying to get rid of the evidence."

"Would've been easier to toss it overboard. Why risk putting it back?"

"That's what the captain said . . . and Jessie. I have to agree. There has to be a reason that makes it important to put it back. And who beat up that guard? Is it related? Oh . . ." he stopped, thinking hard.

"What?"

"I'm so tired I'm stupid. I said just a few minutes ago that someone else had to let Carlson loose, because it had to have been done with a key to open the handcuffs. People don't generally go around with the key to law enforcement cuffs. So, who would be most likely to carry that kind of key?"

"Someone who also carried that kind of handcuffs?"

"Right. And who on this ship?"

"Got any kinky passengers?" Ray grinned.

"I'm gonna ignore that one, thanks. Who else?"

"Well, the captain has restraints, but I think they're those new kind of plastic ones that lock by putting one end through a grip on the other, not real handcuffs. They're unbreakable, and once you fasten them they have to be cut off."

"No good . . . who else?"

"Oh . . . I see . . . yes. The guards for the gold. I've seen them on their uniforms, when they were wearing them," Ray said slowly.

Jensen nodded. "The guards of the gold. Anyone else you can think of?"

"Not unless there's another kind of officer aboard, undercover?"

"Not likely. And who would know where we secured Carlson?"

"Those of us involved in catching and trying to question him?"

"Well, unfortunately not just us. The whole crew

must know—Carla did. And anyone else that we told—I told Jessie, for instance—or whoever they told. Anyone—crew, passengers—who saw us bring him down from the bridge. Could have been a number of people, too many to identify now."

"Including one of the guards from the gold room. There was one in the gangway when we came down."

"Where?"

"The gangway . . . the hallway on Four Deck—this deck."

"Ah, insider names."

"Sorry. All the passageways are gangways to us. The decks that you call the Bridge, Upper, Lounge, or Main Deck, are One, Two, Three, or Four Deck to us, in that order, One Deck being the highest."

"So, there was a guard in the gangway on Four Deck?"

"Right. The one that wasn't beat up."

"Interesting. Guess I'd better have a talk with them. Now, again . . . any hiding places you can think of that we would have missed?"

"Steerage?"

"Got it."

"Chain locker?"

"That, too."

"Linen storage on the upper decks?"

"Yes."

McKimmey smiled. "Bet you even searched the captain's quarters."

"We did."

"You're serious?"

"Deadly."

"Let me think a while. I'll let you know if . . . wait. This's a long shot, but there's a laundry chute."

"Laundry chute? Where?"

"Starboard—all the way down from Two Deck to the hold. Comes out next to the gangway—stairs—that go down from the galley to food storage below, close to the laundry . . ." Unable to resist a bit of needling, ". . . that's washer and dryer to you."

"Right!" Jensen grinned.

"There's also a port-side dumbwaiter that goes up to the galley."

"That, we got. But the laundry chute, we missed. Would he have a chance of hiding there? How big is it?"

"Twelve, maybe eighteen inches wide. But it goes straight down. The only breaks are the doors to the chute on Two and Three. He couldn't hide without something to hold onto . . . a line of some kind . . . and, then, only temporarily."

"But he could slide down and avoid us as we searched decks around him, right?"

"Possibly. Wouldn't be able to climb back up once he'd gone down, though."

"We started at the top, thinking he would get out of the hold as fast as possible, and might be inclined to go up. So, he *could* have waited, holding on at the doors, resting until he heard us coming, then going down another deck?"

"Maybe. Or he could have climbed out on Two, while you were searching Three, or waited, holding that line, taking the chance you'd miss the chute, till you finished Two, or Three, and come out when you were gone. Let's go see what we can find."

"I'll go. You're on sick call."

"The hell you say. Who came up with this?"

"You did, but . . ."

"No buts. I'm tired of being an invalid. When we're through, I'll go sweet-talk my engines. They get cantankerous when they miss me."

Already out of the bunk, Ray was pulling on clean coveralls.

Jensen gave up.

24

6:30 A.M.
Wednesday, July 16, 1997
Spirit of '98
Clarence Strait, Inside Passage, Alaska

IT WAS THERE—A LINE, TIED TO A BRACE ABOVE THE DOOR
to the laundry chute—a thin piece of strong nylon
cord of a kind that Jensen would have expected to
see on a much smaller vessel. Hanging inside the
narrow shaft, it disappeared into the dark. They
hauled it up and found there was enough to reach
the hold, but, of course, there was no way of telling
if Carlson had gone down that far.

"How the hell did you know? If I didn't know
whose side you were on . . ." Alex said to Ray, as
he untied the line and took it to the rail, to examine
it where the light was better.

McKimmey just grinned. "Well, you said you'd
looked everywhere else. At least now you won't have
to search the staterooms."

"Damn. He did it. Slipped around us, didn't he?"

"Sure looks like it."

"But staterooms or not, now the ship's got to be
searched all over again. Where did he get this?" He
thought briefly of the blue and pink line they had
found on the woman in Tracy Arm, and he reminded

himself that he needed to call Commander Ivan Swift
when they reached Ketchikan.

"There's some like that in a rope locker below.
We've got all kinds for different uses. You never
know what you're going to need and it's a long way
to the nearest hardware store."

It certainly was.

Jensen thought of the thousands of square miles of
wilderness between the small points that constituted
communities on the Alaskan and Canadian coast. It
was no surprise that boats, even ships, vanished at
times without a trace—nothing to mark their passing.
The Pacific shores of some of these islands were periodically littered with flotsam that washed ashore; all
that was left of disasters at sea. The old, traditional
Japanese fishing floats—delicate green glass caught
in a knotted web of slim line—that were picked up
less and less frequently, now that the fishermen had
discovered the modern magic of petroleum for ugly,
shocking-pink replacements to support their nets—
were a testament to the distance such things could
travel. There were reasons for the courageous reputation of sailors, and many of the haunting tales of
disappearances that they told were based in fact,
not fiction.

He glanced up at the engineer, who was standing
casually, hands in the pockets of his coveralls, looking out across the water at the rounded shapes of
distant island hills, deep green with morning sun-
light on them, and waiting, comfortable in his silence.
McKimmey was perhaps not obsessed with his engines, but one of the few who quite naturally fit the
work they had found to do for themselves.

He seemed focused on whatever subject he chose
to talk about, and there was an appealing sense of
humor that ran below his quiet, competent surface.
But if you studied him for a few minutes as he went
about whatever he was doing, you might notice that
he had a slightly distracted air, a sense of being else-

where, and might come to understand that this was
an awareness with purpose. For he was always, sub-
consciously, listening to the voice of the *Spirit*—to
the pulse of her engines speaking through the surface
of her decks—to each sound and vibration of her
structure in motion that was an indication of her wel-
fare. He heard, felt, them all, and automatically filed
them away. But let one beat of her regular rhythms
reach his ears, the soles of his feet, or—if he was
sleeping—shudder his bunk, off its timing, and he
would be wide awake and listening intently, almost
before he knew he was on his feet. He was, Alex
thought, one of the true *Sons of Martha*: ". . . it is
their care that the gear engages; it is their care that the
switches lock . . ."

Where had that come from, and what was the rest
of it? He couldn't remember, but the phrase lingered
and haunted him.

This was not a totally unusual occurrence for Jensen; partly as a result of his father's encouragement
and appreciation of literature, he loved the cadences
of some of the traditional poets—Service, Burns, Kipling, Keats, Longfellow, among others—and, thanks
to his mother, many old ballads and folk songs, but
he seldom clearly remembered more than a few lines,
and those not always in the correct order.

I am too tired to go at this any longer, he thought.
I'm simply wandering around in my head—quoting
Kipling, for God's sake.

"I've got to get some sleep, Ray, even a little."

"You've been up all night?"

"Yeah, except for an hour or so before Petersburg.
I'll catch you later, okay? Don't do any more than
you have to, and get someone to spell you, off and
on."

"I'll do that, but let me give you one thing to think
about. We'll talk about it later. All right?"

"Sure. Go ahead."

"Well, here's an idea I can't seem to let go of. I'm

beginning to wonder exactly how and why Carlson got on board in the first place—at the last minute— no one else available. He volunteered—was right there handy to say, "I'll go." Could be that Steve's accident wasn't really an accident? But why? I can't figure why, and it's all reaching, a lot. Paranoia?"

They looked at each other, both considering this concern.

"Let me sleep. Then, yes, we'll definitely talk about that one," Alex told him. "It's a whiz-bang of a thought and worth checking out. Let it ride long enough for me to get my brain back in gear. But it wouldn't hurt to tell Captain Kay that I'd like to find out more about that accident, if you see him."

McKimmey nodded and headed for the engine room.

Jensen walked slowly around to the port side of the ship, heading for the stateroom and a horizontal position on his bed, when he was stopped by Chuck Lovegren, who appeared suddenly, as if from nowhere.

"Hey," he demanded, laying a hand on Jensen's arm to detain him. "I hear you got the guy that stole my money clip. Any cash on him?"

"Mr. Lovegren," Alex said to him, trying to think. Last night seemed so long ago, and he could feel a headache beginning just behind his eyes. There hadn't been much sleep in the last forty-eight hours. "We're not completely sure, sir."

"Not sure? About the cash, or the crook?"

"You know we caught a man in your stateroom, with the clip. He had no cash on him at all. And we aren't sure he was the actual thief, he seemed to be trying to put it back."

"Where is he? Maybe I'd recognize him."

"Ah . . . well, right now that's a problem. You see . . ."

When Alex woke and pulled the curtains aside to look out the window, they were coming into Ketchikan along the Tongass Narrows. It was almost ten o'clock—two hours later than the schedule had called for—and he was alone in the stateroom. Jessie, presumably, was on deck, watching the southernmost community of Southeastern Alaska grow in size as they approached. He quickly shaved, took a shower, and dressed to spend some time in town. There were things he had to do, and fast.

When he had come back into the stateroom, earlier that morning, Jessie had turned over and opened her eyes.

"Alex, it's getting—no, *is* light already. Have you been up all night?"

" 'Fraid so. Ray McKimmey was hurt, fell down the engine room stairs after someone hit him in the head. He's okay, though. The same someone let Carlson loose, and he's hiding somewhere aboard. We searched the whole ship and found nothing except the rope he used to avoid us by going down the laundry chute. We've got people watching and waiting for him, if he attempts to leave the ship in Ketchikan. I'll be up by then. We'll get him."

"The *laundry chute*? You almost have to give him credit for ingenuity. You know?"

"I give him credit for nothing, but keeping me up for hours of futile effort. The bright side is that now I know just about everything there is to learn about how this ship is put together, top to bottom. If you ever need to play hide and seek, just let me know. I can give you at least three places nobody would think to look for you." He quickly named them off for her.

She laughed and propped herself up on one elbow. "I'll remember those, when and if I ever need them."

Jensen had pulled off his clothing and tossed it onto the chair, with no concern for how it fell. With an infinitely exhausted sigh, he dropped into the bed, tugged the blankets over himself, and closed his eyes.

"Got to sleep. Tell you about everything when I wake up, Jess, okay?"

"Sure. Shall I wake you when we're almost to Ketchikan?"

"Please, love."

And he was unconscious, like a candle blown out with the slightest of breaths.

Jessie had snuggled back into her own covers, thinking she would go back to sleep for a few minutes, but her mind was full of ideas that kept her awake. The film needed to be developed in Ketchikan, and she wanted to spend some time with Dallas and Rozie . . . Sitka had been so much fun in their company. Fifteen minutes later, she was stepping out of the shower, rubbing her hair with a towel, aimed at coffee in the lounge and breakfast in the dining room.

As Jensen was putting his wallet in his pants pocket and reaching for his jacket, the door opened, and Jessie came in with a cup of coffee.

"Oh, you're up already. We're almost to Ketchikan. Here, this'll help."

Gratefully, he accepted the coffee and sat down on the now-rumpled bed to drink it. While he did, he filled her in on the happenings of the night before.

"I talked to Ray," she told him when he had finished. "He looks terrible, but seems to be doing okay. You've no idea who hit him?"

"None. But it has to have been someone on board. We may have back everything but the stolen cash, but there's something else going on here. I'm going ashore to call Ivan in Anchorage. When I come back I want to have a chat with those two guards in the gold room. I'll talk to McKimmey about Carlson, too. He thinks Carlson's getting on the ship as a replacement engineer was a little strange and that the guy he replaced could have been put out of commission to allow Carlson the chance."

Jessie's eyes widened. "Nobody does that sort of thing just to steal a few personal belongings, Alex."

"I don't think so either. But we don't know that was even close to the way it happened. I need to talk to Captain Kay and see if I can get in touch with the other assistant engineer."

"Here's an item that may be helpful. I heard at breakfast that, in Ketchikan, four people from the cruise company are coming aboard for the rest of the trip. That's why the owner's suite has been empty— saved for them. The man who started the company, Chuck West, is coming with his wife, his son, and a company public relations person, Gordon somebody. They can probably answer some of the questions without phone calls, don't you think?"

"That's great. Save some time." He looked out the window once more. "We're about to dock. Let's get out on deck."

"Ladies and gentlemen, we are now docking in Ketchikan, last stop before we leave Alaska and, for that matter, before we reach our destination, Seattle. If you have things you wish to purchase for the rest of our journey, or treasures to take home, be sure to get them now.

"We apologize for our late arrival, but we cannot extend your time ashore by more than half an hour. We will be departing Ketchikan at exactly two-thirty this afternoon.

"Soon after leaving Ketchikan, we will be cruising in Misty Fjords National Monument, with its incomparable scenery. Cliffs tower thousands of feet high, and an ancient volcanic plug, New Eddystone Rock, reaches up from the depths of Behm Canal. There are over two million acres of this incredible monument, wild and full of history, as well as deep channels and fjords. Captain George Vancouver explored here in 1794.

"So, enjoy your time in Ketchikan. We'll see you this afternoon. Take an umbrella, if you have one. This is known as Alaska's rain capital. The local weather forecast says that if you can't see the top of Deer Mountain, it's raining, and if you can see it, it's about to."

The *Spirit* tied up at the city dock, next to an enormous cruise ship. A behemoth, it made the *Spirit* look very small: the huge curve of its bow loomed over their ship as if it were examining this curiously diminutive cousin.

Except for Juneau to the north, Ketchikan is the main center of commerce for the people of the southern Alaska panhandle. Like all Southeastern Alaskan towns, it is steeped in the tradition of the native cultures that were there long before outsiders showed up to plunder the furs or search for gold. But, because of their arrival, visitors now find a cultural chowder: modern shopping malls, historic buildings from the gold rush era, and Native Alaskan totem poles, tribal houses, arts and crafts.

Built along the eastern side of the Tongass Narrows, on Revillagigedo Island (locals say "Revilla"—it's easier), it is a long and very narrow town. People may jokingly say that Skagway has only four streets, one of them the airport, but they often say that Ketchikan is three miles long and three blocks wide.

The southern part of the town, just east of the dock, is a tangle of buildings on land and pilings, stairways that all seem to go uphill, and boardwalks that grow invisible slippery coatings in the rain (more than a hundred and fifty inches fall here each year) to toss the unwary on their backs. A sense of humor is requisite to live in Ketchikan, and that quality makes it especially appealing to tourists, because the people are friendly and helpful—and remind them, with buttons and posters, of the Rain Festival: January 1 to December 31.

It *was* raining lightly when passengers began to disembark from the *Spirit*. Down the long *gangway* this time, thought Alex, from *Two Deck*. Although the sights were tempting and varied, with many gift shops and galleries similar to those in Sitka, and in spite of the call of the Tongass Museum, the Totem Heritage Center, restaurants in historic hotels, bars on pilings over salt water, Jensen took a taxi waiting on the dock and headed directly for the Ketchikan State Troopers office.

He left Officer Torenson, McKimmey, and Sawyer keeping watch, along with two crew members minding the side away from the dock, so that Carlson couldn't leave the ship without observation. Until he could have a couple of troopers or city police help him out, it would do.

In less than half an hour he was talking to his commander, Ivan Swift, in Anchorage.

Once again Alex repeated the tale of the last two days of bits and pieces, and the night spent chasing Carlson.

"Bad luck," Swift commented.

"Yeah, he's on there somewhere and we'll get him. Here's one for you, Ivan. Check on a passenger named Bill Prentice. I'm faxing his paperwork from this office. Supposedly comes from Vancouver. Okay?"

"Sure. Anything specific to look for?"

"No, just a hunch. He's just around at interesting times. One other name?"

"Yes?"

"Judy Raymond. Seattle address. The background she's provided just doesn't make sense in light of her age. I can use anything you can get on her. Her paper's heading at you, too. And look for that body I sent up from Petersburg, along with the ax that killed Morrison."

"They're on their way from Juneau. Private pilot brought them from Petersburg in time for the morning plane. I'll have the fingerprints from the ax for you very soon, if there are any. The autopsy will, of course, take a little longer."

"Please tell . . . no, better *ask* John Timmons to put a rush on it. I've got a nasty hunch about this one, so I really need information on this ASAP. There's also a piece of blue and pink rope on the body. It looks familiar, but I don't know why. Have somebody find out if there's anything special about it, would you?"

"Okay. I'll get back to you on the boat as soon as I have anything about any of this. You already know everything we do concerning Morrison's murder, and that her husband hasn't left Phoenix anytime lately. We had a chat with that attorney your man gave us access to, and it doesn't add up that Holden had any part of this personally. Just to be on the safe side, until this gets untangled, we contacted the police in Vancouver to put a regular drive-by and check on Morrison's mother and child."

"Thanks, Ivan. Good thinking. I'll tell Sawyer. It will take some of the worry off his mind."

"This is your last stop before you go into Canadian waters, right? Want to knock around that hunch?"

"No, not yet, it's still coming together, and it's nothing but a hunch and a distinctly uneasy feeling. I'll catch you later with it. All the way down in two days. We'll be into Seattle early Saturday morning. No more stops."

"Okay. Let me know if there's anything else."

"I'll holler if I need you. Thanks, Ivan."

Alex made several more calls, to Seattle this time, and started the ball rolling on some of his ideas. Results would have to wait a couple of hours, or more, before he could even think of expecting answers.

Still, it was something positive and he had only to wait. He realized, suddenly, that he was starving.

25

10:30 A.M.
Wednesday, July 16, 1997
Spirit of '98
Ketchikan, Inside Passage, Alaska

WHILE JENSEN WAS BUSY AT THE TROOPERS OFFICE, JESSIE
went ashore with Dallas and Rozie, leaving them
briefly to find a place to develop her roll of film.
Conveniently, there was one. Straight across from the
dock on Front Street, Schallerer's Photo and Gift ad-
vertised one-hour photo processing. Assured that
pictures and negatives really would be ready for her
in an hour, she left the film and hurried to catch
up with the other two women, who were window-
shopping. They took a taxi to the Totem Heritage
Center, a little ways from downtown. Though she
watched closely, there was no indication of anyone
following them.

They were impressed by the ancient totem poles
that had been collected from abandoned Haida and
Tlingit villages and were preserved in the center.
Close to three dozen were displayed, some mere
fragments of the beautiful wood carving done many
years earlier. Five of the best, over a hundred years
old, stood below a skylight, which showed off the
designs of their worn and weathered surfaces to
best advantage.

"Awesome," Dallas commented, looking up at the complicated details, each telling a story. "You can smell the cedar."

The rain had stopped when they came out of the Heritage Center, so they walked, pushing Dallas's chair, several blocks toward the docks till they reached Creek Street. As its name suggested, this infamous historic red-light district was built in the early 1900s along the banks of Ketchikan Creek, its boardwalk located conveniently near the harbor, where ships and their crews docked regularly. Madams and customers long gone, the street was now colorfully filled with gift shops, art galleries, small restaurants, and a museum in No. 24, Dolly's House, that captured the spirit of long-gone gold rush days.

They went to the railing of the boardwalk, looked down on the creek, and found it full of salmon heading upstream to spawn. Swimming strongly against the current, the large fish leaped and battled in their obsession to find the upper reaches of the waterway.

With a few minutes' observation, it was fairly easy to pick out different kinds of fish—large king salmon and smaller ones with humps on their backs that another watcher told them were pinks.

"Want to adopt one?" he asked, with a grin.

"What?" Jessie grinned, and the other two turned to listen, attention more than caught. Adopt a *fish?* "You're kidding, right?"

"No, you really can. The people at the hatchery have a fund-raising, adopt-a-salmon program. For a small fee you can call one of their baby cohos your very own. Must be a little hard to pick it out among all the rest, though."

"Clever. Will they cook it for me, when it's grown?" Dallas asked.

"Well . . ."

Laughing, they said good-bye to their informant and continued to the end of Creek Street and back into downtown Ketchikan. There they parted, Dallas and Rozie to do a little more shopping before heading back to the ship, Jessie to pick up and look over the pictures she had left to be developed.

"See you later," Rozie called, as she wheeled Dallas toward a large tourist emporium. "I want one of those T-shirts with a salmon on the front. *That* I'm willing to adopt."

When she reached Schallerer's, the pictures were ready for her, as promised. She took them from the folder and quickly sorted through, until she came to three that she had taken in an attempt to get a shot of the man who had followed them in Sitka. Two of them were unworkable—he had either gone into a shop or around a corner when she turned with the camera. The second showed part of his back in a doorway. The third, however, showed a profile view of him in the process of turning away. It was very small and difficult to see, even with the shop's magnifying loupe.

"Do you have an enlarger?" Jessie asked the clerk.

"Sure," she said, pointing. A Kodak Create-A-Print machine stood across the room, ready for public use.

She dropped money and the correct negatives into the appropriate slots, found the picture she wanted, twisted dials to adjust the density and color, and zoomed in on the figure on the Sitka street, cropping the picture to include only about a third of it. She made several enlargements, each with more magnification than the last. One by one, they fell out of the machine, slightly grainy, as the enlargement increased, but reasonably good. One by one, they confirmed the identity of their Sitka follower: Glen Carlson, without a doubt. She stood holding one, staring at the unmistakable proof. Why? What would this possible thief have to do with her?

"Get what you wanted?" the clerk asked.

"Yes, thanks."

She scarcely heard the question. Another thought had occurred to her, as she gathered the results of her half-hour's work. Had he been following her, or could it have been Rozie?

As she looked again at the enlargement, side by side with the regular-sized copy of the same print, she suddenly stopped focusing on the man and saw the other people in the picture with him: someone else caught her eye. Just beyond Carlson, farther along the Sitka sidewalk, was another figure in the process of making the same kind of right-hand turn. It was not a profile—the person had turned too far for that—more of a three-quarter image from behind. If the two figures had been dancers, Jessie would have assumed they were inspired by the same music, performing the same movement. It was impossible to tell if the second figure was male or female, for it, too, wore a hat, slacks, and a jacket, green. But there was something familiar about it. It was someone Jessie felt she had seen before, and recently. She could almost reach a name.

Just in case, she made two enlargements of this second person, but they gave her no further clue to an identity. She found herself wishing she could turn the person back toward her, just a few inches. Damn. Maybe Alex would recognize whoever it was.

In frustration, she pushed the pictures and enlargements into a plastic bag and went out the door, her face in a frown of concentration. She did not notice a figure that hurried into a doorway to watch her walk away from the photo shop, then carefully followed her down the street, passing several passengers and a crew member or two from the ship, all of whom said hello as they went by.

Almost two hours had passed since Jessie had left the ship. Carrying the pictures, enlargements, and negatives, she turned down a side street away from the docks, toward a small grocery she had noticed earlier. There she found several apples and oranges, a ham and cheese sandwich, a large bottle of mineral water, two Snickers bars, and the daily paper. She paid a young Vietnamese boy at the counter, who carefully counted the change into her hand coin by coin. When he finished, correctly, he grinned, proudly pleased at his success in what clearly was a fairly recent acquisition of foreign language and monetary skills. Jessie couldn't help smiling back.

With a little time to spare, and on her own for the first time in several days, Jessie, relishing her independence, spent a few minutes wandering alone through the shops, admiring some of the local crafts and gagging at others. Why did some people go to so much trouble to make trash for sale, when it was possible to make lovely things? Even accounting for differences in taste, some of the things she saw were terrible. And, even more mystifying, why did tourists buy them? Then she forgot to wonder, as one of the lovely things caught her eye; a quilt in wonderful icy blue colors, with tiny silver stars and a delight of subtle, but glowing, colors that swept across it in a representation of the northern lights.

"O-oh," she breathed in appreciation to the clerk, who had noticed her interest and come to ask if she needed assistance. "Did someone here in Ketchikan make this? It's beautiful—one of the most wonderful pieces of patchwork I've ever seen."

"Thanks," said the clerk, with a smile. "I made it myself."

For the next few minutes they talked about quilting, which Jessie had done little of but was interested in learning. She bought a sweatshirt and excused herself to go back to the *Spirit* as it was getting late. She took the woman's card, thinking of the quilt and her large brass bed at home in Knik.

Jessie went out the door, satisfied with her time by herself and the pleasure of finding the quilt. Cheerfully she climbed the *gangway*, as Alex had instructed her to call it—ignoring her grin—and stopped in the lounge to pick up a cup of hot chocolate. Then she went to the stateroom, where she put down her purchases and settled on the bed to read the newspaper she had bought in the grocery store, pushing open the curtains to let in some natural light, rather than turn on the reading-lamp. First, she looked once again at the photographs she had enlarged. The identity of the second person still eluded her.

Jensen came back to the stateroom just after two o'clock, and he found her asleep with the comics over her face. She woke at the sound of the door closing.

"Hey, I'm the one who was up all night."

"Well, it was just so comfortable and, coming in from the damp outside, I just got sleepy. Food coma. I ate half a sandwich I found at a grocery store. You have any lunch? There's the other half."

"I grabbed a cheeseburger with one of the guys at the office. I'm okay. You went to the grocery?"

"Yeah. Found a little mom-and-pop store. Why?"

In answer, he held up a plastic grocery bag and put it down on the bed next to her. "What'd you get?"

"Apples, oranges, bottled water, and Snickers. You?"

"Couple of apples, some cookies, and a package of jerky. Well, we're in high cotton now."

"What's that mean?"

"You don't have to bend over to pick it, I think. Slipped into our family from some southern relative. Doing okay—got everything we need."

"Pass me an orange from that bag on the chair, would you?"

He tossed it across. She caught and began to peel it.

"Find out anything interesting from Ivan?"

"Nothing new. Had a good talk, though. Asked him to check on Prentice and Raymond."

"Why'd you leave the ship to call him?"

"It seemed easier to call him from there than to use the ship's equipment. Besides, I wanted to get some help watching for Carlson in case he attempted to escape. You get those pictures developed?"

"Right." She reached toward the end of the bed, where she had laid the plastic bag that contained the photographs. It was not there. Puzzled, she moved pieces of the newspaper and the bags from the grocery, finding nothing.

"Where the hell is it? I put it right here." Concerned now, she lifted and shook the sheet, blanket, and bedspread, tossing the pillows on the chair. The bed was empty.

Alex glanced around the rest of the room. Perhaps she had laid them on his bed, or the dressing table. He helped her move the beds and looked behind them, searched every corner of the stateroom. The pictures were not there.

"Are you sure you didn't leave them somewhere? Did you stop anywhere after you picked them up?"

"Yes, but I know I didn't leave them somewhere else. I remember looking at the bag as I came aboard the ship, wondering if you were back yet, so I could show you. Then, I looked at the pictures again, just before I ate the sandwich."

She told him that she had identified Carlson and discovered a second person in her picture.

"I wanted to see if you'd recognize the other one. I just know it was someone here on the ship, but I can't think who. Damn it, Alex. I did *not* lose those pictures. I had them here. Someone must have come in here while I was asleep and taken them. They were here, *right here*, in this room . . . on my bed. God. Whoever it was had to reach across me to get them."

"You're sure?"

"Alex," Jessie's temper began to rise, as she swung around to face him, "yes, I *am* sure. Don't you believe me?"

"Hey, slow down. Don't snap at *me*. Of course I believe you. It just seems so unlikely that someone

would risk coming in here. You might not have been
soundly asleep. If you'd woken up and seen them,
they'd have been exposed and positively identified."

"They could have seen through the window that I
was asleep. I don't like the idea of someone in here
when I didn't know it. Damned doors that don't lock.
Makes me furious and scares me a lot, Alex."

She sat down on the bed and scowled at Jensen,
who waited till she stopped speculating, then went
for a glass of water.

"Here, drink this. You can't swallow and growl at
the same time. Let's think it through." He sat down
beside her and took her nearest hand in his, gently
massaging her fingers. "It'll be all right, Jess. It just
sounds so far-fetched, but maybe that was the idea."

She leaned on his shoulder as her anger faded
somewhat, and she began to let go of her fear and
think more clearly.

"So, the picture showed Carlson? Why the hell
would he be following you in Sitka?"

"I don't know. But I wondered . . . could it possibly have been Rozie, and not me?"

"Now there's an interesting thought."

"It was the second person in the picture that concerned me. I couldn't tell if it was a man or woman.
But it was familiar somehow." She described the sim-
ilarity in the motion of the pair portrayed in the
photo.

He gave her a serious look and whistled softly.

"So there *are* two of them."

"You think so, too. Even without seeing the pictures? It wasn't just my imagination."

"Nope. The way you characterize them, it sounds
like they were working together, but who the hell is
the second one?"

"I don't know, but I still think it's someone I've
seen on this trip."

"Well, Carlson had to have help getting away from

us. This other person could be the associate we've suspected."

"Whoever it is, Carlson gives me the creeps. He probably killed Julie Morrison. And I get the chills thinking about someone in here, stealing things from right next to me, when I didn't know it."

"Me too. Don't like it at all. Keep a careful look at who's around you, and don't go off by yourself without letting me know, okay? There has to be a reason for these two shadowing you, and I don't believe it was Rozie. Carlson did *not* get off this ship in Ketchikan, and I expected him to at least try. We've had six people watching, and there's no sign of him. He's still aboard and I'm going to flush him out somehow."

He tweaked one end of his mustache, which was drooping from the Ketchikan rain, and reached into a pocket for his pipe.

"I'm going out for a smoke. Want to come?"

"Pretty comfortable here, thanks. It's raining again."

"That today's paper?"

Jessie handed it to him. "I'm through. Take it with you."

"No, I'll read it later . . . Hey. Did you see this?"

A headline had leaped out at Alex as he glanced over the front page: "*Stolen Boat Burned, Wife of Owner Missing.*" Forgetting his pipe, he began to read the story out loud.

"*A sailboat stolen in Juneau during the early morning hours of Friday, July 11, was located late last night on the west side of Pennock Island, across from Ketchikan, when it burned almost to a shell. Gutting the cabin, the blaze attracted the attention of residents, who called for assistance and battled to put it out. Arson is suspected.*

"*The owner of the ketch, Michael Hazlit, an architect from Seattle, returning sooner than expected from a business trip, late Monday, July 14, reported his boat, the Hazlit's Gull, and his new wife missing from the Douglas marina. The honeymooning couple had arrived in the Juneau/Douglas area on July 3 and intended to sail on to Skagway upon his return.*

"From the name still visible on the stern, the boat was initially reported to the Ketchikan police as the Harry's Doll. *On examination it was determined that the name had been altered,* Hazlit's Gull *unprofessionally painted over with this false name. Matched with stolen boat and missing person reports from Juneau, it was positively identified as the absent sailboat.*

"Mrs. Anne Hazlit, twenty-six, formerly Anne Sheffield of Ashland, Oregon, is still missing. An exhaustive examination of the burned sailboat revealed no trace of the woman, and the police suspect foul play in her disappearance. 'She was just learning; wasn't good enough yet to have sailed the Gull *by herself,' Hazlit told a Juneau* Empire *reporter. According to her husband, she is five foot four inches tall, weighs one hundred and twenty-five pounds, has dark hair, blue eyes, and may have been wearing blue jeans and a blue jacket when she 'left' the boat.*

"Jim Wilkins, bartender of the Sourdough Bar, at the main city dock, informed the police of an angry conversation concerning 'a boat' between two men in his establishment at about five o'clock last evening. One of the two is no stranger to the Ketchikan area, Walter 'Walt' Burns, a local fisherman, who has had more than one run-in with the law, one concerning a fire that destroyed one of his own boats. The other has not been identified.

"In a bizarre coincidence, a powerboat belonging to William Ballard, temporarily employed in Flagstaff, Arizona, through September, was reported stolen from the downtown Johnstown Marina sometime last night. A connection between the two incidents is suspected.

"Police are requesting anyone who has information concerning any of these incidents, or the whereabouts of Walter Burns, to call Ketchikan Police Dispatch at 225-6631, or the State Troopers Office at 225-5118."

"Oh, God, Alex," Jessie said, when he finished reading. "It's the woman from Tracy Arm, isn't it?"

26

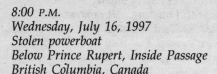

8:00 P.M.
Wednesday, July 16, 1997
Stolen powerboat
Below Prince Rupert, Inside Passage
British Columbia, Canada

AFTER A FULL NIGHT AND DAY OF TRAVELING SOUTH, it was almost dark again by the time Rod had piloted the stolen powerboat across the wide waters to the west of Prince Rupert, British Columbia, aiming for three islands—McMicking, Elliot, and Lewis—at the head of Malacca Passage. Here, with an X on the map, Walt had left instructions to wake him for further orders.

The weather, much to Rod's relief, had remained calm and inspired no seasickness in Nelson, who was also below and asleep. A deep blue twilight had fallen, and the lights of the city to the east twinkled brightly at sea level, miles away, like a handful of jewels on the horizon. That would have almost made the day's trip worthwhile had it not been for the hours of constant, unrelenting roar from the motors of the powerboat, and the overpowering smell of gas and oil. Rod missed the smooth, silent running of the superb ketch he had been forced to leave in Ketchikan, and sighed as he imagined it burned to the waterline. This stinkpot was not at all to his liking.

He had turned on the running lights and eased off on the throttle slightly when Nelson appeared at the top of the companionway.

"Where we at?" he asked, patting down his pockets in search of a cigarette.

"Prince Rupert's over there," Rod told him, pointing.

"Where's *he?*"

"Still asleep. You better go down an' wake him up, like he said."

"Don't like him, Rod."

"I'm not terribly fond of him, myself, but so far he's the boss, at least of this boat."

"Not fond of me, huh? As if that made any fuckin' difference." Walt put in a sudden appearance from his bunk below. "Just remember who's boss. Prince Rupert?"

"Yeah," Rod told him. "Nelson was just coming to get you."

"Right, I heard. I'm here now. Get down there and get us something to eat," he ordered Nelson. "You're good for a lot of nothin', but you can do that much."

Nelson disappeared below.

"You may not like it. He's not much of a cook," Rod warned, mildly.

"Can't screw up a couple cans of chili, can he? Hey, old man, heat up some chili and get out that box of crackers. We'll be putting in here for the night soon. Put some bowls on the table down there."

The powerboat had guzzled a lot of the gasoline they had loaded in Ketchikan, and its tanks were almost ready to be filled again, another thing Rod hated. A sailboat could make way without all this continual refueling.

"We need gas."

"We'll get where we're going, then fill 'em up for morning," Walt told him. "Head for that second island. It's Elliot. There's a sheltered spot to anchor up at this end of it. You'll see another boat there."

Rod guided them along the east side of the first island, McMicking, and slowed to watch the depth finder give him ever decreasing readings as he turned west between the two. Soon they were solidly anchored in a small, but secure, bay just off the northern end of Elliot Island. For the first time all day the motors were silent. His body remembered the vibrations, to his very bones, but now he could hear the sound of the surf and a seagull scream as it swooped past, and the breeze swept away the petroleum fumes, clearing the air. He sighed and dropped to a seat, stretching his shoulders to relieve the tension created by hours of holding the boat on course.

Close by, another powerboat lay at anchor, rocking a little on the slight swell. As they pulled in, the gangway cover opened, and Rod watched a man rise up in it, a silhouette against the light from the cabin below.

"Hey," a voice called through the dark. "That you, Walt? Where you been?"

"Yeah, it's me. Don't get your nuts in a knot. I'll be over in a few, when we get anchored up, and I get something to eat. Everything okay?"

"Far as I know. Got a call this afternoon with the details and times. Bring a bottle, if you got one."

He descended once again into the cabin, leaving the gangway open, and a whisper of music from a radio floated across the water on the still air.

"What now?" Rod asked Walt, who was bending over the navigation maps with a flashlight to double-check their location.

"Nothing now. You fuckin' wait."

"For what?"

"For nothing you need to worry about until I come back."

He wolfed down a bowl of the chili Nelson had managed to heat without burning, leaving them the rest. He tossed the Zodiak in the water, climbed in, and rowed off toward the other boat, taking one of the bottles of whisky from the case he had brought aboard. "Get some sleep," he called back. "We'll be here till sometime tomorrow, and I'll be gone awhile, maybe till morning. When it's time for what comes next, I'll let you know, damn it."

He was, at least, in a more relaxed mood, one that seemed to have nothing to do with the fact that he had slept for most of the afternoon, but rather with the fact that they were now where he wanted them to be, had made up for the delays of the day before, and the pressure was off. Though his language remained foul, he spoke instead of snarling most of the time. Rod was happy to have him off the boat for the moment.

Off and on all day long, he had wondered at what could be behind all the effort they were making. Nothing he could imagine would be worth the trouble of stealing two boats—although one had been sufficient, and he had to admit he shouldn't have stolen the ketch—and come all this way down into Canada, now to tie up and sit here until "sometime tomorrow." He didn't feel like questioning Walt, and he didn't think the man would welcome it, or enlighten him, if he did. But the whole thing made him uneasy.

It plainly made Nelson more than uneasy, but the old man seemed to have accepted the fact that there was nothing he could do about it and might as well go along, without knowing any more, hoping for the best. He treated it much the same as he had the idea of someone looking for them because of the dead woman . . . stayed out of sight, refused to get close to it, hid out below.

It was different for Rod. He wanted to know what he was involved in, however unintentionally. He worried about the locked box Walt had carried aboard at the last minute, and he had a feeling that if stealing two boats seemed a reasonable price to pay for whatever the plan was, it must be something

pretty big. And big meant bad . . . if you were
caught.

He sat in the cockpit, listening to the sounds of
Nelson clearing up below, watching the other boat
with the dinghy tied up at its stern, and he chewed
his lower lip thoughtfully. It was growing dark.
There were no other boats in the anchorage, which
would not have been unusual at other times of the
year, and truly wasn't now. People with their own
pleasure boats often took most of the summer to
motor or sail from Vancouver or Seattle to Alaska,
and back. Considering the enormous size of the Inside Passage, boats could pass and never catch sight
of each other, sink and never know the other had
gone down. But during the day he had seen numerous other boats heading north, more than he would
have expected, and it seemed that there couldn't be
that many places to anchor, though he supposed
there were.

Stars were coming out overhead in a glittering display, and, far away from any city lights that could
fade them, there seemed to be thousands more than
usual. He leaned back to look for the Big Dipper,
and found it, along with Orion, and two or three
more that were the extent of his knowledge of astron-
omy. Getting up, he went below, to reclaim what was
left of his own bottle of whisky, which he started to
take back up to the cockpit. Nelson's hungry eyes on
it slowed him, and, in impetuous sympathy, he
grabbed a mug, poured a couple of shots into it, and
set it beside the gimbaled stove, where the older man
could reach it.

"Hey, thanks, Rod. You're a pal."

Back on top, he sat down and raised the bottle to
his lips for a long pull.

It occurred to him that if Walt had been there, he
would probably not have retrieved the whisky. Why
the hell was he so intimidated by a man that he
hardly knew? He found he was, not without justifi-

cation, angry, had had more than enough of Walt's bad-mouthing.

"Hell, I've been steering the boat all day, and I'm tired. If I want a drink, I'm going to have one."

He took his drink. Then, obstinately and because he could, he had another, and it tasted almost as good as the first. Twisting the cap onto the bottle, he leaned back, watching the lights of a fishing boat slowly passing a mile away, heading toward Prince Rupert.

Maybe Walt wasn't so much after all. When the man came back, he was going to find out just what the hell was going on.

27

3:30 *P.M.*
Wednesday, July 16, 1997
Spirit of '98
Revillagigedo Channel, Inside Passage, Alaska

"CARLSON IS STILL ABOARD. HE MADE NO ATTEMPT TO GET off," Jensen told the group assembled in Captain Kay's office shortly after the *Spirit* left Ketchikan, heading for Misty Fjords National Monument. "Wherever he is, I want him. But right now, I'd like to lay out all the pieces of what has become a real puzzle, so you're all aware and can help."

Besides Alex and Jessie, the captain, Ray McKimmey, Don Sawyer, Carla, the assistant chef, and two of the company men who had come aboard in Ketchikan—Dick West and Gordon Thorn—had gathered on the bridge to hear what Jensen had to say. Tim Torenson, the officer from Petersburg, had left the ship to catch a plane home. Chuck West, retired from active management of the company, had left its representation to his son, and remained in the owner's suite with his wife. "But, if you need him, he is right next door," Dick told Alex.

The trooper quickly brought the two company men up to speed on the unpleasant events that had plagued the *Spirit* for the last two days. They asked a few questions, but, for the most part, they remained thoughtfully quiet, waiting to hear the rest of what he had to say.

"Who is this Glen Carlson?" Thorn asked, frowning. "What do we know about his background?"

"That's one thing I'm trying to find out," Alex told him. "I've asked the Seattle police for help, and they're running a check on him, looking for wants and warrants, and your people in the main office are also working on it. But Carlson may not be his real name. I don't like the idea of him loose on board. He's a dangerous threat, an unknown factor. Got any more ideas, Ray?"

McKimmey gently scratched the bandaged stitches on his chin. "Nothing I haven't already told you, but did you find out anything about how he got the engineer's job—got onto this ship? How about Steve Broughton? Did he have anything to say?"

"I'm waiting for a couple of calls on that. One from Broughton himself, and one from the Seattle police, who are checking the car he wrecked as his ticket to the hospital. They'll find out if there was anything funny about it, and, believe me, they know what to look for. The detective I talked to was already wondering about it, because of some suspicious things about the way it all happened. Had been assigned to find out. He said Steve would be okay, Ray."

McKimmey nodded. "So there was something funny about the wreck. I had a hunch."

"Let's wait for the call and not make assumptions. Solid evidence is important now on all the things that have been happening. How many of you read today's Ketchikan paper?" Jensen asked the group. He spread it out on the captain's desk, where they could see the headline of the article about the *Hazlit's Gull.* I called Juneau on this, to report the woman we found in Tracy Arm. There's not much doubt it's Michael Hazlit's wife. He recognized the clothes she was wearing, and the description fits.

"Now, this seems to have nothing to do with other things revolving around the thefts that have been going on. But I thought we should get that item out of the way, since we were involved in finding her body.

"Captain Kay, did you get anything back from the security company on those two guards?"

"Yes," the captain told him. "But nothing that will help. They've both been in the same job for at least two years. One of them for almost three. Their credentials seem okay. They faxed the application forms they filled out when they were hired, and a list of the jobs they've worked on in the past two years." He passed them across to Jensen, who looked at them briefly, and handed them to Jessie.

"I'll go over them carefully when we're through here. No fingerprints?"

"Not yet. They said they'd try to enlarge them enough to fax, but they're evidently still working on it. They weren't too happy about having any of their people's reputation questioned without something more definite than a suspicion."

"Too bad. I'll give them another call . . ."

As he spoke, the fax machine came to life and three pages slowly printed out and dropped into the basket.

"I don't believe it," said Jessie, with a grin. "Are you a magician, or what?"

The pages were, indeed, the fingerprints of the two guards.

"Hey," said Alex. "Sometimes coincidence actually works. Now . . . Captain, how is the trash collected from the gold room?"

"Carla?"

"They put it outside the door in trash bags. It's picked up and added to the trash from the galley. It all went off the ship in Ketchikan. It'll be dinnertime before any more is collected. Crew usually picks it up when they turn down the beds."

"Okay," Alex said. "Here's what I want. The next time it's picked up, I want it brought directly to me, unopened. Something in that bag, soda cans probably, will give me their fingerprints. I have a print kit from Petersburg. We'll find out if they are who they say they are."

"Why so much attention on the guards?" Dick West asked. "You think they're part of this theft from the three staterooms? I thought all the missing pieces had been returned."

"They have, except for the cash that was in Lovegren's money clip—a little over four hundred dollars, but it'd be hard to identify. Bills are bills. No way to say that any we find are the ones stolen with the clip.

"It's not so much the thefts. We only suspect Carlson on either the theft or the death of Morrison because the two are linked. But someone else let him loose and hit Ray on the head. It's a murderer—or two—that we need to be concerned about here. What bothers me are small things; the attitude of the guard I met in the *gangway* . . ." he glanced at Ray, with a grin, "the condition of his face, and his lie about falling down. Someone beat him up and was good at it. Could be the other guard, but I doubt it. He hasn't a mark on him, and whoever did it would have to have hurt his hands, skinned his knuckles or worse."

"Wayne Johnson came to breakfast this morning with bandages on his hand," Carla commented.

"He cut it pounding on the bar last night," Jessie told her. "He was drunk."

"Well . . . I took a bowl of fruit to the buffet and overheard him growl at his wife that it was already bruised when he cut it, so now he couldn't use it at all. I didn't know about the bar incident, just wondered what he did to bruise it before."

"Worth looking into." Jensen looked around the circle. "Let's all be on the lookout for anyone with injuries to their hands. I want to know who knocked him around, and why.

"The ax that killed Morrison went to Anchorage

and they'll be getting back to me pretty quick if there are any fingerprints on it."

"Well?" said Gordon Thorn, with a long look at the fax machine. "Where is it?" This occasioned a laugh from the rest of the group.

"Sorry," Alex told him. "I can't make it work with mental telepathy. Often wished I could."

"What about the other people you asked Ivan about?" Jessie asked.

"He's looking into them, too, and will get back as soon as he has anything."

"Who's that?" Carla questioned.

"I'd really rather not say till I know something. They're both passengers and may be completely innocent of anything. Just a couple of small things made me wonder. I asked for a background check, that's all."

"Reasonable," Captain Kay said. "Now, what do you need from all of us?"

"Well, the best thing, I think, is to let Carlson and whoever got him loose stew for a while. I want him, but where's he going to go? We aren't stopping now until we get to Seattle. Wherever he's hiding, he's going to have to stay there. I don't think upsetting the passengers with a full-scale manhunt would help them, or us. Besides, we don't know who it was that helped him. If we can figure that out we'll be able to get them both. We could watch again tonight."

He turned to the company CEO.

"Mr. West . . ."

"Dick. Please, just Dick."

"Okay, Dick, I'd like you to call your main office and expedite the things I asked for from there. I took the liberty of telling them they could expect a call from you, when you came aboard."

"Sure. I'll be glad to do that, or Gordon can."

"I'll do it," Thorn said. "I've got to call anyway on a couple of other things. I'll check with Harmony and see what's being done."

Jensen went on. "Captain Kay, will you somehow double up the crew members who do the night watches. I'm not comfortable having them by themselves. If Carlson decides to do some crawling around after dark and runs into one of them alone . . . if he killed Morrison, he's got no reason not to . . ."

"I'll get right on it." Kay opened the door and spoke to the first mate, who was working outside the captain's office on the bridge. "Get out the schedule of who's on watch tonight, please." He returned to his chair. "We'll go over it as soon as we finish here."

"Great. I can't thank you all enough. But what I want to stress is that this is not about any petty theft from some staterooms. This is a homicide. It's all about who killed Julie Morrison, and why." He nodded to Don Sawyer. "We'll get him, Don. Anyone have any questions? If not . . ."

The meeting adjourned, and all but the captain left the bridge.

Jensen and Jessie walked around to the owner's suite with West and Thorn.

"Come in for a minute and meet my father," Dick West invited.

The room they entered seemed enormous to Jessie, compared to the compact size of the stateroom she and Alex occupied.

Chuck West and his wife were sitting at a table, playing cribbage, as the group entered. He got up to meet Alex and Jessie.

"I have your book," Alex told West. "It's a good read. You really started something with this company."

"It's grown a lot. And it's been a lot of fun. We like the way we operate with smaller cruise boats—see more."

"Do you come along often, sir?" Jessie asked.

"Oh, every so often we sneak aboard for a run, or part of one."

They talked for a few minutes about the problems aboard the *Spirit*, then Alex and Jessie excused themselves. Thorn, the public relations consultant for the company, followed them out, and they walked slowly toward the stern, around the waterproof tables and chairs, to the checkerboard pattern on the aft deck.

"It's disturbing to have this trouble on one of our ships," he said, with a worried frown. "Upsets the passengers and doesn't do the company any good either. I'm terribly sorry about the crew member who died, Morrison. Tell me about Sawyer. You indicated in the meeting that he had some relationship to her. Is there anything we can do for him?"

Alex told him the story of Morrison's flight from her husband and how the whole alias situation came to be. He shook his head when he understood. "What a nightmare. Especially with a young child. What will happen to the grandmother and the boy?"

"I don't know, but it will take a lot of legal untangling."

"I got the pictures. Showed Glen clear, but wouldn't give them anything else."

"Good. Our friends make it into Canada okay?"

"Yes. They're waiting exactly where they're supposed to be, ready to follow us down the channel to the right spot and time. Called to check earlier. The message was there."

"Good thing it will be soon. With the big brass on board and all, that cop's getting just a little too nosy to suit me."

"Hey, so what? They'll never figure it out in time, or know what hits them tomorrow. We get what we came for—a big piece of that lovely gold—leave them, make a run down the channel, and before too long . . . bang . . . they're gone. Everyone but you, me . . . and . . . what's her name."

"Never mind about her. You sure Walt got enough stuff to do this boat?"

"Whole box full. It'd do a Princess ship, let alone this tub. Punch a hole right through the bottom. They'll go *down like a rock. No witnesses. And I'll enjoy watching it go. Brought it on themselves."*

"Can we get away without the rest of them?"

"Why not? Takes just a minute or two to untie a boat and take off."

"We'll have to time it just right."

"Of course."

"Okay. I'll see you later. Down here, ready to open the door. Right?"

"Right!"

"He's okay," Jessie commented on Thorn, as she and Alex went back to the bridge to see if anything had come through from Anchorage.

"Yeah. Lot of energy. Seems honestly concerned, not totally worried about overhead, like some company people I've met. Pretty good attitude. I'm excluding Carlson from that category, you understand."

"I sincerely hope so."

A message had come in for Jensen to call Anchorage, and Captain Kay handed him a fax. "I was just coming to find you. This is interesting. Sorry. Can't help reading what comes in over the fax, until they start sending it in envelopes."

The page he had given Alex had the tracings of two partial fingerprints on it. A note at the top gave Commander Swift's phone number both at home and at the office.

Alex went to the phone and called Anchorage.

"Ivan? What's the deal on the prints?"

"No wonder you missed them. We were all looking mostly at the handle. They came out under the lights—on the ax head. He—it looks like a he—wiped it all right, but must have been in a hurry, or flustered. Forgot where he was holding the head while wiping the handle. Got these two from under the pointed spike at the back. They're not perfect, but enough so you may be able to make some comparisons. We'll run them, of course, but don't expect much."

"Good. I've got prints for the guards from the security company and will get right on it. We should know in a couple of hours just what that story is. That it?"

"Two other things. John's doing the autopsy, as we speak, by the way, but says from initial exam he doesn't think there'll be any big surprises. Looks like she suffocated. Choked on her own vomit with the tape covering her mouth. He doesn't expect to find seawater in her lungs. But that's not your problem.

"Second, you asked about that rope on the woman's body. Pink and blue?"

"Yes."

"It's a kind of rope that mountain climbers use, and sometimes boaters. Comes in blue and pink, or blue and black, nylon, dry treated so it won't absorb water, which makes it sensible for boaters. It's 10.5 millimeter line, made by the Blue Water Company. Not particularly unusual, but not widely available either. This boat, the *Hazlit's Gull*, is registered in Nanaimo, B.C. The closest place to get it from there would be R.E.I. in Seattle, or somewhere in Vancouver. But it's not carried in marine supply outlets. Does it matter?"

"Not particularly. Just curious. It looked abraded, like it had rubbed on something. I think she was put in the water with some kind of weight that got loose and let her float to the surface. Does the rope tell us anything like that?"

"Funny you should ask. It seems to have rubbed against rock—some small fragments embedded, and Hazlit says there's an anchor missing from his boat. He flew down to Ketchikan earlier today to see what he could tell, in spite of the condition of the boat."

"That it? Raymond and Prentice?"

"Not yet."

"Thanks, Ivan. Call if you find out anything else. I can use all the help I can get."

28

10:00 P.M.
Wednesday, July 16, 1997
Spirit of '98
Lower Revillagigedo Channel
Inside Passage, Alaska

JESSIE HAD EXPECTED MISTY FJORDS TO LOOK LIKE THE
glacier-scraped cliffs of Tracy Arm, and parts of it did,
but it was much more of a green untouched wilderness
paradise, more welcoming somehow, a place in which
she wished they had time to stay and explore.

The *Spirit* cruised over twenty miles up the Behm
Canal, as far as Rudyerd Bay, a long fjord, as promised. There they slowed and moved through the late
afternoon mists and tree-crowded slopes that looked
as they might have before the hand of man con-
quered the planet. In the canal, before they entered
Rudyerd Bay, a tower of rock, half covered with
brush and a few trees, rose out of the water, once a
plug for a now vanished volcano. It was called New
Eddystone Rock, which seemed a little clichéd to her,
thinking it could have been given a much more ro-
mantic, suitable name. The ship cruised past it and
into the bay, where waterfalls rushed down the green
faces of mountains too steep to climb. So much water
falling was, they had been told, unusual, a result of

251

the afternoon's rain, for it had rained more heavily here than in Ketchikan, and was raining still.

They had put on the slickers they had brought along, and stood together at the rail, holding hands, watching what passed with appreciative eyes.

"We do make a mess of the places we choose to live in," Alex had said, causing her to smile, because it fit so well with her own thinking. "It's nice to see a place like this that sort of rejects us as anything but visitors."

Jessie had been glad the captain had insisted on sailing from Ketchikan in time for them to see this monument to wilderness, though she had heard several passengers complain of too little time allowed for shopping. No one seemed to be complaining when they slowly cruised a few miles into the bay. The ship turned and headed out when Alex spoke suddenly.

"Look. There's a bear. Over there by the edge of the water."

"Ladies and gentlemen. We are slowing the boat because, on the port side of the ship, there is a black bear with at least one cub.

"Look closely just to the left of the large rock, at about two o'clock, for the mother. Behind her about thirty feet is the cub, trying to catch up. Oh, there's another, in the brush above her. It's coming down."

The bear may have heard the boat, or more likely smelled them, for she stopped moving along the water's edge and turned to look out at the *Spirit*'s now crowded decks. Then she sat down and raised herself to a sitting position, watching it grow slowly closer.

"You trained her to do that!" someone laughingly called to the Bridge Deck, where the cruise coordinator had stepped out with her microphone to watch the bear's progress.

One of the cubs caught up with its mother, also stopped, and, considering her posture an invitation, attempted to climb up to nurse. She pushed it away with no more attention than any minor irritation. It bawled. The passengers aboard the ship laughed. At this sound, the mother slumped down once more to a four-legged position and, turning abruptly, disappeared into the heavy brush. The cubs, now together, followed and were gone as quickly as if they had never been there.

"We often see bears in this area, where the fishing for salmon is good in a few places. They are used to boats and our tour ships, because during the summer there are a lot of them every day, as well as the floatplanes that fly in from Ketchikan.

"Black bears are common in much of Alaska, but nowhere are they more at home than in the southeast. They are mainly vegetarian, eating sedges and grass, but are truly omnivorous, eating anything that comes their way, from small mammals and eggs, to honey, along with its bees, and garbage, as you know. They are solitary, unless breeding, hibernate in the winter, and can range up to fifteen or twenty miles. The females usually have two cubs every other year, though they may have only one, or as many as three, and the cubs are born during the winter in the den.

"Bears are measured from the bottom of its paw flat on the ground to the highest point of the shoulder. Adult male black bears are normally between two and a half and three feet high. In comparison, a brown, or grizzly, bear is three to five feet, and a polar bear, up to five feet four inches. Weighing less and having a flexible wrist, blacks can climb trees, unlike their cousins, the browns and grizzlies. So don't climb a tree to escape, if you should ever meet one in the woods. A good whack on the nose or a can of pepper spray will be much more effective, but, whatever you do, don't run. They can easily outrun you, but they can usually be intimidated."

When she finished talking, the ship had regained its speed and was headed once again for the entrance of Rudyerd Bay.

"Wasn't that fine?" Jessie asked. "Have you ever been so close to a bear before?"

"Only once," Alex told her. "Riding a horse in Idaho on the ranch, when I was about ten. I came around a curve in the road and there was the bear, about thirty feet away. The horse didn't like it at all, but neither did the bear. It went one way, the horse went the other, and I walked home."

They skipped going to the lounge for a drink before dinner, in favor of watching more of the scenery as the *Spirit* slipped back down Behm Canal and swung back into Revillagigedo Channel headed ever south. It was, however, getting cold, so they went back to the stateroom and watched from the window.

"I ought to be doing something to find Carlson," Alex frowned.

"Thought you were going to let him stew and get hungry."

"Well, yes, but . . ."

There was a knock on the door, and a crew member handed him a full trash bag. "Captain said you wanted this, sir?" he said with a quizzical expression. "You sure it's what you want? The trash from the guards in 112?"

"Yes, thank you. Don't worry about it, young man. I haven't gone crazy. Honest."

"Okay, sir." He shut the door and passed the window, shaking his head at the oddities of passengers.

For the next half hour, Jensen lifted fingerprints from the contents of the trash bag.

When it was time for dinner, they went down to join Dallas and Rozie at one of the tables next to the windows on the starboard side.

"Wasn't it wonderful?" Rozie asked. "I loved the little bear cubs."

"You wouldn't love them so much up close, I'm afraid, dear," Dallas told her. "They'd love you a lot . . . for dinner."

They had finished soup, and, as the waitress put

hot, delicious-smelling dishes before them, Jessie realized she was all but starving.

"Remember when we were passing the inlets at the bottom of Revillagigedo Island?" Alex asked her.

"How *do* you manage to pronounce that incredible word?" Jessie asked.

"Better to ask how anyone could possibly use it to name anything," Alex responded. "Do you remember an island across on the other side from the inlets?"

"Yes, I think I do. Kind of small, all by itself near the opposite shore."

"That's right. It's named Spire Island, and it's interesting because on December 20, 1905, the SS *Portland*—the famous gold ship this run is re-creating—went aground on it. When they got the ship off, it had to ground itself again on a nearby island—I forget the name—till it was repaired."

"Alex, you amaze me." Dallas smiled at him. "How do you keep details like that in your head and still work full time to solve homicides? But then, I guess your whole job is putting details together into answers, isn't it?"

She turned to Jessie. "What's Lou been up to today?"

"I don't know. Haven't seen her really, just once in town, with her father."

"She going to ask her father for a camera?"

"She said she'd rather find a job and earn it herself. I got the feeling he's having some financial trouble with his bookstore, and I thought it was really mature of her not to want to ask him. Most teenagers wouldn't be aware enough to do that."

Dallas agreed, nodding thoughtfully.

Alex, listening, gave Jessie a look that told her he wanted to ask questions, but would do it when they were alone. It made her wonder about the financial issue, and how, if the Stanleys were in trouble, they could have afforded to come on the cruise. She and

Jensen communicated silently on the subject for a second, aware that they were both thinking along the same lines. Later. They could discuss it later.

She missed parts of the mystery play. Her eyes kept wanting to close, and she yawned several times, till Rozie giggled and poked her in the ribs, when her nose angled toward her coffee cup.

"Wake up Jess, you're missing Alice from the Palace."

She woke up, however, when Alice sang another song. This time a parody, based on one from an old, classic movie, *Rosemarie*. Laurie Trevino and Jim Beal played and sang together this time, he in the red coat of the Mountie, she in her silver and white of the night before. There was some other business with the two miners and another character or two, but the clues they provided to the mystery slipped right by Jess, as she tried, and failed, to concentrate.

"Come on, Jess," Alex said, grinning, when it was over. "Let's skip the discussion they're going to have in the lounge and get you some fresh air."

"I think I'm going to skip it, too," Dallas said, wheeling away from the table. "It's been a full day, and I'm ready for the barn. Rozie?"

"No. I think I'll go listen to some of it. I like the Berrys, and it'll be interesting. He promised to tell all about his great-grandfather, who was in Dawson during the gold rush. If you don't mind," she said. "If you need me, I don't need to go."

"You run along, child, and enjoy it. Alex and Jessie will walk me up, I'll bet." She winked at Alex in delight at her niece's newfound independence. Then, when Rozetta had gone, "This trip has done her a world of good. Best way to spend money that I can imagine. Thanks to Calvin, for leaving me one helluva lot of it."

Alex and Jessie walked her to her door, and she hugged both of them good night and went in to bed. Alex was glad they had skipped the discussion, electing instead a walk on the deck. Alex was physically tired, and Jessie was just tired of people.

"Now," he asked her, "what was that about Stanley having financial trouble?"

She told him what Lou had told her, adding, "I wonder how they afforded this trip."

"That's because the invitation to come included a half-fare break on the ticket, I think," Alex told her.

"Great. What a good idea."

"Yeah. Too bad he's not making it with the store. He mentioned that he had a good collection of gold rush material and books. Want to go in now?"

"Let's go down and sit with Don in Soapy's for a beer, then go to bed early," she suggested. "He would probably welcome a little friendship about now. Having to tend bar right there, looking out on the place where Julie was murdered, can't be much fun."

"Damn. I never even thought of that." Alex stopped and looked down at her. "Why didn't someone replace him, trade with him . . . something?"

"Probably didn't think of it."

"Well, let's get something done about it, right now."

"Let's go down and see how he feels about it first," she recommended.

They found him rearranging the bar, cleaning all the shelves, and rewashing glasses—keeping busy.

"Naw. I'm okay. I'd rather stay here, where there's fewer customers, if you don't mind. I'm angry as hell about Julie's murder, you know. But it's okay to be here. Wish I had been here longer on Monday night."

He poured them each a beer in a frosty mug and came around the bar to sit beside Alex with one of his own.

They stayed, talking quietly—just two good friends taking some of the load from another, new friend.

"Well, guess I can close it down," he said, when

they had finished their beer. "Unless you two want another one."

"No thanks, Don. We're going to call it a night. By morning, we'll be beyond Prince Rupert and into the Grenville Channel. Now there's something I do want to see."

"What about Carlson?"

"Let Carlson sit it out, wherever he is, until morning. We'll dig him out tomorrow. I'm not spending another night like the last, and he can't just walk off, can he? His laundry chute's out of the question now, too."

"Yeah, you're right. Tomorrow is another day, so to speak?" He turned to finish locking up, as Alex and Jessie stood up and waited for him. But, finished, he remembered a question. "What happened with those fingerprints?"

"Oh, right," Jensen said. "You don't know. Well, there's the strangest of all strange things today. To begin with, I got the fingerprints from the security company. You were there when those came in. Then my commander in Anchorage sent me two partials off the ax. Just before dinner, one of the crew members brought me a plastic bag of trash that the guards had put out to be picked up. I took prints off three different soda cans, and then checked them against the company records. And here's the strange part. They didn't match. Then, just for the hell of it, because I had them, I checked both of them against those from the ax. None of them matched any of the others."

There was a silence, while Sawyer thought that over. "Tell me that I'm getting it. You mean the guards' fingerprints off the cans didn't match the ones they had on file with their own company? And that they didn't match the ones from the ax? And that the ones from the ax didn't match the ones from the security company, either?"

"That's exactly what I mean. They're all different.

It doesn't make a lot of sense. I want to think it over for a while, but in the morning, the captain, the CEO, and I are going to have a very interesting conversation with those two guards. And it will include the question of who gave the one a black-and-blue face.''

They all three walked up to the lounge, where they left Don to take in the key to the cash drawer, then the two of them walked on up the stairs to their own deck, stateroom, and beds. Alex was asleep before Jessie finished brushing her teeth, and she was only minutes behind him.

29

4:30 A.M.
Thursday, July 17, 1997
Spirit of '98
Grenville Channel, Inside Passage
British Columbia, Canada

JENSEN WOKE ONCE ABOUT TWO O'CLOCK, AND WENT
down to speak with Ray McKimmey on the status of
the *Spirit*. He found him in the engine room, checking gauges.

"Hear anything? See anything?"

"Nope. Nothing," Ray told him. "Everything's
quiet. I've been down here three times since eleven,
and it's all fine. No sign of Carlson, and I've been
checking the galley, too."

"Get some sleep," he told Ray, and went gratefully
back to bed again.

Sometime later, he woke in the dark, aware of a
sound. He had heard something unusual, almost felt
it, just before he was conscious. What was it? It came
again. A sort of a thump that he felt, a vibration, like
something hitting the ship, or something heavy falling in it, then the sound of the engine changed speed.

Getting out of bed, he quickly began to put on
his clothes.

Jessie woke and turned over.

"What's going on?"

"Don't know, but something's making sounds that are different than I've heard before. I'm going to see. May just be McKimmey's valve."

"Should I come?"

"No, love. Stay in bed. It's probably nothing. I'll be right back." He paused, considering.

"But if I don't come back soon. If . . ."

There was a soft knock on the door, and, when he opened it, Lou Stanley was standing outside, in flannel pajamas, jacket, and tennis shoes. She flew in as if someone were chasing her.

"Jessie. My dad woke up and couldn't go back to sleep. So he went outside for a while, but he didn't come back. So I went to look for him, but I couldn't find him anywhere. There's somebody that I never saw before moving around down by the dining room. Then the elevator started to move, so I ran. And there's another boat tied to this one on the side by the kitchen. Can I be with you? I don't like this."

They stared at her for a minute, astonished at what she was telling them.

"Of course you can be with me." Jessie got up and reached for her own clothes.

Alex went to his bag, took out the holstered .45, and buckled it on under his jacket. He had been wearing it ever since Carlson had escaped. He turned back to Jessie, who was almost dressed. Lou was sitting on Jessie's bed.

"If I don't come back in half an hour, I want you to get out of here. Don't forget this afternoon. Do you remember the hiding places I told you about?"

She nodded.

"Okay, take Lou and go down the back way to steerage. It's a good hiding place, and I'll know where you are, if I need you. Right?"

"Yes, but what about Lou's dad and the rest of the passengers?"

"If whatever's going on is okay, they don't need to know. If it's not, they're better off asleep. We can't round up or warn them all right now. Right?"

"Yes. Anything you want me to do, check the bridge?"

"Not with Lou in tow. Better let me find out what this is all about. I'll come back and tell you in just a few minutes. Or send Ray. Only Ray . . . or the captain. Understand? I wish you could lock this damn door."

"I can put the chair under the doorknob."

"Too low. Besides, it never works. Back soon."

He went out the door, closing it quietly behind him. Going to the rail in a dim space between the deck lights, he looked down. There was a powerboat tied amidships to the lower deck of the *Spirit*, and the thumping sound he had heard was it bumping against the ship between fenders that were spaced too far apart. A man leaned out from the ship toward the powerboat, then disappeared back inside. The outside starboard door was open on Four Deck.

Quickly, he went down the back way, from Two to Three Deck on the aft stairs. From there to the dining room on Four Deck, stairs went down either side of Soapy's, to allow viewing from the large wraparound windows of the Parlour. He went down the one on the starboard side, carefully looking to see if there was anyone in the dining room. It was dark, but there was a light on in the galley.

Quietly, he opened the door to the dining room and quickly closed it again behind him, concerned that the sudden sound of the *Spirit*'s rushing wake outside would alert someone. Crouching behind a waist-high bench at the last cafe table by the window, he waited. There was no sign of anyone.

Swiftly, silently, he moved down the long aisle between the round tables in the center of the room and the cafe tables at the sides, and reached the hallway that led to the corridor amidships. He looked around the corner and saw no one. The door to the engineer's quarters was closed. The one to the engine room, just across from it on his side was, also. Keeping close to the wall, he moved around and cautiously opened it. The light was on, as always, but the engine room seemed empty. He stepped in and stood for a minute at the top of the stairs that the engineer had fallen down the night before.

McKimmey was sitting very still on the floor at the far side of the engine room. He turned his head and saw Jensen at the same time the trooper realized that he was bound, wrists, ankles, and knees, with duct tape, a piece of it across his mouth, very like the woman they had lifted from the waters of Tracy Arm.

Seeing Jensen, his eyes widened.

Alex took one step down, starting toward him.

McKimmey shook his head, then jerked it at the space between the engines, clearly trying to tell Alex that someone was there.

Muffled by the loud sound of the engines, Jensen made no sound as he pulled the .45 from his jacket pocket. He went carefully, slowly, down each step, his attention intently focused on the space Ray had indicated.

Not good enough. The man must have sensed, or seen, the opening of the engine room door, for as Jensen was halfway to the bottom, a figure stepped out from between the engines, facing the trooper on the stairs. *Carlson!* And, to Jensen's astonishment, the missing man was holding an AK-47 assault rifle, aimed at *him*. He grew immediately still, his own gun directed at Carlson.

The exchange that followed took place in gestures, because the enormous, powerful sound of the engines precluded any other form of communication.

Come down, Carlson gestured. *Put down the gun.*

Jensen shook his head.

The *come down* gesture was repeated, more emphatically, with a jerk of the assault rifle. Then Carlson turned it toward McKimmey. His meaning was obvious. If Jensen continued to refuse, he would shoot Ray. The barrel swung back toward the stairs, and he beckoned. *Come down. Slowly.*

Raising his hands in the air, holding the .45 by its barrel, Jensen complied, slowly, carefully, trying to think. What could he do? He was not about to give up his only protection, though it was useless at the moment. He glanced at McKimmey, then quickly back at Carlson, who was waiting for him with an egotistical, satisfied grin on his face.

Under cover of the engine's roar, McKimmey had pulled his legs under him and was deliberately, cautiously rising to his feet.

To keep Carlson from turning to look at Ray, Alex pretended to stumble, caught himself with a hand on the banister.

Carlson jerked to attention, grin vanishing.

Alex resumed his unhurried descent.

McKimmey made it to an unstable, wobbly standing position, paused, and began, slowly, to hop toward Carlson's back, speed increasing as he leaned ahead of himself, jumping faster to keep his balance. Carlson never heard him coming. In the last few feet, just as Jensen reached the last step, he launched himself, headfirst at his former assistant engineer, hitting him directly between the shoulder blades, knocking him forward, flailing wildly.

Carlson fell flat, dropping the assault rifle, which Jensen sprang to kick out of his reach. McKimmey lay on Carlson's legs. Then he was rolling, trying to get out from under Ray, desperately reaching at the same time to grab and hold the engineer between himself and Jensen. Alex stepped forward, fast, held the muzzle of the .45 just above Carlson's left ear, and shook his head. The struggle stopped.

When Jensen released McKimmey from his restrictions, they taped Carlson even more securely and dragged him back behind the port engines. There they taped him solidly to a sewage pump.

"Thanks," Ray mouthed. Reaching for a pair of the protective earmuffs, he placed them on Carlson, who scowled.

"Let's get out of here," Jensen yelled in Ray's ear, pointing to the door. He picked up the AK-47 and started for it.

McKimmey grabbed his arm and shook his head. "They're out there," he said, pointing toward the space between the elevator and the galley.

Who?

He shrugged, turned, and gestured for Alex to follow. Beside the engineer's station, to the rear of the engine compartment, he stopped, pointing upward.

Following the direction of his gesture, Jensen could see a red square on the ceiling.

"Escape hatch," Ray yelled. He pointed at Jensen, himself, then upward. "We go up there." Then he held a finger to his lips. Quiet. "Galley," he mouthed. "Into the galley."

They dragged the nearby workbench under the hatch and pilled a couple of boxes on it. Climbing to the top of the pile, Ray carefully disengaged the fasteners to the escape hatch and pushed, gently. Nothing. He pushed a little harder. Slowly, it moved, upward, just a crack. He pushed it wider, just enough so that he could look through and ascertain that no one was in the galley. Alex gave him a leg up, handed him the assault rifle, and swiftly followed him through the small opening.

The hatch opened into a space at the end of a long metal counter on one side of the aisle between stoves, steam tables, and counter space. The galley was empty, though the overhead light was on. Someone had been there, and could be again, at any moment. Another thump of the powerboat against the *Spirit*. There was the sound of a low voice in the open space by the stairs, between the galley and the long hallway to the forward staterooms.

McKimmey lowered the escape hatch back into its

frame, flush with the rest of the deck, and led Jensen through the door into the darkness of the dining room. There, Jensen caught his shoulder, motioned toward the back bar, and they threaded between the circular center tables until they had reached it.

Standing together, against a wall where they could see the door to the galley but not be seen by anyone coming through it, they could talk for the first time, if only in whispers.

"What the hell is going on?"

"I'm not sure. I was down below, finishing up, when the door opened and I found that thing in my face," he pointed to the AK-47, "and Carlson, with a nasty grin, on the other end of it. One of the guards from the gold room was with him, the one that took the pounding. They hustled me back down the stairs and taped me up like you found me. Then the guard went up and left Carlson to watch me and the engine room. Thanks for the assist."

"They say anything to give you a clue what they're up to?"

"No, but what's that guard doing with Carlson? I'm thinking . . ."

"Probably the same thing I am. They're after the gold. What else could it be? I heard a thump—it was a powerboat tying up and bumping against the *Spirit*. I saw it from the Upper Deck after the sound woke me. Lou Stanley came knocking, scared because her father had disappeared and there were people down by the galley she didn't know. The door on the port side is open, and someone came aboard from that boat. More than one, I'd guess. You only saw those two?"

"Yeah. Couldn't hear anything with the engines running. Just as I started up the stairs, they slowed the speed from the bridge, so I'd guess there's at least one of them up there, too."

"Damn. I know you're right. How many of them can there be? I knew there was something really wrong when I saw that the fingerprints of those two guards didn't match the ones the security company has on file for them. Should have confronted them about it last night, not waited for this morning. I might have suspected something like this, if it hadn't been for the thefts and Morrison's death. Either it's all been a smoke screen, or they got very, very lucky."

The door Alex had used earlier to enter the dining room suddenly opened with a whoosh of sound from outside and quickly closed again. The two men flattened themselves against the wall, waiting.

Jessie and Lou came around the corner into the Parlour. They were carrying a blanket and a pillow each, and one of the plastic bags with the food and water she and Alex had bought in Ketchikan. Lou carried Jessie's camera bag.

"Ugh." Jessie jumped when Jensen stepped away from the wall into her intended path. She dropped the pillow she was carrying and shoved Lou behind her. She had a flashlight in one hand, from which she threw a beam of light into his eyes like a weapon. Seeing who it was, she turned off the light, released the air she had gasped in, and swore in a whisper.

"Damn it, Alex, you scared me half to death. Don't *do* that."

She bent to retrieve the pillow.

"Sorry. Come over here, out of sight." He pulled them around to the other side of the bar.

"Ray." He motioned the other man to come along.

There was a small room immediately behind the bar in Soapy's Parlour. In the floor of it was a trapdoor, larger than the escape hatch, and much more noticeable. He raised it and motioned the other three down. When they had carefully negotiated the steep ladder into the steerage compartment, he followed, closing the door behind him.

"No lights," he said, when Ray reached for the switch. "It might show through into the other end of the hold, and we don't know exactly where they are. This way."

Alex led the others around the heavy Red Fox sewage treatment plant and through a space into the storage section of the compartment. Stacked in it were odds and ends of material used, if needed, for repairs on the ship. He pointed to one stack that all but filled one end of the space.

"There's a hole behind that, where some plate steel leans against the hull of the ship. It'll be a good place to hide for the moment."

"No," said Lou, adamantly shaking her head.

Their attention and light focused on her, and they saw that more than her head was shaking. Her whole body trembled, her eyes were shut tight, and her face was pale. Jessie shut off her flashlight, and they waited.

"What's wrong, Lou?"

"I can't," Lou said, opening her eyes. "It's too small. I get claustrophobia . . . panic and pass out sometimes." Her voice sounded small and frightened in the dark.

"Oh, dear," Jessie said, laying a hand on her arm.

"Yeah. My dad has it, too. I don't even like elevators. So, I'm sorry, but I can't go in there."

"Well, don't worry about it. We don't have to go there. We'll find somewhere else to keep you safe."

"Yes. It's okay, Lou," Alex agreed.

"I wasn't real happy about being down here and not knowing what's going on, anyway," Jessie said. "How about that space behind the bar in the Parlour, at least for now? Is there room?" She indicated the assortment of things they had brought down with them.

"Yes, and it'll come in handy. Could be a little cool in there this time of night. But we won't leave you for very long, unless it's really necessary."

They all worked together to make this happen, climbing back up into the Parlour, where Lou was soon settled behind the bar. Jessie turned to Alex and looked up at him with worried eyes.

"Look, don't do anything dumb, trooper," she said quietly. "I happen to want you back in one piece, please. You took that awful gun away from one of whoever you're hunting, didn't you? And that means there are undoubtedly more."

She referred to the assault rifle, which McKimmey was carrying.

"Carlson," he told her. "We took it from Carlson, who's now secured with duct tape in the engine room." Alex gave her a quick hug. "Will you stay here, for the moment, with Lou? I want to move around some, get a better idea what's going on and who's in on it."

"Sure. But, if anyone comes into the dining room, this place is effectively blocked off."

"I know. If that happens, you might have to go back down in the hold to stay out of their way. That be okay, Lou? Just in the open part?"

"I guess so. I'd rather be here, but, yes, I'll go. Will you look for my dad?"

"Yes. I will. Don't worry. I'm sure he's okay. Just stuck somewhere." He hoped it was true and turned his attention to what they would need to expedite their reconnaissance.

"We'll need a couple of flashlights," Jensen told McKimmey.

"Don't think so," Ray answered from above. "It's getting light out there."

It was, Alex could see, light enough to see the surface of the ocean beyond the deck lights of the *Spirit.* A feeling of foreboding suddenly filled him, and he frowned before he spoke.

"Yes, it certainly is. Soon we'll be able to make out just who's responsible for all this, whatever it is. But if we can see them, they're also going to be able to see us. We've lost our cover, Ray."

30

5:30 A.M.
Thursday, July 17, 1997
Spirit of '98
Grenville Channel, Inside Passage
British Columbia, Canada

"WE'RE IN THE GRENVILLE CHANNEL," ALEX SAID, SOME-
what surprised. He had completely forgotten about
anything but the ship's interior, where his attention
had been focused. The narrow passage through
which they were cruising limited the amount of visible sky, but what he could see had turned a delicate
shade of blue-gray.

Almost as straight as an arrow for forty-five miles,
the Grenville Channel was one of the most well
known and remembered features of the Inside Passage. Seeming hardly wide enough for two large
ships to pass each other, it was, at its narrowest, a
fifth of a mile wide, extremely deep, and the mountains that rose on either side for fifteen to thirty-five
hundred feet were almost perpendicular. Once into
the channel there were no turnoffs except for Lowe
Inlet, fourteen miles from the southern end, an anchorage that was a remarkable haven for smaller
ships and boats. Large ships and ferries made the
entire run, carefully navigating and on watch for oth-

ers passing through. The dense rock of the tall cliffs could interfere with radio transmission, create a blackout zone. Flood tides entered the channel from both ends of the passage at once, and, in the lower, narrowest parts, could attain two knots on the flood and four knots on the ebb, with interesting but not particularly pleasant consequences to small vessels, which timed their trips through it with care.

It was light enough so that Alex could see the green of clinging cedar on the sheer stone cliffs they were passing. As they once more looked carefully into the dining room, it was possible to differentiate chairs and tables from the light coming through the large windows on either side.

The room was still dark and empty, but in the galley beyond, someone was moving, beginning to make breakfast, from the sounds of pots and pans. Who was it? Carla? Did they dare find out? He thought not . . . not yet.

"What next?" McKimmey asked.

Alex shook his head. "I need to know a lot of things fast: how many of them there are, where they are, what they're doing, and what they've got in mind for a whole ship full of passengers who will be getting up in the next hour. We can't just walk up and ask, so we'll have to find a way to answer some of those questions without getting caught doing it. Let's go into that room behind the bar, where our voices won't carry, and talk it over, make some kind of plan."

When they went past, they saw that Lou had gone to sleep, wrapped in one of the blankets. She would be completely invisible to anyone glancing casually into Soapy's Parlour, protected in the shelter of the bar.

Jessie joined them, and the three sat cross-legged on the floor. Ray had picked up a basket of pretzels from the top of the bar and brought it in with him. "I'm starving. You?"

"Yeah."

They ate pretzels while they talked, and washed them down with Seven-Up, which Alex retrieved from the cooler. Not much of a breakfast, especially when they could smell bacon and coffee from the galley.

"They've planned it well," Jensen said. "This channel is one of the few places they wouldn't have to worry about emergency radio transmission. Though, if they've taken over the bridge, as I'm sure they have, there's not much chance of a message going out anyway, unless Captain Kay can somehow manage to contact another boat in the channel."

"That change of speed must have been to allow the powerboat to tie on," McKimmey said thoughtfully, "and however many of them were on it to come aboard."

"The fingerprints that didn't match make a lot more sense, now," Alex mused. "Those aren't the guards that are supposed to be watching the gold. Somewhere along the line they got replaced, and I'm not optimistic about their chances. None of these guys, if they're anything like Carlson, would let anyone escape who could inform the authorities that there's a heist planned for a ton of gold."

"Is that what they're trying to do?" Jessie asked, her eyes wide. "That's a lot of gold."

"And a lot of risk."

"How can they hope to get away with it? There's well over a hundred people on this ship."

They were quiet, thinking that over.

"Well," Ray finally broke the silence, "now we know that Carlson's been in on this from the beginning. I don't have to see proof of that. Somehow he, or someone with him, did screw up Steve's car and put him in the hospital, so he could take his place."

"I think you're right," Jensen told him. "I'm also sure that at least one other person on this ship has been waiting and planning this. The person who turned Carlson loose from the engine room. There may be more than one."

"But who? Passengers? Crew? There's no way to tell."

"Somebody beat up that guard. What for? Whoever it was may actually have been the one who stole those items from the passenger staterooms and killed Morrison, not Carlson. I'm only speculating here, but if someone else was in charge, they'd be pretty mad if something like that wrecked their chance at the gold, right?"

"Right. How're we going to deal with the situation? There's only two of us."

"I beg your pardon," Jessie fired back indignantly. "Two?"

"Sorry. Three. That's still not enough. Can we get anyone else on our side . . . and make sure they're really on it, not one of them?"

"That's not a bad idea, Ray," Jensen agreed. "Where's Don Sawyer? Can we get to him?"

"He's in one of the centennial committee's staterooms. I'm not sure which one."

"Neither am I, except it's on Three Deck. They'll have put guards on the company people in the owner's suite on the Bridge Deck. I'd like to know what's going on on the bridge. Any way to communicate without their knowing where we're calling from?"

"I can call from the engine room, or my quarters, but that's not possible now. Neither is the intercom in the crew quarters. We can't get through to them. There's one in the purser's office on Two Deck, but it'll be a risk to reach it."

"Everything's a risk, but we've got to do something. Look. It's six o'clock. Passengers will be getting up, and I'm trying to imagine what they plan to do with them. A hundred people is a lot to control. My best bet would be they'll hold hostages; the captain and first mate on the bridge, probably everyone in the owner's suite. But I'll bet they'll want the passengers where they can keep them all together. What more efficient way than to just let them come down to breakfast, then not let them leave the dining room? Or they might put them all in the lounge. It's the only other room large enough to hold them all in one place. They'll track down the ones who don't come to breakfast and escort them down to join the others. A passenger list won't be hard to come by on the bridge."

"Some of them will be getting up now," Ray said. "There's supposed to be coffee and juice in the lounge before breakfast. If they intend to . . ."

He stopped speaking as the lights came on in the dining room and a band of it fell into the half-light of Soapy's. The clatter of silverware told him he was right about the breakfast plan. No one would set tables that weren't about to be used.

"We've got to get out of here," Alex told McKimmey, "or we'll be just as trapped as the passengers, even if they don't know we're here."

"How?"

"Let's take a look."

Leaving Jessie with Lou, they carefully looked around the edge of the door. Three of the crew members were setting tables. By the door to the galley stood a stranger with another assault rifle cradled in his arms, watching them work.

"Damn. I think we waited too long."

"No, wait."

"What?"

"Just wait a minute or two. I've got an idea I think will work."

They watched, cautiously, and the man with the gun watched, looking bored. He yawned and scratched his head. In a short time, Jensen got a glimmer of what McKimmey was thinking about. The tables were being set in order from the galley across the room toward them.

In a few minutes one of the table setters, the red-haired woman Jensen had spoken to after the first mystery play, came to the corner in which they were concealed, carrying a plastic bin of silverware. She began to set the window table nearest them. From that angle, they could see her, but they couldn't see the man with the gun; that meant he couldn't see them, either.

"Cindy," McKimmey hissed.

She stopped and frowned, then went on with her work.

"Over here."

She was good . . . didn't stop what she was doing again, but turned her head toward where they stood, making it seem a part of her work. She nodded, once, just enough to let them know she had seen who it was.

"Drop that thing when you go back to the galley."

Again she nodded, understanding what he meant. With her back toward the man with the gun, she raised an index finger, *wait*. When she had set the next two tables, and the rest were completed, she picked up the bin, still half full of silverware.

"Get ready," Ray said, and Alex signaled Jessie that they were leaving.

At the door to the galley, Cindy suddenly appeared to trip. With an exclamation, she all but threw the bin toward the metal counter three feet in front of her. It smashed against it, metal hitting metal, knives, forks, and spoons clanking, crashing to the floor. She went to her knees, silverware falling all around her.

"Now," Ray said, as the man with the gun turned his back on the room and took two steps into the doorway to see what was going on. They moved fast around the corner to the right and out the door to the gangway. Racing to the stairs, they leaped up them by twos and threes. As Jensen's eyes passed the level where he could see into the dining room, the gunman was still watching Cindy pick up the silverware from the tiles of the galley floor.

"Made it. Good going, Ray."

"Good going, *Cindy*."

They were now on the level of the lounge, on the starboard side. The stair came out in a rectangular well that insured that the line of the outer stateroom wall was unbroken as it neared the stern. They stopped, standing in front of stateroom 215. Carefully, Jensen leaned out enough to peer along the deck.

Indeed, three passengers were up, dressed, and moving. Two leaned on the rail to look at the massive walls of the Grenville Channel. The other headed for the dining room. But, as Alex watched, a bulky figure came through the door at the end of the gangway, put his hands in his pockets, and continued toward the rear of the ship. It was the other guard from the gold room. Clearly, they were letting the passengers go to breakfast, but they were keeping a watch all the same.

"Damn," he whispered, under his breath.

"What?"

"One of the guards. We can't move without being seen, and he's coming."

"Can we take him?"

"Not without a lot of noise that will attract attention."

Suddenly Alex remembered. No door on the *Spirit* was ever locked. So, he simply opened the door to stateroom 215 and walked in, pulling Ray after him. He leaned against it, listening. The sound of the guard's footsteps passed and continued beyond the door till they could no longer be heard.

The woman in her nightgown who stood facing them stared with her mouth open, but said nothing for a long moment. Then she turned and walked to the door of the bathroom, through which they could hear the sound of a shower running.

"Lawrence," she said.

"Yeah?"

"Lawrence, you have . . . unexpected . . . company."

Safe for the moment, Jensen explained the situation to the Walkers, Darlene and Lawrence, U.S. Army, colonel, retired, after he and McKimmey had introduced themselves. He had noticed this couple—she, petite and pleasant looking, he, outstanding in his erect military posture—but he'd never met them. After the introduction, she retreated to the bathroom with her clothes in hand, but she left the door open enough to hear. Lawrence dressed as he listened with unbroken attention and no interruptions until they had finished telling why they had appeared in his stateroom so abruptly.

"So, you don't know who these men are, but it's pretty clear they're making an attempt to steal the gold we're carrying, and they may be responsible for the murder of that woman who disappeared from the ship?"

"Right. We think so, sir," Jensen agreed.

"What do you intend to do about it?"

"We're working to figure that out. Right now we're trying to reach the intercom to the bridge in the purser's office. If we can talk to Captain Kay, maybe he can somehow give us an idea of what we're up against. They have clearly taken over the bridge, but I doubt they would do more than make him take this ship where they want, which, right now, seems to mean continuing through the channel. Someone on the ship, besides the guards in the gold room and the assistant engineer, is working with these guys and made him slow the *Spirit* to let the others board. They're armed with very nasty weapons and are extremely dangerous."

"That where you got the assault weapon?"

"Yes. Put one of them out of commission in the engine room, but don't know how long till someone finds him. From what we saw, we think they intend to take the passengers hostage at breakfast."

"We won't go down."

"I think you'd better rethink that, sir. If you don't, they'll probably come looking for you. There are very few places to hide, and they're being careful. They'll undoubtedly keep all the passengers in the dining room, or possibly move them to the lounge. They probably have a complete list of the passengers, or we should assume so."

"That's only a possibility, as you say. What's to keep them from some more radical solution? Are they making any attempt to conceal their identities?"

"No, sir, they're not." Alex realized that, in his attempt to establish communication with the bridge, he was thinking with blinders on. Why weren't they covering their faces? He should have wondered about that. He didn't like the idea of the explanations that occurred to him, and suddenly he couldn't decide if he was glad or sorry he had asked Jessie to stay below with Lou.

He glanced at Ray, who was wearing a troubled expression.

"I think we'd better do something careful and quick," the engineer said, slowly. "I don't like the sound of that."

"Agreed. But first, we've got to get you some different clothes. Those coveralls are a dead giveaway."

Walker solved the problem with a pair of jeans and a sweatshirt that McKimmey swiftly changed into, rolling up the cuffs.

"Look," Walker told them, "you need more help. I will go with you, but my wife shouldn't. She can't stay here. Can't see just giving herself up, but . . . Darlene?" He turned to his wife, who had come out of the bathroom and was listening quietly from a seat on the bed.

"Yes, dear."

"You game to go ahead to breakfast without me,

knowing what we know? You might be able to warn some of the people down there, let them know we're working on it."

"It seems the most reasonable thing to do."

Walker turned back to Jensen.

"They will come looking for anyone not in the dining room, you think? Right?"

"Wouldn't you, in their place?"

"You'd better go ahead, Dar."

She picked up a jacket and turned to a box on the dressing table, which she opened and began to empty into her pockets.

"I'm taking my jewelry. No one gets my anniversary presents."

They smiled at each other, she kissed her husband, and went to the door. "Just keep in mind that I've done a lot of waiting while you fought battles. Be careful and don't keep me waiting too long on this one."

She closed the door quietly as she went out.

McKimmey hid the coveralls he had been wearing in the back of the closet.

"They'd better not find these in here."

"Now, we wait for that guard to go by again," Walker said, listening at the door.

In just a few minutes, they heard him pass, and they peered between the curtains to make sure. Slipping out the door, they raced down the side of the ship, through the door, took a quick look to be sure the inside hall was empty, reached the purser's officer, and were inside when he came around again.

31

6:30 A.M.
Thursday, July 17, 1997
Spirit of '98
Grenville Channel, Inside Passage
British Columbia, Canada

THE PURSER'S OFFICE WAS EMPTY AND, FOR ONCE, LOCK-
able. Alex locked it. The intercom with a telephone
handset was on the manager's desk.

Alex collapsed into a chair and looked up at the
other two.

"What are you thinking?" he asked, noticing
McKimmey's squint.

"Well," McKimmey answered, after a short moment of analysis, "I'm thinking my headache's
worse."

"I'm not surprised. You should be resting."

Ray rummaged through the first aid kit and came
up with the painkiller he needed and Jensen stared
at the intercom, trying to plan his call to the bridge.

"Before I do this, I need to know a couple of
things," he told McKimmey. "If I call from here, does
anything on the bridge indicate where the call is
coming from?"

"No. I always have to say it's the engineer, when
I call up from below."

"Where is the call answered?"

"It can be picked up from the forward section of the bridge or from the captain's office, either one."

"Which is used most?"

"The forward."

"Can someone else listen in from the office?"

McKimmey thought for a minute. "I don't know. Possibly, I guess. Never had a reason to find out."

"Give me some reasons the purser might call the captain."

"Well, to begin with, we don't have a purser, even though this is called the purser's office. This position is called the hotel manager. We just say 'the manager.' I know I said purser's office, but that's what it's called on the blueprints I have to look at periodically, and I get 'em mixed sometimes. The manager might call the bridge to ask for our ETA at a specific location . . . or, if a passenger wanted to make a phone call, he might call to ask before sending them up . . . to adjust the schedule on something, meals, bar openings or closings . . . to give the captain some kind of information . . . lots of things."

"I like the passenger phone call idea. If I say I'm the purser, will Captain Kay catch on that I'm not, just from the wrong term? Is the sound good enough so that he could recognize my voice?"

"I think so. He's used to the sound. He knows that our manager would never call himself the purser. I think he'd catch on, especially now, when he might be hoping for something . . . anything."

"Okay."

While Walker and McKimmey watched silently, he took a deep breath, and, picking up the handset, made the call.

"Bridge."

Damn, it was the first mate, he had hoped for the captain.

"This is the purser. Could I speak to the captain, please?"

A hesitation, then he could tell she had risen to the requirement . . . heard her say, "For you, Captain. The purser's office."

He heard a second pick-up, undoubtedly from the office, and a click as the first mate hung up the handset in the forward bridge.

So . . . the captain was in his office, and it *was* possible for someone to listen in, but there would be a telltale sound if anyone picked up the handset. All the same, he would be cautious.

"Captain speaking."

"Captain, this is Purser *Alex* . . . ander, on Three Deck."

"Yes? . . . Oh . . . *Yes!*"

Great. He knew who he was talking to.

"I have a passenger and a crew member here, who wish to know if I can bring them to the bridge to make a call . . . or do you have too much going on up there at the moment?"

"Yes. We do."

"Can you tell me *how many* calls are waiting, and how . . ." he thought hard for a moment, trying to think how to phrase it. But the captain spoke before he got it together, answering his unspoken question with a similarly coded answer.

"We can't call out from the Grenville Channel. Radio black-out zone. We have *a call* waiting till we reach the other end, and must give it priority. Besides, it may take us longer if that *valve* in the engine room gives us any more trouble and we have to go slower."

Ah . . . there was only one of the gang on the bridge, and the captain wanted to let him know that he thought McKimmey had been captured and the engine room was under the control of the intruders.

"The *valve* has been *repaired*, sir. It's operating *freely* now."

"Good. That's good news. We'll proceed more efficiently with it *repaired*."

"Do you know *how many other calls* may be on hold until we reach the end of the channel?"

"*Two* . . . no, *three* . . ." There was a sudden click, as the second handset was lifted on the forward bridge, but no one spoke. ". . . to the best of my knowledge. But, tell your passenger that *all calls* will wait till we are out of the channel."

"Thank you, sir. I will bring them up to see about it later."

He heard the captain disconnect, the second handset go down, and then he hung up himself.

"Your captain's as shrewd as I imagined," he told McKimmey, through a sigh of relief. "Picked right up, like a pro. There's only one of them on the bridge, but, including that one, he's seen or knows of four. Makes sense. They wouldn't all go up to the bridge. They're waiting to do something till we reach the end of the channel, and he's relieved that you—the *valve*—are out of the engine room. He also knows that there are three of us and that we'll try to help them out up there, later."

"Four?"

"Four that he knows about. We know there are more than that, I think."

"Okay." Ray held up fingers as he counted. "One—Carlson in the engine room, two—the guy in the dining room, three and four—the two gold room guards, five—on the bridge . . . I've run out."

"Well, everyone but the last you've identified has been on the ship all along. Then there's whoever came in that powerboat—numbers five and six, or, maybe five, six, and seven. But we haven't counted whoever was on the ship to make the captain slow it to allow them to board. So, seven or eight, at least. And there could be another one, or two."

Colonel Walker spoke for the first time since they had entered the purser's office.

"Only seven or eight of these guys? I thought we had a lot of them to deal with."

"That's quite a number, sir, on a fairly small ship, with assault rifles."

"You could say so, if you were dealing with them all together at once, Sergeant. But examine the situation in terms of a strategic takeover of their forces spread out, and it's a little different."

All at once, Alex felt as if he had suddenly been demoted in rank, and he had to grin. Colonel Walker seemed to be standing even straighter, if that was possible, and his manner had taken a definite shift into a military command mode.

"Yes, sir. What are you thinking?"

"Our timing right now is good. In order to guard the bridge, hold the owner and his family hostage, assure the desired location of the passengers, and collect strays that don't come to the dining room, they will have to extend their resources to the limit— even if we assumed nine or ten of them. If you can't make a concerted assault on the enemy as a single unit, what's the next best solution for neutralizing them, while conserving, even adding to, the strength of your own forces?"

McKimmey, also grinning, was listening carefully, as Walker stepped easily into a role he had obviously excelled at before retirement. The man had plainly not been a paper-pusher, was actually having a good time being actively included with the good guys.

Jensen knew what he was thinking, and it made sense.

"You take them out one by one, sir," he told Walker.

"Absolutely, young man. Now I don't want to take over your job, but I think I can make some suggestions that might help, if you don't mind."

"Colonel Walker, I couldn't mind less. I'm interested in *neutralizing* these guys, the faster, the better. Suggest away."

"Well, we need two things—three, really—but number two will hopefully take care of number three.

First, we need to add support to our side. Second we need to start whittling down the opposition. And third, we need more weapons, but whittling them down one by one will give us theirs, I think."

"I think so too."

"It's early, ten minutes till seven, and half the passengers are always late to breakfast. We've still got a chance to collect a few more recruits. Let's start by waiting till that guard comes around once more, and we'll take him out of operation. Then we can take care of the one there's bound to be on the next deck up."

It was a good and simple plan. They agreed, and waited, Jensen listening with the door slightly cracked. In a very short time, he heard the guard come past and go through the door to the outside gangway, following the same route as before, with no imagination. As soon as he had gone through the door and his back was turned, they followed quickly, quietly, and hit him—McKimmey, around the knees, Jensen, at his waist, and Walker, grabbing his arms to keep him from reaching for the pistol he carried in his pocket. There was no one on deck. He hadn't a chance. A deftly applied piece of duct tape, from a roll found in the purser's office, kept him from crying out.

"Is the ship held together with this stuff?" Walker had asked, when they took it from a storage cabinet.

"Sir," Alex had assured him, "*Alaska* is held together with it. You aren't issued a resident's permit till you can prove you have your own roll of duct tape and know at least fifty ways to use it."

They used it unstintingly to secure the guard they dragged into the purser's office, taping him to a Pullman bunk so tightly that he could neither pound the wall to attract attention nor roll himself off onto the floor. When he was thoroughly taped and couldn't move, they tossed a blanket over him, concealing him from any quick search of the room.

"Certainly hope we remember where we put 'em, as we catch 'em," Ray commented.

"We'll draw a map," Walker told him without cracking a smile. "Now, get your own personal roll of tape and a couple of extra, and we shall take care of the next one."

"First, let's recruit a couple of people," Jensen said. "I want Don Sawyer. I know he's okay. But I don't know which stateroom the centennial committee's in."

"Oh, I do. It's 203, next to the outside door. We were right in front of it."

They were in luck. Sawyer had not yet gone to breakfast. He looked up in surprise when they walked in and he was quickly clued in to what was happening. Jeff Brady, Skagway committee chairman, was also recruited, and finished shaving in record time.

"Damn it all," he swore. "After all the planning we did to make sure everything ran well, all we've had is trouble."

"Okay," Jensen said. "We are five. Do either of you guys have any kind of weapon?"

They did not.

They split up this time, Jensen, Sawyer, and Brady creeping carefully up the interior mid-ship stair, while McKimmey went with Walker to the more exposed exterior one at the stern.

It went almost as smoothly as before, though Jensen and the two with him were almost surprised when an unknown man came around the corner from the outside deck, just as they exited the stairwell. For no particular reason, Alex had expected this watchman to be the second guard from the gold room, and not the complete stranger who appeared. For an instant, he took him for a passenger. Luckily, Walker and McKimmey came around just behind, to tackle him efficiently and quietly.

Taped and silenced, they secreted him in the con-

venient linen storage room, taping him securely to a
shelf they cleared of clean sheets. When he was as
stationary as the guard a deck below, they replaced
as many sheets as possible on the outer edge of the
wide shelf, effectively building a wall of linen between him and anyone looking for him.

By now, most of the passengers had gone to breakfast, but, leaving his recruits to wait in the linen storage, Jensen went cautiously around to the forward
staterooms to check on the Berrys, and Dallas and
Rozie. The Berrys' stateroom was empty, but he
found the two women about to leave for the dining
room, and he explained briefly what was going on.

"I'd like to get you both down with Jessie and Lou,
but there's no way to get you past the guard in the
dining room now," he told her with regret.

"Don't give it a second thought, Alex. Figured out
a long time ago that, if you want to get anywhere in
this life, you'd better learn to saddle your own horse,
and to take however many tumbleweeds the wind
blows in. I'll take my chances whatever they are. But,
if I have to go down there, Rozie doesn't."

"What do you take me for?" Rozie's look was
grim. "You think I'd leave you to go alone? Besides,
everyone's seen me with you. They'd know in a minute I was missing. We'll go down together, as if nothing was wrong."

It was clear that she meant every word, and that
time arguing would be time wasted, so they left it.

"What can we do to help from the dining room,
Alex?" Dallas asked.

"I'm not sure, because I don't know exactly what
the situation is down there now," he told her. "There
was just one guard, when we made our escape from
Four Deck, but that might have changed. There's a
red-haired crew woman, one of the waitresses, that
helped McKimmey, the engineer, and me get out of
there earlier. She's okay. Just keep your wits about
you, and remember, if it starts to go bad, to put

something solid between yourselves and any guns. Assault rifles are nothing to take chances with. Sit as far to the rear as you can. Those beautiful, old-fashioned, wood-paneled walls are solid metal fireproofing underneath and as good as anything down there for protection, if you can get into Soapy's Parlour. We left Jessie there with Lou, behind the bar. If it's really necessary, try for a trap door in the room next to it. It leads to the steerage compartment."

He had leaned forward to place a hand on the arm of her wheelchair, as he earnestly tried to give her all the advice he could. As he finished, she laid her hand, with the large blue sapphire on her arthritic finger, on his and patted it gently.

"Thank you, Alex. That's a lot more than we'll need, I'm sure. Give me that cane, please, it might come in handy. Let's be off, Rozetta, dear, before someone horrid comes ahunting."

Head high, she allowed her niece to push her wheelchair around the deck to the elevator. Just as the doors closed, she gave Alex a dignified nod and a wicked wink. Then he thought he heard *"Yahoo!"* in a Texas accent echo back up the elevator shaft.

32

7:30 A.M.
Thursday, July 17, 1997
Spirit of '98
Grenville Channel, Inside Passage
British Columbia, Canada

ONE BY ONE, THEY HAD BEGUN TO NEUTRALIZE THE BAD guys, though Jensen knew it would become more difficult as they moved closer to the center of the operation. After the first two, they added one more passenger to their group of five—Vern Repasky, the tall, bald doctor with fuzzy, gray eyebrows.

He came around a corner in a hurry, late to breakfast, and ran full tilt into the center of the small group before anyone could move. Walker and McKimmey instinctively grabbed him and were attempting to wrestle him to the ground, when Jensen hissed, "Stop! I think he's one of ours."

Apologies given and accepted, Repasky volunteered as soon as he realized the reason for their defensive reaction.

"We can't stand here," Walker warned. "The next one around that corner could be one of theirs."

They went back down to the purser's office, where they could lock the door and hold another war council. Somewhere in Jensen's mind the voice of his training and conscience reminded him, once or twice, that he should never include or endanger a civilian in a police action. But there was very little he could do about it. What other way was there? A hundred passengers were a large consideration and changed the equation he tried to work by.

"It seems they're in some kind of holding pattern," Walker analyzed. "None of them have come to see why the guards for these two decks have disappeared, and the dining room must be just about full by now. They really must not have anything planned until we get to the end of this channel. How long is it, Jensen?"

"Forty-five miles."

"And how far do you suppose we've gone now?"

"Ray?"

"I don't know exactly when we went in, but we were already going through when it got light, so we must be somewhere around halfway." He shrugged. "Sorry."

"That's good enough. Can we figure out where the rest of these guys may be? We've got two on ice, or, I should say, in duct tape. Let's count, say, seven more, just to be safe."

Alex used his fingers again to count. "One on the bridge."

"Hard to reach at this time."

"The owner's suite."

"Same."

"The dining room."

"I'll bet with all the passengers there and not wanting to let them out, they'll have at least two there by now. What do you think?"

"I agree. So, two in the dining room."

"Getting them's not a good idea unless we can figure out a distraction, or some other way of splitting them up, so we don't get anyone killed."

"One . . . well, I'd think they'd put someone to guard the gold."

"Why? Nobody could steal it from them, or hide it without being seen."

"True. But I think someone will at the very least look in on it."

"So. That's five. We might be able to take that last one, if we're careful."

"Pretty close to the dining room," Brady commented. "And those two we're counting on to be there. We could be wrong, you know."

"There may be someone still on the powerboat."

"We'd better check on Carlson," McKimmey reminded him. "If he's still there, we can count three out of commission. That's actually nine sort of accounted for. But Jeff's right. Two or three of those may not, probably will not, be where we think they should be."

"I think we should make a try at the . . ."

The doorknob rattled suddenly, startling them all. Then there was a gentle two-knuckled rap at the door, and a soft voice called, "Alex? Are you in there?"

"It's Jessie, let her in, quick."

Walker took Jensen at his word and opened the door.

Inside, she leaned back against it, face pale, hair tousled, the tail of her white shirt pulled out of her jeans, a blue apron tied around her waist. In one hand she held a serving tray.

"What in the world have you been up to?" Jensen asked, stepping forward to hold her shoulders in his big hands, guiding her into the chair he had vacated. "Where's Lou?"

She sat down with a sigh.

"Still down behind the bar. I had to take the chance I could come and find you, Alex. There's another man with a gun in the dining room now. The two of them came back into Soapy's, lit cigarettes, and stood next to the bar talking. I heard every word, and . . . Alex . . . there's a bomb on this boat somewhere."

Everyone in the room stopped moving, and it was dead still for a second or two.

"A bomb? You did say *bomb*, right?"

She nodded, and there was fear in her eyes. "From what they said, they're going to steal the gold, take off in the boat, then, with all of us here, on board, a bomb will go off and sink the ship."

"God. When?"

"I don't know. Just sometime soon after they go away from the ship."

"How did you manage to get out of the dining room?" McKimmey asked.

"After those two men went back to the front of the room, I saw Dallas and Rozie come in and sit at the table next to the Parlour door, so I told Lou where I was going, crawled out, and got under it. When the guards weren't looking, I got up and sat in one of the chairs, like I'd been there all the time."

She looked suddenly at Alex.

"Oh, and while I think about it . . . John Stanley was sitting at a table near the center of the room. They caught him when he went down . . . when Lou couldn't find him . . . I think, because they brought him in and made him sit. I got a chance to signal him that Lou was okay.

"Anyway, Cindy was serving our table, so I whispered to her that I *had* to get out of there and find you. She thought you might be here, or come back here, where the phone is, and brought me an extra apron from the galley. I put it on and took off my sweater. When she moved to another table, she left me the tray. I just stood up and started working at our table, then I followed her back to the galley and walked right on through to the hallway beyond it. No one stopped me, so I came on up the stairs, and past the lounge to here. Thank God you're here. And you've got help."

"A bomb," Repasky muttered, drawing their attention back to the situation at hand.

"Bastards!" Sawyer said aloud, slamming his fist into a filing cabinet.

"They didn't say where it was, or even hint, did they, Jess?"

"No, Alex. Not a word."

"And they didn't say what kind of bomb, or how it will be detonated?"

"No. Sorry."

Brady spoke up. "It seems like there'd be two options. They could leave it with a timing device, or set it off from a remote control of some kind from their boat."

Jensen nodded. "It's the first kind that worries me. They're not going to leave it sitting right out in plain sight. They'll hide it, or already have hidden it, somewhere. We're going to have to find it, unless we can get them before they set it up, if they haven't already done that. Otherwise, it'll be a race to see if we can locate it before it blows."

"It would have to be in the hold somewhere." McKimmey frowned as he considered something that might damage his ship and its engines. "To sink this ship, it would have to blow a hole below the waterline."

"You're right," Alex agreed. "But we can't look for it until we either get these lunatics taken care of, or they leave. I'd rather it was before we're left alone with some explosive device."

"Well," Walker spoke up for the first time in this discussion, "whatever happens, we'll either sink, or not. Let's take things one at a time. Right now, let's concentrate on our goal of catching a few more of them. What else can we do?"

He was right. They could all see that.

"Can you tell us anything else about who's down there?" Alex asked Jessie.

"Not much. The two that I heard talking mentioned a couple of names. Walt and Nelson."

Walt. Walt? Why did that name ring bells, Jensen wondered. Somewhere in the last couple of days he'd run into that name before. Yesterday! It was yesterday, in the Ketchikan paper . . . the article about the stolen powerboat, stolen and burned sailboat, and the woman they had found dead in Tracy Arm. So it might be part of this after all. And he'd thought it had nothing to do with them.

Damn. What a tangle, and how little sense it made. Maybe it wasn't the same Walt.

"What, or who, shall we go after next?" Brady asked.

"The owner's suite, I think," Jensen answered. "They seem to be spread out pretty thin. I can't imagine they'd put more than one man in there. We should be able to take him, if we can just get in fast enough."

"How do we do that?"

Alex gave Jessie a speculative look.

"How're you feeling, Jess?"

"I'm okay. Why? You want me to do something, right?"

"Yes. You looked enough like crew to fool them in the dining room. Would you give it another try?"

"In the suite, you mean?"

He nodded. "You could knock and ask if they want breakfast. Say you're there to take orders. When they open the door, we're in."

She thought about it, but only for a minute. "Sure. I can do that."

"Okay. Take the tray and hold it in front of you. Whoever's in there with them will have a gun."

He turned to the others. "It can't be all of us. Two, three at the most."

"Agreed," said Walker. "More, and we get in each other's way. Have to get through that door. Let's do it military, like we were trained, Alex."

"How'd you know . . . ?"

"Never miss an ex-Marine. Might as well carry a sign that says, Semper Fi . . ."

"Okay. You outline what you're thinking."

"Three of us go; you, me, and Repasky, all military. Vietnam, Repasky?"

The others glanced at Vern, who grinned and rubbed his bald head. "Don't I wish. Korea."

"Right. Can you operate that thing McKimmey's clutching?"

"AK-47? Sure."

Ray handed it over with no reluctance at all.

"I have a pistol we took from one of those guys we put away. You've got your own, Jensen?"

Alex nodded.

"Ray, you take the other guard's pistol. A pistol you can handle, right? You three can back us up, follow a little behind."

"Okay."

"Everybody ready? Let's go."

"Lawrence." Jensen stopped him. "It would be a good idea to have Jessie come along to get us in."

"Oh, right. You're right. Sorry. And we'll be right behind?"

"Exactly, guns and tape in hand. But the most important thing is that we do not want a shot fired, at any cost. Another of these guys on the bridge could hear it and cause problems. The bridge can contact the rest of the ship, and we certainly don't want them all coming to pin us down in the suite, do we? We need to be quick, and quiet, and cause no commotion or sound to attract attention. Got it?"

"Right." They all nodded.

"Counting this one, four of their guys, almost half, will have disappeared and the rest won't know where," Sawyer observed.

"That's right," Jensen told him. "When we get this done, I think there'll be at least three more of us than there will be of them. We're getting someplace now."

*   *   *

It worked almost the way they wanted it to, with one slight hitch. The man who opened the door was not the gunman they had expected, but Dick West, the company CEO. Behind him in the room, in a chair, with another assault rifle trained on Dick's father, was the gunman. As West realized there was more to the visit than a breakfast order, he moved to the side, giving them access to the suite but at the same time allowing the man with the rifle a clear view not only of Jessie, who was still standing just inside the door, but also of Jensen and Walker, who were on their way in from either side of her. He began to move his weapon in their direction, but just before Jensen was about to shoot him, the gun suddenly flew out of his hand and landed on the floor.

Jessie, almost without thought, had swung the tray she carried like a Frisbee, flinging it in a dead-on shot that she would probably never be able to duplicate. It had flown across the room and connected solidly with his wrist, causing him to drop the rifle with a howl of hurt.

Unfortunately, the tray did not stop there. As it hit him, the guard was already swinging his other arm to meet it. He backhanded it away from him with all his might. It sailed back again, missing Jensen by an inch, straight into the face of Repasky, coming fast in the door behind him. The sound, as it made hard contact with his left eyebrow, was an empty metallic *bonk*, but it stopped him only momentarily. With Sawyer and Brady, Jensen had the tray-batter surrounded before the man could recover sufficiently to pick up his rifle.

When they had him stopped, Repasky, for the first time, noticed the blood running down his face. He swiped at it ineffectively, as Jessie steered him toward the bathroom to clean it and use some adhesive tape to temporarily close the wound.

"Bastards, took over our boat," Thorn commented on *his* first priority. "And they're also after the gold."

While Walker and Sawyer taped up their fourth prisoner, and Repasky put some ice on his rapidly swelling eye, Jensen related to the company men all that he knew about the situation, including the explosives that were somewhere on the ship.

Dick West and Gordon Thorn immediately joined the group that was taking back the *Spirit of '98*.

The game was eight to five, and, for the first time, they had the upper hand.

33

8:15 A.M.
Thursday, July 17, 1997
Spirit of '98
Grenville Channel, Inside Passage
British Columbia, Canada

THIS TIME, BEFORE GAGGING THE CRIMINAL THEY HAD CAP-
tured, they questioned him.

"We still don't know who is the leader of this
whole thing," Jensen reminded them. "I'd like to
know just who we're dealing with."

"You're in a world of hurt, here," he told the prisoner mildly. "It would be to your advantage if we
knew just what was going on, and who's in charge
of it. Whoever he is, he's in better shape than you
are. We're going to tuck you away somewhere, the
way we've hidden three others. And if we don't stop
this, no one may ever look for you. We know about
the bomb you've planted somewhere on this ship. If
it blows, you go with it, just like we do."

The man stared at Alex, a troubled frown wrin-
kling his brow.

"They wouldn't go off and leave us."

"No? You think they can get the gold on that boat
you came in? To say nothing of the rest of your
bunch? The gold alone would sink it—forget the rest
of you. They're going to take part of it and split."

"And you're just going to *leave* me tied up someplace?"

"Yes. We haven't enough help to watch you, so we'll have to make sure you can't help them."

"And, if I tell you what you want to know, you'll let me go?"

"I didn't say that. But as soon as we can stop what's going on here, we'll put you and all the others together in one place and keep a guard on you until we can turn you over to the proper authorities. You won't be left alone in a small space somewhere with a bomb ticking."

The man's face plainly showed his growing discouragement and fear.

"Damn it," he finally burst out. "I never wanted to come to Canada at all, did I? Didn't have much choice, did I?"

Alex waited.

" 'Just come to Ketchikan,' they said. 'Steal a boat and bring it to Ketchikan.' "

"They?"

"Well . . . *he*?"

"Who?"

"That's it. I don't know. Never saw him—only talked to him on the telephone. Walt's the only one I ever saw until we got to Elliot Island."

"Walt Burns?"

"Don't know his last name."

"What's your name?"

"Rod . . . Ledlow."

Jensen *had* to ask . . . had to know. "The sailboat? The *Hazlit's Gull?*"

"Yeah. We took it."

"Who took it?"

"Me, I took it, with Nelson. He told me to steal a boat, so I did."

This man, without question, had something to do with the dead woman in Tracy Arm . . . or knew how she had died. Jensen could feel his heart rate increase, but it was a delicate. matter that could wait; they had no time to dig out the details. Now, they needed to know how to derail the rest of the plot, and the gang attempting it, before it went bad and people got hurt.

"Okay. Now, if you can't help me find who's in charge, then tell me how many of you are left, and where they are on this ship."

"I didn't say I didn't know *where* he is. I just don't know his name, or what he looks like. I never saw him."

"Where, then?"

"On the bridge. Making sure everything runs right, while we do the rest, down on the deck with the dining room."

"And how many more?"

"You got me and three others?"

Jensen nodded.

"Then, counting the boss on the bridge, there's four more, and somebody on the ship that helped. My partner Nelson's in that room with the gold. He's scared and he's drunk. Don't hurt him, okay?"

"Will he give up without a problem?"

"Yeah. Probably wet himself when you show up, if he's not sleeping it off."

"The others in the dining room, right? Do they all have assault weapons?"

"Yeah—the boss, and two in the dining room."

Ledlow was the picture of absolute discouragement. Jensen thought there was very little chance of him causing trouble. So they put a piece of tape over his mouth and left him. Chuck West and his wife would be here to make sure he didn't escape, but Alex knew he wouldn't even try.

Taking the bridge was harder than anything they had done so far, but they did it next.

"We really can't go down four decks and leave the mastermind of all this controlling the bridge. Besides, once we have him, the rest will be easier. Then we can track down that damn bomb."

A bomb. The nasty reality set in again. It all made sense. No wonder they hadn't bothered to cover their faces. They meant everyone on board to drown in the icy water, where it would take only minutes. They never meant to shoot anyone, unless they were forced. Assault rifles are seriously threatening, but their purpose here seemed to be just that—threat. Jensen felt a decided chill, wondering exactly where the box that carried explosives of some kind could be located, and what it held. Most appropriate would be a bomb already rigged.

The one comfort was that it probably would not be a bomb with a timer. They would need to control its detonation—be sure they and however much gold they meant to take were off the ship, out of range. It would be a radio-controlled explosion of some kind.

And they meant to leave most of their help, and a large part of the gold, to go to the bottom of the inlet. The latest prisoner had said, in a voice that was very small and scared, "Please, don't leave me here to die."

Alex realized, suddenly, just how angry he was becoming.

"There's almost a hundred people in jeopardy down in the dining room, and I'm more concerned about them than anything else, just now. That damn bomb has got to be found."

He looked around at the group of people who were staring at him, mute with anxiety. Even Walker was no longer having a good time. Nevertheless, he straightened his spine and stepped forward.

"Well, from the sound of it, we've got a rough patch ahead. What do you recommend, Sergeant?"

Jensen sat down at the table with a worried sigh and said nothing for a minute, thinking.

"Forty-five miles. It can't be far until we exit the Grenville Channel," he said finally. "So, it stands to reason, we don't have too much time. We'd better get busy and take back the bridge."

He looked slowly around at his somewhat battered band of recruits; Walker, zealous but past his prime; Repasky with his forehead bandaged; stitches in McKimmey's chin and the lump on the back of his head; Brady, Thorn, and West, who were anything but used to fighting for their lives; and Sawyer, who knew how to escape, perhaps, but had not stayed to confront the enemy. And down on Four Deck were almost a hundred innocent people, many retired, who had no idea what was being proposed as their fate. Alex and this small group of willing souls was all that stood between them and a watery death. It was that simple . . . and discouraging. He wished desperately for the assistance of five or six of the best cops he knew—or the worst, for that matter.

Jessie looked sick. How could anyone have anticipated that something like petty theft could turn this serious, or deadly?

Jensen's temper rose with the lump in his throat that he knew was concern—no, fear—for a lot of people, including Jessie and himself. And, he recalled, he had told Dallas and Rozetta to go to the hold, if things went bad. If things went bad it was the worst place they could be. Okay, enough of that. He let the anger take over again.

"It makes me furious," he said aloud, feeling the need for venting as much as the others needed a pep talk to get them going. "They can't *do this* to us, damn it. A bunch of cowardly, Goddamned *pirates.* And, if we don't make it, I hope their souls rot in hell.

"Now. So much for being angry—we can't afford it, or being afraid. There's a lot to be done. We've caught four of them, with not a shot fired. The only two hurt are Repasky and McKimmey. Both minor injuries. Explaining that you were hit with a flying tray will be interesting, Doctor."

The doctor grinned.

The group was looking a little more enthusiastic. Alex went on:

"We can't let this finish us. There's more of us now than there is of them. We have to get the one on the bridge. Here's what I suggest, but I want all of you to think and make suggestions. We can't afford to miss on this one, can we?"

He outlined what he had in mind. There were a couple of comments, and then they all knew what their parts were.

"Jessie, what do you want to do? Wait here?"

She looked at him for a second as if he had lost his mind. Her expression changed as she realized he was asking, not telling, not trying to protect her. Then she smiled a little and nodded. "You're learning, trooper. I know. I'm not going to do you any good taking over the bridge, or taking care of the two or three left on the dining room deck. So, I'd really like to be back down there with Lou, and Dallas, and Rozie. Maybe I could make it back down, if I went the back way and was very careful."

"You might. You might also run into one of them."

"I could wait for an opportunity to get in the back door. I still look like one of the crew."

"You could. It's risky. Are you sure you want to?"

"Yes, I think so."

"Take this?" He held out one of the handguns they had taken from the men they had captured. "Please?"

She had started to shake her head, but she looked at him, frowned slightly and tucked it in the pocket of the blue apron she still wore. She knew how to use it. Carried one when she drove her dog teams, in case of moose.

He nodded. She laid a hand on his wrist before she slipped out the door, alone.

He turned back to the watching group.

"Gutsy lady," McKimmey commented.

"Yeah. Well . . . here's the deal. It's to our advantage that there's an entrance to the bridge from either side. But we need to create the distraction from one, while going in the other. Ideas?"

"How about just banging on the door," Sawyer suggested. "They'll all be looking in that direction, wondering what's causing the noise."

It was simple, safe, and would probably do the trick. They agreed that Don and Ray should do just that.

"We must not let this guy get hold of either the captain or the first mate as hostages, so it'll have to be quick. Don't shoot unless it's absolutely necessary. It's a wide bridge, but a pretty small space for flying bullets. Everyone ready? Let's do it."

34

9:00 A.M.
Thursday, July 17, 1997
Spirit of '98
Grenville Channel, Inside Passage
British Columbia, Canada

THEY WENT OUT THE DOOR OF THE OWNER'S SUITE BEHIND
Jensen. The towering cliffs loomed ominously over
the *Spirit,* if anything, higher than when he had seen
them at the northern end of the Grenville Channel.
It had grown darker and, looking up, he could see
that dense clouds threatened rain.

So far they had been successful. Could they be
lucky one more time? A lot of people's lives de-
pended on it, but hesitation would gain them nothing. He glanced at McKimmey, who grinned
humorlessly back, waiting for his direction. He nodded. *Go!*

The group of liberators split—Sawyer and McKimmey one way, the rest the other—creeping like com-
mandos, as quietly as possible, past the owner's suite
and up the stairs that led to the doors on both sides
of the bridge. When the larger group heard Sawyer
begin to pound on the opposite side, Jensen led the
rush through the door and onto the bridge itself. The
surprise was total and effective, and they used it to
their advantage, but it was not without resistance.

In the noise and confusion of the harried first few seconds, they were up against a very stubborn and tenacious garden-variety street-fighter, who fractured Sawyer's arm with a particularly vicious blow with the wooden butt of the AK-47 he held onto like death, and kicked Alex so hard in the shin that he was still favoring it a week later.

Walker finally hit him with the butt of the pistol he was carrying, just enough to stun him. McKimmey and Brady once again used the tape quickly and effectively, before he could shake off the effects of the thump on the head and turn to fighting them again.

When it was over, Repasky looked at Don's white face and the way he was holding his forearm, and went to see what he could do to help.

Captain Kay smiled and nodded at Jensen, who was holding his injured shin and gritting his teeth. "Took you long enough," he said.

"You both okay?" Alex asked.

He was assured of their continued good health and gratitude.

But it was the identity of their captive that startled them all.

Bill Prentice slowly regained his senses on the floor of the bridge, where they had laid him down, confined and no longer a threat.

And, near the door to the captain's office, sitting on a chair borrowed from within it, was Judy Raymond, though she did not move—just watched with narrowed eyes and a cynical half-smile.

Alex raised a questioning eyebrow at the captain. "She part of it, too?"

"Not to start with. She followed him up here, and he made her stay. But, when she knew what was up, what they were after, she definitely wanted to be in on it. Lot of money—big temptation. He was having none of her. Wouldn't hurt to make sure she's not going anywhere, I think, till we get it straightened out. You can decide."

McKimmey took care of her with a couple of strips of duct tape, though she spit like a cat and glared in fury.

"What about the passengers?" the captain asked. "Are they okay?"

"We haven't gone down yet," Alex told him. "Thought we should take care of the operating part of the ship, and the boss of this business, first. We need to go down now and get the last three of these bastards as soon as possible. I'm sure the passengers are sick of being there, as is most of your crew, who were probably forced to join them. We haven't seen any."

He walked across to Prentice, who was sitting up, glowering.

"Where's that locked box Walt brought on board, Prentice? We know it's there, somewhere. You might as well tell us where, because we'll find it, and, if we don't, you may wish we had."

Prentice just stared at him and said nothing, as Carlson had.

Quietly, Dick West had been telling the captain what they had learned about the suspected plot to sink the ship. His reaction was as close to temper as Jensen had ever seen in him. He walked across to look down at Prentice. He said nothing at all, but gave the man such a look of contempt and anger that, after one glance, the man on the floor turned his head away.

"We'd better get the Canadian authorities out here," Jensen said. "I know you'd like this bunch off the ship as soon as possible, and so would I."

"We'll be at the end of the channel soon, and able to radio again. But I'm going down with you to the dining room. We'll take that *thing* with us, shall we? When his thugs see that we have him, and they know you've caught the rest, maybe they'll give up. Where are the others, by the way?"

McKimmey told him, and, for the first time, he

laughed. "Not bad. I want to hear everything, but first let's get the job done. I do want these . . . *people* . . . off my ship, and we'll find that box and its explosives, wherever they've put it."

They left Sawyer with Chuck West and his wife. Thorn and Brady, with one of the pistols, stayed on the bridge with the first mate, to guard Raymond and Ledlow, whom they double-taped before leaving. But they released Prentice's legs so he could walk, and, mouth still taped, took him along, as the rest—Jensen, the captain, McKimmey, Repasky, Dick West, and Walker—headed down the three flights of stairs to the dining room level. Deciding against splitting up, they went together, West and Walker last, with Prentice between them.

Walker suggested the elevator, but Alex refused. "I don't want one of them there when the door opens so he can make a trap of what is, effectively, a metal box."

When they reached the last flight, Alex had them wait at the top, while he crept silently down and looked cautiously into the corridor outside the galley. While he looked, McKimmey slipped down behind him and disappeared through the door to the engine room. In only a minute he was back, nodding. Carlson was still there, secured to the sewage pump. None of the conspirators had known he'd been taken, or they hadn't found him, if they'd looked.

The corridor was empty, except for a crewman sitting on the floor beside the partially open sliding door, watching the powerboat. He was startled to see someone besides members of the gang, but he nodded, at Jensen's gesture, to keep still. Waving the others down the stairs, he led them into the corridor and toward the galley door. It remained empty.

With one swift look through the galley, in the doorway to the dining room, Jensen could see the back of one of the gunmen guarding the passengers.

They were still seated at the tables. Stepping back, Jensen gestured to West and Walker to bring Prentice forward, then pushed him to stand in front of them at the doorway.

Shoving him ahead of them, they entered the galley through a small hall with the door to a storage closet and an ice machine. They'd almost reached the guard when he heard them and turned halfway around. The assault rifle he was holding was immediately trained in their direction, and he took a step backward.

Jensen shoved at Prentice, who reluctantly shook his head at the man. Realizing who they held prisoner, the guard's eyes widened, and his expression turned hesitant.

"Step in here and put the gun down," Alex told him. "We have all but you two in custody on the upper decks. We're armed, and you really don't want to try anything. Put it down, right here on this counter." He indicated the section beside the escape hatch he and McKimmey had successfully used, what seemed a long time ago.

The man's resolve wavered. He looked questioningly at Prentice, who glared at him. Then he walked forward and, as told, laid the weapon on the countertop.

McKimmey, with his roll of tape much diminished, was on him in a second, pulling him back farther into the galley, where Repasky could hold a pistol on him, while the tape went on.

Jensen was surprised to see that Walker was missing and that only five of them had come into the galley. Where the heck was he? But he didn't have time now to find out. He was about to move the group into the dining room when a new voice, a woman's voice, startled them all.

"I don't really think that's necessary. Leave him alone. Step back and lay your guns on the floor, please."

McKimmey had managed to tape the guard's arms, and was just starting on his legs. He stood up and, with the rest, turned to investigate this new challenge.

The assistant chef stood in the food preparation corridor of the galley, facing them, the assault rifle the guard had laid down on the counter in her hands, calmly trained on them.

"Carla?" Jensen said.

"Yes, Carla. You never guessed, did you? But why would you. Dumb. Now, put the guns down."

Unwillingly, they complied.

"Just what do you think you're going to do alone, Carla?" Captain Kay asked.

She gave him an angry look.

"Exactly what I was going to do all along. Leave, with the one box of gold I have already had put into that boat out there. I've got it coming. I worked three years on this tub, only to have you hire an outside chef, after I asked for the job. You're about to get what's coming to you. You've earned it."

Prentice jerked around to glare at her.

"You really thought I would take you?" she half-spit at him.

It fell into the equation and made so much sense, as Jensen thought about it. Who else had an excuse to rise early—to get breakfast going? Who could move around the ship without being questioned? Who better to open the outside door immediately next to the galley and let them in? Alex had all but forgotten there was supposed to be a person on board who helped—had assumed it was Prentice—a bad error in judgment.

She had fooled them all, even Jessie, with her crocodile tears over Julie Morrison. Something hot began to burn in his stomach. She had covered her tracks by going to the captain with the tale of her missing roommate, then hunted with the rest of them, all the time knowing the woman had been dead for hours.

The hotness intensified. He glanced at McKimmey, found that the look on the engineer's face expressed a similar loathing, and knew that he was remembering the same fruitless search and Carla's fake reaction to it.

She spoke again to Prentice, bound and gagged. "I should never have picked you to depend on, that's obvious. Well, so much for that. I'll leave you with the others when I go. Good riddance, you dummy."

Prentice's face turned red, then pale. He shook his head, trying without speech to communicate with her.

"Forget it. Shouldn't have got caught, with the rest of the incompetents. I warned you."

Prentice was *not* the boss. Carla had, somehow, organized and planned the heist—somehow conned him into helping. Conned, hell. He had, beyond a doubt, fallen in willingly, disguised himself as a passenger, and helped take over the ship. But, Carla was the Boss. Damn. And damn, again.

"Move. All of you. Into the dining room, and bring them with you." She motioned at Prentice and the guard they had neutralized. "We'll take the tape off the guard, in there, where we can watch the passengers. Keep them still, just like they've been for the last couple of hours. Move."

Slowly, they did, leaving their weapons on the floor where they had been standing. As they passed, moving toward the dining room door, she came out from between the cabinets and counters, to follow them from the galley. For an instant, Jensen glanced back.

Walker and the crewman who had been watching the powerboat were silently closing in on her from behind. To keep her from hearing any accidental sound, he began to say whatever came into his head . . . anything would do.

"You can't really expect to get away with this, can you, Carla? We've got all your men but these two.

You'll never find where we've stashed them. It'll be . . ."

"Ugh!"

Then, without warning, the assault rifle went off, and two bullets were flying somewhere in the room.

Jensen counted them—one—two—as he threw himself to the floor, pulling Repasky, the only one he could reach, down with him. They both rolled behind the counter they had just passed. He knew there were a lot more bullets in that gun, up to twenty-eight more, if it had been fully loaded.

Everything went crazy with the sound of people in motion, and Alex registered a scream from the dining room. He lay without moving for a second, then turned his head to look at Repasky, who looked back in shock.

Then it grew very still in the galley.

35

"It's okay. We've got her. Anybody hurt? She hit anybody?"

Walker's voice brought them up and off the floor, checking carefully to see if anyone had been shot. Miraculously, no one had. Both bullets had gone into the ceiling, as Walker had reached one long arm over Carla's shoulder to lift away the gun she held on the others.

"Pretty big risk," Jensen told him, reclaiming his .45 as they bound her along with the other two.

"Didn't have much planning time. If she'd got you into the dining room, it would have complicated things considerably."

The dining room, Alex thought. There was still one man with a gun in the dining room. Why hadn't he appeared by now?

Stepping to the door, he carefully looked in.

The passengers were on their feet. Moving—surging away from the galley door—but he could see no sign of the other guard. He thought briefly of the

313

steerage compartment, or of being forced to search
the rest of the ship for this one man.

"It's okay, Jensen. They've got him," Bill Berry
called from the middle of the room, where he was
holding Nella's hand. "He's over there."

Alex crossed the room, almost at a run, followed
closely by Walker and McKimmey.

"We're safe."

"There's the captain."

"It's okay now."

Jensen caught scraps of comments as he moved to
the farthest table, next to Soapy's Parlour, where a
crowd had gathered in a ragged circle. It opened to
let him through.

A most incongruous sight met his eyes. Dallas
Blake sat calmly in her wheelchair, every hair in
place, the picture of an aging southern lady, except
for the eager sparkle in her eyes, self-satisfied smile
on her mouth, and assault rifle in her lap.

"Hey," she greeted him. "We got ours. You get
the rest tied up?"

On the floor beside her, the last gang member lay,
plainly unconscious. Jessie and Rozie stood behind
Dallas's chair.

Lou Stanley was taking pictures of the whole scene
with Jessie's camera and the wide-angle lens.

"You made it back."

"Yes, thanks once again to Cindy, who distracted
this one with questions." She looked down at the unconscious man. "We didn't hurt him—really. When
that gun went off, he started for the galley, so Dallas
casually reached out with her cane and tripped him.
He hit his head on the edge of the table as he fell."

Behind Alex, Lawrence Walker began to chuckle.
McKimmey joined in. Then, suddenly, they were all
laughing, with relief as much as anything else. Repasky, who caught up in time to view the entertaining
scene, laughed so hard he had to sit down and wipe
his eyes.

* * *

"Where were you?" Jensen asked Walker, when it was all over.

"Went down to check on that old man. Didn't want him coming up from behind to give us problems."

The old man, Nelson, had slept through it all in the gold room. They found him on one of the beds, the box, with what was a remote-controlled bomb, as they had guessed, beside him on the floor. When they woke him, all he would say was, "I knew it. I told 'em so. I just knew it." Then he threw up.

Mrs. Walker came out of the crowd to join her husband, with her anniversary jewelry still in her pockets.

"Lawrence," she said. "It took a little longer than I expected. Are you all right?"

Her husband seemed almost sorry it was all over, but he kissed her and settled down to tell her all about it.

Repasky took a couple of stitches in his own eyebrow, set Sawyer's arm, and doled out pain pills from his bag to make them both comfortable. He also had another look at McKimmey's head, which he said was hard and healing well.

They rounded up the gang of nine: one each from the engine room, the purser's office, the linen storage room, and the bridge, Prentice, the two dining room guards, Carla, Nelson, and tossed Judy Raymond in for good measure to make an even ten. For two hours, they waited at the south end of the Grenville Channel, until the Canadian police showed up in a swift-moving boat and a floatplane. The police took all ten aboard, to remove to Prince Rupert, where they would initiate legal proceedings. They also took a lot of names, for a lot of people had been involved. With the crimes having been committed in Canadian waters, the whole affair would wind up in Canadian courts. The police also took custody of the bomb and the powerboat, though it would eventually be returned to its owner in Ketchikan.

While they waited for all this to be over, the passengers had an early lunch and watched a crowd of sea otters in the water at ten o'clock off the port bow. A few went back to bed. Some had never been up; Wayne Johnson had not been seen since the breakfast after his drunken display of temper in the lounge, and he would not be seen again. He and Edith would slip off, quietly, upon reaching Seattle, after most of the others had left the ship.

Cindy filled in for the absent assistant chef. "It's a job I've been angling for anyway."

After lunch, the captain talked briefly to those who had been held in the dining room, and answered their questions diplomatically. The Wests and Gordon Thorn came down from the owner's suite to join them, and their willingness to socialize clearly helped unfrazzle many nerves.

The group of rescuers had all agreed not to mention the bomb.

"Seems like adding insult to injury to tell them they might have been blown to bits or drowned," Dick West commented. "Let them settle down and enjoy the rest of the trip. They've earned it."

Jensen agreed, as did Jessie.

"Why didn't you stay in the owner's suite?" he asked her.

"Well," she answered. "I really wanted to check on Lou and her claustrophobia. Behind the bar in Soapy's Parlour was better, but still a pretty small place to spend so much time . . ."

"Any pretzels left?"

"Not a one."

Long after it was over, Jensen would find out that Judy Raymond had indeed stolen the gold nugget chain, that Prentice had beaten the guard from the gold room because he had stolen the items from the staterooms and killed Julie Morrison when she had seen him in passing. The bodies of the two men originally assigned by their company to guard the gold would be discovered just outside Whitehorse, where they had been hijacked on their way to Dawson City, where the gold had started its long trip south. No one confessed to their murders, but their names were added to the long list of crimes committed by the gang.

But none of this mattered during the following afternoon, when everyone felt safe, and glad it was all over.

Cocktail hour was particularly spirited. Dinner was served as the *Spirit* crossed Campania Sound, headed south toward Laredo Channel. The open reach of water, across which they could see for a long ways, felt wonderful to most of the passengers, who couldn't help associating the whole experience with the confining walls of the Grenville Channel that they had now, thankfully, left behind.

The evening was pleasantly filled with the hilarious conclusion to the mystery play. Laurie Trevino, Jim Beal, and the rest of the players outdid themselves in an effort to make everyone forget their unfortunate experience, and, for the most part, they succeeded famously. They offered Alex a second chance at his role of Arizona Charlie Meadows, but he turned it down, deciding, he said, to rest on his laurels.

Bill and Nella Berry won the prize for solving the mystery, which didn't surprise Alex. Berry was an expert in his knowledge of the gold rush, which gave him a head start on figuring out the clues. The prize was a bottle of champagne and a fake brick of gold.

Jeff Smith won second prize—his own bottle of champagne and a bag of dried raisins painted gold to look like nuggets. Once again in his Soapy Smith costume, he recognized the crowd's applause by sweeping off his hat and bowing to them all.

McKimmey disappeared, but Alex found him later, happily tending to his engines in the hold.

"Sure glad I don't have your job," he told the engineer, when they had left the regular roar and climbed back up to the engineer's quarters, where Ray intended to take more aspirin and a nap. "I'd never be able to keep those huge babies running smoothly."

"Well, I'd rather have mine than yours, so we're even. I've had all I want of police work. You can have it."

"It's not all such a lot of work and excitement as this. In fact, a great deal of it's pencil pushing; reports, things like that."

"I'll still leave it to you. But thanks for . . . well, for including me."

"Ray," Alex told him honestly, "without you, it would never have been taken care of. We'd all have died in the icy water of the channel. It took the two of us to get it started, and the whole bunch of us to stop it. But anytime you need anything I can provide, all you've got to do is ask."

McKimmey's face turned red with embarrassment. He held out a hand that gripped Jensen's with surprising strength, but "Thanks" was all he said.

As Alex walked back up to meet Jessie, he thought of Dallas and Rozie, and made a turn toward their stateroom, where he found a light shining between the curtains and an answer to his knock.

"Just thought I'd stop and check on you two giant-killers," he grinned, stepping into the room at Rozie's invitation. Dallas was already in her bed, reading a book. Rozie held a towel and excused herself to take a shower, leaving them to talk.

"We're just fine, thanks," Dallas told him. "Haven't had such a helluva fright, or so much fun, in years."

"Well, you did a great job, Dallas," he told her. "Thanks, too, for taking care of my girl. That guy might not have been so out cold as he appeared. You looked like you could have used that rifle."

"When it comes to my Rozie, or your Jessie, for that matter, I would do just about anything," she said seriously. "But it was you, and that intrepid gang of volunteers, who did the real work. Took a

lot of chances there, Alex. Got damned lucky a few
times too, didn't you? Lot of ridiculous nonsense.
Why can't people just behave?"

"I guess that's it, all right. Some people just don't
seem to be able to behave. Says it pretty well."

"Where's Jessie?"

"Went back to the room for a warmer coat. We're
going to walk a little. She says she feels like exercise
after sitting in the Parlour for most of the morning."

"She took good care of that pretty little girl, Lou.
I was glad when I found out she was with Jessie,
and so was her father. He'd been worried sick."

She gave him the same kind of look she had given
him when they'd returned from Sitka and she'd
asked what Jessie had been worried about.

"What was there about this whole mess that you
and the rest, including Captain Kay, didn't tell us,
Alex? There was the smell of something bad hanging
in the air there for a while. What?"

He shook his head at her and smiled. "Boy, I hope
I never, ever, have to lie to you, Dallas. Might as
well give it up before I start."

"Well?"

"Okay, but it needs to be between us. We all
agreed to just forget it for the rest of this trip."

"Yes?"

He told her about the bomb and plot to sink the
ship. When he had finished, she sat thinking for a
minute or two.

"And you thanked *me*?" she said. "My God, Alex.
You are the most incredibly interesting man. Get out
of here. Go back down to that lovely woman who
doesn't know just how damn lucky she is, and tell
her how much you appreciate her."

He kissed her cheek and left to do as told. As he
was going out the door, she called one last thing
to him.

"Ask her, please, to come and see me tomorrow.
I've got something that belongs to her."

36

11:30 P.M.
Friday, July 18, 1997
Spirit of '98
Queen Charlotte Sound, Inside Passage
British Columbia, Canada

THERE WAS A MOON, JUST PAST BEING FULL, THAT SAILED
along in a clear sky spread with a million stars that
left a reflection here and there on the calm dark water
through which the ship was passing. It was so late,
on this last night of the cruise, that even the Grand
Salon and Soapy's Parlour were closed, and the decks
of the *Spirit of '98* were almost empty of passengers.
Frequent lights visible along the shorelines of islands
and the mainland reminded those still out on deck
that they were back within sight of civilization, leaving wilderness, except for photographs and memo-
ries that would keep it alive somewhere in the back
of their minds for a long time to come. The breeze
created by the ship, as it sailed through the islands
scattered south of Queen Charlotte Sound and north
of Vancouver Island, had warmed slightly since leaving the latitudes with temperatures that suggest to
visitors and residents of the Inside Passage that they
are only visitors and residents at the benevolence of
ice ages past and those yet to come.

Alex Jensen and Jessie Arnold stood at the rail outside their stateroom, leaning together for warmth of one kind and another, watching the night, with its lights, moon, and stars, saying just enough and no more. Jensen's pipe was clenched between his teeth and once again peacefully trailed smoke that was swept away into the dark behind the deck lights. Jessie, her hands tucked into her pockets, smiled once and looked up at him to murmur a word or two, but, for the most part, she was content to let the scenery pass unremarked, standing close in the circle of his arm.

A small sound turned their attention to a more experienced ender of voyages, as Captain Kay stepped up to join them at the rail.

"Evening."

Jensen nodded in return.

"It's so beautiful," Jessie said. "I can understand why some of you are addicted to it."

He smiled. "It's not always this pretty. You folks ready to dock tomorrow morning?"

"Not sure I wouldn't rather turn around and go back with you," Alex admitted.

"Well, after yesterday, you're welcome on my ship any time you like."

"Thanks, but I had a lot of help. Couldn't have pulled it off alone."

"Maybe not, but . . . all the same. And the company agrees."

He stood watching the lights on the water with them for a few minutes longer, then, "We'll stop in Everett, early, about four o'clock tomorrow morning. I'd like you to be on deck when we do, if you don't mind, Jensen."

"Sure. Glad to. Any particular reason?"

"Just to watch them put the gold on board, to take with us the rest of the way to Seattle."

They stared at him, perplexed.

He gave them a rare grin.

"You didn't think we'd really take the chance of ferrying thirteen or fourteen million all the way down the Inside Passage on the ship, did you? In Skagway, we loaded fourteen boxes of rocks, and one of gold we could display. The rest was flown to Everett a week ago."

A chuckle escaped Alex. It grew into a hoot of laughter, inspiring Jessie to similar amusement. "My God," he gasped, "all that for one . . . well, it would have been pretty close to a million, anyway."

Captain Kay laughed with them, a deep rumble that blended well with the sound of the ship's engines. As their mutual mirth died, he nodded and turned away. "Goodnight, now."

"Goodnight, sir."

He smiled slightly at the *sir*, but said nothing more, and walked casually off down the deck, toward the stairs leading to the bridge.

They watched him go with a sense of ironic conclusion, before turning back to watch the lights along the shore.

"I invited Lou and her father to come and visit us sometime," Jessie said after a few minutes. "I hope you don't mind."

"Hey, no, that's a good idea. I'd like a chance to talk gold rush with John Stanley. He's read just about everything that's been written."

"Good."

"What about Dallas and Rozie?"

"Yes, them, too."

"What did she want to see you about this afternoon?"

"Oh, Alex. I should have told you, but I've kind of been hugging it to myself for a little."

"She said she had something that belonged to you. Lose something?"

"No. Just the opposite. Look."

She held out her right hand in the glow of the deck lights. On her finger was the incredible blue sapphire that had been on Dallas's the last time Jensen had noticed it—when she had patted his hand and gone courageously down in the elevator.

"She slipped it on my finger before I knew what she was doing, and wouldn't take it back. She said that after this trip she has to stop wearing her rings because they hurt her hands. She really wanted me to have it. I couldn't say no."

"She's not easy to say no to. You shouldn't try." Alex smiled a little sadly. He thought he could guess why Dallas had given the ring to Jess, it was so *exactly* right. But he was sorry to hear she must give up wearing something that had given her pleasure.

Then he recalled her "Yahoo" from the elevator shaft, and had to explain to Jessie why he was laughing again.

Author's Note

EARLY ON THE MORNING OF JULY 17, 1897, THE NATIONAL *American Trading and Transportation Company's ocean-going vessel, SS* Portland, *steamed into Seattle's Schwabacher's Dock, carrying over two tons of gold from the Yukon and a ragged gang of millionaire miners, most of whom had staked their claims and won their fortunes on Bonanza and Eldorado Creeks near Dawson City, Yukon Territory, Canada. Over five thousand cheering people were on hand to meet the ship and watch as her passengers staggered down the gangplank, burdened with sacks, bags, cases, and even blankets full of gold that they carried or dragged onto the dock. Handles broke off suitcases and bystanders were hired to help transport loads too heavy for their owners to lift.*

The event touched off the Klondike gold rush, a stampede of incredible proportions, and within hours it seemed everyone in Seattle was going—or wanted to go—north to the gold fields. People walked away from their jobs, families, everything, and bought tickets to Alaska. Doctors abandoned patients, shops and businesses hung "Closed—Gone to the Klondyke" signs, streetcars stopped running for lack of operators, newspapers lost most of their reporters. Little more than a week later, fifteen hundred people had already left, and the harbor was full of ships, loaded and ready to sail.

Coming in the midst of the depression that had followed the panic of 1893, the possibility of becoming rich was more than usually tempting to many who were struggling to make ends meet. They sold anything they could for cash, borrowed the rest, and headed north. As the word spread, gold seekers flocked to the Klondike from around the world, and, in a matter of months, Dawson City was, temporarily at least, the largest city in Canada west of Winnipeg, larger than Vancouver, and only little smaller than Seattle. There had never been, and would never be again, anything like it.

Although this book is a work of fiction, it is based on an actual event scheduled for the week of July 13, 1997—the "Ton of Gold Centennial Reenactment" of the voyage of the SS *Portland*, which sailed in July 1897 with the first gold from the incredibly rich claims of the Klondike. This commemorative journey took place aboard Alaska Sightseeing/Cruise West's beautiful flagship, the *Spirit of '98*, just as described in this fictional tale. The setting, the towns, scenery, and locales, from Skagway, Alaska, to Seattle, Washington, are all authentic. A few of the people in the story are also real—with their kind permission—because they will really be on board for the trip. It's also my way of saying thanks for assistance in the research for this book, which is scheduled for publication just before the real reenactment will take place. I am pleased and excited to report that, thanks to the International Centennial Committee and Alaska Sightseeing/Cruise West, when the *Spirit of '98* left the dock in Skagway, bound for Seattle, I had the privilege of being one of the passengers.

When the *Spirit* sailed in July 1997, it was because hundreds of volunteers in the United States and Canada worked for over three years on the celebration, to mark the centennial of this historic event. Arrangements were made to bring an actual *ton of gold* out of the Yukon and overland to Skagway. From there it was transported to Seattle, arriving on July 19, 1997, only two days from the day that, a century earlier, the original Klondike gold arrived at the Schwabacher Dock on July 17, 1897.

This modern ton of gold—a combination of dust, nuggets, and bars from the working mines of the Klondike—was carried up the Yukon River from Dawson City to Whitehorse, overland to Carcross on Lake Bennett, and down to Skagway on the White Pass & Yukon Route's narrow gauge railroad, powered by a rare antique steam locomotive, Engine 73. Protected by armed guards, it was accompanied by parlor cars full of dignitaries and celebrants in period costumes—myself included.

Engine 73, a compact locomotive that glistens with dedicated care, will pull the train to an elevation of almost three thousand feet to receive the gold, and take it back down to sea level in Skagway. One of only a few surviving and operating narrow gauge engines, Number 73 is a great satisfaction to everyone who has the opportunity to ride, or watch it run; cylindrical boiler topped with steam domes, a shiny brass bell, and a forward smokestack that widens slightly at the top. It arrived at the downtown Skagway station in clouds of white steam, whistle screaming, bell clanging, and long, gleaming steel drivers thrusting its wheels steadily around in the unforgettable rhythm only a steam engine can make.

Once Skagway had the gold secured, the townspeople threw a huge party—repeating those in Dawson and Whitehorse—both as a send-off for the reenactment, and in celebration of their own success in making it all happen. They then gathered on Sunday, July 13, to observe or take part in the sailing of the *Spirit of '98*, on its voyage down the Inside Passage to Seattle, where it arrived six days later, at a dock to be renamed in honor of the Klondike gold rush.

Acknowledgments

THIS TIME I REALLY MUST THANK A GREAT MANY PEOPLE, some of whom may be found in the pages of this book. My apologies to anyone I may inadvertently have forgotten. My gratitude and special thanks go to:

As always, my family and the editors and encouragers of Alice's Restaurant and the Friday Night Adoption Society.

Alaska State Troopers and Scientific Crime Detection Laboratory for answers to law enforcement questions.

Dick West, President and CEO of Alaska Sightseeing/Cruise West, "Mr. Alaska" Chuck West, chairman of the board, and Gordon Thorn, public relations consultant, for permission, not only to use the *Spirit of '98* as a setting, but for giving me five wonderful days on board for research, from bridge to bilges. In gratitude, as I promised, I have made an effort to portray the *Spirit of '98* as it really is, with its unique dignity, charm, and delightful turn-of-the-century atmosphere (with only a few small liberties), and, as I promised, with no *gratuitous* vio-

327

lence—though it is a mystery, after all, and we all know that you can't make an omelet . . . etc. And, yes, Gordon, if you read far enough, you'll find yourself on board.

Harmony Crawford, in the Alaska Sightseeing/Cruise West's Seattle office, for schedules, blueprints, photographs, and critical information—all of which arrived *yesterday,* as needed.

Dave Kay, captain, Ray McKimmey, engineer, for permission to let them take their places in this book, and the whole crew of the *Spirit of '98* for their cooperation and assistance in helping me discover the ship from stem to stern in June of 1995. And for answering dozens of questions during and after the voyage.

Jeff Brady and the Ton of Gold Centennial Reenactment Committee for their enthusiastic endorsement of the idea to base this book on the commemorative voyage. Also for their assistance in providing all kinds of information necessary to portraying the setting and sequence of activities as much as possible the way the actual event took place. And, for all their hard work, to the following committees:

    Klondyke Centennial Society, Dawson City, Yukon: Bill Bowie, Akio Saito, Boyd Gillis, Greg Hakonson, Monna Sprokkreff.

    Skagway Centennial Committee/CVB, Skagway, Alaska: Irene Henricksen, Jeff Brady, Bob Ward

    Klondike Gold Rush Centennial Committee of Washington State, Seattle, Washington: Reed Jarvis, Valarie Raya

John Gould of Dawson City, Yukon, for the original idea that sparked the whole Ton of Gold Centennial Reenactment, and without whom there would be no voyage, or celebration, and this book would not have been written. Thanks, John, from all of us. And for your kind assistance to me in sharing the research you had done in locating the descendants of the original millionaire miners who returned to Seattle aboard the SS *Portland*.

Leslie Wilkinson, manager, Passenger Operations, White Pass & Yukon Railway, for great envelopes of material that made going to the mailbox much more interesting than usual.

John Mielke, chief mechanical officer, White Pass & Yukon Railway, for information and pictures of Engine 73 and the parlor cars it pulled between Skagway and Lake Bennett, July 12, 1997.

Donna Whitehead, owner of the Golden North Hotel in Skagway (Alaska's oldest operating hotel) for a warm welcome, generous information, and tours on all three floors and between them, including the haunted ones.

Chad Meyhoff of Oxford: "The Precious Metals People," for information on gold, by the ounce or ton, and its value, then and now.

My brother, John Hall, the family geologist, for figuring out that a ton of gold would fit into three five-gallon buckets or a footlocker.

Norm H. Thompson, M.D., Alaska State Deputy Chief Medical Examiner, for information on penetrating fractures of the skull.

Rich Steiner of the University of Alaska Fairbanks' Marine Advisory Program, for information on the behavior of humpback whales.

Kacey Smith of Schallerer's Photo and Gifts in Ketchikan, for information on Kodak's Create-A-Print machine.

Port Captain Kelly Mitchell, Alaska Marine Highway System, for assistance on the possibilities of radio interference in the Grenville Channel, south of Prince Rupert.

Vic Carlson for judicial information on communities in Southeast Alaska.

Bruce Valiere, Alaska Airlines Reservation Agent, for Southeast Alaska flight schedules and friendly conversation.

The Alaska Department of Tourism, the Visitors Bureaus of Skagway, Petersburg, Ketchikan, Anchorage, and InfoCentres of Prince Rupert, and Vancouver, B.C. for above-and-beyond telephone assistance and great information in the mail about their specific parts of the Inside Passage.

Both the Z. J. Lousaac Library's Alaska Collection, especially David Merrill, for a couple of very special books, and Marcia Colson for locating Kipling's poem, "The Sons of Martha," and the University of Alaska Anchorage Consortium Library, especially Nancy Lesh, who found the words *and* music to "Bird in a Gilded Cage" and set the librarians singing.

Jeff Smith, great-grandson of Jefferson Randolph "Soapy" Smith, II, who, in costume, represented "Soapy" on the reenactment voyage, for graciously giving me permission to use him as a character in this book, to "make me out as a good or bad guy, but please don't make me . . . ugly." And for sharing information on his famous great-grandfather, researched for a book he is currently writing on the "true life adventures" of "Soapy Smith."

Bill Berry, grandson of Fred Berry, for permission to put him and his wife, Nella, into this book as passengers. His grandfather was one of the four Berry brothers (Frank, Clarence, Henry, and Fred) who are a part of Klondike history for their involvement in the gold rush. Clarence struck it rich on Eldorado Creek and arrived in Seattle on the *Portland* with his wife, Ethel D., and $130,000 in gold, one of the only successful stampeders to invest his fortune wisely, and to end his life anything but penniless.

Vicki Doster for her company on a research trip to Skagway—terrible roads, broken windshields, lack of hot water, and all.

Dana Stabenow for her generous assistance in brainstorming a title—for friendship, laughter over lunches, and the continuing empathy of a talented fellow wordsmith.

Trish Grader and Tom Colgan, most talented editors, Andrea Sinert and Coates Bateman, editorial assistants, and all the good people at Avon Books for doing such a great job.

Dominick Abel, wise agent and friend.

IN THE DEEPEST PART OF THE NIGHT, JESSIE FOUND HERSELF suddenly wide awake and staring into the dark, filled with a strange tension.

A breath of wind whispered through the slightly open bedroom window, inspiring a small susurrus in the folds of the curtain. Then there was the soft, dry rustle of flying birch leaves against the glass, like spirit fingers scrabbling ineffectively to come in.

She lay without moving, listening hard. Instinctively knowing that no usual sound had raised her consciousness, she searched past those she could identify for something else. The sound was not repeated though she held her breath till her chest ached with the strain of alert concentration, her body rigid. She could half-remember a sharp noise of some kind, then another—different. All her intuition insisted something was not right.

The wind eased as if drawing its breath, and deep beneath the lowering of it came a distant resonance, a moan . . . no, the pitch was too high . . . a whimper . . . of hurt, or distress? Tank barked, suddenly, twice, and was answered by a yelp or two from other locations in the yard. One of the huskies produced a single howl that faded into yips of disturbance.

Tossing back the covers, Jessie was quickly on her

feet, switching on a small bedside lamp, throwing on
the clothes she had shed on going to bed.

"Wha-at?" Alex asked, sleepily raising his face
from the pillow to see her yanking a turtleneck
sweater over her head. "What is it?"

Hurriedly, she yanked on socks and jeans.

"I don't know. Something's wrong in the lot.
Maybe a moose has them going, but they don't bark
without a reason."

He sat up and swung his feet over the side of
the bed.

"Doesn't sound like a moose. They get crazy for
that."

"I know. I'll go see." She slipped beyond the light
into the front room, wending sure-footed past dark
furniture to her coat and boots by the door.

"Hold on. Let me get some clothes on and grab
the shotgun."

By the time he had snatched the gun from its
hooks on the wall and, shirt-tail hanging, arrived at
the front door, she was anxiously peering out the
window, unable to see anything in the dark but the
square shapes of the closest dog boxes that were a
little paler than their surroundings. He shrugged on
his coat, crammed his bare feet into boots, plucked
one large flashlight from a hook beside the door, and
handed her another.

"Opening this door will automatically turn on the
new lights," he reminded her tucking the rifle in
the crook of his arm. "We could slide out through
the kitchen."

"No, it's okay. We'll need the light. Can't see
much, otherwise, and I want to see, fast."

As they stepped onto the porch, the motion-activated
halogen floodlights on their tall pole blinked into instant brightness, casting a wide, white circle of light
that illuminated both their trucks in the drive and
extended far out into the lot. At a glance, there was
nothing unfamiliar within the area it revealed.

Tank, closer to the cabin than the other dogs, strained toward Jessie as they came down the steps, pacing back and forth at the end of the tether that connected him to the iron stake near his box. He did not bark again, but whined and, when they reached him, turned and trotted ahead, as far as the tether would allow, toward the rest of the lot. There he stopped, and stared intently into the dark beyond the lights.

Several more dogs, inspiring each other, were now barking, making it impossible to hear anything else, though Jessie tried to ignore them, to identify once again the foreign sound that had brought her uneasily searching for its source.

"Let him go," Alex suggested. "He knows what it is, and where."

She unfastened her leader, but kept a tight grasp on his collar, knowing that the temptation of a moose would strain his usual disciplined behavior. Free of the line, he did not, however, hurl himself forward against her restriction, as she had half expected, but calmly, steadily drew her past the other dogs, into the dark half of the lot.

Okay, no moose. What, then? Jessie frowned.

"Show me, Tank. Good boy."

As they moved between individual straw-lined shelters for the dogs, weaving a crooked path through the lot, and left the circumference of the light, her night-vision improved, but not enough. She switched on the flashlight she carried and swung its beam ahead of them. Nothing. She could hear Alex walking quietly, close and slightly to one side. In the narrow beam of his light, she caught the glint of an aluminum food pan, the gold of straw spilling out the door of a box.

The husky pulled her forward until they reached the outer edge of the wide lot, the last row of boxes, close to a hundred yards from the cabin. A few feet from one box in particular, he halted, stared at it, and growled deep in his throat. Hackles rose along his neck and back, bristling under her hand. Her light showed nothing but the wooden side of it.

"Alex?"

He stepped up beside her, the shotgun ready for instant use, should he need it.

Then Jessie could hear it again, a muffled whining that came repeatedly, and the familiar wet sound of a dog licking something, but the sharp crack that had broken her sleep did not come a second time. She shone the light over the outside of the dog box. Alex's light moved over the dirt that surrounded it, stopped and returned to the ground close to the door.

Jessie caught her breath.

It was soaked with red—blotches of blood that continued into the box.

"God. What the hell?"

They stepped forward and leaned to peer cautiously in through the door. Her light found the dog that had struggled to crawl inside and lay on the straw facing them. The straw under it was also liberally stained with scarlet. The dog raised its head to look blindly into the flashlight beam, quivered, then resumed licking, but it had been enough for them to see the ugly metal trap that was clamped cruelly to the flesh of one foreleg.

"Oh, God! She's caught, Alex."

Jessie sprang up to heave the box over, off its base, frantic to get to her dog. The resulting crash startled the next husky into leaping, with a yelp, to the top of its own box.

"It's Nicky. Oh . . . dammit. Where did that thing come from?"

The box crashed away and disappeared into the dark and she dropped to her knees beside the young female that whined again and shivered in shock.

"Oh, Nicky. You poor baby."

Alex held his light, while she raised the dog's head so they could see the trap on the injured leg.

It was the sort of steel trap that was still sometimes used to capture wolves and other animals of a relative size, one that could be spread open, leaving its sharp, wicked, metal teeth turned up, silently ready for the unwary to step into and spring the release. It would then close its steel jaws with a vicious crack, imprisoning the victim, slashing hide and flesh, as it had this dog, probably breaking bone. It was not new, but still strong, though brown here and there with rust and layered with dirt, which made it seem even more loathsome.

"Help me, Alex. We have to get it off her." Her voice was quiet, but terrible with anxiety and anger. "Can you open it, if I hold her?"

"Yes, if you can keep her still."

She slid forward and gathered the trembling canine body into her arms so that the dog's front legs remained on the straw, holding Nicky's head under one arm, the flashlight in the opposite hand, so Alex could see what he needed to do.

Gripping the trap, pressing it solidly against the ground, he threw his weight onto it, forcing it open wide enough for her to lift away the injured leg, then quickly letting it go, allowing it to snap shut again with that awful sound—the sound Jessie had heard in her sleep. She flinched. Nicky yelped in sharp pain, and blood once again flowed from the crushed, severed flesh, but she did not snarl, or bare her teeth, and the bleeding quickly slowed.

Tank whined, then growled again, staring off into the dark beyond the lot.

"Let's get her to the porch and the lights," Jensen said, picking up the trap, "so we can see how bad it is. She's going to need a vet."

Jessie spoke not a word, but handed him her flashlight and rose, gently supporting the dog in both arms.

Slowly, carefully, they made their way back across the dog lot to the cabin. The floodlights that had shut themselves off once again blinked on as Arnold and Jensen came within reach of the sensor.

Two hours later, back in the brightness before the cabin, Alex shut off the truck engine and turned to pull Jessie into the circle of his arms. All the way down the long road home from the veterinarian she had sat beside him, staring out the window into the passing dark, stiff and silent, for the most part, the lines of tears streaking her face, lost in thought and distress. Twice he had attempted to encourage her to talk, failed, and, noting the rigid line of her jaw, let it go, knowing it was better to let her work through her anguish and anger gradually. Now she almost fell, unresisting, to lean against his shoulder.

They had left Nicky with the vet they had roused from sleep with a phone call, and who had been waiting in his small hospital when they arrived in Wasilla. The dog's trapped leg was broken, but the damage that concerned him most was that done to the muscles and tendons, and the possibility of infection.

"That trap may be old and rusty—God knows where it's been—but it did a very effective job. She'll never be able to run with a team, Jessie. I think I can repair some of this, but only so much, and I won't know till I try. The leg may not be salvageable. I'm sorry. Shall I put her down?"

"No!" Jessie had been adamant. "Oh, dammit anyway. No. She loves to run, but. . . ."

She had been ambitious for this dog and in the process of grooming her for a possible leader, but she had also grown more than usually fond of Nicky's sweet nature and patience. Thoughtful for a minute or two, she watched as the vet made a more thorough examination, then frowned as she spoke again.

"She'll be able to get around, right? In the yard, I mean."

"Sure. She'd be fine with three legs, if it comes to that. Let me do what I can and we'll just see how it goes as she heals. She's strong and healthy, like all your dogs, and she's young. Give it a try?"

Arnold had agreed, all her focus on the dog and what was best for her. But on the road home Alex had seen her attention shift back to the idea of the trap and her anger renew itself.

In front of the cabin, he held her, saying nothing, waiting.

In a minute or two, she sighed and sat up.

"Let's go in."

"Yes. It's getting cold in here. Make us a cup of tea, will you? I'll be there in a minute."

When she had gone inside and closed the door, he took the flashlight and walked back through the dog lot to Nicky's box for another, longer look around it, and those closest to it. It had crossed his mind that there might be other traps, but he found none.

The tea was welcome, as was the warm fire she had encouraged in the stove. Jensen sat cupping his palms around the heat of the mug, but Jessie couldn't sit still in her chair at the table and was soon pacing between it and the kitchen.

"Where the hell did that . . . *thing* . . . come from?" she gestured at the bloody trap he had laid on the table on a double thickness of newspaper. "I've never had traps for this very reason. Too dangerous. With dogs around it's a disaster."

"Makes sense. Could Nicky have dug it up from some old trap line, maybe?"

"Was there any sign of digging?"

He had to admit there wasn't. And he had gone over all the nearby ground he could examine with a flashlight in the dark.

Now, looking at the bloody trap in the light, he

saw something he had not noticed before. A cardboard tag hung from one hinge of it on a short piece of string. He pulled it toward him to examine what appeared to be words written in block letters beneath a smear of blood. Aside from the reddish-brown smear, the tag appeared to be new and deliberately attached, as if the trap had been labeled. The letters had been written in pencil. Bending closer, he was able to make it out: *Happy Birthday Jessie.*

"What is it?" Jessie asked.

"Something's written on this tag," he told her, and hesitated thoughtfully, knowing it would disturb her. "I think someone put this trap out there on purpose, Jess."

She came swiftly back to the table, horrified.

"Why would anyone set a trap that near a dog? Knowing what it would do—what it could mean? I hate them—always have. Nasty, evil things. Besides, no animal a trapper might want would come anywhere near a kennel."

Alex frowned, looking across the table with concern.

"It's not the trap that's evil, Jess," he reminded her. "Distasteful, maybe. It's whoever set the thing that deserves the accusation of evil. The trap is just a horror doing what it's made to do."

She stopped to stare at him, dumbfounded, eyes widening with appalled comprehension.

"You really think someone did this intentionally?"

He showed her what was written on the tag, closely watching her reaction.

Her body went completely rigid. "What does it mean? Why would someone do such a thing?" she asked, still struggling with the idea.

A shrug and shake of his head. "I don't know, Jess. But, if it wasn't dug up—and I *know* it wasn't— then someone had to set it, leave it there. This label confirms it. These things have to be set with a purpose. Yeah—this thing was deliberately brought into your lot and set there. And whoever left it knew exactly what it would do—the mutilation it would cause—wanted you to know it had been done intentionally—with malice."

Jessie started to shake her head, but hesitated, as she thought it through.

"But, who . . . ?" she breathed. "Why?"

Her face was pale and her hand trembled enough to slosh tea as she picked up the mug. She clutched it close between both hands, elbows supported on the table, and brought it to her mouth.

"No idea. I looked and didn't find anything. But in the morning I'm going out again, when I have lots of light, and I'll do another thorough search for signs of anyone coming into the back of the lot."

The edge of the cup rattled slightly against her teeth as she stared at him. Slowly, with great care, she lowered it to the table and spoke through stiff lips. Though barely a whisper, her questions sounded loud in the quiet room.

"It's not over, is it? You think whoever did this will come back, don't you?"